THE 95TH DISTRICT

by

Levi Samuel

The 95th District
Eldarlands Publishing
Copyright © 2020

Printed in the United States.

Story and Art by Levi Samuel.

Genre: Urban Fantasy / Action & Adventure

ISBN: 978-1-950541-10-2

First Edition

To the Boys in Blue who never made it home.
This one's for you.

Thank you for purchasing this book. Whether you're reading the print or digital format, I hope you enjoy the story. Your support allows me to continue doing what I love.

This is the second book in my Miami Knights series. If you've not yet read the first book, don't despair. I designed this book with that in mind. You are fully capable of understanding the story without having to read *The Pandora Gambit*. If you've already read the first, doubly thank you.

Miami Knights is an urban fantasy unlike most others in the genre. One might say it falls into the occult detective subgenre, though there isn't much occult about it. Whether this is the case or not, I'll let you decide. I began this series because I wanted to write an urban fantasy unlike most others out there. The market is filled with vampires, werewolves, shifters, and several other tropes that I feel most people are sick of. Instead, I wanted to provide a modern age epic. I believe I've achieved that and I feel this is one of the best series I've written so far.

Be sure to leave a review and if you'd like exclusive access to all the latest updates and details about this book and more, sign up for my monthly newsletter. All subscribers receive a free download for a book unavailable anywhere else. http://eepurl.com/dxRUvL

Levi Samuel
June 2020

Contents

Chapter 1
Missing in Action

Knobby tires roared against the asphalt. The K5 Blazer was a streak of flat black, showing olive drab where the paint had chipped away. Its analog speedometer was maxed at eighty-five but it was moving much faster than that. Rattling steel and rushing air shook every part of the M1009, as it was known when it was in service.

Hitting the intersection a little too fast, Crum tightened his grip on the steering wheel and the old SUV took flight. It bounced roughly, the oversized tires and heavy-duty suspension groaning to absorb the sudden strain. Subtly was a word rarely associated with such a machine, though for its flaws it managed it well. In the dead of night, paired with the dull and uneven paint, it could all but disappear beneath the glowing moon overhead.

The tires chirped, sliding around the corner and Crum saw his target come into view once again. It was quite a distance from the only other taillights on the road but it pressed him to go faster. The victims were running out of time. If only he could catch up, maybe they'd have a fighting chance.

Watson Island loomed just ahead. Crum watched the red dots disappear into the Port Miami Tunnel. It took a moment to reach the entrance himself, but he was right behind them. Unfortunately, he had to let up on the throttle. It was a double-edged sword. The tunnel was the perfect place to gain ground but, to his knowledge, he hadn't lost the element of surprise yet. He needed to maintain a safe distance if he was to avoid suspicion. At least until he located the victims anyway. Once they were found, anything was fair game.

Exiting the tunnel, Crum flipped the switch mounted beneath his headlight controls. A green screen, roughly eight inches wide, flashed to life at the right of his steering column and a display of the road, as seen from his front bumper, appeared. Were he human it wouldn't have done much for fast maneuverability. It was designed for little more than keeping it between the lines during blackout mode. Fortunate for him he didn't suffer the visual drawbacks of human sight. Crum was an orc. His eyes were capable of adjusting to his surroundings and granting visibility in the darkest of places. Ignoring the screen, Crum hit the throttle again, moving into what he hoped was a blind spot.

The target, an F-250 Transit van, turned onto Port Boulevard. He was now closer than ever. Reading the license plate he recalled the numbers from the surveillance photos a few days prior. It was a perfect match. Unfortunately, tracing the plates had been a dead end. They were reported stolen from some town up north he'd never been to.

Realizing he was a little too close for comfort, Crum slowed to the speed limit, allowing them to gain some ground. The RPMs settled and the diesel engine began to purr. It was amazing how much quieter the SUV became when it wasn't being pushed for everything it had. That didn't mean it was silent by any means. There were still plenty of sounds being generated, but at least he could hear the radio again.

"—I don't think you fully grasp the situation here, Frank. People are in fear for their lives and you treat it like it's a conspiracy."

"It is a conspiracy! One side of government says one thing. The other says another. You have state leaders threatening to arrest the President if he refuses to adhere to their decree. How can you sit there and pretend like this is anything except political?"

"I'm not pretending anything. I'm stating the facts. This pandemic has ravaged our country, it's ravaged the world, and I believe isolation is the only answer."

"It's been six months! Open your eyes. Do you expect us to hide in our homes for the rest of our lives out of fear for something that has no lingering death toll? What about the essential workers? These people are going to work every day. They stock our grocery stores and prepare our take-out. They deliver your packages. Don't you find it strange they're not dying by the thousands?"

"These people are putting their lives at risk every day and they deserve a—"

Crum turned the volume knob until it clicked and the voices went silent. It was a shame really. Pretty much all the stations were talking about it nonstop. Aside from upgrading, basic radio was the only option he had and it wasn't worth listening to anymore. As usual, the media had it all wrong. Crum had been there. He'd had a larger hand in it than he cared to admit. It had been his failure that allowed the current strife to begin.

He worked for a covert organization which maintained and enforced laws between the mundane and magical worlds. It sounded more complex than it really was. Simply put, criminals existed in all walks of life. It was his job to ensure they didn't affect the humans. The last time they'd coexisted the humans had hunted them to near extinction. In response, the elves sacrificed what was left of the wellspring, the source of magic, to create the Veil. The magical races slowly drifted into myth and legend until they were all but forgotten, though that didn't stop them from continuing their existence parallel to the age of man. Unfortunately, all that had changed about six months prior.

A drug called Pandora had been released into the world. It gave humans the ability to see through the Veil. Since then, crime rates on both sides had skyrocketed. The human world was divided.

Many believed, encouraged by their government, it was a pandemic. That instigated mass hysteria and, strangely enough, a worldwide shortage of toilet paper. Fear became the driving force. Many states ordered quarantines and mandatory lockdowns. The general public was split into two demographics, essentials and nonessentials.

Personal safety became a controversial topic. Those in fear criticized those who weren't. And those who weren't mocked those who were. In a matter of months latex gloves, sanitizing wipes, disposable face masks, and several other such protective items became the number one source of discarded litter across the country. Everyone was terrified of 'catching the disease', when in truth, there was no disease. That is if you didn't count the people themselves.

The most dangerous aspect of the entire situation began slowly at first, though now it spread like the wildfire the 'pandemic' was constantly being compared to. Hate groups arose on all sides. This had led to many innocent people, both human and otherwise, being targeted. It was this very element which Crum was battling at the moment.

A large number of the nonhuman population had gone missing over the past several months, most of them isolated to a twelve-block radius. It had taken weeks but he finally had a lead where the victims were being held. All he had to do now was follow this van to the drop off point and he'd have a location.

Watching intently, the van veered onto Bahama Drive. Crum had been on this stretch enough in recent months, he now had a general layout of the roads. From their current position, they could only go east or west. Considering they'd come this far it made no sense to turn west now. Anticipating their actions, Crum stayed straight on Port Boulevard. The decision would not only eliminate any suspicion if he'd been spotted, but it would also allow him to get ahead of them for the intercept.

Glancing into the side mirror, Crum watched their headlights turn left onto Antarctica Way and disappear behind a wall of stacked shipping containers. Gently pressing the brake, he slowed to a crawl, searching the gaps between rows. Their headlights ran parallel to the ocean, passing the first street. Second street. Arriving at the third street, Crum came to a full stop. His query was nowhere to be found.

Something wasn't right. There was no place else for them to have gone. That could only mean they stopped short. Pulling into a small lot on the side of the road, several other vehicles were parked here and there. Crum selected a dirt patch between two flatbed trucks and disabled the blackout system, instantly killing the headlights. Turning the key toward him, the 6.2 diesel chugged a few times and then fell silent. It was on foot from here.

Opening the door, he grabbed his keys and stepped out. Cautiously, circling behind his SUV and onto one of many forklift paths, Crum drew his Desert Eagle and stalked down the path.

He was nearly halfway to the sect of bay known as Fisherman's Channel when two pops echoed in the distance. They sounded eerily like gunshots. Small caliber but gunshots nonetheless. He hoped he was wrong. He'd come too far and put too much into this case for it to be over now. If they'd killed his contact he'd be back to square one with nothing to go on. Not to mention the loss of another innocent life. Unable to ignore the possibility, Crum raced between two stacks and across the next run.

The salty breeze rushed him. It was a strange scent, one he believed he'd grown accustomed to by now, though there was something different about this one. It was more than the usual salt smell. It had a sweet tinge to it. Blood maybe? It was typically sweet in a sort of coppery way, especially blood from someone in fear. That was the sweetest blood there was. Though it couldn't be that. He couldn't detect the copper scent.

Crum paused, searching his surroundings. He could hear voices somewhere, echoing between the metal boxes. They were on the next row, maybe the one after that. It was hard to tell. Carefully, he rounded the corner, scouting ahead. There were two armed guards at the far end of the row and at least one more atop the next stack. He was far enough away, the two on the ground weren't much of a threat. Not yet anyway. The one overhead however was going to be a problem.

Watching, waiting, learning the routine in as little time as possible, Crum saw his opportunity. He darted across the opening and ducked into the shadows of the next row. The sweet scent was much stronger here. Suddenly, he knew what it was. He was in more trouble than he realized, though it was too late to turn back now.

Taking a deep breath, Crum worked his way around the side, watching for other guards. They were here somewhere. He could smell them. Reaching the front, a short sand covered road separated him from the ocean. Carefully, he peeked around the corner and located the van. To his relief the informant was nowhere in sight but that didn't mean anything. For all he knew he was already dead, his body tossed roughly in the container where the men lingered.

The van was backed against one of the intermodals, both sets of doors fully open and bridging the gap. Crum watched the two humans transport several large sacks from one to the other, though he didn't have a clear enough view to see much else. It didn't add up. These men were human—or more accurately—nonhuman traffickers. Whatever they were moving didn't make much sense to the grand scheme of their plan, whatever that was.

Overhead footsteps alerted Crum and he ducked into the shadows, awaiting the armed patrol to make his rounds.

The lookout casually walked the edge, gradually sweeping everything in view. A faint melodical whistle echoed from him as he passed directly overhead and down the side of the long metal box. At his current pace he'd reach the end in just under a minute, which, if following his previous routine, meant he'd turn the other way.

That would be his que. Once the guard turned, he could advance to the van. It was going to be tricky to get between it and the box but he had a plan for that. Once inside, the two men would drop with relative ease and from there it was only a few short actions from isolating each of the guards and sending them to a similar fate. Though unless the victims were inside the container, and he desperately hoped not, it was best to hold action.

"What's your count?" One of the men asked.

"Just loaded the last one. Let's get out of here."

Crum watched one climb through the back and hop into the driver's seat. He pulled forward just enough to close the doors, though to his surprise, the other held fast. The driver climbed out, leaving the engine running, and returned to the rear. He couldn't see what they were doing but their footwork suggested they were lifting something. A moment later they reappeared, working in tandem with short staggered steps, carrying a long vaguely humanoid shaped and clearly heavy item wrapped in black plastic and duct tape.

It wasn't conclusive but it was worth checking out. He watched them toss it roughly into the container and slam the heavy metal doors shut. The lock rod squealed, clamping them tight. Crum stole a glance overhead. He could just barely see the lookout guard at the end of the row. Like clockwork he turned as expected and Crum saw his mark.

He broke into a full sprint toward the van and the two unsuspecting men. Sudden movement caught his attention at the far end of the run. That wasn't part of the plan. With no other option, Crum straightened his legs and he stepped down hard. His boots dug into the sand and he dove sideways into a narrow gap between containers. It wasn't the optimal place to be stranded. He was blind on all sides except straight into the bay. It minimized his options, not to mention if he was discovered he had literally nowhere to run.

He heard the van doors slam shut and a moment later, with the brief spinning of tires and flung bits of debris, the humming engine became distant, driving away. Crum cursed himself. Not only had he lost his only lead but he'd trapped himself. Shaking his head, he inched toward the edge of the gap and peeked around, hoping the guard was gone. He'd already sacrificed too much time with his detour, he didn't have much more before the patrol would be back around.

The coast was clear, both literal and metaphorical. Stepping into the open, Crum started toward the container. He needed to know what was inside. One way or another, his case depended on it.

Fresh tire tracks and a missing padlock told him exactly which one it had been. Doing a quick scout, ensuring the guards weren't too close, Crum grabbed the latch and lifted it from its retainer. The lock rod groaned under his strength but he held tight, minimizing its call. The keepers released the door from its seal and he pulled it open as quiet as possible. Nothing would tip the guards off more than a loud squeaky hinge in the middle of the night.

Peering into the gap between doors, Crum took a step back and scratched his head. His night sight was near impeccable, yet he couldn't see a thing. A cloth of some kind was blocking the entrance. Fortunately, most of the noise had already been made and nobody came running. A little closer investigation wouldn't hurt.

Craning the door toward him, Crum could now see the mesh curtain. It was black and had little reflective specks in the fabric. It was secured to the frame by a taut rod and plastic rings like a shower curtain. He grabbed hold of the thin shroud and pulled it aside.

Before he could respond several sharp pains burned into his chest and stomach. Crum stared blankly at the team of armed men inside the container, weapons trained on him. His strength was waning rapidly. Glancing at the holes in his shirt, he stumbled backward, his gun slipping from grip. The world spun around him and he found himself staring at the night sky. Dark silhouettes entered his fading vision. He felt the men latch on to his shoulders and legs and for the briefest moment he was weightless.

The impact of the cold steel floor was of little concern. There wasn't much that could concern him at the moment. A voice echoed somewhere off in the distance, close but so far away.

"We got the orc. Bring the others around."

Ray groaned, hearing his alarm sound in the dark. He rolled to his side, securing the annoying device. Unplugging it from the charger, he desperately swiped at the screen trying to shut it up. Finally, after about the third attempt it fell silent.

His eyes burned from the night before. Rubbing the puffy surfaces, trying to dislodge the sleep from them, he squinted at the bright display in a vain attempt to focus on the numbers. It was entirely too early to be awake. A heavy sigh escaped him and he tossed the meddlesome phone back onto its makeshift table.

It hit and skidded to the floor with a metallic thud. He didn't notice. His pillow had already reclaimed him.

The alarm sounded again, further away this time.

"All right already! I'm getting up!" He yelled, as if somehow it would listen. Ray stared into the darkness for a long moment. He grunted and pulled himself up, spinning to place his feet on the cold concrete floor. Ray groggily got to his feet, his blanket falling away as he stood, and walked across the small dwelling. The alarm continued to sound, though it wasn't quite so loud from where he stood.

Extending his hand, unable to see in the total dark, Ray reached for the dangling cord he knew was there—somewhere. Making contact, he gave a firm tug and light erupted from the twin incandescent bulbs mounted to the ceiling.

Ray stood near the center of a small storage unit. Extension cords were tucked into nearly every corner, supplying power throughout the dwelling. An old canvas cot with a wadded blanket and a single pillow rested in the corner behind him. Beside it, an overturned milk crate served as a nightstand with phone charger, lamp, and a few trinkets. In the corner to his right a cheap clothing rack leaned heavily to one side. A few suits, a uniform, and a couple outfits were hung neatly from the upper rod. That seemed to be the only thing neat about his surroundings.

Boxes of overflowing paperwork were stacked around a plastic folding table that rested middle wall in front of where he stood. Nearly twice as much paper was heaped on the table, leaving only a small section uncluttered.

Ray stood tall, arching his back. A few light pops echoed and he released, scratching himself. He wore light blue boxers and a stained wife beater that would have fit perfectly a few short months ago. Now, it was just shy exposing his lower belly. A short brown beard clung to his face, though there was no word to describe how unimpressive it was, and his usually combed and kempt hair was just the opposite.

Glancing around, Ray's eyes fell on a coffee cup that rested near the edge of his desk. He snatched it up and glanced inside, finding the dark liquid near the three-quarter mark, along with an added bonus. A drowned fly floated helplessly on the surface.

Ray sauntered, half asleep, across the narrow hovel. A small microwave rested atop another stack of boxes at the foot of his cot. He pulled the door open and placed the cup inside, hitting the start button.

Lost in the microwave's hum, Ray surveyed the chaos around him. It hadn't always been like this. In fact, prior to a few months ago, he'd been organized and tidy in every way that mattered. His eyes darted to the metal wall above his desk. A collection of pictures, newspaper clippings, and old police reports were taped here and there. Expansive trails of multicolored yarn jumped between the groupings, each one eventually ending at a single paper with a large question mark posted at the top.

Ray studied the paper for a long moment, lost in the question he'd been asking himself since everything turned sour. The microwave's ding pulled him from his all-consuming focus. Mindlessly, he opened the door and grabbed his coffee.

Trotting back to his desk, Ray pulled the metal folding chair tucked under the table's edge and took a seat. He located the newspaper he'd left on top the night before and began scanning the words. Lifting his coffee, he paused, reciting the headline aloud. "Mystery Man donates eleven point two Million toward Pandemic Research." The paper was over a month old. He'd read it numerous times. There was something about it he couldn't shake. It was one of those cop instincts he had sometimes. There was no explanation for it, he just knew it was connected. Though that connection continued to elude him. Ray set the paper aside and brought the warm cup to his lips.

A knock echoed through the thin metal door.

"Dammit!" With a deep breath, Ray set his cup aside and drew his pistol from beneath a stack of papers. It felt good in his hand. It had been a gift from his Command Sergeant Major when he got out of the Army. Since then, it had been upgraded a few times. The wooden grips were tailored to fit his palm, and the fiberoptic sights delivered that last bit of accuracy when things got heavy. It had been a good companion when he was still a real cop.

Quietly picking himself up, Ray stalked toward the door. He wasn't expecting anyone, and no one was supposed to know he was here. He'd arranged to rent the unit off the record and money had been paid upfront for the year. If someone was here, they didn't belong.

Pressing the muzzle of the nickel-plated Colt against the thin metal, Ray leaned close and stole a glance through the peep hole he'd drilled a few months prior. He sighed and lowered his weapon, taking a step back. Unlatching the door, Ray pulled it overhead revealing an older man in a generic suit and a pair of sunglasses. His graying hair was neat and he wore a knowing smirk on his lips. Ray inspected the large envelope he carried under his right arm. It had been stamped numerous times with thick red and black ink.

"Good morning, Detective."

Tucking his gun into the exposed bracing of the wall, Ray turned and retreated into the shadows of his lair. "I should have known you were keeping tabs. I take it Martinez and Jenkins weren't circling the block for my protection." Ray plopped down in his chair a second time, snatching up his coffee. Tipping it back, he took a long draw, feeling something that didn't belong. He was faced with a choice. He could expel the coffee and whatever else was in it, or he could swallow it and save face. Decided for the latter, Ray forced himself to swallow and slammed the empty cup onto the table. "What can I do for you, Captain?"

"If you would have answered my calls I wouldn't have had to come all the way down here." Captain Anderson walked into the small hovel and extended the heavily stamped envelope.

"What's this?" Seeing it up close, all the stamps said *Confidential* and covered every available surface in big bold letters. He grabbed hold of the red string holding it shut and quickly unwrapped it from the cardboard tabs. Breaking the tape that sealed it beyond that point, he overturned the envelope and a file slid out. Ray inspected the outer flap.

Thick black bars covered the subject tab as well as the agency from whom the file had come. The inside was much of the same. Almost every bit of information he could have gained was blacked out, leaving little more than a general scenario. He didn't even know what day or time the events transpired. "What am I supposed to do with this, sir? The whole thing's been redacted so much, I got about every other word of it."

Anderson, careful of where he stepped paced the small room. He turned to look upon the confused detective. "Bradley, why are you staying in this rat hole? The department's still paying for that beach loft of yours. This place stinks."

"It's quiet here. I can focus better. Besides, there's a fine line between suspension and being fired. I thought it best to leave department resources alone for a while. You didn't answer my question."

"What do you make of it?"

Ray sighed. "It looks like a missing persons case. But I don't have a name, time, last known location, or really any of the important things needed for such a case. That makes me wonder why you're showing it to me."

"The case file pertains to William Crumble. His superiors tell me he was on assignment here in Miami. He's been officially missing for a little over two weeks now. His agency—"

"The DEA." Ray interjected, recalling the fact that Crum had posed as a DEA agent when they met.

"The DEA." Anderson repeated. "—thought that since you're the last to work with him, you might have some insight in locating him. I've been requested to have you report."

"I'd need the unredacted file."

"That's between you and them. I'm simply relaying the request." Withdrawing a folded piece of paper, Anderson handed it over.

Ray opened it. Hurried scribbles were written at an angle in blue ink. It was an address, someplace downtown.

"They're expecting you, but I'd recommend taking a shower first." Without another word, Anderson turned and made his way out the door.

"Does this mean my suspension's over?"

Refusing to look back, Anderson opened the door on a gray convertible BMW Series 7. "Go to the address. See what they have to say."

Mimicking his captain, Ray lifted his arm and sniffed himself. "Damn! I do need a shower."

Chapter 2
A New Gig

Ray stared out the window of his Uber, watching the bustling city fly by. As much as he'd hoped for an uneventful and quick ride, it was turning into more of an adventure than he'd desired.

The backseat was covered by a thick plastic liner. It was uncomfortable and full of wrinkles. Between that and the fact that he kept sliding every time they hit a bump, went around a corner, or, to be honest, drove in a straight line, it was starting to wear his patience thin. On top of that, the driver was wearing latex gloves and a paper face mask which muffled his voice greatly.

The only saving grace, he was nearing his destination. He'd taken to counting the addresses like a silent timer announcing his escape.

The car turned onto a circle drive and came to a stop in front of a tall bricked building.

Ray couldn't open the door fast enough. Stepping out, he inspected the address, confirming a match. Even if it hadn't matched, he knew he was in the right spot.

Like most federal buildings, named after some long-forgotten politician, this one was called The Charles Downing Building. The name, like the address was posted in small black lettering on a white marble sign that sat in the middle of a perfectly manicured lawn. It had been the sign that confirmed everything for him. Ray stared at it for a long moment, not exactly sure what he was seeing. It was similar to the lenticular cards he'd played with as a child. He could see what was intended for the general public, the sign as he'd already read it. But there was something more, something most people weren't meant to see. Suddenly it popped out at him. *World of Mystical Descendants – South East District.*

Approaching the building, Ray couldn't help but notice how underwhelming it was. That wasn't to say it was in disarray. Had it been standing by itself it would have been a sight to behold. It was simply the elegance of the surrounding skyscrapers of downtown Miami's Central Business District that made it seem bland. It was too normal. Too mundane. It blended into its surroundings too well, nearly disappearing into them. Then again, what better place for a secret organization to hide?

The Uber driver shouted something muffled and pulled off.

Ray started for the paved walkway leading to the front doors when his phone vibrated. Unlocking it, an email receipt from Uber popped up. "Would I like to rate my experience? Why, yes. Yes, I would!" Quickly typing out his complaint he submitted the review and pocketed his phone just as he reached the tinted glass doors.

Stepping inside, Ray found himself in a short foyer, an automated door at the far end. He walked through and entered the lobby.

It didn't feel much like the entrance to a secret organization. The walls were simple and bare. There were no paintings or pictures of any kind, just plain white paint. A narrow hall rested left of the entrance and ended at a set of restroom doors. The lobby itself was little more than a wide corridor with a stainless-steel elevator on the far end, and seemingly no push button, floor display, or placard of any kind. There was, however, a door that said 'stairs' to the left of it, though it had a keycard lock.

The only real area of interest was in the dead center. There was a single grouping of plastic chairs with a fake tree in a wicker basket at one end, and an old man with wrinkled and dark skin quietly reading a newspaper on the other. Directly across was a small glass window in the wall. A woman with crescent-shaped glasses and a pink knitted sweater stared intently at a computer screen on the other side.

Approaching the window, Ray leaned toward the metal filter at the center of the thick glass. He could see several other people in the large office behind her, each doing whatever it was their jobs were, and that clearly didn't extend to paying him any attention. "Excuse me, ma'am. My name is Ray Bradley. I was told you were expecting me."

"Ah, yes, Mister Bradley. Please step into the elevator. It will take you to your appointment." Her voice was squeaky and polite, though her eyes suggested she was tired of interruptions. She grabbed a file from the top of a stack and dropped it into a slot beside the wall.

He couldn't be sure, it had disappeared too quickly, but he was fairly convinced his name was on it. A ding from the elevator called his attention. Confused, but more curious, Ray turned and hurriedly stepped into the elevator, the doors closing as soon as he was clear.

He stood there a long moment, staring at his reflection in the polished surface. There was no music to break the monotony, and aside from an occasional bounce, he wasn't entirely sure the elevator was moving. What was worse, there was no access panel or buttons of any kind that he could see, simply a card scanner to which he was ill equipped to operate.

Out of nowhere his stomach churned and he felt the familiar bounce he'd been expecting. The doors opened and he found himself standing near the center of a small reception room. A round wooden desk sat straight ahead. Behind it was a beautiful woman with golden hair twisted into a bun. Her long and pointed ears poked through the golden locks and a single diamond sparkled from each one. She wore a tan blouse, cut low in front, and her milky skin was free of the slightest blemish. He didn't have to ask to know she was an elf. He'd only met a few of them but there was no mistaking it.

"Detective Bradley?" The elf asked, staring at him inquisitively.

"Yes, ma'am."

"This way please." She smiled softly and stood, grabbing a file from her desk. He suspected it was the same one he'd seen downstairs, though how it had beaten him here was anyone's guess.

Ray marched toward her, taking in the sight of her shapely form the moment her back was turned. Her legs were covered in flesh tone pantyhose that disappeared beneath a form-fitted skirt that clung tight to her hips. Suddenly, he remembered elves had some influence over humans. He didn't know exactly how far that went but decided it best to avert his gaze. The last thing he wanted was for her to read his mind if it was focused where it had been moments before.

Quickly he glanced to the TV mounted above the seating area. It wasn't anything of interest but Ray recognized the guy displayed.

Frank Elliott had been everywhere over the past few months. It was annoying. He couldn't use the internet without seeing or hearing about him at least once. He was this overly religious fanatic who'd been extremely vocal about his views on the pandemic. Every time he popped up he was constantly preaching about the connection between the sins of man and how the faithless were responsible for all of it.

Having seen enough, Ray turned away and followed her down a corridor, past several insets, and to the very end where a set of wooden doors waited. A bronze placard was fixed to the left side. *Arthur Roderick – Deputy Attorney General.*

The receptionist opened the door on the right and stepped in, gesturing him to follow.

Ray was astounded at the sights within. This had to be the largest office room he'd ever seen. Two full walls were nothing but huge windows overlooking the city. Standing in just the right place, he could see the ocean between two of the skyscrapers off in the distance. By his estimate, they were at the southwest corner of the building. A minibar and small kitchen took up one of the alcoves on the right. Another held a futon and a full entertainment center, complete with surround sound and a projector. It had its own bathroom just right of the entrance, and of course the desk was the central focus of the business side of things that occupied the entire left side of the room. It may as well have been an apartment in addition to an office. It certainly had enough space. But then again, almost anything was better than the storage unit he'd occupied over the past few months.

Nearing the large oak desk, Ray spotted who he was here to see. He was an older man, though his posture and muscle tone suggested he was still fairly agile. He wore a pair of gray trousers and a white button shirt with a set of red suspenders.

The receptionist signaled for silence and waited patiently for the old man's attention.

Ray studied him. He straddled a green turf that didn't seem to like the fact it wasn't rolled up.

Rotating his torso, the man brought his putter dangerously close to the yellow ball resting peacefully on a punched out dot. Exhaling, he repeated the process, adding just a bit more swing. The putter connected and the ball gently rolled forward, headed straight for a hole at the far end. Watching in anticipation, it slowed, teetering on the edge. Finally, the ball fell in and the man threw his hands into the air. Smiling his victory, he set the putter aside and turned to address the newcomers. "Thank you, Elaine. You can set that anywhere."

The receptionist laid the file on his desk and hurried out the door, closing it behind her.

"Thank you for joining me, Detective Bradley." He extended his hand and gave a vigorous handshake before gesturing to the cushioned chairs opposite his desk. "My name's Arthur Roderick. Please, have a seat."

Selecting the chair closest to the door, Ray paced himself, waiting for his host to sit. Such was proper etiquette in his line of work. People were silly like that. Hurt feelings over something small could be the difference between a botched deal or even death in some cases. Seeing Roderick start the descent, Ray quietly sat.

"Scotch?" Roderick grabbed two glasses and a crystal decanter, pouring before Ray could answer.

Accepting the glass, Ray swirled the amber liquid, unsure if he should drink. Work experience told him yes. There was one big difference though. This guy wasn't a drug dealer so far as he knew. If the placard on the door was accurate, that made him a politician, someone far more dangerous. Placing the glass atop the desk, Ray stared straight at the old man who was now preparing a cigar. "Sir, with all due respect, what am I doing here? I've agreed to look into the disappearance of William Crumble, but I—"

"Crum'Bul." Roderick corrected. "Yes, Agent Crum'Bul of Tactical Divisions within the WMD is missing. We thought you'd like the opportunity to find him considering you two worked so well together with that whole Pandora thing. Granted, it was an ultimate failure but you can't win 'em all." Setting his unlit cigar aside, Roderick snatched the file that had been delivered moments before. He flipped through the pages within.

Now that it was before him, Ray had no doubt it was his name printed on the subject tag.

"Let's see here. A few insubordination remarks, destruction of police property, multiple traffic violations on and off duty, and enough criminal complaints to solve the toilet paper crisis. Though you've never been brought up on charges, and with commentary from one Captain James Anderson I believe you'll make an exemplary candidate."

"Candidate?" Ray asked, glancing around the room curiously. He couldn't help but feel like this was all some big joke. Like any moment now someone was going to jump out and announce they got him good. "Sir, my apologies, but if this is some kind of RTD interview? I already met with IAD. They cleared me of any misconduct."

The file clapped shut and Roderick tossed it unceremoniously atop his desk. He placed his elbows at the edge and interlaced his fingers. Staring intently, a mild smirk formed. "How would you like a job?"

"Excuse me? I already have a job, though as I'm sure you're aware I'm currently on suspension."

"Son, let me put it another way. You've come into contact with things—creatures—beings of this world you never knew existed. We have riots in the streets. The media is spreading panic. The general public is snatching up hygiene products by the pallet in fear of some imaginary contamination they can't explain." He shook his head, thinking about the state the world was in. "There are two types of people. Those incapable of keeping their mouth shut, and those who can. Even after you were fired and tossed on your ass. Even after the world went to shit. You had many opportunities and you kept quiet. Can you imagine the temptation that comes with a world altering revelation like that? I can. And I know you can too. You were stripped of all your resources and left in the cold. Yet here you are, still working the case months later. That takes someone either extremely stubborn or extremely dedicated. My guess, it's a little of both."

"I was suspended."

"What?"

"I was suspended, sir. Not fired."

"Semantics. You're a cop whether you've got the badge or not. You don't just wake up one day and quit being something because someone says you must. I called you here because I believe you've got what it takes."

"For what?"

"How would you like a badge that won't evaporate? You'll be in a job that will allow you to do what it is you do and won't kick you to the curb the first time things don't go as planned. You'll have the full and complete backing of the United States Government, as well as close ties to the WMD."

"Um—Do I have time to think about it? I mean, I really don't know what you're wanting me to do. I don't have any details."

"Son, this is one of those situations that require a leap of faith. I can't provide any information until you're on board. All I can say is this is a once in a lifetime opportunity. If you turn it down, I can promise you'll spend the rest of your life wondering about it."

Ray stared out the windows behind Roderick. The view was phenomenal. Golden rays of sunlight reflected off the glass, creating a rainbow that disappeared into the deep blue water far in the distance. Sighing, he drew his focus in and settled on Roderick once again.

Everything he was saying raised more questions than answers, but he was always the curious sort. That's what landed him in law enforcement in the first place. He wanted to say yes. That was the nature of intrigue. On the other hand, he hadn't been a detective long. Sure, he'd landed a few good cases in that time. But he'd been suspended after the first big fail. It wasn't even a total fail. He caught the bad guy. Just not before the bad guy released a bunch of drugs into the world. What did that say for his career?

Six months was a long time. He hadn't been fired. That was true. He was suspended. But how often was someone brought back after a half year suspension? Ray stared straight into Roderick's eyes, searching for any sign of deceit.

Whether it was hidden due to training or because it didn't exist, he didn't know. "I'll need two things."

"Am I to take that as a yes?"

"Perhaps."

"List your demands."

"First, I need the unredacted file for *Special* Agent Crum'Bul." Ray added emphasis to the tag at the front of his friend's title.

Roderick pulled his lower right drawer open and retrieved a sealed envelope. "It's already been pulled and is awaiting your review. What's the second?"

"I need some new wheels. My last one— Well, I suppose I can understand why they suspended me."

Roderick chuckled and slid the envelope across the desk.

Opening it, Ray noticed what appeared, at a glance anyway, to be little more than a standard employment contract and a round metal badge. He overturned the packet feeling the small accessory drop into his hand. It had a star at the center and the outer ring, like the hidden image outside, had a glowing set of runes that rotated clockwise.

"Welcome to the US Marshals Service. Once your paperwork is on file, Elaine will get you an ID badge and escort you to Tactical. Director Kel'Gos has the file you seek. Now, if you'll excuse me, I need to get back to work." Roderick stood and made his way back to his putting green.

The elven receptionist handed Ray his ID badge. Glancing it over, it listed little more than his physical description, name, and an embedded U.S. Marshals Service badge with a chip.

"If you'd follow me." She led him across the waiting room and to a door on the backside of where the elevator ejected. It opened into a bright white corridor which seemed to glow despite no evident lights being present. It was a relatively short hall intersecting another, though he didn't get to see where it led.

Instead, Elaine pushed a chrome button on the wall and another elevator door opened. "This is the internal elevator. It has access to any floor you may need to access." She stepped inside and took position in front of the control panel.

The doors closed as soon as Ray was clear.

"You'll insert your card into the panel." She inserted her own and a digital display appeared. "It takes a while to learn the floors, but I'm sure you'll figure it out in no time. Just remember the cafeteria is seventeen and eighteen and the entrance is on G. Anywhere else, someone will show you." She pressed the sensor for the eighth floor.

Ray counted nine sub levels and twenty stories, excluding the ground level. Considering they were in Miami, something wasn't adding up. The doors opened almost immediately, derailing his train of thought. He never once felt the elevator move, yet suddenly they were at the edge of a bustling office filled with cubicles.

Dull chatter filled the air and Ray was suddenly unsure what he was supposed to be doing. The chaos was familiar. The bullpen at the precinct was much worse on many occasions. Still, it was something new. A place he'd never been before. Hesitantly, Ray stepped out, lost in the unknown.

Elaine leaned out the elevator, holding the door open. "This is Department 7, Tactical Division. Director Kel'Gos is the last door on the right."

"Thank you." He was glad she directed him. It made it a little easier. If nothing else, at least now his legs were moving. Breath constrained, Ray followed the path along the right side of the large room. He was somewhat taken back by the number of humans around. It was a silly thought. Prior to half a year ago he hadn't known anything except humans. He simply assumed the WMD was comprised of nothing but orcs and elves. Though Crum had mentioned that some people knew of their existence, it made sense they'd hire outside.

Avoiding the crowd as best he could, Ray rounded the corner and stopped dead in his tracks. A single row of large windows ran the width of the wall displaying the most unexpected sight. Unlike the sunshine he'd seen from Roderick's office not long before, this view was filled with low hanging clouds, fog, and a fair amount of rain. He couldn't see more than a few buildings through the haze, though the ones he could were not what he expected. Especially in Miami. They were dark and foreboding.

"Excuse me, sir. Can I help you?" A small voice asked.

Ray jumped, turning to see a short man in a pair of thick glasses and carrying a red stapler. "I'm sorry. I was just looking for—" Ray glanced around, seeing the office he'd been directed to. The placard, like the sign out front, had a dual message. *Mark Kelly – Director of Operations*, shifting to *Kel'Gos – Director of Tactical Divisions*. "—Ah, there it is." Ray hurried to the glass door, watching the squat man continue onward to one of the many cubicles.

His knuckles rapped against the metal frame and movement caught his attention through the dark tint. The door opened and Ray found himself staring up at the largest creature he'd ever seen.

Kel'Gos was a few inches taller than Crum with quite a bit more muscle, though his light brown skin was wrinkled in places suggesting he'd once been bigger. The massive orc had a scar across the right side of his face and the tusk on the same side was broken and dulled from age.

Ray recalled a discussion he'd had with Crum about how orcs aged. It had something to do with their sur name, though he hadn't heard which century *Gos* stood for. One thing was certain though. Kel'Gos was much older. What was more confusing was the skin tone. Crum'Bul was green. This orc was brown. It stood to reason that humans had different skin tones depending on where their ancestors lived. Was it the same with orcs? It was a question he didn't expect to ask. This orc could pick him up and break him in half with little more than a thought. "Dir— Director Kel'Gos, I presume?"

"You presume correctly. Come on in." Kel'Gos stepped aside, holding the door open.

Ray entered, instantly recognizing the scent of a burning cigar. The lingering haze had been an afterthought. He glanced around the surprisingly organized office, locating the source of the stench. A half burned Macanudo rested in an ashtray on the desk. Ray wasn't much of a cigar guy, though he'd been forced to suffer through his fair share of them. He was more suited for the rapid smoke of a cigarette. It had been a few months since his last one and while the craving still came from time to time, he wasn't thinking about it as often anymore. That was until someone lit up beside him. That always triggered the desire.

Looking around the office, Ray spotted a number of awards and decorations resting neatly atop a row of file cabinets on the left wall. It appeared to be mostly time of service plaques, but there were a few military awards he recognized as well. All were long before his time, more commonly seen in a museum than an office. Behind the desk, mounted to the wall was an ancient shield that had several deep gouges in the metal and wood. A worn battle axe hung blade down beneath it, though both appeared easily secured if the need arose. Three shelves rested together on the right, decorated by all manner of trophies, though none stood above a broken talon that stretched across the top of the three shelves and continued more than a foot on either side. Whatever it belonged to was a creature of gargantuan size.

Finding his own chair, Kel'Gos gestured to the seat in front of his desk and brought his cigar to his stretched lips. Taking a steady draw, he blew a thick cloud into the air and snuffed the rest.

Ray fell into the designated seat, realizing it was oversized to fit the girth of an orc. He felt like a child sitting at the grownup's table.

The old orc's gaze settled on the human. He watched him for a long moment, finally exhaling and letting his shoulders sink. "I wish we could have met under better circumstances. After that fiasco with Wright, I told Anderson I wanted you to come work for me. Unfortunately, the brass wouldn't have it."

Ray remembered Wright all too well. He'd damn near been shot by the traitorous elf. It had been Wright who'd arranged for Pandora to get out in the first place.

"Politics—" Kel'Gos scoffed, shaking his head. He grabbed two files, both atop two perfect stacks and handed them to Ray. Watching the human open them, he continued as if speaking from a textbook. "In the months following the release of Pandora one-hundred- and thirty-nine descendants were reported missing from the Miami Gardens area alone. Expanding another ten-block radius, the number climbs to two-hundred- and eight. Those numbers have been on the rise ever since.

"I had Crum looking into the disappearances. He made contact with numerous eyewitnesses, only for them to disappear before he could get anything solid. Finally, he caught a break. An informant contacted us. At twenty-one-nineteen, on September 4th, Crum left the WMD to meet the informant. He called me at twenty-three-thirty-seven announcing the informant had been snatched and that he was in pursuit. I haven't heard from him since.

"Two days later I received a call about a vehicle registered to one of our shell corporations. It was Crum's, abandoned in a lot at the South Florida Shipping Yard. We pulled his phone records. The only listed contacts were between he and I. His phone signal went inactive twenty-two minutes after his final contact."

Ray flipped through the files, looking at the details of Crum's case, as well as the case on Crum himself. "It says here you have an informant on Crum's disappearance but I'm not seeing a report."

"That's correct. About a week ago we received an encrypted message through an old channel. It said, 'I know who has Agent Crum'Bul.' There was a catch, however."

Ray stared blankly awaiting whatever the old orc had to offer.

"They requested you specifically."

"Why me?"

"That I cannot say. Information through those channels is often one-sided. The WMD is not authorized to operate outside the United States. Fortunately, the Marshals Service does not have that limitation."

"I understand, sir. Wait, outside the US?"

"You've got an eight p.m. flight to Brussels."

Chapter 3
Special Delivery

The elevator doors opened and Ray found himself standing in an entirely different lobby. This one looked a little closer to what he'd expected to see. It was still desperately lacking color but that seemed to be a common element throughout. Near the middle of the room there was a round receptionist desk with three people sitting with their backs to him. Numerous doors led off the side walls and a large glistening chandelier hung overhead. Stealing a glance, he could see that at least two floors above had a three-sided balcony that overlooked the lobby.

Making his way around the desk, a security checkpoint blocked access from a glass wall that held the exit doors and a foyer on the other side. Armed guards, metal detectors, and what looked to be an x-ray machine were all required for entry. Fortunately, leaving appeared to be a much simpler process.

Ray approached the right side waypoint. They had a turnstile in the middle of the guarded path and a single guard standing over it.

"Identification?" The muscular elf extended his hand.

Until this point Ray had assumed all elves were frail looking. The few he'd met weren't lacking strength or sickly or anything like that. They simply didn't appear overly strong. In hindsight it was a stupid thought. Stereotypes were based on reality but it didn't mean they were one-hundred percent accurate all the time. They certainly weren't in this case.

Handing his newly printed ID to the guard, Ray waited as he plugged it into the computer. His picture appeared on screen with, judging by the seemingly unending block of text, every detail ever known about him.

The guard reviewed the information, removed the card, and returned it. "Have a nice day." He gestured to the rotating gate which now displayed a green light instead of a red one.

Pushing his way through, Ray quickly navigated back to the central path and passed the inner and outer doors. The sun was beaming and the few lingering clouds were light and fluffy. It confirmed his suspicions. Something wasn't right on the eighth floor.

Ray turned to study the building. It was even less inviting than the public entrance at the front. This was little more than an unmarked door on the north face. It didn't even offer a city view, instead, staring directly at the bricked side of another building. The most attractive element in sight was an Audi A8 parked curbside on the narrow road.

Ray noted the engine was running, though the mirrored tint prevented sight inside.

The driver's door opened and a young man poked his head over the top. He was dressed in a simple black suit and a pair of sunglasses and fingerless leather gloves.

Ray prepared to take cover, though aside from a few short bushes hugging the wall there wasn't much cover to be had. This kid didn't look like much of a threat but he'd just entered a new world. There was no telling what to expect.

"Are you Marshal Bradley?"

"Yes?" Ray was slightly taken back by the title. It was something he was going to need to get used to.

"I've been directed to take you to the impound yard."

"What for?" Ray slowly made his way forward.

"Something about picking out a new car."

That made sense. The U.S. Marshals Service was responsible for nearly all seized assets. He hadn't even thought about that when the request was made. Of course, he didn't know he was going to be made a Marshal moments later either. The prospect brought an uncontrolled smile to his face. Reaching the Audi, Ray opened the passenger door and climbed in.

The driver started slow, pulling away from the curb. It didn't last long. The moment they were on open road, he was passing cars, sliding around corners, and doing just about everything short of breaking the sound barrier.

Clutching the 'oh shit' handle, Ray stomped the imaginary brake, finding a moment between certain and possible death to buckle his seat belt. He was used to driving fast, he was just more accustomed to being the one behind the wheel while doing it.

Traffic was starting to thin by the time Ray got his stomach settled. He glanced out the window realizing they were at the city's edge. All kidding aside, the kid was an excellent driver. He handled the car with perfect precision, no detail left unaccounted. Wind direction and strength, other cars, slickness of the surface, as well as loose objects and people in the cab. He calculated every factor in an instant, handling their execution with the skill of a professional.

Ray suspected the coffee test he'd failed when he first got his license would have been no trouble for this kid, even at a hundred miles an hour.

The cityscape passed, its expanse dwindling moment by moment. Buildings were replaced with trees, neighborhoods became marshland, and before long they were deep in the Everglades.

Ray had only been to the Glades a few times. It seemed the type of place one could easily get lost. He certainly didn't want to be on foot. That was just asking for trouble.

As if the universe were confirming his thoughts, they swerved, dodging a huge alligator basking on the warm asphalt. It was the first of many such encounters. Various snakes slithered across their path. Bugs splattered against the windshield, some so large he expected they'd survived the encounter. One thing was certain. He was glad they were in a vehicle. With all the critters along the road, there was no telling what existed out of sight.

The Audi slowed, transitioning from blacktop to gravel road. They traveled several miles before their destination came into view. It looked like an old airplane hangar at the head of what might have once been an airstrip. A tall chain link fence filled with privacy slats and topped by razor wire ran the perimeter. It blocked all sight as they neared. A guard shack sat at the entrance and a row of thick rods barred all access in or out.

Stopping at the shack, the driver lowered his window just enough to extend a card to the attendant. Without a word his gaze returned straight ahead and both hands locked on the steering wheel.

Ray wasn't sure what had been handed over. It looked too large to be an ID, though whatever it was clearly had the guard baffled. He inspected both sides, punched details into his computer, radioed his superiors, and even made a phone call to someone who spoke exclusively in a yelling volume. Finally, nodding vigorously as if whoever was on the phone could see him, the guard placed the card in a metal box under the counter and pushed a button somewhere out of sight. Lights began to flash on the boom in front of them and the steel barricades blocking their path retracted into the ground.

Ray felt the engine rev. The smirk growing on the driver's face announced he needed to hang on to something.

No sooner than the barricades seated, the flashing lights went out and the boom raised. It all happened so fast. Ray was plastered to his seat. Things flew past so quickly all he saw was a flash. It was possible they'd done a few donuts, though that was purely speculation. All he really knew was that before his takeoff reaction had registered, they were already coming to a stop. A huge bay door sat before them and a massive cloud of dust drifted past and engulfed them.

Coughing his nuts out of his chest, Ray glanced over. "I assume you don't open her up very often?"

The driver shrugged. "Not as much as I like. That's one nice thing about this place. The runway has plenty of room to see what a car's capable of. Take this little beauty, for instance." He patted the dash. "The body and interior are stock. Nothing else is."

"What's she top-out at?"

"The fastest I've been able to get her is two-twenty-six, but I know she can go faster. Unfortunately, it takes a bit to get her there."

The bay door split down the center and both sides slid outward, revealing a large man dressed in desert fatigues.

Ray recognized them. They'd just begun circulating the digitized ACUs about the time he was getting out. Prior to that it had been BDUs all the time. Everything about this man said military. He was standing at parade rest, staring intently at them.

Once the doors came to a full stop, the man snapped to attention and began formally marching. Right turn, left turn, left turn, halt!

The driver rolled his window to the bottom this time.

"You boys have clearance to inspect any piece of equipment on the yard. Pull ahead and park in the designated zone."

Ray watched him do an about face and march back inside, disappearing into the shadows.

The car slowly rolled forward and entered the huge building. Flickering white lights flashed into existence no sooner than their tires hit the concrete floor. They could have been on before but the blinding sun prevented him from realizing that. In truth, Ray couldn't pay much attention to anything. He was too enthralled with the contents of the massive warehouse around them.

There were five rows that ran the entire length of the hanger. He was just estimating, but each one had to be at least two football fields long. Each row consisted of a heavy metal shelf. He couldn't help but think of those orange pallet racks, only these were much larger, gray, and had several large hydraulic pistons between the runs. The outer two rows were comprised of three stacks, while the inner three had four. It was like Christmas, and he had his pick of toy. They had everything. Cars, motorcycles, ATVs, SUVs, trucks, boats, amphibious vehicles, planes, helicopters, and even a small selection of manned and unmanned tanks, as well as drones. It appeared to be sorted by type, but just when he thought he had it figured out, some strange combination would reset the pattern.

Barely able to contain his excitement, he turned to his driver. "Are you telling me I can pick whatever I want?"

"I believe Roderick used the words 'within reason'." He finger quoted. "For obvious reasons you'll want to stay away from tracked vehicles and aircrafts. You know what? Let's just make this easy and limit your selection to wheeled vehicles only. Boats aren't necessarily out of the question but they're typically reserved for special use and won't take you very far on land. And while motorcycles are fun it's hard to balance a bunch of stuff while operating."

"I take it you've tried?"

"Once or twice." He smiled, ensuring the seriousness of his statement.

"Sorry to ask, but what's your job? You act like a professional wheelman or stunt driver or something like that."

The driver pondered the question a moment. "Yes." He finally answered. "Something like that. Anyway, each vehicle has a spec sheet attached to the exterior. Take as long as you need."

The lack of answer was both humorous as well as intriguing. He wasn't entirely sure what to make of the kid but he liked him so far.

Climbing from the Audi, Ray began his search for the perfect vehicle. He looked at hundreds of cars. McLaren, Lamborghini, Ferrari, Rolls-Royce, even a Bugatti caught his attention. In the end only one spoke to him, and it wasn't even the most expensive one he found. The bond between car and driver was a special one. Not just anything would suffice, especially when such a selection was at his disposal.

Ray circled his new partner once again, taking in the elegant beauty of the matte black paint and sexy sleek design. The Aston Martin Vantage Roadster was a bit of a mouthful, but it was the one he needed. It was a convertible, which was nice. Unfortunately, it wasn't a manual transmission. They'd reserved that option for the hardtop variant. Still, this was the only car that spoke to him, and from the total of eleven miles on the tachometer, it was basically brand-new. That meant no one had had the opportunity to mess it up yet. How such a beautiful car had found its way into lockup, he couldn't say. These were all seized from criminals. He could only imagine the bad day its original owner had had.

Ending his final inspection at the driver's door, Ray grabbed the spec sheet hanging from a rubber band on the mirror. Ensuring the key fob was inside he opened the door, hearing it unlock with his touch. The sound brought a smile to his face. It was the sound of consent, as sweet as that little pelvic lift women did when he removed their panties. Never mind the proximity feature. This was a relationship between man and machine, though he had no intentions to screw his car.

Pressing the cycle control on the lift, Ray opened the door and settled inside. He had about thirty seconds before the lift would place him and the car on the ground. That was the perfect time to adjust the mirrors and seat, though now that he was here she didn't need adjustment. She was already perfectly attuned to him. If that wasn't a sign he didn't know what was.

Hearing the lift come to a stop and ensuring the ramps were in place, Ray consecutively pressed the brake pedal and the center dash start button. The engine purred to life. The low rumble sent chills down his spine and butterflies frolicked in his stomach. Pressing the drive button, the car crawled off the platform.

The unworn tires squealed no sooner than they touched the polished concrete. Ray straightened, slowly making his way toward the entrance. He wasn't sure what details were needed to complete the transaction but he desperately hoped there were no problems along the way. If it wasn't this car, he didn't want any other.

The driver was leaned against the hood of his Audi and playing on his phone when Ray appeared. Glancing up, he tucked his phone away and gestured at the space beside him.

Ray parked where directed. It nearly broke his heart to turn it off. Opening the door, he stepped out, smiling ear to ear. "This is the one. What do I do now?"

The kid chuckled. "Sounds like it's time for a test drive. Afterward, if you're certain, they'll have you fill out some paperwork."

The rest of the day passed quicker than expected. Ray updated his passport only to discover it wasn't needed when he arrived. He had no clue how long he'd be gone, which resulted in packing a week's worth of clothes and about three extra pairs of underwear and socks. And he spent as much time getting used to his car as possible. That pretty much covered saving his preferred stations and syncing his phone via Bluetooth, though he did manage to get in just over a hundred miles in the few hours before his flight.

After a short briefing which covered simple things about the plane, estimation times, lodging arrangements, and that he was going to be meeting a contact from some offshoot branch of Interpol that he'd never heard of, Ray was off the ground and in route to Brussels.

For his first experience in a private jet, he was deeply disappointed. To begin, there were no attractive flight attendants. No stripper poles. And no cabin music or disco lights converting it into a mile-high nightclub after takeoff. To be fair, there were no flight attendants of any kind, attractive or otherwise. Just himself, the pilot, and copilot were onboard. But still, he'd hoped it would be somewhat like it was in the movies. It turned out to be just another example of Hollywood lies.

This was the final test run for the newly crafted Cessna Citation Longitude. They were awaiting another few hours of flight time before they'd be officially awarded some certificate or license or something about the fuel tanks. In truth, Ray hadn't really been paying much attention to the logistics. The pilot assured him the plane was safe. That was all that mattered. Besides, if he'd declined the trip, which had been offered on numerous occasions during the briefing, it would have taken another week minimum to lockdown the next available flight, a Gulfstream G650. Crum didn't have that kind of time.

Getting comfortable, Ray turned on the TV. They had a decent selection of movies to choose from, though not much he hadn't seen several times over. Mindlessly, he selected Mel Brook's Young Frankenstein and got up to inspect the bar. Another disappointment. He'd seen hotel minibars with a wider selection than this thing had. Sighing, he started a bag of microwave popcorn and made himself a rum and coke.

The microwave dinged. Grabbing his drink and popcorn, Ray plopped onto the flatbed. It seemed more like a couch without arms than a bed but it was comfortable nonetheless. Securing his phone, he leaned against the backrest and passively watched the movie.

"The time is one-thirty-seven p.m. We'll be arriving at Brussels-National in approximately five minutes. I'd like to thank you for joining us on our first FAA Certified flight. Please return to your seat and prepare for landing."

Hearing the voice over the intercom, Ray jumped. He wasn't sure when he'd passed out but the TV was off, his drink was empty except for melted ice, and a crumpled popcorn bag rested beside him. Wiping the drool from his chin, he sat up and moved to the chair where his bag was located. Glancing out the window he could see land far below. None of it looked familiar, though he was sure he could say the same about the land back home. From this elevation major landmarks were about the only noticeable indicator as to where he was and he didn't know any of them.

Buckling his seatbelt, Ray heard the toilet flush behind him. He glanced back seeing the door open and the copilot step out.

Stopping near Ray's seat, he offered a warm smile. "Did you have a good rest?"

He was in his mid to late twenties with short brown hair and a freshly shaven face. He wore a uniform, though Ray never learned pilot insignia. He didn't even know if it fell within the same realm as military insignia, though the lack of name tag sparked a dilemma. He knew he'd been introduced to both pilots, and one of them was Charlie. For the life of him the other name escaped his memory. "Slept like a baby. Any idea how long I was out?"

"No clue. We've been in the air for almost thirteen hours. The tanks are running on fumes but we've got enough to land."

"Thanks, Charlie." It was a risk but one he felt inclined to take. When he departed, it wouldn't be appropriate to address them as dude, guy, fellow, or some other liquid label.

The copilot's smile dropped. "I'm Doug. Charlie's in the cockpit. It's okay though. I forgot your name too, Ray."

"My bad. In my defense, I did just wake up." A mild chuckle escaped him.

"I'm just messing with you. We're all good."

"If I heard *Charlie* right, he said it's one-something. I thought you said we've only been in flight for about thirteen hours?

"Time zone difference. They're five hours ahead here. GMT time."

"Ah. I guess that makes sense."

"Yeah. Anyway, I need to get up there an' do my job. I don't know how long this job of yours is going to take, but we'll be departing this evening. You're welcome to ride back if you need."

"I'll have to play it by ear. Though if I get what I need I'll do my best to be back in time."

"No worries." Doug glanced out the window seeing the airstrip on approach. He dropped all formality and rushed into the cockpit and closed the door behind him.

Ray tugged against his seatbelt, making sure it was secure. It was silly really. All the nylon strap would do was make his body easier to locate in the event of a crash. That's really all any seatbelt did, though it felt more important at the rate they were approaching the earth.

The plane touched down with a mild bounce and the tires squealed. They were on a small strip adjacent to the main terminal. Ray wasn't sure if this was for private crafts or something special. It didn't matter. He was here now. With any luck he'd get what he came for and be back on the plane in no time.

Watching out the window, they made a sweeping arc and turned toward a row of hangers. The plane came to a stop, which didn't result in the best view. It was open grassland on one side and tin covered shacks on the other. He did notice one thing of interest. A glossy Bentley Continental GT with beaming headlights parked about ten feet from them. The tinted glass made it difficult to see who was inside, but this had to be the contact he was told about.

Listening to the engines wind down, twin Honeywell turbofans he'd learned during the briefing, the cockpit door opened and both men stepped out. Charlie was much older, probably mid-sixties. He wore a uniform identical to Doug's, only he had more patches sewn to his.

"Enjoy the flight?" He asked, stepping aside so Doug could open the door.

"Honestly, I slept through most of it."

The older man chuckled. "Happens to the best of us. I managed to get a few hours myself."

Ray started to question, though the presence of a copilot answered for him. He would have felt stupid if it had escaped his mouth. Unbuckling his seatbelt, Ray grabbed his bag and stood. It took about three steps to realize he'd been sitting for too long. His legs felt like jelly. He staggered toward the doorway, nearly in reach when they gave out. To his surprise he didn't meet the floor. Ray didn't know an old man could move that fast. He looked up from Charlie's arms, trying to get his feet beneath him.

"You all right, sir?"

"I'm fine, thank you. Damn legs fell asleep."

Charlie laughed, though he didn't release immediately. Helping him to the steps, he slowly released seeing him take his own weight. "Hold tight to the handrail. Wouldn't want you missing a step and tumbling to the ground."

"Yeah, that wouldn't feel very good. But if it's gonna happen there's bound to be witnesses. It's hard to make a fool of yourself when no one's around to see it."

Charlie chuckled. "Very true, sir. Just so you know, we'll be refueling and taking a break for a few hours. Departure's scheduled for ten p.m. You're more than welcome to join us on the return trip."

"Thank you. I'm not sure what my schedule's going to be, but if I'm not back by then, assume I won't be going."

"Understood. Good luck."

"Thanks."

The first couple steps were somewhat tricky. Each one felt like his knee was hitting the ground. The tingling was starting to set in which didn't feel any better but it made walking a little easier. Ray slowly made his way to the base of the steps. No sooner than he hit the ground, the car door opened and the most beautiful woman he'd ever laid eyes upon stepped out.

He stared in stunned silence, unsure what to say. Naturally, the first thing that came out was the last thing he'd intended. "You're an elf!"

"Half-elf actually, thank you for noticing."

Even her voice was sexy. The language rolled off her tongue. If he had to guess, he would have said Romanian, though he was no expert in accents. Ray was lost in her dark glossy hair, nearly matching that of her car. Her brown almond shaped eyes held a sparkle he hadn't seen elsewhere, not to mention the pensive depth within them. Her perfect skin was smooth and colored like that of golden sand. It was a shame the light gray suit she wore covered so much of it. A metallic badge hung from her left breast pocket, saving him from ogling longer than appropriate. Women were like a fine wine. You didn't just pop the cork and go to town. You had to let them breathe a bit first.

Quickly reading the badge, he noticed *Interpol – ICPC* cresting around it. Ray could narrowly see a glowing ring around the center sigil, similar to that of his own badge. It made him wonder if his Sergeant's badge had the same thing. Unfortunately, it'd been taken when he got suspended.

"Marshal Bradley, I presume?"

"Uh—Yeah." The fact he was already making a fool of himself did not set well. First, he'd nearly fallen down the steps. Now he couldn't even talk without the words sounding stupid.

"I'm Senior Agent Lilian Lambrino, Interspecies Criminal Police Commission. I'll be your chaperone while you're with us."

"Cool." For the first time in his life he wished he would just stop talking.

A knowing smirk peeked onto Lilian's lips, disappearing just as fast. She gestured to the car. "Shall we?" Refusing to wait, she opened the passenger side door and climbed in.

Ray stood there a moment, confused. "I guess I'm driving." He slowly circled the car, hoping his legs would behave. They were beginning to regain feeling. That wasn't a good thing. Feeling at the moment was horribly tingly. He opened the door and climbed inside, instinctively reaching for the steering wheel. It wasn't there.

"First time in the UK?"

"I spent a little time in Germany, Iraq, and Afghanistan. The usual hangouts. Never in the UK to my knowledge. Though, we aren't exactly in the UK, are we?"

"Not exactly. There's an embassy here though, so it still counts." Lilian put the car in gear and let out on the clutch.

"By that logic, the US would be part of the United Kingdom. I'm pretty sure we had a big war to ensure that didn't happen. 1776, the British are coming and all that."

It could have been the start of a laugh that escaped the beautiful woman beside him, though she stifled it immediately. "Americans are funny." Exiting the airport, she turned onto the road and into the right side lane.

"Um, why are you on this side of the road? I thought you guys drove on the left?"

"A few countries are left side. Belgium is not one of them. Actually, more countries drive on the right than on the left."

"Then why do you have a right controlled car?" Ray hoped he wasn't asking too many questions.

"I like this car. Do I need more reason than that?"

"None whatsoever. I was just curious." A long awkward silence followed. After a few minutes, the urge returned. "So, how many Americans have you met?"

She shrugged. "A few. How did you know I wasn't human? It's usually only the true believers or the junkies. You don't fit the mold of either."

"It's a long story. Someone should write a book about it. Short form, I was drugged semi-voluntary and shown the truth. Hard not to believe when you've seen it firsthand."

"I guess that makes sense. At least now I know why they sent me."

"Why's that?"

"Clearly you haven't been in this job long." Lilian accelerated, whipping around from the A201 and onto Zaventem R22. In no time they were flying down the E40.

"I like the way you drive." He desperately hoped he would just shut up. This had never happened before. Usually he was pretty smooth. Something had to be wrong.

"Thanks. Most people complain I go too fast."

"I like fast. So, where are we going?"

They cornered and shot onto N23. "Interpol. We have to get you a visitors' pass before your meeting."

"Okay. So, what did you mean by why they sent you?"

"I don't know how things work where you come from. Here I'm the senior investigating agent. Not to be rude, but this is— How do you Americans say it? —below my pay scale. They wouldn't have brought me in for babysitting unless you were someone who causes problems."

"What kind of problems?" Ray knew he was walking a fine line but his intrigue told him there was more to the situation.

"If they send an elf. They're applicable to the same laws as the rest of us. If they send a normal human, they can't see anything beyond their realm of comprehension. But when they send a human who can see through the Veil, secrets aren't so easily hidden. They want me to make sure you don't get involved in anything *above* your pay scale."

"I suppose I get that. Kind of like playing in someone else's backyard without letting them know."

"I don't know what that means but for the sake of simplicity, we'll go with it." Lilian squealed the tires, drifting into what appeared to be an abandoned parking lot in front of an old rundown building. Slowing only when necessary, she slipped between two fence posts where the mesh was missing. It was a steep grade but she handled it with precision. No sooner than her tires hit the asphalt, she pulled a U-turn and circled behind the building, pulling straight into an open garage door. It closed behind them.

Chapter 4
The Other Guys

Beaming headlights shone on the blank concrete slab. Metal conduit ran vertical along the wall, disappearing at the light's edge.

A sudden ground shift caught Ray's attention. He could hear metal clanking somewhere in the shadow. Turning his attention to Lilian, her angelic face reflected paradise by the dashboard lights. She showed no concern. The tubing brackets began to move, stealing his interest. They traveled up the wall— or more likely, the car was going down.

An eternity passed, staring blankly at the plain wall. Hundreds of better pastimes flashed through his mind, a great many of them involving parked cars. Before he could make a bigger fool of himself, Ray was relieved to see the end of their voyage come into view.

Yellow lights erupted, burning away the shadows. A moment later the car touched down with a metallic thud. Ray glanced around. They were in the farthest left of a four-bay garage, near identical to the one they'd pulled into. A waist high barrier divided them. It was a good thing. The next two bays were little more than a bed of springs and thick chains that disappeared up into darkness. He guessed those two were at the top. The far right bay had a solid floor like the one they were parked on. There was only one real difference, as far as he could tell anyway. Now, the open door stood ahead of them.

An oddly smooth road with bright yellow markings lay just ahead. It turned in front of them and headed off to the right. The space between the garage—lift— and road was occupied by two identical booths, stationed between the outer runs. A black and white striped boom protruded from both sides blocking all traffic.

Lilian crept forward, stopping at the downed bar in front of them. She reached into her pocket and retrieved a brown bifold wallet. Stretching out the window, she presented her ID and a moment later they were on the move.

Ray stared in wonder at their surroundings. At first, it didn't appear to be anything more than a common parking garage. Rows of cars were parked here and there. Concrete slabs comprised the walls. And the familiar echo known in such places was ever-present. That had been a façade, eradicated no sooner than they left the main road. It was then he realized they were in some kind of massive subterranean complex.

Fallen water droplets left the ground continually wet. Large humming lights glowed from ceiling mounted cages, their flickering luminance greatly diminished by stalactite shadows and dark moisture. Numerous buildings cropped along the sides, growing out of and comprised of the surrounding rock. The maze of roads, each worn smooth from years of use, jutted between massive pillars of rough stone, some disappearing into and around walls of the same. Dust covered curtains blocked entire sections. Sometimes the roads cut straight through columns or ran along seemingly natural bridges that straddled expansive overhangs.

The constant turns and sudden intersections, unseen until upon them, would have been pure chaos if not for the painted lines and numerous signs dangling above. Ray was beginning to recognize when the traffic was growing thicker or some unknown danger was near. The fluorescent yellow always became exceedingly heavy in those areas. They were doing so now.

Out of nowhere, they exited a tunnel and passed in front of a large waterfall. A gentle mist coated the windshield and glossy paint of Lilian's car, requiring the wipers to engage. Ray peered into the shadows below, hearing the roaring water crash somewhere out of sight. The road curved around, circling behind the fall before it entered another tunnel. It was marvelous to behold.

As far as he could tell the entire place was a blend of masterfully carved stone and metal. It became increasingly difficult to identify what was natural and what had been crafted. Seeing it for the first time, a single question rose above the rest. What was the purpose? Surely it would have been easier to build above ground.

Almost every building was labeled by a letter and number combination, written in a language he didn't understand. Many had concrete or metal faces, especially near the entrance, but the bulk of their entirety was hidden within stone. And while he hadn't seen any in the last few sections, most had several rows of docks that were filled to capacity with parked and running big rigs.

Seeing Ray's interest, Lilian offered some insight. "This is our main distribution hub. It's primarily a cold storage facility but they handle almost all trade goods."

"How do they get the trucks down here? There's no way they'll fit through the doors we came in."

She laughed at the simplicity of his statement. "There's more than one entrance. Two others, actually. We used the lift because it was the closest to where we're going."

"And where's that?"

"I already told you. ICPC." Lilian turned on to a narrow road wholly different from the others. It was rougher, pitted in many places. A fair amount of dust and debris made the usually dark surface look more of a dirty tan. The overhead lights ended at the main road, their glow rapidly fading. The path twisted and passed under one of the tunneled columns. It was this point the headlights became the only source of light, doing little for anything not directly ahead of them.

Jaw locked and fists clenched, a weird feeling churned in Ray's stomach. There was a growing anxiety in his chest. Suddenly he realized he was scared. He hadn't noticed it when there was plenty of light but now, lost in the near dark labyrinth of underground corridors beneath an equally unfamiliar city, he was starting to feel phobic. He wasn't afraid of caves. It wasn't the dark. It wasn't necessarily even the enclosed space they were traveling through. He'd experienced all independently on numerous occasions. It was simply the fact that there was no telling how far underground they were and the condition of the road was getting worse by the moment. What if a tire blew? What if they had to walk? Did Lilian know how to guide them on foot? What if something happened to her and he had to navigate it alone? Sure, his cellphone had a light, but the battery would only last so long. It wasn't like he could simply call somebody.

Finally, the headlights landed on something other than a dark void. It looked like one of those dirty vinyl curtains he'd seen further back. That relieved some of his concern.

Reaching into the center console, Lilian grabbed a garage door opener and pressed the large gray button. The curtain shuttered and began to slide to the left. Light spilled from behind and another road was revealed. Waiting for it to open completely, Lilian inched forward and transitioned back to the smooth floor.

The narrow road was just wide enough for two vehicles to squeeze past. It curved and wrapped further into the cavern, finally opening into a large chamber. Seeing no other tunnels, Ray assumed it was a dead end. A single building was partially inset to the wall on the right. Large protruding letters arranged in *I.C.P.C.* were fixed across the front. Smaller lettering formed a line beneath, spelling out the abbreviation. *Interspecies Criminal Police Commission.*

Parking in one of the numerous open spaces on the left, Lilian turned off the ignition and stepped out.

Climbing out, Ray circled the backside of the car and fell into step behind her. The air was crisp but far from cold. He suspected, pretty much like all caves, it was this temperature year round. Walking across the road, he instinctively grabbed his phone and swiped the screen, checking his notifications.

Starting up the short series of steps, Lilian spoke over her shoulder. "You aren't going to get much. We're too far below ground. Only landlines work down here."

"I guess that explains why I have no signal." He tucked the phone away and continued after her.

It was a short walk, lined by painted handrails. The entrance was a single door, glass with metal frame. A decal was plastered high-center bearing the earth with a vertical sword behind it. It had a wreath wrapped beneath the lower half and a set of balanced scales at the bottom. The banner on the globe's base said *Interpol* and another across the top, overlapping the sword, matched the initials on the building. It wasn't the official logo, at least not among the human world, but that was to be expected. Especially if they were anywhere near as secretive about things as the WMD.

Lilian pulled the door aside, allowing Ray to enter first.

"Normally I like to be the one holding doors for pretty women." He smiled, though it didn't appear to have the effect he was hoping for.

Lilian shrugged and stepped inside, letting the glass barrier close on him.

Chuckling to himself, Ray pulled the door open a second time and followed her inside.

The temperature was a bit more friendly than it had been. Only a few of the overhead lights were on, leaving it darker than he preferred. It was also much quieter than he'd expected. But it didn't look or feel much different than the numerous police stations he'd visited. Aside from the quiet anyway. If not for the subtle clicking of unseen typists and a few hushed voices in the distance, he would have thought the place empty.

A wooden receptionist desk sat just inside the door. The counter was the perfect height to lean against, though he refrained. His visit was already off to a rough start. He didn't want to give them any more reason to dislike him.

To the right, a long hall stretched on forever. Numerous doorways lined the right, greatly disproportionate to the few on the left. Of the handful of open doors, only a couple had their lights on showing any sign of life.

Signaling him to follow, Lilian started down the hall ignoring the first several offices. She passed the first opening on the left, one of the few providing light, and continued.

Ray took the opportunity to inspect. It looked to be more of a lounge style breakroom than anything. A couch, coffee table, and a few recliners were angled around an old style TV along the back wall. The center was occupied by a round table with four wooden chairs, all tucked neatly under. A vending machine and refrigerator rested side by side in a gap between the rear wall and a countertop. The opposite counter was cluttered with a sink, microwave, toaster, espresso machine, and regular old coffee pot that was heavily stained.

Realizing he'd fallen behind, Ray had to take larger steps to catch up. He nearly ran her over, unprepared for her sudden stop.

Refusing to cross the threshold, Lilian leaned around the doorframe and peeked inside. "Do you have time to authenticate a visiting officer's badge?"

"Of course! You know my day exists only to suit your needs."

Ray didn't like the response one bit. He was a pretty decent judge of character and he already knew he wasn't going to get along with whoever this was.

Ignoring the condescension in his voice, Lilian smiled. "Great." She turned and gestured Ray into the room.

Skeptically, Ray entered. His immediate impression was wrong. Not about liking the guy. That wasn't likely to change. He was wrong because he'd expected an elf. It was another of those stereotype mistakes he'd made so frequent of late. Since his introduction to this world he'd spent a vast amount of time learning everything he could. There was one piece of information the numerous books, granted most of them RPG or game manuals, agreed upon. Elves were always pompous. The demeanor was accurate. This guy clearly fit the description. He was wrong because this guy was not an elf. He was something—different.

Ray stared up at the creature behind the desk. It was the tallest humanoid he'd ever seen, and it was sitting down. Even Kel'Gos, who had to be at least seven-foot-two would have had to look up at this guy. But he wasn't stocky either. Quite the contrary, he was exceptionally slender, more so than any elf he'd seen. The man—creature—thing, was little more than glistening skin and jagged bone. His shoulders were pointed and hooked, as were all his joints. His hair was slicked back and sparkly white, almost like he'd used glitter glue in place of gel. But what really set him apart from every other creature Ray'd come across— This guy had thin iridescent wings that sprouted from his back and draped down like a cape. They looked almost insectoid, like a cicada or a dragonfly.

"Um, what are you?" Ray couldn't help but ask, the insolence of his question not lost upon him. "I apologize— I've just— I've never seen your kind before."

"Fantastic! I'm pleased to have expanded your knowledge of beings different than yourself. Do you have your identification?" The winged man stood, his slender and pointed head nearly touching the ceiling. His bony fingers extended, beady dark eyes glaring complete and total indifference at the visitor.

Ray handed his driver's license to the strange creature.

A heavy sigh escaped the winged being and he returned the plastic card. "Your other identification."

"Oh. I'm sorry. I'm not quite used to having more than one." Ray handed over his Marshal ID card.

"We can't all be of superior intellect." The creature took the badge and returned to his seat. Placing a jeweler's lens to his eye, he studied every detail. "Ah, yes, I see." Lowering the device, he twisted and grabbed a thick tome from the shelf beside him. Opening to the center, he began flipping page by page in search of something.

Peeking over the contraptions cluttering the desk, Ray noticed the book was filled with several incarnations of the glowing runes he'd seen around both his and Lilian's badges. It didn't make any sense why that mattered. He'd inspected the card thoroughly and hadn't seen one. Even if he had, those in the book looked no different. Though he had to admit it was difficult to tell with such fine detail. "What's all that mean?"

Sighing deeply, the winged creature glared up from the book, his gaze burning a hole through the pesky human. "It means the more you talk the longer this takes. I know my time means nothing to you, but I'd like to go home sometime today. Even if I had the desire to lower my intelligence by consorting with you, I have not the time nor the patience to explain it in a manner of which your feeble brain is capable of comprehending."

"You're a bit of a dick. I wonder if your superior intellect is capable of comprehending that?"

The creature held his gaze for a moment before returning his focus to the book.

Leaning beside Ray, Lilian spoke just over a whisper. "Don't mind him. He's always been an arrogant prick. He's identifying your rune magic."

"Rune magic? What's that?"

"It's a protective ward inscribed on your badge. All cops have them. That's why it became known as a shield. It's supposed to protect you when nothing else can, but the effects are different on each one. He has to make sure the runes are an exact match. If they aren't, they can conflict with each other and create any number of problems."

"Oh, okay." Ray focused intently on the runes, trying to identify the differences between two seemingly identical sets.

"You still don't understand, do you?"

"Not really, no." A laugh escaped him, which brought a smile to Lilian's face. That was a pleasant sight.

"Children, please. I need to concentrate. In fact, why don't you two continue your schoolgirl crush elsewhere. I'll let you know when you're needed."

Standing upright, Lilian glared, daring the winged man to say anything further. "Come on. The air's better out here anyway. It doesn't smell so strong of pixie."

Growling his discontent, the winged creature chucked a wooden pipe stand at the doorway. It shattered on impact. "I'm not a damned pixie. Pixies and sprites are like four inches tall. I'm a faerie, gods damn it. If you're going to insult me get it right!"

Lilian chuckled, pleased with herself. "Do you know how many things he's broken that way?"

"My guess is quite a few." Ray entered the break room and approached the espresso machine. Lifting the cup rail, he glanced into the reservoir and grabbed the coffee-stained pot from the much simpler unit beside it.

"You don't know how to use that thing, do you?"

"Am I that obvious?"

Lilian smirked. "Step aside."

Ray returned the pot to its cold plate and took a seat at the table.

Replacing the top rail, Lilian inspected the Profitec 700 Dual Boiler. Checking the switches, the machine began to gurgle and heat. She worked with such prestige, it was difficult to know what all she was doing. She lifted the drip pan with one hand, working tandem with a grinder in the other. Stretching for the cupboard, Lilian secured a small burlap sack.

Seeing her stretch like that sent improper thoughts through Ray's mind. He had to force himself to turn away or risk an audible grunt of manliness.

Filling the grinder, Lilian returned the bag to where it belonged. The machine came to life and a coarse powder settled where the loosely packed beans had been an instant before. Her left hand returned to the espresso machine. It took little more than the twist of her wrist and the chrome-plated basket handle came free. She inspected it, lifting the brew lever at the same time. Steaming water spilled from the underside, purging the head. She dropped the lever and turned her attention to filling the basket with the fresh grounds. A few firm taps settled the heaping mound and she pressed the tamper, firmly packing it. A quick flip told her it was ready. "Are you straight espresso or more of a latte kind of guy?" Lilian asked, setting two cups beneath the reinstalled basket.

"I lean toward the sweeter side of things, but I'm willing to take it however you want to give it." The double meaning brought a smirk to his lips, though she either didn't catch it or chose not to comment.

Lilian spun toward the fridge with such grace she may as well have been floating. Locating a jug of milk, she returned and poured a fair amount into a metal pitcher.

He had no idea what she was doing or why, but it was enjoyable to witness, like watching an artist work. The fact that random containers and levers and knobs all seemed to respond to her with such elegance added to the mystery.

Hissing steam became a gurgling echo and a reddish-brown liquid began to drip into the twin cups. Lilian rotated the pitcher, creating a whirlpool within the metal container. She placed her hand against the side, checking the temperature. Certain it was hot enough, she turned off the steam wand and tapped the pitcher against the countertop, removing any lingering bubbles. The espresso finished with just enough time to clean and purge the wand before tucking it away. Topping the cups with steamed milk, Lilian glided across the floor and took a seat. With a flip of the wrist, the cup danced across the table and settled perfectly in front of him.

Ray stared at the intricate pattern swirling atop the brown liquid. He'd seen various latte art before. It was usually something like a leaf or a flower, sometimes even a cat or a series of hearts. None were as amazing as this. A bird sat in its nest, calling to the sky. The nest disappeared and wings formed, taking flight. After four or five visible flaps, it dove under the surface never to return. Ray was in awe, watching the swirl end in a perfectly blended mix of espresso and cream. "That's amazing! It's so— I'm not—Just wow!"

Lilian smiled, taking a sip of her own.

"I assume it's a safe guess you've done that a few times." Ray brought the cup to his lips and sipped the creamy concoction.

Lilian shrugged. "A few."

"So tell me a little more about this rune magic."

"There isn't much to tell. It's not exclusive to law enforcement, but we're about the only ones who use it anymore. Our side anyway. I think the humans forgot about it. I haven't seen it on their shields in a long time. Even before law enforcement became what it is today, knights of old used it. The old code, which all knights were sworn to uphold. That was basically the same thing. If they broke the code the runes quit working for them. You could always identify law enforcement of one kind or another by their shield."

"Okay, but how does that work for protection. I was under the impression magic went away when the Veil was created."

"Arcane magic did, yes. But there's more than one type. Have you ever heard stories of a mother lifting a car to save her child, or even something so simple as a coin for good luck?"

"Of course."

"This is magic, just a different kind."

"How many kinds are there?"

"I don't know. I think four, maybe?"

"What are they?"

"You ask a lot of questions."

Ray smiled, taking another sip of the delicious goodness in his cup.

Gesturing to the latte mustache on his lip, Lilian couldn't help but return the smile. "Arcane was the most widely known. But nobody has seen it in so long. There's been reports of divine magic, but likewise it's rarely talked about."

"Divine, like gods and stuff?"

"Exactly. Most believe the gods are dead. Or they simply don't care anymore. It's hard to say."

"So you believe in god?"

"*A god*, not really. *The gods*, it would be foolish not to."

"Why's that?"

"Think of the relationship between an ant and your people. Sure, some ants have seen humans, but the vast majority have never ventured outside what they know. When an ant finds its way into a house, a human will typically smash it without a second thought. They never consider that it had a life. It could have been there for any reason, food, shelter, searching for its mate. But a human will step on it simply because it ended up in a place it didn't belong, among creatures it can't possibly hope to understand. A human lifetime is nothing compared to that of a god, like the ant is nothing to a human. If enough ants gather, they can kill a human. As can one individual ant, but it's unlikely it will survive the process. It's all a matter of perspective. Humans cannot understand a god any better than an ant can understand a human. It's for that reason I believe it's foolish."

"So, elves are immune to this relationship between gods and man?" Ray asked, noticing she only used humans for her example.

"No. I selected that term because I believe you'd be better able to understand it."

"So, what are the other magics?"

"Mind and soul. A mother lifting a car is using her soul. The person with good luck is using their mind."

"Well, how does rune magic work then. Clearly it can't be mind if most don't know of its existence. They can't will it to protect them."

"They can. Having unwavering faith in something is a form of mental prowess. It creates a force of mental energy which leads events toward the desired outcome."

"But that doesn't always work." Ray added, realizing they were getting deep into something he'd need a lot of time to understand.

"It does if one's will is strong enough. When their belief is not solid, that's when it fails."

"Okay. So how does one control soul magic? If mental power is a trained ability, surely the others are as well. And how does rune magic tie in?"

Lilian sighed, setting her cup on the table. She leaned forward, staring deep into Ray's eyes.

Meeting her gaze, he felt a pull. It was like she was tugging at the door, trying to get him to open it. The spark he'd seen deep within her beautiful brown orbs was more present than ever, more intriguing than anything he'd seen. He was lost, traveling in their eternity, refusing to look away. A longing burned inside him, something he'd never felt before. And suddenly, he was thrown out, returned to the present.

Lilian leaned back, looking away. She wasn't sure what she'd been looking for. Whatever it was disappeared the moment she tried to isolate it. Slowly, she turned toward him and continued. "I believe they are all learned abilities. I believe they can all be obtained through training and discipline. As for how they work, I cannot say. Rune magic is not one of those four. It belongs in the realm of innate ability, which borders on arcane. Faeries are one of the last remaining races with access to their innate powers. They are believed to be born of magic. A truly magical race. It's as much a part of them as their body or voice. The Veil is constantly keeping the well spring empty, using any new magics to recharge itself. Faeries are their own little generator. It allows them access to what's been lost to most others."

"So, you're saying that right now faeries are the only ones capable of using magic?"

"Not entirely. They're simply the only ones unregulated in its use. Others have innate ability. Pureblood elves are another *born of magic* race. But no one's seen or heard from them in almost a thousand years. Long before the Veil. The closest is a handful of second generation elves, and about thrice as many third gens. But they have little more than a few parlor tricks."

"What do you mean by generation? I know with orcs it's like a way of telling how old they are."

The sarcastic faerie leaned out his office door and around the corner. "I've finished the inscribing. Please return and waste more of my time."

Lilian smiled, getting to her feet. "Come on. Once we're done here we'll go get some food."

"Food is good." Returning to the office, Ray took position where he'd been before. A bright flash blinded him just as he was about to sit.

"You need to sign this." The faerie extended a wireless pad with a pen protruding from the top.

Quickly scribbling his signature, he plopped down and his original ID was returned. A moment later he was handed another with a metal clip on top.

The faerie watched in interest, bringing his jeweler's glass to eye. He studied Ray from head to toe. "Pity."

"What's that?" Ray asked, unsure what was supposed to have happened. He studied the new ID badge. It contained the worst picture he'd ever taken, along with the ICPC logo and the word 'Visitor' across the top in bold blue letters. Unfortunately, he still couldn't see the runes.

"I was hoping you'd explode. Taking pride in one's work is so often a curse." The faerie shook his head in disappointment, returning his tools to where they belonged.

Lilian took the card and clipped it to Ray's suit jacket. "You'll have to keep this with you at all times. It's embedded with a tracking chip in the unlikely event you're misplaced or abducted."

"We couldn't be so fortunate." The faerie interjected.

Glaring at the winged creature, Lilian continued. "When you're ready to return home, we'll out process you here. Any information collected, including the badge, will be destroyed." Checking the time, seeing they were approaching three o'clock, she gestured for him to follow. "Let's go get some food. Your meeting is arranged for five."

The 95th District

Levi Samuel

Chapter 5
Stout Evidence

The trip to the surface wasn't nearly as fascinating as the trip down. Now that the initial shock had worn off, Ray was noticing things he hadn't paid attention to before. Notably, the number of people present. Near the larger collections of warehouses and other assorted buildings, foot traffic and golf carts seemed to be the primary means of transport, though he'd spotted a couple shuttle vans in service. The dock areas were filled with semi trucks and forklifts. As far as he could tell, most of the normal vehicles were parked in various lots, used only for arrival or departure.

They were in a different part of the massive underground system. Ray couldn't recall seeing any of this from his earlier venture, though that wasn't saying much. How was he supposed to identify one section of stone from another when it all looked the same? Still, they hadn't passed any buildings in quite some time and the tunnel seemed to be getting straighter.

The car glided atop the wet floor with precision, not so much as a squeak calling from its tires. Lilian stepped on the throttle, racing through the narrow channel. Pillars separated the parallel roads, revealing the other side here and there. This part felt more like an underground highway than a road. They passed under tunneled arches, around sudden curves, and over bridges that spanned seemingly unending chasms of darkness. She never once showed the slightest sign of fear.

Ray on the other hand held tight to his seat, though it wasn't nearly as fast as his previous escort.

Sunlight exploded into view. Before his eyes could adjust they launched from the mouth of a large cave, blowing past the security checkpoint. Leaning forward, Ray stole a glance through the left side mirror, seeing two massive black holes in the side of a cliff face. A long line of eighteen-wheelers awaited entry at the tunnel opposite the one they'd escaped.

Refusing to slow, Lilian reached the top of the subtle incline and cranked the wheel, sliding onto the highway. The tires never made a peep.

Now that they were in the open and on proper blacktop, Ray sat back and relaxed a bit. He had no delusions Lilian had increased in speed. He didn't need to look at the speedometer to know they were running upwards of ninety. Somehow, it was less nerve-racking knowing the threat of sudden rocky protrusions was diminished.

For several minutes Ray studied his surroundings, as best he could anyway. Sights weren't available long, but he was finding a beauty to the exotic city. He wasn't sure how long they'd been on the road— a few minutes maybe— but the car was slowing.

Lilian turned into a near empty gravel lot. An old looking building with slated wood trim and a tavern feel sat just the other side and the blue and white sign mounted above the entrance read, *Café Novo.*

"You sure they're open?"

"They're open." Lilian assured, climbing out. She walked with purpose, as if the place was nothing new to her. Pulling the door aside, she stepped in and glanced around.

Ray followed, forcing himself not to stare at her backside. He wanted to. That was the only thing he wanted—well, not the only thing. There was something unusual about her. Something that demanded more than his typical treatment. Whether it was because she was a cop, like him, or something more, he couldn't say.

A woman came through the opening behind the counter and stared at them. "Het spijt me, maar onze lobby is momenteel gesloten. De patio is beschikbaar of wij bieden uit te voeren."

"We gaan op de patio zitten." Lilian responded, turning left along the bar. She passed a few pub tables, high top and booth style, and pushed open the side door.

Ray had no idea what either of them had said. He followed regardless. Stepping out the door he found himself on a wooden patio. Thick ivy clung to the lattice boards tacked along the side walls. A thin canopy offered shelter from the sun while allowing the outdoor breeze to circulate. Numerous tables, some wood, others metal, were scattered about, and a small stage was erected in one of the corners.

Lilian took a seat at one of the metal tables, adjusting the matching chair to her comfort.

Selecting the seat across from her, Ray sat down. "Come here often?"

"Sometimes. I usually eat inside. This stupid pandemic thing is getting out of hand."

"I couldn't agree more. Though I'm surprised you guys have that issue over here. I thought Pandora was exclusive to America."

"It grew in America but the threat is everywhere." Changing the subject, Lilian grabbed a folded menu from the center display and turned to the inside flap. "Are you familiar with Danish or French food?"

"I like danishes, if that's what you mean. Especially when they're filled with cherry and cream cheese. But under no circumstances am I eating snails."

"You're an idiot." Lilian laughed, unable to help herself. "They have many amazing dishes. The carbonnades are to die for. And if you've never had frites you don't know what you're missing."

"Whatever your favorite is, I'll have that." Ray interjected, saving her a long list of recommendations.

Thinking for a moment, Lilian nodded. "All right."

The lady from inside emerged, carrying two glasses of water. "Wat kan ik voor je halen?"

Returning the menu to where it had been, Lilian looked up at her. "Twee bestellingen van Vlaamse stoofpot, friet en een bestelling van garnaalkroketten. Oh, en twee biertjes, alstublieft."

The waitress scribbled onto a note pad. "Ik breng het naar buiten als het klaar is."

"Dank u."

Staring blankly, Ray's mouth decided to talk. "I don't know what you said, but I like the way you said it."

A smirk crept to the surface. "I told her my companion is an idiot and to pick through the garbage for the nastiest slop they can find."

"Yum! Sounds tasty." Ray joked, hoping she was too.

"No, I ordered us Flemish Stew and Frites, and a basket of shrimp croquettes. And beer to drink."

"It sounds interesting. What language were you speaking?"

"Flemish. It's basically Dutch but spoken with a French accent. Most people here speak French. I only ordered in Flemish because that's what she speaks."

"How many languages do you know?"

"More than I care to count. They start to blend sometimes. It gets harder when you have a mixed language, like Flemish for example."

"That makes sense. I only know two languages. English and Bad English."

Lilian sighed, shaking her head. He really was an idiot.

The waitress returned with two frosted mugs of golden liquid and set them on the table. "Je eten is zo klaar."

"Dank u."

"So, Senior Investigating Agent. How long have you worked for the ICPC?"

Lilian glanced upward, as if recalling the details. "1914. But we didn't become enforcers until 1945."

He wasn't sure which part of her statement was false, but at least some part had to be. He'd been schooled in basic psychology when he went through the academy. Most people looked up and left when fabricating a story, whereas recollection of facts typically resulted in down and right. "Why the thirty-one year gap?" That made him feel young. He wasn't quite thirty yet.

"The organization was created as a meeting ground for various law enforcement agencies. In 1923 it became official and, in many ways, retains that purpose today. When the World Court was established the Eldar Council ruled that any criminals beyond the Veil were subject to the court's ruling. The ICPC was tasked with enforcing this. The human branch changed names in 1956, allowing us to continue in secrecy."

"So you've literally been with the organization since day one."

"Yes." Lilian glanced around, looking for anything else to talk about. Her prayers were answered when the waitress appeared with a basket in hand.

Inspecting the little puffs of fried bread, Ray grabbed one of the crustaceans and tossed it into his mouth. His teeth broke through the crispy outer layer and into the soft creamy center. It nearly melted in his mouth. Unable to resist he grabbed another, and another. "Dis is weally good. Wat is it?"

"Shrimp Croquettes" Lilian answered, stealing a few for herself before he could eat them all.

Swallowing, Ray took a long draw of his beer. "I don't think I'll ever be able to eat regular popcorn shrimp again."

"Popcorn and shrimp?"

Laughing at her response, Ray set his mug on the table. "No, not popcorn and shrimp. It's an American thing. They basically call anything bite sized and fried *popcorn*. Like popcorn shrimp or popcorn chicken. I don't know why. This is basically the same thing but it tastes so much better."

Just before the shrimp ran out, the waitress arrived with their entrée.

Unsure what he was getting into, but excited to find out, Ray was somewhat surprised when it turned out to be little more than thin slices of steak in a thick gravy-like sauce and french-fries. Carefully, he took a bite. The meat was tender and the sauce had a unique flavor. It reminded him of a Guinness gravy he'd once had, but was still very different. Of everything, it was the french-fries that stood out the most.

Ray had had french-fries from hundreds of places. It was no exaggeration to say none compared to the fried potato sticks before him. They were crispy on the outside and smooth and creamy on the inside. A better description would have been mashed potato sticks.

"What's this?" Ray asked, spooning a small tray of tan colored sauce on his platter.

"Andalouse sauce. It's basically a mixture of mayonnaise, tomato paste, and peppers. You dip your frites into it."

Ray was slightly taken back hearing mayonnaise. It reminded him of the conversation between John Travolta and Samuel L. Jackson in the movie Pulp Fiction. Uncertain but willing to give it a try, he dipped a fry and ate it. To his surprise it was exceptionally good, though the beer sauce from his stew was better.

Stuffed and about half through his second beer, Ray leaned against the back of his chair and admired the beauty before him. She'd kept pace every step of the way and looked amazing doing it.

Lilian glanced at her watch, checking the time. "We need to get going. It's better to be early than late." Slamming the remainder of her beer, she stood and made her way inside.

Glancing over his shoulder, Ray watched her disappear through the door. A sudden realization hit him. She was going to pay. That was unacceptable. He jumped up and raced after her, slowing when he reached the door. Approaching the counter, he realized she'd already covered it. Sighing, he said the most logical thing he could think to say. "How much do I owe you?"

"Don't worry about it." She smiled and collected the receipt from the waitress.

He hadn't expected her to pay. Quite the contrary. He'd been raised to always pick up the check. Granted, he didn't have whatever the local currency was, but a Google search while he was on the plane suggested Visa was widely accepted here.

"Shall we?" Lilian gestured to the door.

"Ladies first."

She chuckled. "You just want me to go first so you can stare at my ass again."

"True."

They stood there, staring at each other for a long moment. Finally, Lilian twisted and made her way for the door, adding a slight flourish for good measure.

It took every ounce of control he had not to look. It was one thing to openly admit to doing it, but to do it knowing she was aware was something else. Shaking his head, he turned and followed, inadvertently surrendering to his desire.

In the car, they flew along the city streets. Ray tried to catch a glimpse of the names, though they were moving too fast and turning too frequent to study the foreign letters. It wasn't until they were on the longest stretch of the trip that he recognized N201.

"This guy we're meeting. Be careful what you say to him. He's known to have a bit of a temper." Lilian warned, turning onto N1.

"So, don't call him a dick?" Ray joked.

"Correct. Don't call him a dick. Even if he's being one." She smiled.

They pulled into a fenced gravel lot at the head of a huge metal-plated building. Several motorcycles were parked tightly together near the front. There were a few rundown trucks and old cars here and there and not much else. Heavy layers of dust clung to every available surface, and from the look of the place it hadn't been mowed in quite some time. Lilian's car was easily the newest, cleanest, and prettiest thing to look at. Next to her of course.

A weatherworn sign, written in a language Ray didn't know, stood just inside the gate. He recognized the word *steel*, though whether that was because of the word itself or the remnants of a roughly painted I-Beam beneath it, he couldn't say. Between the sign and the fact that rows upon rows of rusted metal were piled beside, behind, and around the large building, he suspected it had to be some kind of metal factory.

Weeds grew tall around the edge of the building and many places in the parking lot. The piles of metal looked nearly inaccessible from the growth.

A dry heat burned through the car's tinted windows, making him want to stay inside. It was odd. The weather outside the café hadn't been bad. Slightly chilly if anything. Looking around, Ray found the source of the unexpected heat.

A row of bay doors faced them. Heatwaves poured into the fading sunlight, disappearing somewhere near the building's roof. Inside, just beyond the large openings, several thick metal containers resembling giant buckets could be seen. Metal frames, dangling chains, and conveyor belts, contrast to the glowing orange lights, seemed to be the bulk of what was inside.

"Shall we?" Without waiting for an answer, Lilian opened the door. Heat poured in immediately.

Sweat began to build on his skin. Despite his desire, Ray climbed out and followed. They approached a metal door at the side of the building, not far from the front bay doors.

What had been hot before became a melting pot the moment Lilian twisted the knob.

Ray stepped into the oven, feeling as if he was going to melt. How anyone could survive in this heat was a mystery. Though strangely, Lilian didn't appear to have a single drop on her. He wanted to ask her about it but the noise was nearly unbearable. It made it hard to think. He'd heard it from the parking lot but it wasn't anything compared to now. Buzzing machinery, clanking metal, and an ungodly deafening roar that shook the ground echoed off the walls. Flashing lights danced across the ceiling, some orange, some blue, some white. Some were constant and others strobed. Between the lights, smell, and noise, he could feel a headache coming on.

To make matters worse, the place was filthy. There was probably enough dust here to fill a dump truck if anyone had a lifetime to clean it. Had it not been for the fresh boot prints intersecting the painted yellow lines along the floor he wouldn't have seen them. Equally dirty rails guarded their path, blocking access to anywhere except a rickety shack with an equally rickety door to the right, and a set of metal stairs that when up and disappeared around the corner of the crude structure. There were two openings in the railing but both were blocked by draped chains and signs that might have been legible had someone wiped away the grime.

Lilian pressed a small black button mounted to the wall and grabbed a hard hat and reflective vest from the wooden shelf beside it. She handed a set to Ray and quickly applied her own.

Ray accepted the accessories, staring at them for a long moment. These things were as dirty as everything else around here and with the amount of perspiring he was doing, he was a magnet for filth. The last thing he wanted to do was ruin such a nice suit.

Noticing his distaste, Lilian leaned close to talk without shouting. "They won't let you go any further unless you have them on."

Begrudgingly, Ray wrapped the vest around him and set the hat atop his head. It was officially the worst day ever. "What do they do here?"

"Structural metal manufacturers."

The door at the end of their path opened and a stout man with a thick black beard came hobbling out. He was shorter than the average man but not by much. "What can I do fer ye?"

"We're here to see Berlan." Lilian answered.

"Aye. Just need ya ta sign on the line." He grabbed a clipboard from a protruding nail on the side of the shelf and handed it to her.

Lilian quickly scribbled her information on line thirty-two.

"Ye too, lad."

The pen had once been white but due to handling was stained black. A string had been taped to it, the other end attached to the clipboard. Carefully, hoping to get through this with as little soiling as possible, Ray filled out line thirty-three and returned it.

"Ye'll find Berlan up the steps, second door on the right." Hanging the clipboard from its nail, he marched back into the room from once he'd came.

Lilian started up the stairs. A metallic ring echoed with each step, though they didn't bounce in the slightest.

"What are they?" Ray asked, quiet enough to keep the question between them but loud enough for her to hear.

"What?" Lilian glanced behind her, unsure what he was talking about.

"That guy. What is he?"

"Oh. They're dwarves."

"Dwarves? He's a little tall for a dwarf, isn't he?"

"How tall did you expect them to be?" Lilian reached the top of the stairs and ascended the catwalk. It was little more than a c-channel frame. Jagged metal mesh bridged the top and the elevated platform lined the majority of the north wall. Several office entrances were connected to it but only one set of lights was on.

"I don't know. I guess I thought dwarves were like—" Ray motioned about waist high. "—you know, really short. Like midgets."

"He was average height for most of the dwarves I've met."

Ray shrugged, dropping the conversation. She'd know better than him. Looking out over the factory, Ray could see the vast majority of the main building. There were two other sections that were less visible, but equally active. Several of the huge metal bowls were filled with a glowing orange liquid. Spots of black floated on the surface. Occasionally a small flame would erupt, burning until the moth, dust particle, or whatever had landed in the vat burned to nothing. Now that he could see them in action, he realized they were smelting pots.

It was even hotter here than it had been on the floor. Wiping his brow on the sleeve of his jacket, Ray watched the watery liquid steam as it soaked into the delicate fabric. A horn echoed right above his head and he jumped.

One of the cranes began to raise, its chains clinking with each link, and the pot furthest to the left began to tilt. Numerous workers, all of similar stature to that of their dwarven greeter, scrambled for positions. The molten metal spilled into a giant mold.

Ray watched the men—dwarves—go to work pushing and pulling the metallic sludge toward the edges with long tools. Within a few minutes the glowing metal was spread evenly across the form and turning a glossy blue-gray.

Lilian knocked on a flimsy wooden door with a small window at face level.

A gruff voice shouted from inside. "Come in!"

Realizing he'd fallen behind, Ray hurried to catch up. He stepped through, instantly feeling some relief. His damp perspiration was cut mildly by the cool breeze of an air conditioner working overtime. He'd never been so pleased for anything in his entire life. Unfortunately, his suit was more than likely a total loss.

A dwarf sat behind a cluttered metal desk. He was much older than the first Ray had seen. His fully gray beard and thick long hair was braided over his shoulders and intersected into a single thick braid about mid chest. Ancient tattoos covered his weathered and scarred arms and what could be seen of his neck. His dirty and cracked fingers were wrapped around a sandwich that was overstuffed with meat and cheese, which he unceremoniously took a large bite of. Chewing, he took the opportunity to speak. "Is dis 'im?"

Ray glanced around the crowded office. An overflowed bookshelf rested beneath a blind covered window just inside the door. Magazines and books alike were piled horizontally atop the already full collection. The vast majority appeared to be metallurgy in nature, though some of the magazines were outdoor living or hunting based. The cluttered desk sat at an angle on the other side of the shelf, its occupant residing in the corner where he could look out the window at the sights below. Another door faced the desk from the opposite wall. Judging from the protrusion, it was most likely a small restroom. A chrome framed couch with black leather cushioning sat between the protruding wall and a tall file cabinet in the corner. The cushions were ripped and a moderate amount of stuffing hung out. Atop the file cabinet an old black and white TV displayed some '90s sitcom, barely visible through the static.

"It is. Ray, meet Berlan Steward. Berlan, this is Ray Bradley." Lilian introduced, taking a step back so they could get onto business.

Berlan laid his sandwich atop the plastic bag he'd removed it from. He kicked his chair from beneath him and got to his feet, extending a meaty hand. "Pleasure ta meet ya, laddie." Returning to his seat, he grabbed the sandwich once again and tore another huge bite from it.

"Um—good to meet you. Does anyone want to tell me what this is about? I thought we had a meeting?"

"This is it." Lilian offered, unsure what the question was.

"This is where I get information about Crum's disappearance? No offense, but I expected something a bit— nicer. I mean, it's been a nice vacation so far. And I learned, not only that faeries exist, but now dwarves do too. I—I don't know. I guess I just thought things were going to be a bit more formal than some factory in BFE where I'm sweating my balls off."

The room was silent, all eyes on Ray. Lilian watched closely, wondering how the dwarf was going to respond. She'd warned the human about his temper. If he took offense to the statement, there wasn't much she'd be able to do. Dwarves had their own laws. And they weren't known for recognizing the ICPC as authority. She was surprised they'd contacted them about this meeting to begin with.

Out of nowhere a hearty laughter filled the air. Berlan leaned back in his chair. It groaned under the movement. After a moment, the old dwarf corrected his posture. He sniffed, wiping away the tears on his cheeks. Reaching for a green thermos on his desk, he quickly unscrewed the cap. Steam rose from the black liquid, dispersed by the final cackles of his fading laughter. "I like 'im!" Nodding to himself, the old dwarf put the thermos away and brought the cup to his lips. Staring intently at Ray, he took a long draw. "Take a seat, lad. Let me tell ya a tale."

Reluctantly, Ray glanced around seeing only the torn couch or perhaps a few stacked boxes. "I think I'll stand, thank you."

Lilian sat on the couch, waiting to hear the big reveal. It was odd the dwarf reached out in the first place. Even odder he'd requested the young human. She was curious to know why.

"There was once a greedy king who set out ta rule the world. No matter 'ow much power 'e collected, twas never enough. Though that didn't stop 'im.

"One day, a noble knight was passin' through when 'e stumbled upon one o' the king's plots. Knowin' twasn't right, 'e destroyed what the king 'ad built and returned what was taken ta the people.

"The king considered this a mild annoyance at first, one easily ignored. But the knight didn't leave. Piece by piece, 'e began ta systematically tear down the king's empire. The more 'e destroyed, the 'arder twas fer the king ta ignore 'im.

"Finally, after a few months, the king decided twas time to get rid o' the knight fer good. But 'e couldn't kill 'im outright. The people loved 'im too much. 'E needed ta destroy 'im first. Once the people lost faith in 'is strength, 'e could be done with 'im once an fer all.

"The king, knowin' the knight 'ad a taste fer good deeds, 'ired the strongest mercenaries 'e could find. They set a trap fer 'im, a trap so temptin' not even the most cowardly o' 'eroes could resist. When the knight came, twould be 'is demise."

Ray waited in silence, wondering if that was the end of the story. Unable to take it anymore, he lashed out. "What the hell does that have to do with Crum, or really anything for that matter? I mean, cool story and all, but it doesn't tell me anything."

"Yer sure 'e's the guy?" Berlan asked again, turning to Lilian.

"It's him." She assured.

"'Umans—" Shaking his head, Berlan threw the remainder of his sandwich into the trash bin and got to his feet. Marching around the desk, he leaned against the top, staring at the comfortable elf across the room. "Ya know, this be the problem with the world today. Nobody enjoys a good story anymore. They want it all spelled out fer 'em. There's no mystery." With a sigh he returned his focus to Ray, his piercing eyes staring through him. "Yer partner, Crum— 'E's the knight from me story. And the king be a drug lord by the name o' Thomas Ezekiel. If yer the guy, ye know 'im as the force behind Pandora."

A spark ignited inside Ray. He'd been searching for a name for months. All it had brought was more questions. His mind raced, searching for dots to connect. Suddenly, he stopped, realizing exactly what he already knew. He'd searched for months with no leads whatsoever. How did some dwarf halfway around the world come up with a name? His police brain kicking into gear, Ray started his search for evidence. "How do you know that?"

Lilian perked up. She'd heard the name before, but never in conjunction with the drug.

"There's very few things I know. Among that extremely limited list is who me enemies are. Tis no secret I 'ate 'im with every fiber o' me bein'. Thomas Ezekiel 'as many enterprises. One o' them 'as targeted me people, not ta mention if this little plan o' 'is works, all o' us are in the spotlight." Leaning back, Berlan shuffled through the mounds of rolled blueprints and scattered papers cluttering his desk. Locating his query, he retrieved a bubble envelope. Handing it to Ray, he circled the desk and returned to his seat.

Looking over the package, Ray noticed the USPS stamps adorning it, though the date was from a few years back. He peeled the tape that held it shut and peeked inside. A micro SD card clung to the bottom. He retrieved it, inspecting the small storage device. It was covered in some kind of film and the plastic housing was discolored. The contacts looked good though, despite some minor corrosion.

Grabbing his phone, Ray quickly removed the outer case and his own card. Inserting the worn one, the contained files began to display in his gallery. There were hundreds of them, though most were nothing more than a gray thumbnail with an error icon. Flipping through the available files, most were pictures of various tourist attractions in Miami, as well as a few nightclubs and parties. The guy in several of the pictures had a large brown beard but he looked normal—human. Running out of pictures, the screen went black and a white circled triangle appeared. It was a twenty-three second video clip. Curious, Ray adjusted the volume and pressed play.

The picture faded from black, showing a large man unconscious and surrounded by several sets of slender legs. The unconscious man's arms were locked in metal sleeves and chained to his manacled legs. A voice spoke quietly somewhere off screen, but Ray didn't understand the words.

Turning the volume as high as it would go, he restarted the video. Ray recognized the man on the floor. He'd been introduced as William Crumble when they first met. That was before Ray could see through the Veil. How was it Crum looked human? Before he could ponder the question, the voice began, louder than before.

Berlan translated. "I recognize this orc. 'E works fer the WMD. I don't know where they're taking us. I was able ta 'ide me phone before they grabbed me. Me battery is almost dead and I can't get signal. I 'eard one o' the guards call us a shipment fer Ezekiel."

The screen went black once again and returned to the gallery display.

"How did you get this?" Ray removed the card from his phone and dropped it back into the envelope.

A stern expression settled on Berlan's face. Taking a deep breath, he pulled open one of his desk drawers and retrieved a folder. Handing it over, he looked away as if he didn't want to see what it contained a second time.

Tucking his reassembled phone away, Ray took the folder and opened it. A series of pictures, along with an elegantly written, yet blood stained letter were all that was inside. The signature at the bottom, despite his lack of understanding the context, was signed, *Thomas Ezekiel.* He flipped through the pictures, studying the horrific scene before him.

What could have been the bearded man from the other pictures, or what was left of him anyway, lay dead. His tongue had been cut out and black charring remained where his eyes had been. The fingers were removed at the knuckles, leaving both hands completely useless. His legs were shattered below the femur, suggesting he'd been partially crushed. The remnants of a thick beard were little more than a few patches of stretched and damaged hair, and the skin around his face was battered and bruised. Judging from the coloration, most of the damage had been caused while he was still alive, though without a coroner's report there was no way to be certain. Ray closed the folder, understanding why Berlan didn't want to look. He handed it to Lilian.

"That's the one who made the recordin'. Once 'e realized what they were doin', 'e swallowed the card. I got a call from 'im two days after 'e disappeared. They were bein' 'eld someplace underground with 'undreds o' others. 'E told me about the card and that it 'adn't passed yet. I was on with 'im when 'e was discovered." Berlan peeked through the blind covering his office window and stared down at the smelters. "'Is body was found at the base o' smelter number two. That letter pinned ta 'is chest. It says—"

Lilian interrupted, reading it for him. "This is what happens to those who refuse Elven rule. I'm coming for you! Thomas Ezekiel" Looking up from the folder, Lilian glared at the old dwarf. "Why didn't you report this to the ICPC?"

"We take care o' our own, lass."

"So why me?" Ray asked. He was glad to have a lead on Crum, but he hadn't heard anything that tied him to it. Why did they want to speak to him directly?

"Karin was a good lad. A bit 'asty at times, but a good lad, nonetheless. 'E moved ta Miami two years ago in 'opes o' chasing the American Dream. We spoke every few months. When Pandora 'it, 'e told me 'e wanted ta come 'ome. Said twas getting' too dangerous ta stay. I arranged a plane ticket but 'e never showed. I was already lookin' fer 'im when I learned about ye and the orc. I 'eard ye 'ad a 'and in takin down Ezekiel's number two. Before I could find 'im, I was called back 'ere fer business. A week later I got the call from

Karin and then we found 'im two days later. I knew if anyone 'ad a chance of cripplin' Ezekiel, it'd be ye."

Turning to Lilian, Ray realized she was doing everything she could to contain her composure. He hadn't known her long but it was long enough to know she was ready to snap. Risking her wrath, he gently placed his hand on her arm, feeling the softness of her skin beneath the jacket. A static pop shocked his fingers but he didn't mind. "Lilian, do you have anything on this Ezekiel guy?"

Turning her attention to Ray, the burning rage softened slightly. She took a deep breath, calming herself. "He's had a few minor run-ins. Mostly conflicts with humans that escalated. I think he's been arrested once for money laundering, and once for something else. I just remember we had to release him due to circumstantial evidence. The guys a snake. We've never had anything hard on him until now. Honestly, from what I know about him I wouldn't have guessed he was smart enough to be behind Pandora. But we'll certainly inquire."

"You know where to find him?" Ray asked. He usually had to hunt down the bad guys. It was rare for one to be so easily located.

"Last I heard he's at his estate in Amsterdam, but that was about a month ago."

Chapter 6
On the Run

"Satellite surveillance shows three outbuildings around the main complex. He's got a single guard shack at the entrance gate and onsite barracks. We're looking at thirty-plus militarized security guards with an untold number of firepower." The elf announced to the assembled agents, analysts, and team leaders.

Ray sat next to Lilian at a simple table. The room reminded him of a classroom, complete with a large dry-erase board mounted to the front wall. Each table had two chairs, and the side walls were filled with monitors, each one labeled across the bottom by location. Faces stared into the room, silently listening in on the briefing.

It had been called the moment they arrived back at the ICPC office.

Ray surveyed the assembly. Elves made the bulk of attendance, with a few faeries scattered about. There was only one orc, green like Crum but less muscular. He was sitting near the rear wall, scribbling vigorously on a piece of paper. For an orc he looked exceptionally nerdy with his thick glasses and loaded pocket protector.

Inspecting the side monitors, Ray realized he was the only human present, excluding the possibility of the few blacked out silhouettes gracing them from afar. Why they chose to hide their identity during a confidential briefing was a mystery in itself.

"We're going to have to be vigilant, people. This guy is likely to go down the hardest possible path. Watch your battle buddy's back and keep your eyes open. Teams in England, Germany, and France will join us in Rotterdam. We'll travel to Amsterdam as a collective unit and strike in unity. I already have a team in position watching the site."

Ray raised his hand, noticing they were forgetting an important detail.

"Whatcha got?" The elf asked, pointing to him.

"Yes, Superintendent Callon, I'm just noticing you have all these people on the screens, listening in and making their own preparations."

"And?"

"Well, sir, it seems to me we're missing one major factor in all of this."

"Which is?"

"You can't apprehend a suspect without physical evidence. We have a letter which has been handled by many people, and the word of a dwarf. Regardless of how respected that dwarf may be, that's hardly enough to hold this guy for long. The way I understand it, you've already had to release him once for lack of solid evidence. I'd hate to do so a second time." Getting to his feet, Ray marched around the desk and neared the front of the room. How these guys had operated so long without basic procedures was beyond him, but then again most of these countries didn't allow firearms or adopt the motto of shoot first ask questions later.

"And what would you recommend?"

"We need to expand the raid, sir. Strike multiple locations in unison. Target his estate and enterprises simultaneously. With the element of surprise he won't have anywhere to flee and we'll be able to secure any evidence before it can be relocated or destroyed."

"I agree with your opinion, which is why we have so many listening in via video conference. Though I'm please we have you here, I'm not sure we could have done our jobs without you."

Ray heard the stifled laughs from those around him. "In that case, sir, would you mind answering one final question?" It was clear his opinions weren't welcome here.

The Superintendent gestured for him to continue, glaring his increasing annoyance with the outsider.

"Thomas Ezekiel has property in America. Don't you think the WMD should be involved in this raid?"

"We do not answer to the WMD. You're here as a guest simply because the informant refused to discuss evidence with anyone else. I recommend you remember that for the remainder of this operation. You're free to leave anytime you wish." Callon's eyes narrowed, daring him to push the topic.

"If that's your official stance, sir, do you mind if I call my office and update them on proceedings? At the very least they need to know what *I've* found thus far." Ray was certain to emphasize his participation in the events up to this point.

Sighing, the elf gestured to the door. "Do it."

"Thank you, sir." Ray glanced at Lilian.

She mouthed the words, 'I'm sorry', and watched him head for the door.

Ray moved to the side of the room as to avoid distracting anyone else, though he could feel all eyes upon him as he left.

The hall was eerily quiet, most of the field agents being in the rally room, as it had been called. He could hear a few of the desk workers typing away in the surrounding offices, though he didn't have any reason to interact with them. It was a complete shift from his first experience here. What had seemed a dead office building was now lively and full of people. The only thing he could figure was people came in specifically for the raid.

Making his way to a small outcropping he'd seen on the way through, Ray approached the wall mounted phone. It was old school, black plastic with a coiled wire connecting the receiver to the base, though fortunately it was new enough to have actual buttons. He wasn't sure he could handle a rotary phone at the moment.

Glancing at the piece of paper taped above the device, Ray lifted the receiver and placed it to his ear. Reading the directions, he pressed the Belgium exit code of zero-zero followed by one, and seven-eight-six for the Miami area code. Scrolling through the contacts of his cell he located Roderick's number and quickly punched it in.

A series of loud grating tones echoed in his ear and an automated voice came through. "We're sorry, the number cannot be completed as dialed. Please check the number and try your call again."

Hanging up, Ray repeated the process, certain he'd followed each step correctly. Again, the error message played. Giving it one final try, he dialed Kel'Gos, hoping the orc would be easier to reach than some old politician.

"We're sorry, the number cannot be completed as dialed. Please—" Ray hung up the phone. It seemed he wasn't going to be able to notify the WMD until he got above ground. He glanced at his phone, hoping the time was accurate. It should have been. Lack of signal didn't typically interfere with that. It was nearing nine o'clock. By the time he got to the surface it would likely be too late to call them anyway. He recalled the time shift, solidifying his thought.

With a heavy sigh, Ray turned and headed back toward the rally room. Stepping in, he suspected they'd been discussing him in his absence as the room was deadly silent. It didn't matter. As far as he was concerned, aside from Lilian, the rest of them could go to hell.

Superintendent Callon continued no sooner than Ray was seated. He was holding a Kel-Tec KSG shotgun and had a table loaded with various weapons in front of him. Explaining the features and usage, he laid the weapon on the table and grabbed another, beginning again.

Ray had bared witness to a few of these pregame rundowns before. It was pretty typical, discussing tactics, equipment, and mindset. Everyone involved needed to be at their best and prepared for every outcome. That was the safest way to ensure they all made it home.

A knock echoed at the door and an elf rushed into the room. The newcomer carried a file in one hand and a look of caution upon his face. Approaching the Superintendent, he whispered something into his ear and handed the file over.

"You're shitting me?" Callon asked, clearly displeased with whatever news he'd just received.

"No sir. It's been confirmed from three sources."

"God damn it!" Waving the newcomer away, Callon opened the file and scanned the information within. Shaking his head, he slowly looked around the room, setting his sights on Ray. "Everyone can stand down and return to your regular duties. Someone tipped off the target. He boarded a private jet not five minutes ago and went dark after ignoring air traffic control."

Whispers filled the room and several people turned to look upon Ray.

"Clear the room! Marshal Bradley, would you stick around for a moment?"

The screens began to go dark as bodies made for the door. The chatter of screeching chairs, shuffling boots, and talk was deafening.

"I'll be right outside." Lilian placed her hand gently upon Ray's arm. She offered a comforting smile and disappeared into the crowd.

Getting to his feet, Ray marched to the head of the room where the Superintendent was waiting. He didn't say a word until the last being crossed the threshold and the door was closed.

"Do you mind telling me what the hell happened?"

"I'm afraid I don't understand, sir." Ray suspected what the elf was insinuating but to admit it aloud would do nothing to help his case. If anything, it would be received as an admission of guilt.

"How is it you step out to make a call and moments later the man we're targeting hops a plane and leaves the country?" Callon's face was red, though he was doing remarkably well containing his anger.

Ray selected his words carefully. This was one of those moments where the wrong choice could impact the rest of his life. "Sir, you and I both know this guy is slippery. You've not been able to get anything substantial on him. Hell, prior to my arrival, you didn't even suspect he had anything to do with Pandora. People like that don't just get lucky. They craft the illusion of luck with informants and consultants of their own. If I were to speculate, he has an informant within the ICPC who alerted him of the pending raid. I also believe, sir, whoever this informant is waited for the perfect opportunity to send their message. What better opportunity than an outsider stepping out to contact his home office?"

"You're suggesting I have a mole in my department?"

"I am, sir. Intentional or not."

"Elaborate." The elf peered down his long nose at the unyielding human.

"I noticed a few of the monitors had concealed identities. Who's to say the person on the other end isn't working for, or god forbid, has been intercepted by Ezekiel. There were enough security risks happening that any one of them could be responsible. Obviously, I have no evidence on this matter. I simply don't believe in coincidence.

"It's clear somebody used my phone call as a window to redistribute blame. Which is really kind of clever. I'm an outsider here. Nobody knows me. It makes me the perfect patsy. But it had to be somebody in this room, in one manner or another. To my knowledge nobody else knew about the raid, and cell phones don't work. That means, provided it was someone physically in attendance, it happened over a landline. I haven't noticed any landlines in this room and we would have noticed someone dragging a hundred foot of cord with them.

"That leaves only two options. One of your taskforce people on the other side of the screens or an automated message timed and triggered within this building. In all, your list of suspects is pretty slim."

Callon handed the file to Ray, a victorious smirk forming on his lips. "Well explained and agreed completely. Have a look at this and tell me what you think."

Ray opened the file, revealing time correlations between a phone call received at the Amsterdam estate of Thomas Ezekiel and a numbered terminal within the ICPC Brussels, Belgium location. The terminal number matched the phone he'd unsuccessfully used. Scanning the information provided, it showed his three calls, including the numbers he'd dialed, but it did not relay the outcome of those attempts.

Realizing there was nothing further he could say, the elf having already made his mind, Ray did the only thing he could. "Sir, as this file shows I did make three calls from the terminal listed. I attempted to call my direct superior, as well as Director Kel'Gos of WMD Tactical. All three of my calls were undelivered for reasons I do not know. You're welcome to confirm the numbers for yourself. I believe if you were to conduct a thorough investigation you'd see that my phone call was hijacked by means beyond my understanding. However, I also see that you've already judged me. Therefore, as a federal agent of the United States Marshals Service, authorized by your authority and here for the express diplomatic purpose of acquiring evidence from an informant, I, Marshal Rayford Scott Bradley, evoke the rights of diplomatic immunity to arrest and prosecution without a thorough investigation performed by an unbiased party. As no such party with proper clearance exists, I strongly urge you to oversee my transportation to the airport and upon the aircraft by which I arrived. Send whatever information you wish to my home office. If they decide to pursue this matter in detail I will cooperate fully and completely with whatever decisions they make."

Superintendent Callon snatched the file out of Ray's hands. "Lambrino, get in here!"

Lilian opened the door and stepped inside. "Yes sir?"

"Escort Marshal Bradley back to the airport and see him safely aboard his plane. I don't want to see him in my city again." His eyes never blinked the entire time he spoke, staring intently into Ray's soul.

"Understood, sir."

Ray did everything he could not to smile. He knew how thin the ice was, and he'd completely pulled that out of his ass. He didn't know if federal agents were permitted diplomatic immunity but he'd made it sound good nonetheless. More importantly, he'd achieved his goal. He needed to get stateside. If they arrested him here there was no telling how long it would take to get back, provided Crum would even last that long.

Ray slammed his visitor's badge on the table for good measure and stormed out the door. He couldn't explain how he felt. It was one thing to be accused when guilty, but to be accused when innocent created emotions he wasn't aware he had. Part of him wanted to do it just for spite. The other part wanted to catch whoever was responsible and make them pay. Neither was feasible. The best thing he could do was make it home and ensure the leak was reported.

Refusing to wait for out processing, Ray marched out the front door, across the street, and into the lot where Lilian's car was parked. Grabbing the left side door handle, he pulled. The door didn't budge. A defeated sigh escaped him. Ray spun around and leaned against the car, staring up at the stone ceiling. Could things ever go as planned?

A click echoed inside the car and Ray looked around, finding Lilian at the top of the steps. He pulled the door open and climbed inside.

Lilian glided into her seat with far more elegance than Ray possessed even when he wasn't pissed. There was a long pause. Searching for the words, she sat quietly staring straight ahead. Not knowing what else to say, she twisted in her seat to face him. "I'm sorry."

It was hard to be mad when she was near. "What for? You didn't do anything."

"I'm sorry you had to experience that. You have my empathy. I'm neither accepting blame, nor offering apathy. It sucks you were treated with such disrespect. I wish it were different."

Managing something other than a stoic glare, his face settled into a solemn expression. That was the best his mood would currently allow. "It does suck."

Lilian started the car and put it in reverse. Within moments they were in the garage lift and headed for the surface.

Ray wanted so much to get rid of the anger. This was likely the last time he'd spend with Lilian. He didn't want to spend it in anger and silence. Forcing himself to breathe, he glanced over at her. "Thank you for everything. It's been a pleasure being chaperoned by you. Even if you were babysitting."

A smile escaped her. "Well, despite my initial reluctance to the task, it's been—interesting to be your chaperone."

"Honestly, you were probably the best part of this trip. If you ever find yourself in America, be sure to look me up. Maybe I'll show you some of my favorite food places."

"As long as they have good beer." Lilian added.

"Nothing but the best."

The garage door began to open and they were off before it reached the top.

Brussels had been beautiful during the daylight. He hadn't seen much of it, but what he had was filled with history and architecture, as well as a vibrant and rich culture that inhabited the city. Now that the sun had set Ray was able to see just how beautiful it actually was. In many ways, Brussels and Miami were the same. Both served as waypoints for their various cultures. Both were filled with wonderful structures and history. And both came to life at night, displaying beautiful colors and interesting people. But

Brussels had something Miami did not. It had a warmth he hadn't felt elsewhere. It wasn't the heat. This place was substantially colder, though not uncomfortable. It was more akin to a warm embrace absent in other places. Brussels was the Crossroads of Europe, always inviting those who traveled. And now that he was leaving, a part of him would miss it.

Arriving at the airport, Lilian parked where she had hours before. The engines were running and both pilots were outside, inspecting the Citation for takeoff.

Ray glanced at his phone, checking the time. In just a few minutes he'd be in the air, never to see Lilian again. He sat there quietly, unsure what to say. He was still angry about the situation. How could they believe he'd had anything to do with it? He wanted to catch the asshole responsible for Crum's disappearance as much as anybody, not to mention the man behind Pandora. He'd sacrificed months of his life in that pursuit. Hell, his entire life had been changed because of it. If anybody wanted this guy to go down, it was him. But he also understood how evidence worked, and the evidence against him was suspect at best. Circumstantial didn't mean anything when judged by your peers. That had been proven time and again with various celebrity scandals. Once the media labeled you a monster your career was over. It didn't matter whether you were innocent or not. Far too many had been wrongly accused of misdeeds, their lives and careers destroyed by it. It didn't matter what a court said, once society believed you were guilty, that was the end of it. Of course, all they discussed now was the pandemic, but they always had time for a social lynching.

Taking a deep breath, Ray reached into the back seat and grabbed his bag. Pausing, he settled his gaze on Lilian, meeting her all-consuming eyes. There was so much he wanted to say, so much he'd never get the chance to say. "Thanks again, Lilian."

A wounded smile settled on her lips and she extended a folded manilla envelope.

"What's this?" Ray asked, surprised by the offering.

"Your evidence. You came all this way to get it. I couldn't let you leave without it."

"Really? Wow. Thank you. I thought for sure I was going to have to file a formal request."

"It isn't much but it's the least I could do. I wish things had gone differently."

"I do too." Ray wanted to hug her, or kiss her, really any physical show of appreciation would do, but such intimacy was likely frowned upon. Extending his hand, he took comfort in her warm grip. "Be safe, Lilian. Don't hesitate to look me up if you ever make it stateside."

"I won't." Lilian smiled and leaned in, gently kissing his cheek.

His face flushed red. He was floating, vaguely aware of his surroundings. Ray opened the door and climbed out, nearly forgetting his bag. Swooning, he glided to the steps that led into the plane. Charlie— or was it Doug? —The younger of the two was standing there when he arrived.

"Welcome back, sir. We're performing the preflight inspection now. Takeoff is in eight minutes."

"Thanks, Cha—, Doug." He second guessed himself.

"My pleasure, sir."

Grabbing the handrail, Ray climbed aboard.

"Hey, Ray!"

He stopped, turning around to see Lilian standing halfway out her car. "For what it's worth, I believe you."

"Thanks. Unfortunately I don't think they care what anyone else has to say." He waved goodbye and entered the jet. Tossing his bag into one of the empty seats, he selected one on the left side. Laying his head against the window, he watched Lilian. She was waiting outside her car, seeing him off.

The dual turbofan engines began to roar, increasing their RPMs. Doug climbed aboard and sealed the hatch. He glanced back into the cabin, locating Ray. "Are you all set, sir."

"Yes, thank you."

Nodding, the copilot turned and made his way into the cockpit. The jet began to roll, slowly at first. It reached the end of the small strip and made a one-eighty, aligning to the tarmac. Gaining speed, it lifted off.

Ray watched the black Bentley and the gorgeous woman who owned it grow distant. She continued to wave until he could no longer see her. Just a blip far below. He wanted so desperately for her to come with him. If nothing else it would make the return trip much more enjoyable. Once the jet leveled out, Ray got up from his seat and fell onto the flatbed couch. Closing his eyes, he drifted off to sleep.

Chapter 7
A Brief Debrief

Twelve chairs rested around a large conference table at the center of the room. Vertical blinds draped over the row of windows, blocking the midday sun. Numerous LED satellites ran along the tiered ceiling, providing illumination. An odd shaped device covered in buttons and indicator lights rested at the center of the table, seemingly dormant.

"What do we know about this Steward guy?" Roderick asked from the table's head, furthest from the closed wooden door. He was leaned against the soft backed chair, one leg crossed over the other.

"He's the closest thing the Ironhull Dwarves have to a king. All reports suggest he's well respected among their kind. It gets a little murky beyond that. The dwarven clans operate like motorcycle gangs. They work hard and play harder. Turf disputes have resulted in war between various clans as well as other races, but for the most part so long as they're left alone you don't typically hear much from them." Kel'Gos offered. He was sitting to Roderick's left, scanning a stack of papers in front of him.

"So he's a criminal." Roderick decided. "It's hard to run with the word of a criminal."

"With all due respect, sir." Ray interjected at his superior's right. "I saw the look on his face. He was conflicted when he was telling me about Karin."

"Who?"

"The dwarf in the pictures, sir. I believe him. He wants what's best for his people. This Ezekiel guy may be stepping on his toes but I don't believe he's the type to have someone else handle his problems."

"I second that." Kel'Gos added. "Dwarves are extremely proud. I'm surprised he was willing to talk to Ray in the first place. Under stereotypical circumstances we wouldn't have heard anything about this until after the fact."

"All right. For the time being we'll run under the assumption this dwarf is telling the truth. As for this leak in the ICPC. Do we know where it originated?"

Ray shook his head glumly. That was still a tender subject, though he was pleased his own people believed him. He would have been awfully salty had they not. "I only met a handful of them. All I can say is whoever it was, they were part of the planning. They knew when to move and how."

"Until it's resolved, we'll limit what information we can." Kel'Gos assured, staring at Ray. "They're already pushing for your records."

"Request denied. Bradley is a member of the USMS. Any requests pertaining to my operatives goes through me!" Roderick demanded.

"That's what I told them. They didn't take it well."

"Tell me about this senior agent. Lilly Anne or something like that."

"Lilian Lambrino, sir." Ray corrected. "What's to know? She was a model representative. Punctual, polite, she maintained a strict schedule. We wouldn't have the evidence from Berlan if not for her."

"My point exactly. After everything that went down why would she sneak evidence away from her affiliation and give it to you?" Roderick arched an eyebrow.

"She agreed they made a mistake and was attempting to make it right?" When put that way, Ray wasn't so sure he knew her motives.

"By stealing evidence and delivering it to an accused mole?"

"I'm not saying it was the correct choice of action but I understand why she did it. I'm grateful she did it. Without her we would have had to wait for those arrogant pricks to decide when to give us our evidence. Who knows how long that would take?" Ray pleaded, letting his emotions run a little stronger than he'd intended.

"Did you screw her?" Roderick asked flatly.

"What? No! I was only there for a few hours. Most of it was spent at the ICPC office."

"Just be careful. Don't start thinking with the wrong head. That's a quick path to trouble." Roderick warned. Turning his attention to Kel'Gos he continued. "What have we got on this Ezekiel guy?"

"Not much. He has a handful of legitimate businesses. Two of them in Miami, along with a mansion just off Millionaire's Row. No official record on the mundane side. On our side he's been arrested thrice and released thrice due to lack of evidence. Charges in all three cases were 'willful manipulation of the human psyche'."

"What's that mean?" Ray asked.

"Use of suggestive mind control." Roderick added. "So he's an elf. What led to the arrests?"

"First offence, March 1998, Dubai World Cup. Accused of altering odds on a horse race. None of the witnesses were able to identify him. Second offence, February 2011, Cambridge, Massachusetts. Racial manipulation in opposition of a hostile takeover for a biotech company. Once he was caught, the acquiring pharmaceutical was able to seal the deal. There was no paper trail suggesting he'd been hired. Evidence was circumstantial."

"Biotech and pharmaceuticals! How was this guy not already on our radar for Pandora?" Ray asked, surprised by what he was hearing.

"Pandora wasn't a threat at the time. We believed it was safely locked away. It seems this was being planned longer than we realized." Kel'Gos added.

"Tell me about the laundering case." Roderick asked, flipping through his own notes.

"Not much to tell. June 2013, Scotland Yard, in cooperation with the ICPC, arrested six individuals, including Thomas Ezekiel, only to release them four days later. Roughly fifty-thousand-pound sterling was confiscated and the case was dropped in October 2016. Lack of evidence." Kel'Gos scrunched his nose, pausing in confusion. "He has a Code-thirty-five-twenty-one association, though it doesn't elaborate. I'll have to look into that."

"Has forensics turned up anything new on the evidence?" Roderick asked.

"They're still identifying prints on the letter and pictures. The blood was a match to the victim, confirmed against the sample submitted during his Visa application. As for the memory card, they've been able to recover some of the corrupted photos. They're still working on it though." Kel'Gos grabbed a small remote from atop his stack of paperwork. Pressing a button, light erupted from the device on the table and a blue screen appeared on the wall. Pressing it again, a picture appeared.

It was a selfie taken at a nightclub packed with people. The dwarf, though he looked human in the image, was dressed in a baby-blue jersey-style shirt and a pair of loose blue jeans. A thick silver chain hung around his neck, partially hidden by his braided waist length beard. A white flat baseball cap with a straight bill rested atop his head.

Kel'Gos flipped through the pictures. Several were at the same club, showing the events of the evening. They became increasingly risqué, centrally focused on a woman as more clothing disappeared.

There were a few random shots, a flock of geese taking flight, the back of a driver's head in another. One by one, the large brown orc brought the recovered images up, allowing ample time to review them.

One in particular jumped out at Ray. "Wait a minute! Go back."

Kel'Gos returned to an image of a white Lamborghini Aventador with suicide doors. A pretty black haired girl with a short black dress was climbing out.

It wasn't the car or the girl that caught Ray's attention. It was the guy in the background. "I know that guy. Rez Morales. Local gangster turned police informant. I busted him about a year ago for distribution. Got him to turn state's witness for a clean walk."

"Do you think you can find him?" Roderick asked.

"He runs an auto performance shop in Miami Gardens."

"Same area the victims are centered." Kel'Gos added.

"It sounds like we have a plan." Roderick pulled himself up. "Gentlemen, I have a meeting in Washington first thing in the morning. I should be back by the end of the week. Kel'Gos, if you'd be so kind, please email me the rest of the pictures."

The old orc nodded, turning off the screen and gathering his paperwork.

"Ray, walk with me."

Getting up, Ray followed the Deputy Attorney General, wondering what he wanted. He hoped it wasn't further lecturing about a specific female he'd been thinking about. "Where are we going, sir?"

"It's time to inspect your new office."

"Oh, cool!"

"We don't say *cool* here, son. We're the government. We have no hip lingo or sense of humor that we're aware of."

Ray couldn't help but laugh, which he promptly buttoned up with a stern gaze from Roderick.

They walked a short distance from the briefing room and stepped into the elevator. Scanning his ID, Roderick pressed his thumb against the fourth floor display.

Almost instantly a roar of chatter assaulted them and the doors slid open.

Ray stared into a massive clutter of desks that filled an expansive but otherwise open room. Every race he'd learned about, including a few he hadn't, fed the chaos. Voices talked over one another, each speaking louder than the next in order to be heard. Excessive clicking keyboards echoed.

Hundreds of phones were ringing from all directions, seemingly nonstop. This was not the place he wanted to be. It was louder than a crowded bullpen on New Year's Eve. "What happens here?" Ray shouted over the noise.

"Public Relations!"

"That seems like a bit of an oxymoron considering what we do."

"Even shadow work has to be spun. Who do you think explains the unexplainable and makes sure the general public never knows what happens here? These guys." Roderick nodded to the pandemonium. "The majority of tabloid press, fake news, clickbait sites, and coverups originate in this room. Once approved, they're circulated into the general public. They've shown time and again they cannot be trusted with the truth." Casually, Roderick stepped from the elevator, following the only unobstructed path through the center of damnation.

Clinging to his heels, desperately hoping his desk was located literally anywhere else, Ray glanced around seeing some of the things Roderick was talking about. One guy was on the phone, pitching a cheesy movie idea about a buddy cop team with a human and an orc. Another was drawing on a digital tablet. Ray detoured just enough to catch a view. It was one of the winged creatures he'd met in Brussels, though this one wore a tight green dress and had blonde hair like Tinkerbell, despite male dangly bits clearly visible under the hem. With so much noise around him, it'd be difficult to think, let alone take a phone call in this place.

Roderick reached the end of the desk islands and stepped through one of many doors along the rear wall. It opened into a silent corridor, miraculously blocking all noise from the pit of hell. "We're back on the public side of the building. From here the elevator is only capable of accessing the first eight floors, as well as the cafeteria on floors seventeen and eighteen."

"Understood."

Roderick turned right and led him down a long corridor to another intersection. Turning right a second time there were seven doors on the left wall, each with a name plate on the solid wood barrier. Roderick stopped at the third door, pausing just outside.

Ray read the brass placard engraved with his name. *U.S. Marshal Ray Bradley – 95th District.* "Sir, I think there's a mistake. I thought there were only ninety-four districts."

"Known to the general population, there are. Why do you think you're stationed at the WMD?"

"I hadn't thought about it."

"Beyond the Veil is the ninety-fifth."

"Are there others?"

"Not that you have the clearance to know about." Roderick cracked a smile and twisted the doorknob, stepping inside.

The office was fully furnished with thick gray carpet. It was nowhere near the size of Roderick's office, but would put Anderson's to shame. Behind the glass and metal desk three full length windows made the entirety of the wall, overlooking Miami. Biscayne Bay could be seen at a distance, though it was several miles off. There was a black leather futon with wooden frame along the right wall. A bookshelf rested on each side of it, loaded with a mixed collection of legal, fiction, and occult books. The left wall was mostly open aside from a mounted flatscreen that was nearly as wide as the wall was tall. Another shelf rested just to the left of the door, though this one was empty.

Ray approached the desk. A wooden placard with a brass plate stared up at him, repeating the message on the door.

Roderick gestured to the chocolate brown swivel chair between the desk and windows. "Take her for a spin. See how she feels."

He didn't have to be told twice. Ray circled the desk and plopped down, feeling the hydraulic piston catch him. Grabbing the right side lever, he made a minor adjustment and got comfortable. Rocking back and forth, he noticed a thin bar at the corner of his desk. A tiny blue light occasionally flashed from it.

Rolling the chair around, something hit his right knee and the bar lit up, projecting the USMS logo. "Holy shit! Is that a monitor?"

"It is. State of the art perception projection monitor. It cannot be seen from any angle or location than in that chair. Even if you were to roll over here and sit by the door, the display will follow you. Both the keyboard and mouse are wireless. So long as you're in the chair, you can work from any location within this room."

"Interesting." Ray peeked beneath the desk, looking for whatever he'd hit. A kydex holster was mounted to the right side near his leg. Beside it, there was a small black button.

Seeing a protruding piece of wood from the trash bin, Ray grabbed the discarded device and inspected it. The name *Arthur Roderick* and a title matching his own was displayed. Glancing up from his newfound toys, Ray locked sights on Roderick. "This was your office?"

"It was. Not too long ago. An opening came up and I was forced to find a replacement." Casually walking around the office, as if he were acquainting with an old friend, Roderick approached the bookcase to the left of the futon. "The Beretta under the desk has fresh ammo but it could use a good cleaning. I never had to use it. With any luck you won't either. The button activates a silent alarm. Hold it three seconds to call security. Three consecutive presses will announce a lethal threat. And five consecutive presses will alert all departments to vacate the premises."

"This is some spy shit right here."

Roderick chuckled. "You don't know the half of it. Come here."

Picking himself up, Ray joined him at the bookshelf. "Next you're gonna tell me there's a secret room behind this."

"Not quite. I couldn't get approval to demolish the next office over." Roderick grabbed the book labeled *The Art of War*. Lifting it vertically, the outer sleeve revealed a hidden keypad. "It's a little cliché I know, but I couldn't help myself. I cleared the code when I left. All you have to do to set a new one is type the code you desire and hold the pound sign. That's the one I believe your generation calls a hashtag."

"I knew it as a pound sign, sir. I'm not *that* young."

Roderick pressed the asterisk-star button and the shelf clicked. The top four levels started to rise, tilting into the wall. Within a matter of moments it was completely out of the way and a not-so-hidden weapons locker remained. It was backlit with glowing white lights and a wire rack covered the entire surface. Several hooks were connected to the rack displaying a vast assortment. It had everything a paranoid agent could want. A tactical vest was rolled and secured on the base shelf. Two pump action shotguns, one pistol grip, the other carbine stock with a seven shot mag hung vertical. A SIG MPX, four Beretta 92F pistols with a total of eight extra mags, a combat knife, two smoke canisters, a CS grenade, and three M67 grenades, and so much more were meticulously organized and ready for action.

"Were you planning to go to war, sir?"

"I believe in being prepared. As unlikely as it may be, if I *have* to shoot my way out of this place, I'd prefer as little improvisation as possible."

"Where's the escape hatch and the panic room?" Ray joked.

"Haven't you been listening? If I had an escape hatch I wouldn't need all these weapons." Pressing the star button again the shelf returned to its former state, securing the locker. "Anyway, I'm running late. I had all your cases transferred to your desk. You'll find them in your right side drawer. Get them cleared as soon as you can, but this

Crum'Bul situation is our top priority. We can't afford to let anyone touch our operatives without penalty."

Waiting for Roderick to leave, Ray set the locker code and did a quick test run. He was pleased to see it worked. Sliding the book cover over the keypad, he returned to *his* seat. He'd never had such a nice office before. Hell, he'd never had an office of his own before. Like everything else, it was going to take some getting used to.

Giving his chair a couple test spins, Ray lifted his feet letting the momentum carry him around. After a few revolutions it came to a stop at a window view overlooking the city, *his* city. Crum was out there somewhere and he was going to find him. He'd played enough. It was time to get to work.

Opening the right side drawer, Ray grabbed the metal basket packed full of case files. There were more than he'd anticipated. It was nearly overwhelming. If he could manage to convince all the criminals to take a vacation for a few years and complete a single case every day, maybe he'd have about half of them done by the time he retired.

Not sure what else to do, Ray heaved the bulk of paperwork to his desk and set it over the leg brace. There was no telling how much weight the black tinted glass could hold but he didn't want to break it on his first day in office. With a heavy sigh, he grabbed the top file and flipped through, memorizing what details he could. He needed to keep them in front of him. So long as he did that he was more likely to review them often.

One by one, Ray picked through the files, inspecting the details. Homicide of human by other. Homicide of other by human. Ritualistic sacrifice. Gang activity, disturbing the peace, rape, prostitution, several narcotics cases. The list went on.

A narcotics file caught his attention. The name Ramirez 'Rez' Morales was mentioned as an eyewitness. This was the second time in under an hour the name had come up. Ray didn't believe in coincidence. In one way or another Rez was tied to two separate cases. It was time to have a chat.

Grabbing his phone, Ray scrolled through the list of contacts. Locating *Snitch Number Four*, Ray hit the call button. It rang several times before a Spanish voice came through.

"What up? You got Rez."

"Rez, how the hell are ya? You don't call, you don't write."

"Who is this?"

"I'm hurt, truly. And after all that time we spent together. You in handcuffs, me working a plea bargain in exchange for cooperation."

"Ray." The tone of his voice sounded less than enthusiastic. "What do you want, homie? Our business is done. I'm legit now."

"Don't lie to me. I know better. Besides, all it takes is one call to the prosecutor and you go back in the hole."

"Why you threatening me like that? I ain't done nothin'."

"Give me some information and you won't have to worry about it."

"I'm telling you, man. I ain't in that business no more."

"I've got your name on a report in front of me that says otherwise. Just give me a name. Who's supplying the new stuff?"

"I don't know. I'm out!"

"Rez, quit jerking me around. I want a name."

"I ain't got one, homes, but maybe I can give you somethin' else. You know that church on 2nd and 179th? Trinity or somethin' like that?"

"I'm listening."

"Be there at five-thirty. I hear a deal's goin' down. Maybe one of them knows what you're after."

Ray thought about it for a moment. He didn't want to chase a cold lead but it was more than he was getting elsewhere.

"So, we good, esse?"

"It better pan out, otherwise I'm paying you a visit. And don't even think about skipping town." Ending the call, Ray glanced at the time. It was nearing five o'clock. Stacking his cases, Ray stood and made for the door.

Chapter 8
Hit and Run

The matte black Aston Martin sat in the parking lot of an auto parts store on 2nd Avenue. Ray watched from the driver's seat, listening to music through the Bluetooth in his phone. A row of hedges and a large parking lot separated him from the church next door.

Checking the time, a heavy sigh escaped him. It was nearly a quarter till six and he hadn't seen the slightest sign of activity. There were several cars parked along the road, as well as a white delivery van that hadn't moved since before he arrived. Whatever he was waiting for had already happened, or he'd missed it. The latter was not possible.

Shaking his head, Ray started the engine and began to back out when something caught his attention. The buzzing exhaust of a group of imports raced down the street. They ran in a tight formation, headed his way.

Studying the cars, Ray recognized the first as a Mitsubishi Lancer Evolution, 'Evo' as it was known on the street. It had a cherry red paint job and a carbon fiber hood. That, mixed with the winged spoiler on back and the pulsing red neons beneath, told him these guys were part of the street racing crowd.

He didn't know much about the industry, other than an appreciation for fast cars, but it answered one question he'd had. Rez owned a performance shop on 183rd. If these guys were involved with whatever was going on, it made sense how he knew about it.

The other two cars weren't nearly as impressive. A Subaru Impreza WRX and a Toyota GR Supra ran side by side. The Supra had a custom black and lime green paint scheme but appeared stock in all other ways. As for the Subaru, it didn't even have aftermarket valve stem covers, running a boring factory gray paint and the standard seventeen-inch rims all around. Ray suspected it belonged to whoever was driving's mom.

The trio dropped out of formation and parked in the street, not far behind the delivery van.

Ray watched them spill out, five bodies in total, two in the Evo and two in the Supra. The guy in the Subaru was running solo. What was more interesting, they all had bandanas covering their faces like a wild west train robbery. Had this been literally any other place he could have written it off as pandemic paranoia. Bandanas were being worn as face masks all over the place. However, they were here. This had to be what he was waiting for.

The five men gathered at the rear of the Evo. No sooner than the trunk popped, guns came out.

It was time to act. Ray pressed the drive button on the dash and mashed the gas pedal. His tires broke traction and he drifted around the corner, headed straight into the mix.

A gunshot echoed and the thugs went running back to their cars.

The step van took off down the road ramming anything in its path. The imports were hot on its tail.

Reaching the scene, Ray spotted a body in the street. One guy, an elf with half his head blown off. It was too late. If only he'd known to watch the van a little closer maybe he could have done something to prevent it. Sighing, Ray stepped on the gas and took off after them. They were murderers now. They would face justice.

The step van slid around the corner onto Miami Gardens Drive, slamming into a Jeep Gladiator. The Jeep rolled onto its side and slid into the grass. The street racers were right behind it, Subaru and Supra flanking the sides and the Evo at the rear.

Rapidly catching up, Ray slid around the corner. In just a few seconds he'd be parallel with the tail car.

Gunfire riddled the side of the step van, punching holes through the sheet metal and white paint. From the timing, Ray guessed they were using semi-automatics. That was fortunate. He wasn't equipped to deal with full auto today. All he had with him was his 1911 and two extra mags for a total of twenty-two rounds including one in the chamber. "Note to self, stock up first chance I get." He said aloud. Dodging an oncoming car, Ray gripped the steering wheel in his left hand and retrieved his extra mags in the right. Tossing them into the passenger's seat, he drew his Colt. There was no telling what all was going to happen during this chase and he didn't need to be distracted trying to grab a mag from his belt.

Ray pulled beside the Evo and rolled down his passenger window. Displaying his badge, he shouted. "Pull the vehicle over!"

Gunfire answered his demand.

Slamming on the brakes, Ray dropped back. His car was too nice and too new to have bullet holes in it already. The simple fact they tried was enough to piss him off.

He maneuvered into position a second time, taking aim. Suddenly, the speakers in his car echoed out loud billowing rings, startling him. A message scrolled across the central display. 'Incoming Call from DAG.' Ray held fast, tapping the green button on his steering wheel. "Hello!"

"Ray, this is Arthur Roderick."

"I apologize sir, but some major shit is happening and my hands are a bit full at the moment."

"I'll be brief. I just learned the ICPC has decided to conduct their own investigation. They got the sign off—"

Another two shots forced Ray to swerve, drowning out whatever Roderick had said. Swinging wide, he accelerated into oncoming traffic, passing a stopped car. Seeing his opportunity, he swerved between two others and moved into position closer than before. Ray fired two shots into the carbon fiber hood.

Steam began to roll near the windshield and the car started to slow. The driver was beating his steering wheel, either encouraging it to go faster or angry his car got shot. Ray couldn't tell which.

"Listen, it sounds like you've got a lot going on right now. Give me a call as soon as you're free."

"Understood, sir." Ray hit the red button and glanced into his rearview mirror. The Evo was still following, though at a much slower speed. With any luck he hit something vital, preventing them from pursuing any longer. Of course, that meant they were going to get away since he couldn't arrest them and pursue the others at the same time. On the bright side, how many cars matching that description could there be?

Returning his focus to the forefront, Ray cranked the wheel, narrowly dodging a wrecked minivan. It was too close for comfort. He glanced around realizing they were nearing the I-95 overpass. As if the realization triggered it, traffic came to a sudden and complete halt.

He slammed both feet on the brakes. The antilock kicked in and the pedal pulsed under pressure. He came to a stop less than an inch from impact. Labored breaths and profuse sweating assailed him. Unable to do anything else, Ray patted his dash. "That a girl." He took a second for himself, catching his breath. There was too much happening entirely too fast to allow any more distractions.

As ready as he could be, Ray hit the reverse button and spun around, doing a reverse three-sixty. Systematically he hit drive just as he came to a stop and took off again, realigned along the right side of the road. He was glad he'd taken the wheelman's advice and hit the airstrip. Not only had he worked out shifting times, but the kid had taught him a few tricks as well.

Ray jumped the right side wheels onto the curb and raced past the stalled traffic, nearing the 6th street intersection.

Several cars were piled up at the center. The step van had t-boned an old Chevy Suburban, bringing it to a stop. Both had been rear ended, and at least two of the wrecked cars were on fire.

Searching the cluster of broken fiberglass, plastic, and crumpled metal, Ray located the remaining two cars. The Supra wasn't hard to find. It had been sideswiped and collided with the back of a garbage truck. It was down for the count. The driver on the other hand was nowhere to be seen. As for the Subaru, it was three cars behind the wrecked step van and buried under a mangled bumper.

Movement caught his attention. The occupants were tactically surrounding their target. Even after all this they weren't giving up. It made him wonder what was in the van. Unfortunately, he wasn't in a position to do anything about it here. There was no cover.

Seeing an opening in traffic, Ray dropped off the curb and inched through the channel. Gunshots echoed to his left. He glanced over seeing the thugs close in. One of the men jumped on the hood of a crashed car and climbed to the van's rear door. He peeked through the broken glass only to jump back almost immediately. A shotgun blast peppered the frame where his face had been. The other two responded by shooting up the sides, making their way toward the cab.

Inching into the right turn channel off of 6th, Ray blocked the lane as best he could and parked. There were far too many civilians here. Even in the 'lockdown' state the country was in, bullshit or not, there shouldn't have been so many people out and in the way.

Opening the door, Ray ducked low and rushed toward the metal light control box. He peeked around, identifying his shooting lanes. Most were no-go. There were too many chances for unneeded casualties. He had a few clear lanes though, and a clean sight on the guy at the right of the van. There was no telling where the other two were. Taking aim,

Ray released three consecutive shots at the guy nearing the passenger's door.

His target spun, searching for the source of the shots. It was too late. They'd already landed. His back hit the side of the van and he dropped.

Ray heard shots returned from somewhere on the other side but he couldn't see the shooter. One down, two to go.

The passenger's door flew open and Ray watched someone jump out, disappearing behind the westbound cars and rubble almost instantly.

A bandana covered face appeared through the driver's window and ducked out faster than Ray could take aim. Even if he'd had a shot, he would have hesitated. There were too many unknown factors to shoot anything that moved. That was precisely why so many cops were in trouble lately. Well, that and perceived use of deadly force in non-deadly situations.

Ray watched, searching for movement. It was suddenly too quiet. Out of nowhere bullets whizzed past him, landing somewhere off to the right. He ducked to the left side of his cover and stole a glance around, lower than he had been. Movement beside the van told him who was shooting. The guy he'd dropped was still alive, the only explanation being body armor. There was no doubt he'd hit center mass.

Ray took cover as another round missed him entirely. It was a shame to kill a man who was already defeated but sometimes they didn't leave much of an option. He moved to the right side again, waiting for the man to raise his gun. Refusing him time to squeeze the trigger, Ray made sure he wasn't getting up.

Seeing his slide locked to the rear, Ray dropped the empty mag and reached for his backups. "Dammit!" They were still sitting in the passenger seat of his car. He tactically retreated around the nose and reached through the passenger's window.

For the moment nobody was shooting but he could hear the high winding rev of a motorcycle engine. Tires squealed and a red and white Yamaha R1 screamed past him, easily dodging the few cars blocking the eastbound lanes. He'd only seen the bike for a heartbeat before it was gone but the operator looked too feminine to be male. It was difficult to tell with the enclosed helmet but he was almost certain it was a woman. Hell, with all the targeting of police and social justice warriors on high alert, he'd likely face execution if he were to state the suspected gender in his report.

Slamming the fresh mag into place, his thumb hit the slide release and it snapped forward chambering another round. Ray tossed the empty into the floorboard and returned his attention to the pileup. A guy wearing a red and white armored jacket was picking himself up near the front of the van, where the suspected driver had disappeared. That answered who was on the bike, but it did little to tell him where the thugs had run off to?

As if in answer to his question, a crash exploded in front of him launching the tail end of a pickup into a row of previously undamaged cars. Ray ducked. Fortunately, the flying debris didn't make it anywhere close to him or his car. Unfortunately, he'd located the remaining two thugs and they'd escalated the threat higher than he could have imagined. They'd added carjacking to their ever expanding list of infractions and were once again in pursuit.

Abandoning all grace, Ray slid across his hood and jumped into the driver's seat as fast as his legs would carry him. Hitting the drive button, he floored it, hoping to catch up with the stolen one-ton pickup.

For a chase vehicle, they could have done better. The truck was slow and heavy, and it wouldn't maneuver very well. It had a metal flatbed and heavy metal rails around the back that added to the weight, not to mention its load. If they used it as such it was an effective battering ram.

Unfortunately, that wasn't its most dangerous feature. The load itself was.

It didn't take much effort to catch up. He was right behind them in a matter of seconds. One guy was in the bed, the other driving. Ray realized he was probably in the worst possible position he could find himself in. Seeing a liftgate tucked neatly under the rear, a unique opportunity crossed his mind. He searched the undercarriage, locating what he was looking for.

A metal box was mounted to the right side frame just behind the dual rear tires. If he could somehow compromise the system, there was a likely chance the gate would drop. It wouldn't stop them, but it would drastically slow them down.

In full pursuit of the fleeing motorcycle the truck rocketed left, onto the I-95 ramp.

Ray was close on its tail.

The bandana wearing criminal in the rear of the truck grabbed a slender green bottle from a small cage toward the front. It was only a couple feet long and about three inches in diameter. It had a chrome plated nozzle at one end and was concave on the other.

"Don't do it!" Ray pleaded, preparing for the worst.

He did.

Ray swerved, dodging the rapidly flipping and bouncing oxygen cylinder. There was no telling how many times it hit but he both heard and saw it shoot into the sky behind him. Glaring his irritation at the criminal, he clenched the steering wheel, feeling his knuckles pop. They were dead set on messing up his ride.

Arcing wide, Ray mashed the gas and pulled up beside the truck. Unfortunately there wasn't enough room to stay there long. The motorcycle could narrowly be seen in the distance, nearing the top of the I-95 ramp. There was no way they were going to catch it. Why they'd even bothered was a complete mystery.

The truck darted over, nearly on top of him. Ray slammed on the brakes, back into the danger zone. Another green cylinder hit the road right in front of him. Spinning the steering wheel, he slid sideways and shot into the far left lane. Another spin the other way sent him sliding around, the front of his car facing the left side of the truck. He corrected just as the second bottle went off. It shot like a torpedo, flying inches over his hood and passed the truck with ease. An explosion of concrete dust showered them and an overhead sign began to fall.

Ray sat there stunned. His gut churned. His heart raced. His breath short. There was no one to help. He was alone, stuck in an impossible situation. Taking a deep breath, he worked a mixture of gas and brake, whipping behind the truck just as the sign crashed down.

It landed hard against the truck's rails, crinkling them but they held fast. The guy in back was forced to drop, but the truck kept going, ripping itself free.

Ray cleared it with less than an inch to spare. Had he not been so close his car would have been permanently convertible.

Reaching the top of the ramp, Ray's nightmares became a reality. He watched helplessly as the bandana wearing thug got back to his feet and craned one of the rachet strap release levers. It popped loose and the entire group of large cylinders began to rattle around.

With no other option, Ray dropped back and prepared himself. The chain gate came open and the first cylinder hit the road. It flipped end over end and slid off to the side. Another landed, going straight into a bottle spin. He had to swerve to miss it.

Realizing his error, the guy unscrewed the cap on the third cylinder and rolled it toward the rear. It hit the road and flipped, sheering the valve almost instantly. Faster than anyone could see, the loose torpedo launched into the air and disappeared.

He needed to stop this now. Once they reached the highway there was no telling how much carnage they could inflict. Ray stomped the gas as hard as he could, accelerating up beside the truck in the blink of an eye. Taking position on the right side he slowed, matching speed but kept enough of a cushion in case they tried to run him over again.

Stealing a good look at the hydraulic box, Ray could see a handful of hoses and wires coming from a hole near the top. If he could hit it maybe he could slow them down. At the very least, a slow moving target was easier to hit than a fast moving one.

Grabbing his pistol, Ray laid the rail atop his left forearm. Considering he was using it to drive, it wouldn't be the steadiest shot but it was better than nothing. Aligning the sights as best he could, he squeezed the trigger. It hit just beneath the bundle. "Dammit!"

Police sirens echoed in the distance.

Ray glanced in his mirror seeing blue lights merge into heavy traffic. He shook his head. There was no reason for all these people to be out. Nearly every state had issued a stay at home order. Essential personnel, meaning mostly medical, law enforcement, food, and supply companies were about the only ones technically allowed to work. It was highly unlikely all these people belonged in that group. It was simply ridiculous. He didn't care so much about the lockdown. As far as he was concerned that fell within the realm of personal freedom. What bothered him was all the people who clearly realized bad stuff was happening and couldn't be bothered to get to the side of the road or even stop in most cases. It was things like this that made him question why he even bothered protecting them.

Another bottle hit the road. It was shorter and wider than the others, with a black paint job and a hint of red around the collar. No sooner than it flipped a massive fireball exploded, launching the cylinder through the side of an RV that had ignored police presence. The cylinder hit with such force the elongated vehicle flipped sideways.

Ray took a deep breath, aligning his shot once again. Exhaling, he squeezed the trigger. The nickel casing ejected and bounced off the dash, landing in the passenger's seat. A slow trickle of red fluid ran down the side of the box.

One of the brown bottles hit the road and collided with one of the many Miami PD cruisers swarming in. It nearly tore the car in half.

One after another, stray cylinders went rolling, spinning, or flipping through the pursuing cars. Some exploded, some shot off, a few hit and spun, or rolled harmlessly to the side of the road. They'd only just arrived and at least five cars were permanently out of the chase, likely their drivers as well, and the thug had just released the strap on another group.

Biting his lip, focusing every bit of effort he could muster, Ray squeezed the trigger. One of the hoses whipped around oozing red fluid from the ruptured line. The gate slammed down, unfolding as it went. The sudden jolt threw four of the cylinders out the back before their caps could be removed. It was a small victory but a victory nonetheless.

Despite the anchor the truck kept going, tearing deep gouges into the pavement. Sparks danced behind the downed gate, bouncing and dragging as it went. The man in back was picking himself up, climbing over the loose and fallen bottles. He narrowly caught himself on the rear rail and was getting to his feet.

One of the patrol cars closed in just as a bottle was rolling out. It hit dead center of the grill and the car imploded, flipping on itself. Two others crashed into the back of it.

Accelerating, Ray shot ahead of the truck. It swerved, trying to hit him but he was too quick. Using that to his advantage, he cut sharp into the left lane and slammed on the brakes. Pistol extended, Ray waited for the truck to pass. No sooner than he saw the front bumper he pulled the trigger and emptied the mag. There was no telling where each of the remaining bullets hit but he could see at least two holes in the driver's door.

The truck veered left, then suddenly shot right, straight into the concrete barrier at the edge of the Ojus area lake bridge. It hit, throwing the guy in back, along with several of the uncontained cylinders over the cab and into the water below. The rear of the truck came off the ground and twisted. It teetered on the edge for a brief moment before falling over the side.

Ray sat in the middle of the road, watching the truck disappear. There was nothing he could do for them. With Miami PD closing in if he stopped to answer questions, he'd never catch the motorcycle. Scouting ahead, he spotted the red and white bike in the distance. He was surprised it wasn't long gone by now.

With no traffic to contend with, Ray caught up in no time.

The evading R1 turned into a gravel lot just past the Ives Dairy Road sign and got onto a narrow dirt path between the lake and a row of palm trees.

Seeing no alternative, Ray followed. He had them. There wasn't anywhere to go. The road ended under the bridge where the truck had flipped.

The motorcycle hit a patch of gravel and came to a stop under the bridge. Revving the engine, waiting for the Aston Martin to present itself, it shot forward, aimed for a narrow path between two piles of loose gravel. From there it'd be able to get back on the dirt road and leave before the car could turn around.

Ray cut the wheel hard blocking the bike's path. It went down, sliding on its side. In that moment he saw something he never thought possible. The operator, verifiably female now that he had a good view, climbed atop the overturned bike and surfed it to a stop. She stepped off as if it were as easy as exiting a stairway, gun drawn and aimed at his windshield.

Opening the door, his own pistol aimed and ready, Ray shouted the first thing that came to mind. "Miami Vice, Freeze!"

"Miami Vice, huh?" A familiar voice echoed beneath the tinted helmet. Lowering her gun, she peeled it away, revealing long dark hair and pointed ears.

"Lilian?" Ray was stunned. He lowered his firearm and took a step forward. "What the hell are you doing here? I thought I'd never see you again. I—Wait a minute. What's all this about?"

She holstered her gun and reached into a compartment under the bike's seat. "We got confirmation Ezekiel was headed to Miami minutes after you left. I was told to hop on the first jet and see it to the end. I'm surprised your superiors didn't notify you."

"I—um—I'm guessing they tried. Things were kind of hectic back there and I had to end the call." He gestured to the bubbling water to his left. Debris was floating on the surface and many of the remaining cylinders were bobbing. "Why'd they try to hit you? What's the connection to Ezekiel?"

"I was setting up a sting. Cash for drugs. The guy they shot was my contact. This was the preliminary meeting before I could deal with the supplier. I was just about to get the location and time when they hit. Guess I'll have to try a different approach now." Lilian pulled a small black bag from the compartment and unzipped it revealing three thick rolls of hundred-dollar bills. "Three-hundred-thousand to get me in the door."

"How do you think they found out about it?" Ray stepped within arm's reach, lost in her presence. His heart pounding, he wanted nothing more than to embrace her. They'd both nearly died back there. If that wasn't cause for physical affection, nothing was.

"I don't know. It was supposed to be discrete. How'd you find out about it?"

"I pushed a local narc into giving me information. I didn't know what was going down until it happened."

The sound of tires on dirt echoed and a black Escalade pulled in behind Ray's car.

Ray lifted his pistol, ready for the worst.

Casually, Lilian placed her hand upon his chest. "Relax. That's my extraction." She stared deep into his eyes. "Thank you for the help back there. It was good to see you again." Removing her hand, she walked past and climbed into the passenger's seat. The SUV turned and left, a trail of dust floating in its wake.

Ray watched it disappear. "I think I'm in love— This is gonna suck!"

Chapter 9
Old Friends, New Enemies

A pulsing beep echoed from the tow truck backed to the lake's edge. Its wench groaned, slowly retracting the taut cables and fishing the flipped truck from the water. Flashing lights were everywhere, both above and below the bridge.

"So, to recap. You witnessed the suspects approach a white delivery van. They opened fire, killing one victim before the van took off. It then led to a car chase down Miami Gardens Drive and escalated into the pileup and shootout at the 6th street intersection, reverting to a second car chase which ended here. Is that about right?" The officer asked, confirming Ray's statement.

"There was a bit more to it, but yeah."

"Okay. And the person who stole the motorcycle. Where did they go?"

"I don't know. By the time I got here they were already gone." Ray lied. He couldn't rightly explain that a secret organization of elves and other magical races existed, let alone that they were working a case. It seemed better to say she got away without identification than to admit he knew who she was, spoke with her, and risk creating more lies.

"Ray Bradley, why am I not surprised to find you here?"

Recognizing the voice, Ray turned seeing her usual curly brown hair. She was wearing an off-white blouse tucked neatly into a pair of tight blue jeans. A detective's badge was clipped to her waist, and a holstered pistol rested behind it. "Hello, Katelynn, how are you?"

The inquiring officer turned away, realizing he was no longer top dog on site.

"Suspended narcotics detective to U.S. Marshal." Shaking her head, she smiled playfully. "How does that happen?"

"Just lucky I guess."

"So, what happened here?" Katelynn asked, fully aware his official statement had already been given.

"Just like I told the officer, attempted robbery, turned murder, turned chase, turned shootout, back to chase until here." Ray grazed over the question he'd answered so many times already. It was exhausting trying to keep so many details straight, but he was starting to gain proficiency in telling the tale. "Am I free to go? It's been an eventful day and I need to call the office."

"Yeah, Ray, you can go. Though, I'd like you to swing by the department and fill out an official statement. We still have procedures to follow. You remember those, don't you?"

"Yeah. I remember. I'll swing by when I get a chance. It was good to see you again, Katelynn."

"You too." The homicide detective turned to the officer who'd been standing there and began collecting information from him.

Ray crossed the now crowded dirt and gravel lot to his car, still parked where he'd left it. He climbed in and closed the door, laying his head against the leather wrapped head rest. The memory foam absorbed him. He closed his eyes, taking a moment for himself. He was one with the machine, simple and enduring.

A heavy sigh escaped and he sat up, looking around the scene before him. Investigators, forensics, coroner, and so many others worked tirelessly in an attempt to determine exactly what had happened.

Knowing he couldn't delay any longer, Ray started his car and backed out, his focus shifting between the mirrors and the center dash backup camera. Putting it in drive, he started up the narrow road, squeezing through the row of cars parked along the side. It was a tight fit but he made it back up and onto the blacktop.

Ray grabbed his phone and flipped through the contacts, debating who to call. It was more a question of who he preferred to talk to at the moment. Kel'Gos reminded him of an old Command Sergeant Major he'd once had. The same man who'd given him his Colt. Gruff on the outside but a big softy inside. Not to say the orc or the CSM didn't have the capacity to cause some damage. That was a given.

Roderick on the other hand reminded him of a Lieutenant Colonel. Calm and collected most of the time, but a temper like no other when pressed. There was no denying the day's events were certain to elicit a certain amount of rage.

Decided, Ray hit the call button. The six speaker system echoed out and a moment later the old orc's voice came through.

"Tactical. You've got Kel'Gos."

"This is Ray Bradley, sir. I apologize for the interruption. I wasn't sure who else to call."

"What can I do for you?"

"Where to begin?" Ray stated aloud, thinking through what he was trying to say. "It's probably already hit the news. I was following a lead. It ended up creating quite a bit of chaos on I-95. These thugs came out of nowhere and opened fire on an unmarked step van. It turns out ICPC is in town and was running a sting-op. I wasn't sure if you were aware, sir."

"I found out they were here just a little while ago, but if they're already running an op I'm guessing that notification was delayed for quite some time. Am I to assume you made contact with their operatives?"

"Yes sir. The half-elf I met in Brussels, Lilian Lambrino. She was arranging a meet and greet when the van got hit."

"ICPC is refusing to coordinate with us. I'm being fed as little as they can get away with at the moment, though that's going to change— One moment, Ray."

Shouting erupted in the background, though it didn't belong to the orc. Waiting patiently, Ray tried to listen, picking up a few choice words here and there. Between outburst he could hear Kel'Gos offer retort, though the deep voice was too quiet to hear in detail. Whatever he said didn't seem to sit well. The other voice unloaded loud enough to hear every word. "Two point eight million in damages! Twenty-three cars totaled, eight critically wounded, and seven dead! How the hell does someone cause structural damage to a bridge? Wait, he's on the phone? Let me talk to him!"

Kel'Gos, calm as ever spoke into the phone. "Ray, Deputy Attorney General Roderick would like to speak with you."

Roderick began unloading so quickly, Ray assumed he'd ripped the phone out of Kel'Gos' hand. "Bradley, what the hell is going on out there? I'm halfway to Washington when I have to turn around and come back over this ICPC fiasco. Before I can even get back to my office, I start getting phone calls about one of my operatives. You're supposed to find Crum'Bul, not blow up half the god damned city! Did I make a mistake in hiring you?"

"No sir. There are extenuating circumstances. I contained the situation as best I could, though if you'd like someone else to take over, let me know."

"Are you giving me lip, Bradley?"

"No, sir. I'm simply relaying the facts. Bad guys do bad things. Sometimes it takes longer to bring them down than we like."

Grumbling echoed at a distance. Ray suspected his boss had removed the phone to vent. Taking a deep breath, calming himself, Roderick continued. "Just do your damned job. No more explosions. No more blowing up bridges. Do you understand me?"

"I'll do the best I can, s—" The phone clicked before Ray finished speaking. He didn't have to guess to know he'd been hung up on.

The sun was nearly set when Ray pulled into the parking lot of an old auto parts store turned performance shop. It had been a while since he'd last seen the place but it looked the same now as it had back then.

Parking in front of the first of three overhead doors, Ray turned the car off. He found it odd they were closed. Then again, things had just gone south for the hijackers and at least two of them were still alive. It was possible Rez was taking precautions.

Climbing out, Ray made his way to the glass door at the corner of the showroom. A paper sign was taped inside.

We apologize for the inconvenience but we're temporarily closed.

City Ordinance has labeled us a Nonessential Business. We cannot afford the fees of defiance.

We'll reopen as soon as possible. If you're in need of parts or service before that time, please call us. We value our customers and wish to make the best of this unfortunate situation.

Ray scanned the phone number and turned away. Despite the closure, he could hear music playing inside. Rez had to be here.

Leaving the front door, he made his way along the cinderblock building, passing the overhead doors, and to the chain link gate at the rear corner. Ray reached over and hit the latch on the inside. The gate swung open on its own.

Stepping through, a dirt trail ran between the rear wall and fence. Heavily overgrown grass and weeds lined both sides of the path and thick leafy vines intertwined the crosshatched fence to his left. Three leafed groupings were turning yellow from green and stretched out toward him. Wanting no part of them, Ray stepped off the trail and hugged the wall to his right.

Walking as close to the rear of the building as possible, the stench of engine grease assaulted him. He'd smelled it earlier but it was nowhere near as strong. Hearing an air wrench echo inside, Ray knew he was on the right path.

The ivy covered fence continued another ten feet before turning and heading away from him. He realized he was in somebody's backyard. An assortment of car parts laid here and there, seemingly abandoned in the urban jungle. It was a fair distance from the house at the opposite end of the overgrown field. Just ahead Ray saw an overhead door at the back of the shop. It stood open at the center wall.

He stepped into the opening and glanced around. Classic rock echoed from an old radio on a workbench. Ray recognized the song, though the lead singer's voice was drowned out by another less talented individual with a tendency to mispronounce the words. The tail end of a 1964 Barracuda rested just inside the door. The fastback was beautiful in all ways save for one. The back glass was busted out and the trunk lid was concave, ruining the metal flaked paint.

The shop owner was hunched over the front left fender, buried to his elbows in the engine compartment. The hood had been removed and was standing on end a short distance away.

"Nice car." Ray said, hoping not to startle the man.

Rez jumped, his head snapping around to see who'd spoken. Spotting Ray, his worried expression turned to one of displeasure, though it was nowhere near as strong as the look of shock on Ray's face.

"Come on, man. I told you on the phone I didn't know nothin'." Rez pleaded, withdrawing his dirty hands from the engine and wiping them on a shop towel.

Two very distinct details jumped. The first was severe bruising around Rez's right eye, along with a fresh cut that had been pulled together by butterfly bandages. Secondly,

Rez wasn't entirely human. "What the hell?" Ray asked, finding no other words. "What kind of orc are you?"

Rez paused, staring curiously at the cop. "Orc? What's an orc?"

"Um—What you are. I guess?" His features weren't nearly as harsh as those of Crum or Kel'Gos but they were clearly orc features. "Who were your parents?" Ray asked, lost in the discovery.

"My mama is Rosario Morales. Never met my pa. Mama said he was killed before I was born."

"I bet one of them was an orc. I hadn't thought about orcs breeding with humans but it makes sense. Elves can do it. Why not orcs?"

"Orcs, elves? You ain't tappin' into the evidence locker, are ya?" Tossing the dirty rag over the fender, Rez stood to his full height, which clearly wasn't a trait from his orcish heritage.

"No, nothing like that. You really don't know?"

"Know what? Homie, I got work to do. I told you I was legit. This city closin' thing has me workin' day and night on commissions just to keep the lights on. What do you want?"

Ray thought about it, stuck on the question. How could anyone not know their heritage? Granted, Rez clearly wasn't fullblood. He looked human with the exception of a heavy underbite, two little tusks, slightly pointed ears, and an upturned nose, not to mention his skin, brown like that of Kel'Gos but a little lighter. Ray had just assumed he was an ugly Mexican. That was before he knew what was out there, before he could see through the Veil. Half-breeds were something he needed to ask about when he got back to the office. "Um—I was hoping you could tell me a little more about the street racers you sent me after. They're your kind of clientele. Is that how you knew about the hit?"

"No. And they're not my clientele. Not anymore. I used to do a lot of work on that Evo. A few months ago they came in to order some parts. I knew somethin' wasn't right by the way they were lookin' at me. Started freakin' out and smashed up my place. I called the cops and they took off."

"So how did you know they were going to hit the truck?"

Rez grabbed a ratchet and returned his attention to the car. Going to work, he kept talking. "I'm legit now, but that doesn't mean I don't hear stuff. Old friends want to hook you up, get you gigs and stuff. This mornin' a buddy of mine called. Asked if I knew anyone runnin' the new stuff."

"Pandora?" Ray asked.

"What's Pandora?"

"New drug. Hit the streets about six months ago. Liquid, usually served in wine."

"I don't know nothin' about that. This new stuff is kind of like ecstasy, or so I've been told." There was a long silence, broken only by the clicking of the ratchet.

"Go on." Ray prompted.

"Anyway, so I get this call askin' about the new stuff. I tell the guy I'm not in that business no more, cause, you know, I had to get clean after that last deal." Removing the carburetor, Rez turned and set it gently on the workbench.

"Get to the point, Rez!"

"So, I don't want to leave him hangin' cause he's my boy and all. I tell him to go to this place on Brickell, La Mosca. You know it? They got amazing taquitos."

"Rez, I don't care about the food. Get to the point."

"Sorry, man. You know how it is. I love me some good taquitos."

"Rez!"

"All right! So, I tell him to go down there. If anyone knows who's dealin', it'd be them. But that's where it got all messed up."

"What happened?"

The look on his slightly orcish face became suddenly serious. "Jared and his boys came here about an hour later. They wanted to know who I talked to, like I knew somethin' else. They put me through the back glass there." Rez pointed to the rear of the car. "This isn't even my car. Now I gotta pay for a new trunk, window, and paint."

"I'm sorry about that, but I need to know how you knew about the hit."

"I was layin' in the backseat, bleedin' all over the place. One of 'em grabbed my torque wrench. He was gonna finish the job. Right as he opened the door, Jared got a phone call. I heard him confirm the details. Trinity on 2nd, five-thirty. He stopped the one who was about to hit me. Said they didn't have time."

"Why didn't you tell me this when I called?"

Rez shook his head. "Get real, man. If I gave you a name, you know as much as I, first chance they got they'd come back here and finish the job. I did the only thing I could. You wanted somethin'. I gave you what I had in the only way it wouldn't lead back to me."

"They hurt a lot of people before I was able to stop them. Three ended up in body bags, two remain on the loose. Do you have any idea where I might find them?"

"I don't know if it's still the same, but I had an address on file back when they used to order parts. Give me a minute and I'll look it up."

Ray nodded.

Setting his ratchet aside, Rez stepped through the service office door and turned on the light.

Ray grabbed his wallet and quickly counted out ten hundred-dollar bills. He returned the bifold to his pocket and concealed the money in hand.

Turning off the light, Rez returned with a piece of paper and handed it over.

Ray inspected the written address and extended his hand, dropping the folded bills into the half-orc's palm.

"What's this for?"

"To help pay for the glass and trunk lid. You're probably looking at around three-hundred for each, and who knows how much to match the paint."

"I can't take this." Rez offered it back.

"Sure you can. Think of it as a thank you for the information." Considering the issue over, Ray folded the paper and pocketed it. "Take care of yourself, Rez."

"You too, homie."

The streetlights kicked on just as the sun disappeared behind the distant cityscape. Ray sat in his car, parked at the side of the street a few houses from his target. Thus far it had been slow. He'd watched the place for the better part of an hour. So far, no lights had come on and no vehicles had showed. It was dead quiet, but he couldn't go in yet. He hadn't been given permission. Instead, he did the only thing he could. He continued to watch and continued to wait.

Baby-blue siding covered the exterior. The fascia, trim, and support columns of the covered porch were painted white. It sat quite a way off the road. There were two double windows on the front wall, the larger of the two overlooking the porch. Ray guess the living room was behind that.

The remnants of a circle-drive were lost to grass. Both it and the yard were long neglected and grown about shin high. An empty trash dumpster sat near the road despite pickup having been several days prior.

Out of nowhere Ray's phone began to ring through the car's speakers, interrupting his music. He didn't recognize the number but answered it anyway. "Hello?"

"Marshal Bradley, this is Deputy Marshal Kershaw. I understand you're awaiting a warrant to enter the premises of a suspect."

"That's correct."

"It's been processed, reviewed, and signed. You have a green light to freeze the location. I'm on my way with a physical copy.

"Understood." Pocketing his phone, Ray climbed out of the car. Passively, he patted his Colt making sure it was locked and loaded. It was, along with the reloaded mags clipped under his jacket.

He stuck to the shadows, cautiously making his way toward the house. A streetlight beamed down directly above the dumpster but a minor detour through the neighbor's yard would mostly avoid it. Closing in, Ray kept a close watch on the windows. He was fairly certain no one was home but it wasn't worth the risk.

Approaching the front door, he slowly grabbed the knob and applied pressure. To his surprise it wasn't locked. Ray drew his gun and gently pushed the door open, peeking inside. No sounds called his attention. With a final inspection of his surroundings, he ducked in and closed the door behind him.

He was standing in a small foyer. A closet door stood closed directly across from him and the living room entrance was on his right, the only direction he could go. He was already having second thoughts about going in.

The stench of body odor and rotten food was nearly unbearable. Pizza boxes, empty soda bottles, and dirty dishes rested on every surface and in nearly every configuration. Clothing was discarded along the floor or draped roughly over furniture.

Despite his desire Ray inched into the living room. There were two exits, both along the rear wall. The one adjoined was a kitchen and small dining area. It appeared to go all the way to the northwest corner. A set of sliding glass doors off the dining area led to a patio and the back yard beyond that. Judging by the exterior design, the garage entrance was probably along the east kitchen wall, somewhere.

Now that the primary rooms were located, that left only bathrooms and bedrooms to be explored. Quietly Ray stepped forward searching the premises. He needed anything that could tie these guys to the shootout earlier, and hopefully something to tie them to Ezekiel.

The southwest living room wall opened to a vestibule. There were four choices, two doors along the right, what appeared to be a bathroom straight ahead, and a narrow hall to the left. Ray recalled his training on the matter. It was best to sweep the perimeter and work in. Unfortunately, he was alone. It was hard to watch the flank and check everything at the same time. In this instance, there was no right answer. Regardless of which direction he chose, his back was going to be exposed to unsecured areas.

Decided, Ray twisted the doorknob nearest and peeked inside. It was the first organized and clean room he'd found. It looked to be a bedroom though the contents had turned it into an office. A particle board desk sat in the corner with a flat screen monitor that was too large for the hole. Chromed car parts and a variety of metal or plastic signs hung from the walls or were displayed on shelves. There were a few items of interest resting atop the desk but he couldn't justify checking it out until the rest of the house was secure.

Closing the door, Ray backed out and moved to the door beside it. This one was clearly being used as a bedroom. It was covered in filth and a stained mattress lay directly on the ruined carpet, covered in clothes and trash.

Shaking his head, Ray moved onto the next. How anyone could live this way was beyond him. It was one thing to be disorganized. Hell, even clutter wasn't too terrible so long as it was clean. This place was horrendous and it smelled like curdled milk.

Quickly sweeping the bathroom, Ray entered the hallway and approached the final room. There was a sliding closet door directly across from what appeared to be the master bedroom entrance. A quick glance revealed numerous boxes and clothes. Nothing of much importance as far as he could tell. Then again, with all the discarded clothes on the floor he was surprised to find any in the closet.

Directing his attention to the master bedroom, the bed was empty save for a few random items tossed roughly on the unprotected mattress. At least this one had a box spring and frame. Another door sat in the west wall. It took little more than a glance to realize it was a master bath. Nothing seemed to jump out at him.

With the place secure, Ray rushed back to the office and approached the desk. He lifted the two bags lying atop an envelope. They were filled with little pink tablets that left a chalky powder on the inside of their container. Each one was a little smaller than an antacid and a coiled snake logo was pressed into the center.

Ray had seen a lot of designer drugs in his time as a narcotics cop. He'd never seen these, though it looked remarkably like ecstasy tablets. Was this the drug Rez was talking about? He was curious to see what the lab would identify them as.

Noticing a small hole near the top, Ray removed one of the tablets and inspected it closer. It had a strange scent, reminding him of fruit. The texture was firm, though the chalky residue stuck to his fingers.

Returning it to the bag, Ray grabbed the envelope and bent the metal prongs holding it closed. Inside was two stacks of bound hundred-dollar bills and a stapled bundle of paper. He emptied it on the desk and inspected the document. It appeared to be a shipping schedule. Several of the units, both arrival and departure, were highlighted yellow and a price amount was handwritten in black ink next to them. Judging by the occasional smudge and identical deformations on the pages, he guessed it was a photocopy rather than an original.

A rattling doorknob demanded his attention.

"Did you leave the door unlocked?" A male voice asked.

"Nah, man. I think Walter did."

Ray stuffed the money back into the envelope but the paper wouldn't cooperate. Unable to delay any longer he placed the bags back on top and skated out of the room, pulling the door closed behind him. The voices were in the living room and drawing closer. With nowhere to go and the schedule still in hand, Ray rushed down the hall toward the master bedroom and climbed into the closet. He pulled the sliding doors shut, leaving just enough gap to peek out.

"What kind of moron leaves the door unlocked? We've got entirely too much shit lying around for that."

"A dead moron." The second voice answered.

"Don't remind me. That job was a huge mistake. We shouldn't have taken it."

Ray could hear them heading toward the office. Peeking through the cracks, he could see the back of the one nearest the door and a side profile of the other. The door opened and they disappeared inside. Hearing the crinkle of the plastic bags, Ray suspected they were loading up.

"Hey, Jared?"

"Yeah?"

"You know where the boat schedule went?"

"It was in the envelope. Why? Is it not there now?"

"Not that I'm seeing."

"Screw it. Doesn't matter anymore. We'll be long gone before the next shipment comes in anyway. Just grab the cash."

Ray heard a loud crash, like a hammer striking the wall.

"Holy shit, that's a lot of money!"

"I know. Do me a favor and grab a duffle bag from the closet across the hall." Jared asked, hitting the wall again.

Sweating and his heart racing, Ray readied his gun. He watched the man approach, hand extended and ready to discover his presence.

A timely knock at the door halted his advancement. Ray watched him go into the master bedroom and come sneakily running back through.

"Shit, man, it's the cops." He whispered.

"Grab the sawed off and get behind the door. Next time they knock, blow a hole through it." The one named Jared ordered.

The sound of a pump action echoed. Ray knew what was about to happen. Listening to both men head into the living room, he quietly opened the closet door and stepped out, pistol ready.

Ray approached the corner and peeked around. The guy who'd been driving the Evo was huddled in the corner. He had an AR-15 aimed through the window and ready to fire. The one with the shotgun was nowhere to be seen but Ray suspected where he was.

Silently counting down, knowing whoever was at the door had limited time, Ray stepped around the corner. "US Marshals, drop your weapon!"

Jared turned, bringing the ArmaLite rifle to bear. He was at a disadvantage, his focus being on the people outside.

Before he had time to complete the action, Ray put two rounds in his chest. Jared fell backward over the arm of the couch and didn't get up. Ray moved further into the room, locating the guy behind the door.

"Oh shit, man! Oh shit!" He dropped the shotgun and threw his hands up.

The door busted open and Miami PD rushed in. "Freeze! Drop your weapon!" Two others grabbed the guy at the door, dropping him face first to the floor and handcuffing him.

Ray put his hands up, palms exposed, letting the pistol hang harmlessly by its trigger guard. It rotated upside down, dangling by the index finger of his right hand.

"I said drop the weapon!" The armed and aimed cop demanded, slowly moving toward him.

Slowly, carefully, Ray bent at the knees letting it slip off his finger and fall a controlled short distance to the floor. Unlike most modern firearms, the Colt 1911 Series 70 was one of the few without a drop safety. The last thing he wanted was to toss a locked and loaded firearm and risk an accidental discharge toward whoever was misfortunate enough to be in its trajectory. "I'm a US Marshal. You'll find my ID and badge in my inner left breast pocket."

Miami PD flooded into the room and secured the scene. Verifying Ray was who he said he was, they lowered their weapons and allowed him to collect his own.

"What are you doing here, Ray?" Katelynn asked, stepping through the door. "Twice in one day. You're going to have to stop interfering in my investigations. And you still haven't filed that report like I asked."

"I said I'd get to it when I had time. I haven't had time yet." Ray offered. "If it helps, I have a warrant to be here, it just hasn't arrived yet."

"That's good. I have half a mind to bring you in for obstruction of justice."

"Obstruction of justice? Had I not acted you'd have at least one dead officer. They were waiting for someone to approach the door."

Katelynn glanced around the room, verifying Ray's story. Whether she believed him or not, she didn't say. Looking to one of the investigators, she arched an eyebrow. "What have you got?"

"A bunch of money and what appears to be a couple bags of drugs."

"They had this as well. It ties them to *my* investigation. I guess that means we're going to have to work together." Ray snidely remarked, retrieving the now folded schedule from his inner jacket pocket. He liked Katelynn. Hell, at one time he used to date her. All that ended when he became a detective and she decided it couldn't work.

Katelynn ignored him. "How much money?"

"At least half a mil. Maybe more. There's a bunch more stuffed inside the wall. Without tearing them all down it'll be hard to know how much is here."

"All right. Have forensics start working on that." Katelynn turned to Ray and gestured to the stapled papers. "May I see that?"

He handed it to her.

"Thank you. Now, I need to see your warrant."

"I already told you, it's on its way. I didn't expect them to show up while I was inside."

"Okay." She addressed the investigator once again. "Sergeant, will you kindly detain Marshal Bradley until his warrant arrives?"

"Will do, Lieutenant."

"Feel free to smack him around a little if he resists." Katelynn smiled her victory.

"Really, Katelynn?" Ray asked, knowing she was doing this just for spite.

"Really. Once your warrant arrives and I've verified its authenticity, I'll consider sharing any evidence found. Until then, you're just a perp who was apprehended at the crime scene."

"You realize this could be construed as interfering with a federal investigation, don't you?"

"Are you intending to file a formal complaint? I simply want you out of the way while we do our jobs. If everything checks out, which I'm sure it will, I have no problem with your involvement in this investigation. Until then I'd like you to wait outside."

A heavy sigh escaped him. He was a federal agent now. It was well within the duties of his job to deny her request, though he wasn't sure it was worth it. "Whatever!"

"This way, sir." The sergeant gestured to the door a little too late. Ray was already on his way out.

The 95th District

Levi Samuel

Chapter 10
Sins of the Past

"How many times do I have to explain it? You would have done the same thing if it was your investigation." Katelynn defended, climbing the stairs of the department's headquarters.

"First off, it is my investigation! Secondly, no I wouldn't. I may not like the idea of having to work with an outside agency but I would have put the job above my personal feelings and done what was required. You're just trying to get even for some imagined slight." Ray demanded.

Most of the accompanying officers had already passed the bickering pair. The few who lingered wore humored smirks upon their faces.

"What imagined slight? What could I possibly want to get back at you for?"

"Oh, I don't know, Katelynn. Maybe the fact that you've been a bit of a pain in the ass since I became a detective. Maybe you're jealous for some reason. Hell, I don't know. Maybe you're pissed off because we never took things any further when we were going out."

"Going out? You think that's what all this is about?"

"You tell me!" Ray demanded. He hadn't realized their conversation had gotten so heated until he glanced around to see everyone staring at them.

"Bradley, Slack, get in here!" Anderson yelled from his office door. It wasn't often he yelled but when two supposed professionals were acting like children—

The pair marched to the captain's office, refusing to say another word without mediation.

Anderson closed the door once they were clear. "Take a seat."

Ray waited for Katelynn to sit. He was pleased it wasn't in his preferred chair.

Making his way around the desk, Anderson took his own seat, his pensive glare lingering on the pair for just a moment longer. His calm demeanor had returned though disappointment was plainly visible in his eyes. "Would either of you mind telling me what the problem is?"

"Well, sir, apparently Katelynn doesn't think I should be allowed to work my case."

"I never said that!" She demanded, her temper flaring. "I simply asked you to wait outside the crime scene until you had a signed warrant in your possession."

"My badge isn't good enough? I told you it was on the way. I did everything by the books. I think you simply can't handle the fact that I outrank you now." Ray's volume was beginning to raise once again.

"Bullshit! I don't give a damn about that. I was following evidence in connection to a case which you managed to interfere with not once but twice in one day. And let's not forget that I had my warrant on hand."

Anderson raised his hand, calling for silence. "Okay. It's clear we have some underlying issues here that need to be worked out. You're both doing your jobs. It just so happens those jobs have overlapped. Lieutenant Slack, you've cooperated with the FBI on more than one occasion. If memory serves, you've also assisted in a Marshals case. Removing any personal connection, is there any aspect of this case which would justify your expulsion of a badge carrying federal officer?

Katelynn took a deep breath, realizing the captain was right. "No, sir. Aside from being inside the house when we came in there was no justification. Marshal Bradley responded reasonably and informed SWAT of his affiliation, which was verified on scene."

"Good. If there's a personal issue which needs resolved, I would appreciate you handling that off-duty. As it stands, the state of Florida as well as the Chief of Police are in conjunction with the use of federal task forces. Sometimes the best course of action is to use the most valuable weapon at our disposal. Restraint and common sense."

"Understood, sir."

"You're dismissed. I wish to have word with Marshal Bradley."

Katelynn stood and made for the door. Grabbing the handle, she paused and turned back to face the men. "I'm sorry, Ray. When you have a moment I think we need to have a conversation."

"I agree." Ray smiled at her, hoping there were no hard feelings.

Katelynn left the room and closed the door behind her.

"Wipe that stupid grin off your face. You haven't won anything!" Anderson snapped. "I like you, Ray. I really do. But I can't have that shit happening in the middle of a crime scene. Then you bring it back here in front of the entire floor?"

"What was I supposed to do? She wanted to have a pissing match. I didn't like it but I did what she asked. By the time my warrant arrived they pretty much had the scene wrapped up." Ray retrieved the folded paper from his pocket and laid it on Anderson's desk.

Having regained his calm, Anderson inspected the warrant. "These parameters are pretty vague. Did you find what you were looking for?"

"They had a couple bags of dope, a bunch of money, and a schedule. So far, the schedule is the only thing that ties into my investigation. It's the same shipping yard where Crumble disappeared. And the night he vanished is on the list. I didn't get a chance to see if anything else was found."

"Paired with the report I received earlier today, am I to assume you were first on scene in both instances?"

"Yes, sir. The I-95 incident, I was following a lead when the hit took place. The second was a follow up from my informant."

"That makes it your case above ours. If you wish the evidence turned over, it's yours."

Ray thought about it for a moment. "Sir, my case is ongoing. This was a detour which yielded a lead. I don't care about the money or really even the drugs for that matter. The department can claim both for all I care. I just want the schedule contents. Though I wouldn't mind reviewing the finished reports. Maybe they found something I missed."

Anderson nodded. "Understood. In any case none of it will be ready tonight. I recommend going home and getting some rest. It looks like the WMD is running you pretty hard. I'll make sure everything's ready for you in the morning."

"Thank you, sir." Ray paused a moment, realizing what he'd just heard. "WMD, sir?"

Anderson smiled. "Who do you think gave them the greenlight?"

"How long have you known?

"Longer than you've been alive. Kel'Gos and I used to be partners back in the '70s. Things were much different back then." Anderson seemed to drift into memory.

"How so?" Ray asked, piecing it together. He recalled looking at a report from that time frame when he'd first been partnered with Crum. Anderson's name had been on it, though the other agent in question was— The double sign on the old orc's door flashed to memory. "Mark Kelly!"

Anderson chuckled. "Yep. That's what that old bastard was going by when he turned up. I'll tell ya, I didn't have Pandora to help me see through the Veil. I had to do it the old-fashioned way. I spent months thinking I was going crazy. Just as I reached my breaking point I gave in and stopped questioning all the crazy shit I was seeing. Then one day it happened. I realized there was more out there than I'd been told. Everything sort of fell into place. It's funny how acceptance can trigger belief."

"I bet that was difficult. I can't imagine what it must have been like. Though without Pandora at least you didn't have to worry about any random person off the street complicating it further."

"That's true but there were also a lot more hippies in that era. You'd be surprised how many of them were either part of the coverup or believed just enough to slip through the cracks. Either way we've got some dark days ahead of us. Keep your head down and your eyes open. I've a feeling things are going to get a lot worse before they get better."

"I will. Thank you, sir." Ray left the office and headed downstairs.

Feeling an odd sensation in his pants, Ray rolled over and grabbed the vibrating cellphone from his pocket. Swiping the green icon, he placed it to his ear. "Hello?"

"Hi Ray. This is Alice, MPD Forensics."

"Hey Alice. I remember. What's up?"

"Oh, nothing much. I was just going over this evidence from Lieutenant Slack's case last night. Captain Anderson said you'd want to review it before I submit the report."

"Okay. I'll be there in about thirty minutes. Thank you, Alice." Waiting for her to acknowledge, Ray's arm fell limp, ending the call. He slowly opened his eyes. It took a fair amount of effort but he forced himself to get up. Unbuttoning his shirt and dropping his pants, he undressed and climbed into the shower.

The hot water felt good, rousing him from his slumber. Performing a few quick rituals, he dried off and stepped into the room sized closet where he would pick the suit of the day. The array of choices had been provided courtesy of Miami PD. Only a few had been specifically tailored to him but most fit well enough. That was one of the many perks to working undercover. He got first access to any confiscated apparel. Expensive suits, watches, jewelry, briefcases, pretty much anything that could sell the image of successful entrepreneur was his for the picking. Of course, that didn't apply anymore. But they hadn't asked for them back. Like the loft itself, it was his until it wasn't.

Making his selection, Ray settled on a Stefano Ricci pinstripe with baby blue button up. Grabbing two ties, one red and white striped, the other blue and silver, he held them up inspecting the overall scheme. Unable to decide, he returned both to their hanger and adjusted his collar. He preferred the casual look of a few loose buttons anyway. Slipping his loafers on, Ray grabbed his effects and made for the door.

It took a little longer to reach the station than it had to leave the night before, but not by much. Pulling into the secluded lot around back, Ray climbed out and chuckled to himself. Even now, months after his suspension, he continued to parked discretely, walking the added distance to the side door. Old habits die hard.

Entering the building, he followed the path he'd taken so many times in the past. Passing Katelynn's desk he was somewhat relieved she wasn't there. He needed to talk with her at some point but right now wasn't the time. Ray detoured and approached the elevator, going down to the forensics lab.

The downtown station was one of the few buildings in the city which had a partial basement. In truth, it wasn't underground, but rather along the rear half of the building on the first floor. It simply couldn't be accessed without stairs or an elevator from anywhere other than the second floor or higher. The same could be said for the interrogation rooms and a few holding cells. It was more secure that way.

Pushing through the whitewashed doors with a glass pane in the center, Ray stepped into the forensics lab seeing Alice near the back wall, peering into a microscope.

Ray approached the timid woman. She looked the same as always, long blonde hair pulled into a high ponytail. A pair of wide brimmed glasses magnified her brown eyes and she wore a dark blue sweater beneath her lab coat that depicted a row of white kittens walking from right to left. "What have you got for me, Alice?"

"Oh! Hi. I didn't see you come in." She started one way then turned and went the other. Reaching into a plastic tray at the side of her workstation, Alice grabbed a printout and handed it to him. "We just finished analyzing the drugs that were brought in last night."

Ray looked at the graphs depicting a composition report. It was about as useful as talking to a doctor in technical terms, which was to say he didn't understand hardly any of it. "What am I looking at, Alice?"

She bounced lightly on her feet, seemingly waiting for him to ask. "It's a new compound!" She squeaked with excitement.

"Which means?"

Seemingly disappointed in his inability to keep up, Alice moved beside him and pointed at the names on the sheet. Flipping the page, she denoted the same names once again at similar levels. "This drug is an exact match to that stuff you brought me several months ago. Pandora."

"You're sure?"

She didn't have to answer. The look on her face told him that question was an insult.

"Sorry. But—If they're the same, what's the other stuff on this one?"

"Oh. Okay, so you know how water and ice are so different when viewed under a microscope, but they're practically the same thing?"

"No."

Alice sighed. "We'll, they are." She separated the papers for comparison. "Composition A, liquid Pandora. Composition B, solid Pandora. They're the same with a few minor exceptions. The solid form is a much higher concentrate but it also has insanely high levels of calcium and magnesium, as well as trace amounts of chlorine, fluoride, lead, iron oxide, sodium, and several other chemicals commonly found in water." Her excitement returned and she began to bounce again.

"So—they're using water to make the drug?" Ray stated slowly, still missing the connection. Lots of drugs required water during manufacturing. He didn't see how this was any different.

"Bam!" Alice shouted, slamming another paper atop the other two. "Chemical analysis of city tap water taken from my wash sink this morning." She pointed to the aforementioned sink.

Ray scanned the details realizing the names were the same as what was listed on the solid Pandora breakdown, the only difference being much lower levels. "So Pandora is already in the water? They aren't using it to make the drugs, they're making the drugs from it?"

"Exactly. Whoever's manufacturing this stuff is filtering hundreds of gallons and collecting what they take out."

"Holy shit! That means there's no way to limit production. All anyone has to do is filter the water."

Alice looked around, making sure no one was paying attention. "You know what I think? All this pandemic stuff is just a cover. When's the last time you heard of anyone getting sick because of it? More than that, think of how much water the average person consumes on a daily basis. Even if they don't drink the recommended eight glasses, they're still consuming it in their coffee, tea, and foods. Not to mention personal hygiene. There's literally no escaping it. The entire population is infected and they don't even realize it. They simply have to consume enough to trigger the hallucinations and suddenly there's an outbreak."

"That's quite the theory, Alice. But wouldn't confirmation be as easy as running bloodwork? If they ingest it, it would show up wouldn't it?" Ray asked, buying time to think. Alice was getting dangerously close to the truth and he wasn't sure what would happen if she unlocked it. Of course, he didn't know it was in the water. That was news to him.

"That's the thing about Pandora. Do you remember when I got infected? I never got sick or felt any different than usual. Some things were simply—weird. Like that DEA agent. He was big and green, kind of reminded me of the Incredible Hulk. Really, that's as far as my symptoms went. Once I got to the lab I was perfectly fine. I drew my blood and ran the tests myself." Alice approached a dry erase board standing near the wall. Grabbing a marker she went to work explaining it. "There are four steps to any imbibed substance: absorption, distribution, metabolism, and excretion.

"The first stage is how it gets into the body. Administration can occur orally, injected, inhaled, transdermal, or rectally. Regardless of how it enters, it's eventually broken down and ends up in the circulatory system." Alice began drawling a crude river with little angry face blobs floating in it. "This is the distribution phase where it's carried throughout the body. Most prescription drugs are designed to target specific areas by binding to the receptors, tissues, or intracellular fluids, but due to inefficacy they often target other things which is why side effects occur. Before it can enter the central nervous system, it has to cross the blood brain barrier. There's a lot more that happens on both sides, whether it's successful or not.

"What I'm getting at here is my bloodwork did not show any sign of Pandora. That means one of two things. Either it defies the laws of nature and doesn't enter the bloodstream, or it does the opposite so efficiently that it enters and is consumed almost instantly without any, or so little rejected waste that it does not show up in a report."

"Which do you believe is the case?" Ray asked, realizing she'd put a lot more thought into this than he'd considered.

"Honestly, both are equally implausible. Every nutrient, chemical, or substance we take has to be absorbed into the bloodstream. Biologically that's how our anatomy is designed. The same holds true for the second scenario as well. Cells absorb the nutrients and chemicals they need from the bloodstream and eject waste back into it for excretion. I would have to do additional testing over time to get solid evidence. Of the two, I believe the second scenario is more likely. I simply haven't found where or when the waste is being expelled."

"What do you plan to do about this discovery?" Ray asked, wondering how far she was willing to go. She was hinging on obsession. And with the discovery, she not only had proof but resources to conduct further tests.

"What can I do? The government said it was a series of random gas leaks and mutation. Never mind L.A., St. Louis, Huston, NYC and several others who experienced the same *leaks* at the same time. Not to mention how the infection radius spread from each of those cities." Alice shook her head, seemingly battling with herself. "No. The government knows what's happening. They're either letting it happen or covering it up, I don't know which. But I'm not about to go poking around to find out. I'll just stick to bottled water until I've done proper testing."

Ray was pleased to hear that. He wasn't overly thrilled with contributing to the coverup himself but he understood why it was necessary. Like Roderick said, the general population wasn't ready for such change. "That sounds like a plan." He smiled, hoping the defeat registered on her face would fade. "Is there anything else I need to know?"

"Just that the money is real, and most of it is covered in a mixture of Pandora dust and dirt. The dirt is specific to southern Miami. I imagine whoever's manufacturing is also handling the money."

"Okay. Thank you, Alice. Go ahead and file your reports. I'll have the drugs and the shipping schedule transferred from evidence."

"Shipping schedule?" Alice questioned. She grabbed a report and began scanning the information. "I never received a shipping schedule, boss. I see the note in Lieutenant Slack's report where it was collected, but it was never included in the evidence lift or submitted to us."

A heavy sigh escaped Ray. "Okay. I need to go talk with the Captain." Shaking his head, he turned and started for the door.

"Ray!" Alice called just before he reached it.

He turned.

"I'm glad you're back."

"I'm not back but I'll be around. It was good to see you again, Alice."

Ray made his way to Captain Anderson's office. Knocking on the glass, Anderson waved him in. "We have a problem, sir."

"What kind of problem?"

"An internal one. The schedule I needed for my case. It was never submitted to evidence. Katelynn did her job in reporting it but it never made it beyond that."

"If I'm understanding what I think you're saying that's a pretty serious accusation, Ray."

"I'm aware. Unfortunately, I believe that to be the case. Alice said it never made it to her. She doesn't even have record of it being collected."

Anderson took a deep breath. Nodding a few times, he finally spoke. "Give me a day or two to look into it. If it appears to be anything larger than a simple mistake I'll inform IAD and have a full investigation opened."

"Okay, sir. Until then, that puts me back at square one. Without the schedule I have no way of knowing when the next shipment is scheduled to arrive."

"I understand. I'll try to get this resolved as soon as possible."

"Would you mind if I have the suspect from last night pulled for interrogation?"

"I would not but I fear you're going to have difficulty getting anything out of him. He bit his tongue off last night."

"What? God damn it! Why does every aspect of this case keep getting pulled out from under me?"

"Welcome to law enforcement." Anderson offered, finding no humor in the joke.

Ray picked himself up. He didn't want to be here right now. "Please give me a call if you find anything. I guess I'm headed back to the drawing board."

"Will do."

Ray made his way through the bullpen. Spotting Katelynn at her desk, he sighed. "Now's as good a time as any." It wasn't like his day could get any worse.

Approaching her desk, Ray noticed a similar expression on her face. "Katelynn, do you have time to grab a coffee? Maybe we can work out whatever issues we have."

"Yeah." She grabbed her badge and gun, clipping them to her belt. Slipping a brown leather jacket over her shoulders, she fluffed her dark wavy hair from beneath it. "The place down the street, or do you have somewhere else in mind?"

"Down the street is fine. I know you have a job to do, as do I."

Katelynn nodded agreement. "Walk or drive?"

"I could use the air. Besides, maybe we'll get to the root before we get there." Ray smiled at the prospect.

The pair made their way outside and onto the sidewalk. Heading north, the coffee shop was two blocks away. After several uncomfortable moments of silence and about half a block of wasted distance, Ray sighed and began speaking.

"Okay, so just to clear the air I want to say I appreciate you. When we were dating I saw potential for a lasting relationship. Whether that attributed to the way I responded to you or not, I don't know. I liked you and it hurt when you broke things off."

"I liked you too, Ray. The problem was we were both working all the time and I couldn't allow myself to get emotionally attached. Then you got promoted and it complicated things further."

"How so?" Ray asked as they neared the end of the first block.

"The random girls for one. You were working undercover. I knew— I know that sometimes it requires separation of emotion. I wasn't comfortable knowing you'd have to entertain them from time to time. I wasn't comfortable with what you had to do to survive. I thought it best to simply release any commitments we had. I didn't like it but I understood it. Then, after you got suspended and weren't around anymore I began to question if I'd made the right choice. Whether I did or not is irrelevant." Katelynn paused for a long moment. "I really am sorry about last night. I've thought about it quite a bit. I agree I overreacted."

Ray smiled. "I'm sorry too. I could have handled the situation better myself. I felt you were trying to pull a power trip as a way of gaining some kind of superiority. I think it's best if we just call it even and move on."

"I can do that." Katelynn agreed.

"And maybe, on those lonely nights we can do the things I know you've been dreaming of since before we split." Ray joked, pleased to see a smile return to her face.

"You wish!" She bumped into his shoulder, sending him off the edge of the sidewalk.

Sharing a laugh, they reached the coffee shop. It only took a moment to order their drinks and settle at one of the outside tables. No sooner than they got seated, Ray heard a familiar voice.

"Ray!"

He glanced across the street, seeing Lilian headed toward them. "Um—" He was frozen. He turned from the beautiful half-elf to Katelynn and back again, wondering how this was going to go over. Lilian was gorgeous in every way. She had the perfect body, the perfect face, the perfect hair. Even the way she spoke was sexy. Katelynn was much of these things as well. She was outspoken and playful, though serious when needed. She resided within the realm of attainable. Lilian was a ten on all scales. She could have been a supermodel if that was her choice. She was unattainable and that was part of what attracted him.

Ray paused, realizing he'd been comparing the two. It wasn't so much a difference that one was superior to the other. They were both wonderful in various ways. Katelynn was from his old life, his life before he opened his eyes. Lilian was part of the new world. It was that revelation that told him he'd moved on. "Hi." He said, not knowing what else to say. "What are you doing here?"

"I heard this place has the best coffee in town. I had to see for myself." Lilian answered, approaching the pair. "Who's your friend?"

"Oh, my apologies. Lilian, this is Katelynn. Katelynn, this is Lilian."

Katelynn stood and shook Lilian's hand. "Nice to meet you. How do you two know each other?"

"I used to babysit Ray." Lilian offered, laughing at the inside joke.

"Really?" Katelynn asked, glancing at Ray. "You have to tell me your secret. You don't look a day over twenty."

"Oh? It's in the blood."

"She didn't babysit me." Ray interjected. "I had to go to Europe a few days ago. Lilian was the agent responsible for keeping tabs on me."

"Like I said, babysat." Lilian repeated.

"Well, he certainly needs it sometimes." Katelynn replied. "So, you're an agent? What department?"

"Interpol"

"That must be interesting."

"Sometimes. It mostly depends on what's going on." Lilian smiled at Ray and turned her attention back to Katelynn.

"I'm going to get another drink. Can I get anything for either of you?"

"I'm good, thanks. I need to be getting back to the station." Katelynn replied.

"I'll take a double shot latte, if you don't mind."

"Coming right up." Ray made his way inside, wondering what kind of hell he was going to suffer leaving them alone to gossip. With any luck they'd find their own topic of discussion, though he suspected it'd be about him. They certainly wouldn't be passing the Bechdel Test today.

Approaching the counter, Ray placed the order and returned outside. Katelynn was already gone and Lilian sat comfortably in his chair. Handing the beverage to her, he took a seat in the opposite chair where Katelynn had been moments earlier. "I assume she returned to the station?"

"Yeah. She seems nice. Were you two ever an item?" Lilian asked, taking a sip.

"Briefly. It didn't work out." Ray offered, hoping the subject would shift. "How's your case coming along?"

"Slow. I've found a few leads but nothing substantial. Yours?"

"Dead-end after dead-end. I almost had something last night but it slipped away."

"Well, I may be able to help with that." Lilian stated casually.

"How so?"

"Not here. Join me for dinner, seven o'clock?"

"Is this a date?"

"If you'd like it to be." Lilian smiled.

"Where?"

"The Rusty Pelican? Most places are closed but they're not."

"I'll see you there."

"It's a date." Lilian winked. Picking herself up, she finished the rest of her drink and tossed the empty cup into a trash bin. "Don't be late, Ray Bradley."

"I won't." Ray watched her hurry across the street and disappear around the corner.

Chapter 11
Getting Acquainted

The Metro Dade garage was packed with cars. Ray was nearing the roof and he still hadn't seen a single open lot. Taillights caught his attention just as he rounded the final corner. He pulled to the side and waited, watching a Buick Regal vacate the spot. He wasted no time to fill it.

He was somewhat surprised how close the WMD was to Central Police Headquarters, though that wasn't to say it was right around the corner. In truth, it was just over two miles due east and a couple blocks offset. It seemed so far removed had he not just driven it.

Getting out of his car, Ray grabbed a nylon garment bag and an extra pair of shoes from the passenger's seat. Slinging both over his shoulder, he made for the elevator and pushed the button for the ground floor. The enclosed lift jolted and for the first time he realized he was getting accustomed to the smooth ride the WMD's private system provided. Anything lesser left him slightly unnerved. The ride came to an end and the doors opened. Hurriedly, Ray stepped out onto the pavement.

It was a short walk to the ambiguous building surrounded by magnificent architecture in the Central Business District. Had he not known what he was looking for he could have easily walked right past.

Ray turned onto the small road that ran beside the Charles Downing Building and approached the north entrance. Stepping inside, he had no trouble getting past security, though this was his first official visit through the entrance. They scanned his badge, had him step through an x-ray machine, various metal detectors, and finally allowed him on his way without question. He didn't even have to remove his sidearm which had come as a shock.

Ray climbed into the much smoother elevator, silently promising he would forever cherish it, and scanned his ID. He placed his finger over the sensor for the fourth floor and prepared for the noise that was about to assault him.

The doors opened and he found himself at the edge of the public relations offices. Ray cut through the center as fast as possible, retracing the steps he'd walked seemingly a lifetime ago. The fact it had been just yesterday made no difference. Reaching the end, he navigated the public corridors and found his office.

Ray was surprised to find the knob had no obvious lock. Instead, it had a hard plastic surface on the back side, out of view. The moment he touched it, he felt a vibration and the door clicked. He wondered if it was unique to him or just certain people. If it worked on the same concept as a magnetic key, his ID could be linked. But then why not just use a key lock? There was also the proximity keyless entry like his car. Of course, they'd taken his fingerprints during processing as well. If it was fingerprint base that would answer it, but what if someone else needed in?

Realizing it didn't make much difference, he pushed the door open and stepped inside. Locating the clothing rack just left of the empty shelf, Ray unzipped the bag and retrieved two sets of clothes. He hung them neatly and placed the shoes on the bottom rack. His job had been fairly demanding thus far and while he hadn't needed them yet, having a few extra suits seemed like a good idea.

Removing his jacket and hanging it as well, Ray fell into his brown leather chair and grabbed the case files he'd reviewed the day before. Something had been nagging at him since then but he couldn't place what it was. Repeating the procedure, Ray opened them one at a time, reviewing the contents.

About three-quarter through the stack, he found the one he'd been seeking. It was a smaller case. Human on elf homicide with witness descriptions and video evidence.

Scanning the witness reports Ray began to piece together the scene.

There were too many commonalities for it to be coincidence. Searching the bottom of the file, locating the evidence block, Ray spotted a file number for the video clip. The description box read *CCTV footage.*

Reaching under his desk, he pulled the keyboard slide toward him and moved the mouse. The USMS logo appeared in the air in front of him. Clicking once, he was prompted for his ID number and password. Having already remembered both, he quickly typed them in and the desktop appeared.

The system was fairly straightforward. There were a few differences from what he was used to but for the most part once you learned one LEO database, you pretty much knew them all. Ray located the evidence archives and typed the reference number. It showed a single entry, an mp4 video file.

Ray didn't need to push play to get positive identification. The thumbnail alone was enough for that. For good measure, he hit play and the forty-three second clip began.

It was a nighttime scene, overlooking a small section of road and sidewalk. Ray could see the victim walking, clearly away from the street. The report said he was an elf by the name of Sean Harris, though from the footage he looked human.

Suddenly, a red Mitsubishi Lancer Evo with a dark hood and winged spoiler came out of nowhere. It turned, intentionally by all accounts, and jumped the curb, plowing into the guy. The victim landed near the edge of the screen and rolled a few times.

The car stopped and the man Ray recognized as Jared climbed out, tire iron in hand. He casually approached the victim and hit him several times. Then, as if he hadn't done anything, he calmly returned to his car, threw the murder weapon into the backseat, and drove off.

Closing the video, Ray pulled the autopsy report. It had been performed by the WMD and plainly stated his race. Though the pictures, both pre and postmortem appeared human in all ways.

Scratching his head, Ray stared at the file for a long moment. There were a few details he needed to ask about, but even without those answers he'd accidentally completed his first case as a federal agent.

It took only a short time to fill out his report, covering much of the previous day's adventures, though he was less than forthcoming about the involvement of MPD. He'd agreed to give Anderson a few days to straighten everything up. He didn't want to damage that by being completely honest. 'In cooperation with Miami Police Department, evidence has been requested' seemed to be a good way to cover all sides. If nothing else it would buy a few days before questions started to arise.

Closing the file, Ray realized he had no idea how and where to submit the completed report. Getting to his feet he grabbed his jacket, as well as the file, and marched out the door.

The elevator door opened and Ray stepped out, making his way across the cubicle filled office. He had no idea what these people's jobs were but that was something he could add to the list of topics he was about to discuss.

The ever-present gloom that seemed to exist exclusively outside the eighth floor's windows greeted him. Ray paused to study it. It wasn't as hazy today but it was still raining. Several massive skyscrapers could be seen in the fog, though most were little more than dark shadows with an occasional glimpse. Ray suspected it had to be a screen of some kind. That was the only explanation. You didn't go from bright sunny days to eternal despair over the course of a few floors.

Though why anyone would opt for this instead of sunshine was a mystery.

Continuing toward his destination, Ray knocked on the door hearing it click. He could just barely make out the shape of the old orc through the tinted glass, waving him in. "Apologies for the intrusion, sir."

"What's on your mind, son?" Kel'Gos exhaled a large cloud of smoke into the air and placed his seemingly endless cigar on the ashtray.

"There are a few things of late, sir. I have a few questions and concerns I'd like to address. More imminently though, I've completed this case but I don't know where to file it." Ray handed the file over.

Kel'Gos scrolled through the details, seeing Ray's input. "Have you submitted the digital?"

"We have to file digitals as well?" A heavy sigh escaped him. What was the purpose of having paper then?

A hearty chuckle echoed through the small office. Kel'Gos grabbed a remote from the edge of his desk and pushed a button. A beam of bright light erupted from the wall behind him. "Our server is piggybacked to the one you use. Most of the features are the same. About the only difference being we have our own database."

Ray twisted in his chair, getting a better view of the projected desktop. Watching intently, Kel'Gos navigated the menus, showing Ray where he needed to go to access the live files, in addition to where he would file his reports. "So, I have to file the report digitally and manually? That seems a little repetitive."

"I don't require it. My people have their choice. We have people who get paid to do the sorting and organizing. Of course, such an answer isn't up to me. That would be a question better suited for your direct superiors. Cross agency, I serve as little more than advisory."

"Understood, sir. I'll talk to Roderick about it when I get the chance."

"You have other questions?" Kel'Gos prompted, ending the projection.

"Yes, sir. For starters, how common are half-breeds, particularly between orcs and humans?"

"Orcling children are exceptionally rare in general. If the general public knew of our existence our population would be on every endangered species list known to man. We used to be one of the most common races to walk this planet. As to why procreation for our kind has dwindled, I cannot say. That holds true for dual or single orcish parents. Why do you ask?"

"I know a guy who until recently I believed to be human. When I saw him yesterday I recognized orc features. He had brown skin, a little lighter than yours and small tusks with the tapered ears. He has plenty of human features as well, it was just the first time I'd seen anything like that. I asked him about it and he couldn't answer my questions. I gathered he was raised by his mom—human."

"Aside from the procreation aspect, that's not overly surprising. It used to be quite common actually."

"What do you mean?"

"Well, my kind haven't always been the most friendly of sorts. Like all races, we had good, bad, and those in between. At one time our culture was centered on a rule by strength philosophy. The strongest among us was given leadership until someone even stronger took it by force. Oftentimes this led to tyrannical clans that preyed on anything or anyone weaker than themselves. Many half-orc children were a result of these raids. And most of the time they weren't accepted by either culture, being too orcish for humans, and too human for orcs."

"What about half-breeds with other races?"

Kel'Gos shrugged. "I can't say it's never happened. In known cases when an orc bred with an elf, neither the child nor an elven mother survived the birthing process. It's a conflict of anatomy. There are other instances where an abomination presented threat to everyone."

"Can you elaborate on that, sir?"

Kel'Gos shook his head. "I cannot. Such things are forbidden, even in discussion."

"Okay—" Ray paused a moment, not certain he liked that answer. "So my friend, him not knowing what he is— is normal?"

"Unfortunately. Though I'm somewhat surprised he exists in the first place. Since we integrated, crossbreeding laws have been established. They're less enforced for the more human looking races, elves and faeries and such. But orcs don't look human. As for your friend, be careful what you say around him. Even if he's half-orc, he's also half-human. The Veil will protect him until that door is opened."

"Understood, sir." Ray paused, running through his mental list. "On the topic of elves, Crum once explained orc generations to me. Would I be correct in the understanding that elves use the term differently?"

"That's correct. Orcs operate on a hundred-year cycle as a generation. Our surname is essentially our age. For instance, I'm from the century Gos, which happened in the 1600s according to your Gregorian calendar. Funny enough, that was the same century that calendar was introduced. Well, 1582 anyway. The way I understand it, it's not much different than the Julian calendar that preceded it, accounting for your leap years if I'm not mistaken. It was a big deal back then. Apparently, it had gotten ten days off track which is what prompted the change in the first place. I remember it being a huge scandal. Many were still complaining about it long into Rae." Kel'Gos chuckled as if he'd told a joke that was lost on Ray. "Anyway, elves refer to generation as how close they are to pureblood. For them it's all about status. The purebloods have been gone longer than I've been alive. Most think they're either extinct or sealed away in some long forgotten cathedral under torpor. Whichever the case—"

"Excuse me. What's torpor?" Ray interrupted.

"It's a long rest, like hibernation, though involuntary. Many animals do it, though not to the extent of elves. The more powerful an elf becomes the more they require torpor. The stories I've heard suggest an elder pureblood would have to enter torpor no less than every one-hundred years or so, spending anywhere from three- to five-hundred in a deep slumber. Whether that's the case or not, I don't know. What I do know is they're forced to do it or their bodies will begin to breakdown."

"That doesn't sound fun. Though I guess it's no worse than humans having to spend a third of our lives in an involuntary sleep."

"Agreed." Kel'Gos paused. "Where was I?"

"You were talking about blood being a status symbol."

"Right! Elves aspire to be as close to pureblood as possible. The closer they are, the stronger they become, which is a silly desire if you ask me. You can't rightly become more of something like that. You're either born to it or you're not. But that's a different discussion. All an elf really has control over is who they mate with. If they aren't content with their own status, they'll often seek a mate to increase the blood strength of their offspring. Pretty much every elf we know of is less than a third total elven blood, leaving them around seventh generation or greater by their standard."

"How do they achieve that?"

"By mating with humans." Kel'Gos announced as if he'd already answered that question. "Elven blood is powerful. It overrides the human traits. If a pureblood were to mate with a human the resulting child would be first generation half-blood. They would be nearly as strong as a pureblood, but if that half-blood were to mate with another pureblood and the elven blood overpowers as it always does, the result would be a second generation half-blood, stronger than the first generation and near equal in strength to a pureblood. Anything beyond this point, aside from the continued mating with purebloods would be weaker."

"That sounds—" Ray searched for the right word. "—complicated. Like some primetime royal bloodline drama happening there."

"Indeed, it is. Royal hierarchy was often inspired and occasionally infused with elven rule."

"No shit?"

"No shit. Just keep in mind that blood status plays a major role in their motives. Most elves will never admit to being anything less than elven. They view human parentage as a weakness."

Ray's mind jumped to Lilian. The first thing she'd ever said to him was that she was half-elf. If what Kel'Gos said was true, why was she different? "Sir, I've one further issue to report. I promised Captain Anderson a couple days to fix an issue."

"Knowing James, he'll likely do everything in his power to keep his word. What issue are we talking about?"

"He said you guys were partners a long time ago. Anyway, last night I acquired a shipping schedule. It contained the date and location of the night Crum disappeared. It *was* my first real lead in the case."

"Was?" Kel'Gos asked.

"Yes, sir. Due to complications with Miami PD I was unable to oversee the evidence myself. It disappeared somewhere between the time it was noted in the detective's report and being checked in as official evidence."

"If James is anything like he was back in the day that's bound to have him in an uproar. A crooked cop was something he could never stand."

"Well, there's more to it, sir. At the scene there were two bags of an unidentified narcotic. Forensics ran the labs. It came back as a new form of Pandora. Somehow the old strand was dumped into the water supply. That's how it got out. Whoever's manufacturing this new stuff is filtering it straight out of the city water. Not only is it more concentrated, but literally everybody has access to it. Containment is going to be a nightmare."

"Containment is already impossible. I would ask how they introduced it in the first place. More importantly, how is it still there?" Kel'Gos tested.

"I don't know, sir. That part has me stumped."

"Think about it. If I understand the water system in Miami, the entire southeast of the state is atop the Biscayne aquifer. Most of that area you can't dig more than a few inches without hitting water."

"Exactly, sir. The water table is extremely high. That allows for filtered access once it passes through the ground. Even if they were to get past all the security and dump hundreds of gallons straight into the aquifer, they can't expect it to last. It would take hundreds of gallons each day to maintain the levels it's reported at."

"And what does that tell you?"

Ray thought about the question for a long moment. There was clearly something there Kel'Gos wanted him to see. Hesitantly, he began to piece together a scenario. "That they have someplace where they're still dumping?"

"And?"

"And there's either no security to stop them or they own the security."

"Right. The first places I would check is all of the canals, wellfields, and rock pits. Those are going to be the easiest to inspect and rule out. Once they're checked off, you'll have only a few options remaining."

"Understood, sir."

"And another thing."

"Yes, sir?"

"Quit calling me *sir* all the time. I work for a living, dammit. My name's Kel'Gos. You can call me that, Kel, Kelly, Mark, or if you insist on formality, Director."

"Understood, sir."

Kel'Gos arched an eyebrow, suggesting he was ready to bring his battle axe off the wall.

"Kelly." Ray corrected. "As for the MPD issue, I told Captain Anderson I'd like the drugs and schedule formally requested so the department can sign off on the case. There was also a shit load of money but I didn't figure the USMS needs to tap into that." The statement triggered something Alice had said to him. "Alice said the money was covered in dust from both the powdered form of Pandora and dirt. What do you think the chance is of the dump site being underground?"

Ray paused, considering his own question. Before Kel'Gos could respond, he answered it himself. "No, that wouldn't be feasible for the same reason hardly anybody has basements here. The water table would make it stupid expensive to build. It'd have to be completely waterproof and excessively anchored to keep from moving. Even then the likelihood of success would be low."

"Perhaps. Perhaps not." Kel'Gos offered.

"What do you mean? Something like that is guaranteed to be noticed. Look at the Port Miami Tunnel. They're still bitching about that and it took four years to build after decades of discussion."

"It's hard to say. All we know is somebody with a lot of money and influence is running that operation. We now know they have direct access to the water supply. I'll have our guys pull some samples to determine if the pollution is happening before or after treatment. That should narrow the search significantly. From there, once we've checked the locations we discussed, there's only a handful of places remaining. With that, we'll be able to narrow the search by any major contract jobs and various water samples. It stands to reason the strength would increase the closer to the source we get."

"Sounds like we have a plan." Ray got to his feet. "Thank you for the advice and for showing me a few areas of the system."

"No problem. They like to throw people into the fire and see if they swim."

"I'm not sure that analogy works, but I get what you mean." Ray laughed, glancing out the door. "One more question, if you don't mind?"

"Go for it."

"What's up with the windows? Every time I come here it's foggy or raining. Outside my window it's sunny and eighty-five."

Kel'Gos chuckled. "That's a story for another time. I fear I don't have a way to explain it that'll make sense."

Chapter 12
Date Night

Six-thirty rolled around and Ray had just finished getting dressed. He'd put so much time into the affair that he'd lost track of it. It all began with the simple idea that he'd been wearing nothing but suits for so long, he'd forgotten other clothes existed.

The Rusty Pelican was a business casual upscale joint off the north west tip of Virginia Key. It was the sort of place suitable for most affairs, especially if you had money to throw around.

He needed to retain his suave appearance but lose the formal approach. A simple pair of blue jeans and a white tee shirt under his Eurostyle leather jacket would have achieved that effect but it wasn't flashy enough. The jacket was a must. The night air was cool enough to get away with it. More importantly, it provided both attributes he was looking for.

Instead, he'd elected on a pair of dark blue dockers, brown belt, brown boots, and a gray sweater over a light blue collared shirt. For style's sake, he had the sleeves bunched to mid-forearm. Quickly tucking his essentials away, Ray gave his hair a final once over and made for the door.

The parking lot was nearly empty when he arrived. Glancing at the time, he was ten minutes early. He remembered Lilian telling him it was better to be early than late. Parking his car, Ray made his way across the lot and under the colonnade where the doors awaited.

Pine colored hardwood floored the foyer and a large earth tone rug rested at the center with rectangles growing progressively smaller. Small potted trees and a towering lamp rested along each side of the door, but the most noticeable attribute in the room was the orange and wooden benches that ran along the wood plated walls. Odd looking devices that reminded him of short skis were plastered above them, and a glowing chandelier style lamp hung mid room.

Ray approached the front counter where a woman stood waiting.

"Welcome to the Rusty Pelican. Do you have a reservation?"

He found the question amusing. Ray glanced back at the door, just in case someone had arrived whom he couldn't see. The place was barren. What use was a reservation? "I'm meeting someone. Lilian Lambrino?"

"Right this way." The greeter turned and marched through one of two adjacent openings, talking as she went. "As I'm sure you're aware, we're open under the stipulation that social distancing will be followed. For that reason, no two adjacent tables will be seated."

"I'm aware of the ridiculousness of it all." Following, Ray surveyed the wine cases that made the hall she'd selected. It wasn't overly large, basically just the two initial walls and then a third that forced them to go left or right.

Turning left they followed the path to the outside patio.

Ray noticed Lilian the moment he stepped through the door. Every light within view was dimmed by her beauty. She wore a sparkling red dress which hugged every inch of her amazing figure. Her dark hair had been braided and ran elegantly down her exposed back. Even from a distance he could see the spark in her all-consuming brown eyes.

Approaching the table, the greeter pulled out the chair and gestured for him to sit.

It took a moment to comprehend, lost in Lilian's beauty. Finally, he understood. Removing his jacket, Ray hung it around the back of his chair and took a seat.

"Your server will be right with you." The greeter turned and disappeared the way she'd come.

"Wow!" It wasn't much but it expressed how he felt. "You look amazing."

"Thank you. I feared I was over dressed. I'm happy to see you know how to wear something other than Armani." Lilian jeered.

"I'll have you know this is a Tom Ford jacket. It easily retails for five-grand." Ray replied, expressing his seriousness.

"I think you should have saved your money."

Mimicking a tearful sniff, Ray forced himself to look away from her. "You hurt my feelings." Using the moment to look around, it was a magnificent location. They sat at the water's edge. The sun would be fading any minute leaving the horizon a beautiful mix of blue, orange, and pink. Yachts motored by in the distance, though much closer than most beachfront diners offered. A rock waterfall sat not far from them on the right, glowing blue on one side and purple on the other. Mood lighting ran overhead from the building to the palm trees, and stone basins rested between every few tables, though he didn't know for what reason.

"Relax, you big baby. I'm just messing with you."

Chuckling, Ray returned his attention to her. "I know. Fortunately, I didn't buy this jacket. It was seized during my first bust. This drug dealer named Carlos something or another."

"You wear stolen clothes to a date?"

"So, it is a date, huh?" He couldn't help but smile.

"Did I say date?"

"Yeah. Not once but twice now."

"Slip of the tongue. You didn't answer my question."

"All my clothes are borrowed. All the ones worth wearing anyway. I do own these boots though." He kicked his foot out to show them off. They were nothing special though disuse ensured they were well taken care of. If not for the slightly worn tread they could have passed for brand new.

"Put your foot down you heathen. We're at a restaurant." Lilian jokingly smacked his leg.

A young male approached their table and set a menu in front of each of them. "Good evening, folks. Welcome to The Rusty Pelican. What can I get you started with this evening?"

"I'd like to start with a Bay Blossom and a beer." Lilian answered.

"Any particular type?"

"No. Just a plain beer. It doesn't have to be anything fancy." She lifted the menu and began inspecting the items.

Scanning the drink menu, Ray found one that looked interesting. "I'll try a Wilson."

"Anything else?"

"Not at the moment, thank you." Lilian responded before Ray had a chance.

"All right. I'll be right back with those drinks." The waiter rushed off.

"So, I was doing a little recon and I remember you telling me you were—" Ray glanced around making sure no one was listening. "—half-elf. The way I understand it, most elves would never admit to that."

"I'm not like most elves."

Ray nodded knowingly. He didn't have much basis for comparison but he'd certainly never met anyone quite like her. "How are your parents?"

"Really?"

"I guess? I don't know. I'm just trying to have a conversation." Once again his inability to shut up was haunting him.

"I don't have much to do with my family. For that reason I feel no desire to discuss them."

"Okay. No problem."

The silence was awkward for a long moment until Lilian finally broke it. "I'm sorry for just showing up here the way I did. I wanted to see you again but I hadn't planned for it to be like that."

"No harm. It was a surprise but a pleasant one." Ray noticed a slight blush in Lilian's cheeks that made him smile.

"Still, that wasn't how I wanted it to happen."

Ray shrugged. "Things rarely happen the way we intend. We can just be glad it did happen. I didn't even get your number before I left. That's something I wish I'd done."

"We can remedy that. Give me your phone." Lilian slid hers across the table to him.

"Okay?" Ray handed his lifeline to her.

She began punching in her number. Bringing it up, she took a selfie and saved the contact.

Understanding, Ray dialed his number and handed it back.

"Wait a minute. You can't not take a picture, especially right after I just did." Whipping her phone around, she took aim. "Smile!"

It was difficult not to. The bright flash caused him to blink and suddenly he wished he'd just done it himself.

"Perfect!" Lilian announced, showing it to him.

Next to the horrible picture on his Interpol visitor's badge, this was the second worst picture he'd ever taken. "No! I demand a reshoot. My eyes are half closed and I look like I got stung in the face by a wasp."

"Fine, you big baby. We'll take one together." Lilian stood and rounded the table. Without warning she plopped into his lap.

Instinctively, Ray caught her and held her close for a long moment. It felt amazing despite the innocence of it.

Lilian placed her face beside his and lifted the phone. "Are you ready?"

"Yeah."

Lilian turned her head and planted a kiss on his cheek as she snapped the picture. Picking herself up, she inspected it and smiled. Spinning it around, Ray's face was in complete shock mixed with a hint of euphoria. "This is the one."

Ray was too giddy to decline.

"So, food. I was thinking the Board for Two looks good."

Jarring his senses to return, Ray scanned the menu finding the item to which she was referring. It appeared to be a seafood dish consisting of fried snapper, lobster risotto, steak, and whatever smoked sweet plantain mash was supposed to be. "Looks good to me."

Lilian set the menu aside. "So, tell me about the case you were working on. You said you hit a dead-end. What happened?"

"Oh, nothing much. You remember those guys who hit your deal?"

"Yeah."

"I followed up on them. Turns out they were into some bigger stuff."

"Like what?" Lilian leaned in, clearly interested.

"Typical bad guy stuff. Drugs, money, murder. That reminds me. There's a new strand of Pandora out."

"Powder or pill?" Lilian asked.

"Pill, or tablet actually, though it makes sense there would be a powder as well. How'd you know?"

"It hit Europe about a month ago. I'm surprised you didn't know about it yet."

"Well, truth be told, I was out of the game for a while after the first wave landed. I was suspended from local PD shortly after that investigation."

"What happened?"

"We were tracking the guy we believed to be responsible. Ended up in a shootout which turned into a pursuit over land and water. Long story short I ended up driving a hundred- and fifty-thousand-dollar car off a bridge and crashed it into a stolen seven-hundred-thousand-dollar cigarette boat. Apparently, that was the price of my job even though we caught him. Unfortunately, he wasn't the man at the top and the drugs still got out."

"Now I understand."

"What's that?"

"Why you want Ezekiel. I could tell you were personally invested. I think that's why Berlan asked for you specifically."

"I simply don't like people who think they're above the law. Everyone must be held accountable for their actions, myself included."

The waiter returned with their drinks. "Have you had a chance to look over the menu?"

"We have. The lady and I would like the Pelican Board for Two, please." Ray ordered, taking her subtle nod as approval.

"We'll get that right out. While I'm here, would you like to order another drink?"

"We're in Miami. I think I'll have a mojito. Oh, and a Miami Vice!" Lilian requested with a smile.

Ray simply waved his off.

"Coming right up." The waiter rushed off to update their ticket.

Ray waited a moment before he spoke again. "Not that I don't enjoy our conversation. Quite the contrary actually, but you alluded to a potential lead when you invited me here."

"Did I?" Lilian asked, a smirk forming on her lips. "Well, I have a bit of a confession to make."

"I'm not a priest. I don't do confessions." Ray joked.

"Good. Because I'm not the confession type." She smiled. "I lied about the lead. I needed an excuse to get you here."

"Now why would you go and do a thing like that?" Ray leaned in, looking deep into the almond eyes before him.

"Because—" Lilian met his gaze, leaning in herself. "I needed to do this." Without another moment's hesitation, she kissed him.

Ray stayed there long after she pulled away. It was heaven. A fraction-of-a-second action that consumed a lifetime. Coming to his senses, an uncontrollable smirk rooted itself, refusing to go away. "Wow!"

"You already said that."

"I meant it."

"I suppose I do have one lead I've been having trouble locking down." Lilian added casually.

"What's that?"

"Well, there's this casino."

Before she could say more, the waiter returned with a large wooden cutting board loaded with amazing looking food. Laying both it and two glass plates on their table, he took a step back. "I'll be right back with your drinks."

The night continued. They ate, drank, and conversed. Just as the sun disappeared completely and the last slither of orange faded from sight, several bright flashes erupted and flame shot from the stone basins. It danced brilliantly, swaying in the breeze. Music had been playing at a low volume, though now that the crackling fires added to the ambiance, it became a little louder.

Perking up, Lilian looked around. There were only two other tables seated, a family of three seemingly on vacation and an elderly couple sharing a bowl of ice cream. "I want to dance." Without another word, she stood and grabbed Ray's hand, pulling him toward her.

Holding each other, they slow danced beside their table, swaying in time with the music. Ray stared into her eyes, taking pleasure in their returned gaze. It was so easy to get lost in them. He could see years of experience behind them but more importantly a youthfulness that was so often absent.

Lilian laid her head upon his shoulder, enjoying the moment. The song ended and she stared up at him. Gently, their lips contacted a second time. "Let's get out of here." She whispered into his ear before releasing him.

"I'll get the check." Ray signaled the waiter, who came rushing over. "We're ready to cash out." Handing him his credit card, Ray was glad he hadn't spent much money over the past few months. With the price of some of these items, there was no doubt they'd racked up several hundred bucks.

The night air was cooling off. Grabbing his jacket, Ray gently placed it over Lilian's exposed shoulders. She showed no sign of being cold but it seemed the right thing to do.

She smiled and laid her head upon his chest again.

The waiter returned with a black leather booklet. The card and a pen protruded from the top.

He hated having to step out of her embrace. Ray took the booklet and reviewed the receipts for a moment. Sighing his disbelief, he quickly calculated the hundred- and twenty-dollar tip and signed his name. Grabbing his card and a copy of the receipt, he closed it and walked hand in hand with Lilian toward the exit.

Out front, they stopped near Ray's car. He glanced around seeing only a few others, none suitable for the beauty in his arms. "Where's your car?" He asked, gently kissing her forehead.

"It'll be arriving tomorrow."

"You had your Bentley shipped? Why didn't you just rent one while you're here?"

"I like my car. In case you've forgotten, I told you I got it in England."

"I remember. What's that have to do with anything?"

Lilian shook her head. He really was an idiot sometimes. "England's an island, silly. I have it shipped everywhere I go."

"Oh. Okay." It still didn't make any sense but she seemed confident in the decision. He couldn't fault her for wanting a piece of home. "I wouldn't consider myself *under the influence*, but I think we've had too much to consider driving home. Do you want to get an Uber? My loft is about twenty minutes away." Ray blushed, realizing he'd just invited her back to his place, though in his defense he'd assumed that was her intention when she said she wanted to leave. On a different note he wasn't sure what was happening to him. He'd talked hundreds of women into staying over for the night. Okay, maybe not hundreds but he'd certainly lost count. Why was talking to her so difficult?

Lilian hugged him, squeezing playfully. "So responsible."

Grabbing his phone, Ray searched for the nearest car and hit the call button. "Yes. I need a ride from The Rusty Pelican. Thank you." Returning his attention to Lilian he took the opportunity to kiss her wonderful red painted lips. "Someone will be here in about five minutes.

Holding the door, Ray followed Lilian inside and turned on the lights. They slowly came into existence, beaming from the vaulted ceiling.

The large living room was simple yet strategically arranged. It provided plenty of places for easy cover in the event of an unexpected shootout while equally maintaining the comforts of home. The couch and wooden coffee table rested center room, facing a digital fireplace and wall mounted flat screen above the mantle. The entire right side wall was one large glass window with two sliding doors that granted access to the balcony. A dining area and kitchen rested to the left, partially divided by a wooden bar top. Beyond the living room a wooden barn door on hanging sliders stood open, leading to the master bedroom.

Lilian glanced around. "Nice place. Let me guess, it's borrowed?"

"Pretty much. Though I've been here for about a year now." Ray approached the coffee table and grabbed a remote. Pressing a couple buttons, the fireplace came to life and mood music echoed from unseen speakers. The lights dimmed to match the audible tone. "What do you think?"

"I think you've got the music, lights, and fireplace preset for specific guests." She inspected the layout. If she noticed the defensive measures, she didn't say anything. "It's lacking a woman's touch."

He chuckled. "Can I get you anything to drink?" Hearing no response, Ray turned, finding Lilian right behind him.

She threw her arms around him and pressed her lips to his. His jacket dropped from her shoulders and hit the floor. "No—thank you." She whispered between kisses.

Ray held her, taking in her scent. She was the most wonderful creature he'd ever encountered. Her lips tasted like honey and her warmth could have ignited the most resilient cold. Holding her tight, he kissed her deeply, passionately.

Lilian turned, her hand in his and gently pulled him toward the bedroom. Reaching the bed, she spun around to face him again. Her lips met his collar bone and her fingers went to work loosening his belt.

"Lilian." Ray pleaded, hating himself. "I can't believe I'm about to say this but I think we should wait."

"What? Why?" She asked, ripping the leather strap from the loops of his breeches.

"We've both had a lot to drink tonight. I don't want to do anything you're going to regret in the morning."

She whipped the belt behind him and caught the loose end in her other hand. Gentle yet commanding, she tightened it behind his shoulders and pulled him toward her. Staring deep into his eyes, she spoke with a tone he'd only heard her use on occasion. "You listen here, Ray Bradley. I appreciate your concern, but nobody makes me do anything I don't want to do." The look in her eyes was deadly serious. "Not now. Not ever!"

"Even babysitting?" Ray asked, surrendering to her pull.

"Even babysitting." A smirk came to her lips and she pressed them against his. Dropping the belt, she grabbed the bottom hem of his sweater and undershirt and began working the pair over his head. Inspecting his exposed chest, he had less hair than she'd expected but considering his choice of clothes he was likely one of those who was always well groomed. Beginning at his sternum, she drug her lips across, kissing, licking, and occasionally nibbling her way toward his chin.

Aided by her, Ray removed his shirt, happy he'd left a few buttons undone. Taking a deep breath, he felt the clasp of his pants loosen. They dropped to his knees and her hands caressed his hips. They ran up his chest and back down again. He bit his bottom lip feeling his boxers fall free and she took him into her mouth. Involuntarily, he looked up at the ceiling, lost in pleasure.

It could have been hours, minutes, or even seconds, he didn't know. He was lost in the ecstasy of it all. All he noticed was suddenly Lilian released him. He peered down at her, staring deep into those pensive brown orbs that stared back at him. He wanted nothing more than to take her here and now. She was calling the shots though. He wouldn't deny her that.

Smiling wickedly, Lilian got to her feet. Gracefully, she slipped her shoulder straps and the red dress cascaded down her body and crumpled about her feet.

Ray was dumbfounded, lost in her natural form. He'd seen more than his fair share of naked women but none compared to the sheer perfection of what stood before him. Her dark complexion glistened in the low light, though from sweat or some unknown racial trait he couldn't say. Placing his hands on her hips, he pulled her to him and brought his lips to hers.

Lilian kissed him passionately, clinging to him. Releasing the embrace, she stepped out of her dress and grabbed hold of him. In a single fluid movement, she twisted and spun.

Unprepared for the sudden maneuver, Ray tripped and fell, landing atop the bed. The soft and thick mattress sprang beneath the sudden impact and he bounced a few times. He watched her intently, seductively climbing onto him. Her bare breast drug across his flesh as she kissed him from knee to waist, waist to abdomen, and up to his lips.

Straddling him, Lilian leaned forward and placed her body against his. She slowly worked back and forth, rubbing him, teasing him. Kissing his neck, she worked her way around near his ear. "Do you have protection?"

The heat of her breath paired with the whispered tone of her accent sent shivers down his spine. Every hair stood on end and he had to fight to answer her question. "Yeah. Yes. It's in the nightstand." He vaguely gestured to the right of where they lay.

Lilian stretched for the small table, pressing her bare body against his. Locating her prize she tore the package open with her teeth and prepared him.

Before he could respond she slid onto him. Slowly at first. Saddling fully, she worked into a rhythm. It was amazing. Her body contorted and rolled against him, bringing each of his senses to life. Her moans were ecstasy to his ears. He caressed her, fondled her, squeezed her. His hands ran along every inch and curve of her silky skin, each movement in time with hers.

The pace quickened and Ray felt her begin to tighten. He grabbed her hips, keeping rhythm. When she pulled, he thrust. And when she thrust, he pulled. It was a constant give and take, ebb and flow. Breathing heavily, unaware of any sounds he was making, Ray held her tight, feeling the internal convulsions. It was then the oddest thing happened.

He could feel her in every conceivable way. It was more than just the physical. They'd become one. The physical, the mental, and the spiritual. In that moment he knew her better than he knew himself. He could feel the pleasure she felt, see what she saw, hear what she heard. For the briefest moment it was as if they were no longer two separate entities joined as one, but rather one complete being trapped in two intertwined forms.

Lilian fell limp, heaving upon his chest. Her panting breath was a cool fire and for the first time in his knowledge she was covered in sweat.

Finding some strength, Lilian kissed his chest. She lay there in the comfort of his embrace, feeling at peace.

Chapter 13
An Old Score

Rolling over, Ray's arm landed on the empty mattress where Lilian had been. He sat up and looked around. She was nowhere in sight. A folded piece of paper on the nightstand caught his attention. Grabbing it, he read the words written in an elegant script.

I'm sorry I can't be here when you awake.
I received some information that can't wait.
I'll call you as soon as possible.

Lilian

P.S.
I had a wonderful time last night. Thank you!

She'd turned all the dots into little hearts and a lipstick kiss rested at the bottom of the page.

Catching a whiff of her scent from the pillow beside him, Ray hugged it, calling the memories to the forefront of his mind. A smug grin settled on his face. It was going to be a fantastic day!

Picking himself up, Ray climbed out of bed and danced toward the bathroom. He whistled a melodic tune to himself and stepped into the shower.

His morning ritual took no time whatsoever, though time was meaningless. He was still reeling. The only thing he couldn't explain was what had happened toward the end of their first time. The more he thought about it the more confusing it became.

Getting dressed, he grabbed his effects from his clothes the night before, still where they'd been discarded. A final look around told him there was nothing further here except longing. Ray made for the door, killing the lights on his way out.

The trip to the WMD was a pleasant one. Traffic was unusually heavy for a Thursday, though before Pandora it would have been a total nightmare. He parked his car and made the trek into the plain building on 1st Street.

Within a few minutes, Ray settled into his office. A notification displayed on his projected desktop in the form of a sealed letter. Grabbing the mouse, he clicked it. A single message rested in his inbox from *Captain James Anderson. – Felony Investigations*. Ray opened the email and quickly read the message.

> *Ray,*
>
> *I tried calling a few times. We found the leak. Though I'm sorry to say not before the evidence in question was destroyed. A formal investigation has been requested and any future information on this matter will be relayed immediately.*
>
> *I apologize for the inconvenience this has caused. However, there's a small amount of good news. In review of the suspected officer's digital communications, we were able to recover a picture of the item in question. It's not much, but hopefully it will be enough to get you started.*
>
> *Captain James Anderson*

Ray clicked the attachment and a crude picture popped up. Anderson was right, it wasn't much at all. The lighting was terrible, most of it being in shadow. It had been taken at a weird angle and displayed only the top sheet. Zooming in didn't help. The small section that was any form of legible was so blurry he couldn't make out half the characters. It was better than nothing, but not by much.

Unlocking his phone, he noticed the missed calls. There were three of them, two from Anderson and one from an unknown number. None had taken the liberty to leave a voicemail.

Selecting his old bosses name he hit the call button and listened to it ring.

"Anderson!"

"Sir, this is Ray. Sorry I missed your calls. I was—" Ray paused, selecting the right word. "—occupied. I got your email. Who was it?"

"I've been barred from disclosing their identity until after the investigation has concluded. I wish there was more I could give you." Anderson replied solemnly.

"I'll do what I can. Thank you for the picture. It looks like I'm going to have my work cut out for me."

"That was recovered from a sent text message that had been deleted. The accompanying message suggested it was proof of acquisition. We investigated the number. It was registered to a fifty-six-year-old man who's been dead for nearly a decade. It had been active for less than a week and service was terminated two minutes after the text was received."

"Good to know burner phones are still a thing."

"Some tactics never expire. As for our leak, they claim they never met with anyone. Said they got a call in the middle of the night instructing them what to do or their family was going to be targeted. So far we haven't been able to get anything else."

Ray sighed. "Okay, sir. Thank you for the update. I sent REF yesterday. I figured that would buy you the time you needed."

"I received it. I've arranged pickup for what we can provide and a delay request for the schedule until the investigation can be completed. You're clear to file officially however you choose to do so."

"Understood, sir. Thank you."

"Be safe out there, Ray."

The call ended and Ray returned his attention to the picture. Zooming in partially, he was able to find a happy medium. It still wasn't perfect but a little deductive reasoning never hurt anyone. Grabbing a piece of paper, he started writing.

After about an hour of constant squinting, looking through a magnifying glass, and a throbbing headache, Ray glanced at the paper as a whole to see what he'd written. Three of the shipments appeared to be complete, aside from a single number here or there. Two were departures and one receiving. One of the departures was circled but the destination was some business that didn't make any sense. Some place called Buccal Invoices.

A quick Google search yielded no results, though apparently buccal was another word for cheek. That added to the confusion. He scrolled through the results seeing something about halfway down the page.

It was purely a hunch but a word scramble site being on the top page was worth checking out. Curious, he clicked the link. The page went white and a moment later several results began to fill it. Most were just as if not more useless than the initial name. Cubical novices, occlusive cabin, the list went on.

A search perimeter appeared at the bottom of the results, likely designed to keep him on a moment longer. Most websites had something similar. It was how they upped their SEO ranking. Ray looked at the options. Language barriers and number of words in the result were the primary functions. "What the hell." Ray shrugged and hit the *Find Words* button for three-word results.

The page loaded and it was then he realized his hunch had paid off. The top result was the name of a place he'd driven passed every time he'd gone home. Club Vice Casino. Granted, it wasn't much to go on but it was more than he had before.

Staring at the name a memory from his dinner with Lilian flashed to the forefront. She'd mentioned something about a casino. That couldn't be a coincidence.

Scribbling the name onto his paper, Ray pulled his phone and scrolled through the contacts. He paused, seeing her name and picture pop up. It brought a smile to his face. He could feel her presence that very moment.

Taking a deep breath, his finger hovered over the call button. He wanted to ask about the casino. That was the intention. Unfortunately, he genuinely liked her. That was the problem. He couldn't call. Not yet. Not after what they'd done last night. If he called too soon she'd think he was being clingy and he'd never hear from her again. No, he needed to wait a bit. At least twenty-four hours. Locking his phone and tucking it away, Ray returned his focus to the computer screen projected in front of him.

Club Vice Miami didn't yield much. There was no website, no social media, and no pictures aside from Google Street View. Even that showed little more than what he already knew, a rundown factory warehouse. The assessor's office had some generic company listed as the owner, though a search with the license bureau turned up nothing on that end. All legal details aside, it sounded like the perfect place for illicit activity.

Expanding his search, Ray found a single blog post on the location. Like everything else, there were no pictures of the interior. It did however provide more information than he'd found elsewhere.

Some business guru out of L.A. had purchased the property and converted it into a nightclub a few years back. It was originally saddled with the name, *The Factory*. A few pictures showed the typical nightclub scene. Drinks, dancing, multicolored lights. Since the warehouse had two levels, most events took place on the main level and the upper portion became the VIP room.

It seemed a bustling investment, though easily overlooked by most. Ray recalled seeing it but never took the time to stop. It wasn't prestige enough for the type he consorted with. That didn't make it any less a successful enterprise. Still, about six months ago and seemingly out of nowhere, they closed their doors and went out of business. The property was sold, though no one knew to whom. And about three months later the building itself was rebranded.

The blog writer went on to talk about his dissatisfaction. Vice City refused him access without a membership, and nobody would tell him how or where to obtain one.

Ray smiled. He knew just the person for such a task. Retrieving his phone a second time, he scrolled through the contacts and located the one labeled Score Keeper.

He was the owner of a downtown club called The Palm, and an informant for Miami PD. Ray met Score Keeper days after he'd been promoted to detective. Katelynn had introduced them. In a weird way Score Keeper was the one who designed his persona. Before Ray Bradley smuggler and playboy, he was this shy kid who'd joined the Army right out of high school and had no idea how to talk to women. It was those details which shaped who he'd become.

Ray pressed the call button, hearing the familiar voice before the first ring.

"Ray Bradley, how are you going to make me regret answering your call today?"

"I need some information."

"What a surprise. Although if it's concerning the disappearance of one Mister William Crumble, I'm unfortunately in the dark on this one. Nobody's talking, nobody's been hired off the street. Whatever happened, it's been kept completely internal."

"Of course, that would have made things too easy. No, I'm actually calling about a place called Club Vice. Any leads on how I might get in?"

Score Keeper was quiet for a moment. "Give me about thirty minutes. If I can do it I'll call you back with my price."

"And if you can't?"

"Everything has a price, my friend. It's a matter of how far you're willing to go for it."

"We aren't talking about money anymore, are we?"

"Who says you can't teach an old dog new tricks?"

"Can you give me an idea? It's hard to promise something intangible."

"I assure you, Mister Bradley, whatever I ask for will be within your meager means of attainment. That's one of the perks of knowing everything that happens in this city."

"And you don't know what happened to Crumble? You're losing your touch."

"Remember, Ray, you called me. Not the other way around. I'd keep that in mind if I were you." Scorekeeper ended the call.

Ray stood and approached the rack where his jacket was hanging. Quickly throwing it around himself, he gave a little bounce to ensure it settled properly. With a final glance around making sure he hadn't forgotten anything, he stepped out the door.

Hurriedly, Ray crossed the noisy PR floor and rushed into the private elevator. It was becoming quite the annoyance having to walk so far to access the majority of the building. Why they couldn't have put his office behind the line or even built a secure elevator on the public side, he'd never know.

Scanning his card, Ray hovered the digital display, trying to decide which floor to select. Roderick was likely the person to talk to, but he couldn't remember which floor his office was located. He'd only been there once, and from the public elevator. There was no way he was crossing that madhouse again. On the other hand, despite his size, muscle, and general appearance, Kel'Gos was much less threatening. Sure, the old orc could break him in half without much effort. That was intimidating. But the chances of him doing so seemed slim. Roderick was too easy. He appeared transparent. That made him dangerous.

Having made his decision, Ray hit the eighth floor button and the doors opened.

Ignoring the sights and sounds along the way, they never seemed to change and his questions were never answered to his liking, Ray approached the last door on the right. The door opened just as he prepared to knock.

To his surprise, both Kel'Gos *and* Roderick were inside. The perpetual cloud of smoke was thicker than usual, swirling near the ceiling before disappearing into a small vent working overtime.

"What have you got for us?" Roderick asked, extending his cigar over the tray just as the long tail broke free and fell apart.

"Oh, I hadn't expected to find both of you here?" Ray stammered, unsure what to do. It made his relaying of information easier, though he hadn't planned for this encounter. "I—Uh—I possibly have a lead in the Crum'Bul case. There's a place off 24th street called Club Vice. It's a member's only type of joint."

"I've heard of it." Roderick replied, blowing a perfect smoke ring into the air.

"Well, I'm awaiting a phone call that could open that door for me. Unfortunately, I don't know what it's going to cost. I was wondering what sort of assets or guidelines I have to work with."

Roderick chuckled. "Son, we're the US Government. There isn't much we don't have access to."

"I understand that, sir. This is more for my knowledge going forward. When I was with MPD I knew the department's budget. Even when I had to talk my way into major deals I knew what my limits were. I'm afraid I haven't gained that familiarity here just yet."

"Let me put it this way. If you need something, no matter how outlandish, make the request. If need and availability are an option, we'll make it happen."

"He should see Department 13." Kel'Gos interjected.

"I can't grant him that authorization."

"I can." Kel'Gos reached into his desk and retrieved a reflective card that was inset with both a magstripe and a chip. Handing it to Ray, he continued. "That's a platinum card. It works everywhere within the WMD, as well as most ATMs if you need money fast."

"You're giving him a platinum card?" Roderick shook his head. "He's brand new and you just handed him the keys to the kingdom. I would have started him with copper. Maybe silver if I was feeling generous."

"I think he'll manage. Remember, I was going to hire him directly. You're the one that said he had to go through you." Kel'Gos retorted.

Roderick threw his hands up. "Rules are rules."

"Does someone want to tell me what's going on?" Ray felt like they were having a different conversation altogether, one pertaining to him.

"Don't worry about it. You'll know what you need to know. Anyway, I need to get going. I have a committee meeting to get to." Roderick stood and snuffed his cigar. He turned to Ray. "Kid, take care of yourself and try to use that card sparingly. Something given has no value. Remember those words." Without another word, he stepped around Ray and was out the door.

"So, what's this for?" Ray asked, holding up the card.

"It's getting a little stuffy in here. Let's take a walk." Kel'Gos took a final drag from his cigar and laid it to rest in the ashtray. Grabbing a few items from the desk, he followed Ray out the door. "Have you ever been to the parking garage?"

"We have a parking garage? I've been parking over by the government building and walking. I wondered why security always seemed so bored."

The orc laughed, which somehow seemed more frightening than a full blown rage. Kel'Gos stepped into the elevator and pressed the *B7* button. It wasn't lost on Ray that he didn't have to scan an ID first.

The door closed and the elevator sat stationary, or so it seemed. Ray could never tell when this one was moving. It was usually so fast the doors barely had time to close before a new floor came into view. "Sir—Kelly—" Ray corrected almost immediately but not before getting *the look*. "Two questions. First, how is it that you don't have to scan a card to make the elevator work. And second, I assume the B stands for basement. Per our previous conversation, how is that possible? I mean, I can see maybe one sublevel if someone were to spend a ton of money. But not nine floors. That borders on the seemingly impossible."

"The first part is simple. I'm a director. Identification is no longer required. As per your second series of questions, I must respond with one of my own. What do you know about the WMD?" Kel'Gos asked, his tone patient as ever.

"Not much. Really only what I've learned from you or Crum'Bul."

"That isn't much at all. Well, we don't have time to go into full detail at the moment. I will tell you the entirety of the WMD is divided into thirteen departments. Most own entire floors, though there are a few that share. I am one of three directors for Department 7. I oversee all field and tactical operations. My department also has a search and rescue division, and an investigative division.

"We're going to Department 13. They handle all storage and munitions, as well as supplies. Most of the crazy stuff the guys in Department 9 come up with ends up in Department 13 as well, but good luck getting approval on most of that." Kel'Gos paused a moment, letting the statement simmer.

"It's best to think of them as a commissary. If you need something, they either have it or have a line on where to get it. Some requests require a director's approval but most reasonable needs are approved without question. That's where the platinum card is best served. It works in all WMD vending machines, the gift shop on the first floor, the cafeteria, and pretty much every other currency based transaction within these confines. All of which are stocked by Department 13."

"You guys have a gift shop?" Ray laughed. "What do they sell, tee shirts that say 'Welcome to Area 51—You didn't see anything!'?"

"They don't have any like you described but they do sell shirts. It's mostly stationery and novelty items for visiting dignitaries." Kel'Gos answered seriously, clearly missing the joke.

The doors finally opened after what seemed a lifetime, especially with their usual haste.

Stepping out onto the polished concrete floor, the orc continued. "What you see here is the medium level parking garage. Be careful operating anything larger than an APC beyond this floor. The ceiling below isn't tall enough and you'll get stuck. That one is reserved for smaller cars or motorcycles."

Ray glanced around at the rock walls and iron reinforced concrete ceiling. Many places were barricaded by chain link fencing that ran floor to ceiling. Several trucks and SUVs were parked between the many painted lines on the floor and numerous lights beamed from above, though inset to the point their source was unable to be seen.

Kel'Gos approached a rough rock wall to their right. The metal door and frame was embedded in the stone and painted gray to give it that professional feel. He pulled the door open and stepped aside, letting his human companion enter first.

Inside, Ray found himself standing in a relatively small chain link cage within another larger cavern. This one seemed to go on forever. Only a few of the unseen lights were on, but even in the distant darkness he could see thousands of overstocked shelves arranged in neat rows. Many of the items that were too large to fit on shelves were covered by thick canvas tarps or stacked neatly on heavy frames and tables. The intimidating sight suggested he could spend years inspecting the warehouse and still not find everything they had.

Kel'Gos closed the door behind him and approached a stainless countertop beside the locked gate. It was the only part of the cage that wasn't completely sealed off. Pressing a black button mounted beside the framed gate, the orc turned and leaned against the counter.

A few moments later a wooden door opened on the side of what looked like a guard house. To Ray's surprise it closed without anyone walking through. He studied the building for a long moment. It was adjoined to both the floor and ceiling, seemingly melded into both. From his vantage point, it appeared to only have a front and side wall, where the door was located. The cavern wall wrapped around, absorbing the rest.

"Wha de ya want?" A squeaky voice asked.

Caught off guard by the sudden question, Ray looked over the counter seeing a small humanoid creature staring up at him. Between the mismatched clothing, pointed ears, and the excessively large nose, Ray couldn't help but think of a Christmas elf.

"This is Marshal Bradley. I've authorized his use of a platinum depot card. Anything he needs, make sure he gets." Kel'Gos instructed.

"Oh, great. Another one." Climbing up the support braces of a bar stool, the creature placed his hands on the countertop and got to his feet. Even standing on the stool he had to look up to meet the human's gaze. Squinting, he raised his fist in warning. "Let's get somethin' straight ya round headed small nosed imbecile. This is my warehouse! Ya want somethin', ya talk ta me. And don't go gettin any ideas about the flame throwers, or grenades, or rocket launchers. Those are mine! Ya can't have em. And another thing—"

Ray's phone rang. Having already had enough of the insulting little rodent, he lifted a finger in silence. "Excuse me. I have to take this." Hurriedly, he made his way out the metal door and into the garage on the other side. "Hello?"

"Are you trying to set me up?" Score Keeper bellowed, sounding more arrogant than usual.

"Not that I'm aware of. Why, what happened?"

"I made some inquiries about Club Vice. Not ten minutes later I had some thugs at my door. These guys hit fast and hard. I've got two men in the hospital and another three with minor injuries. Mercenaries if I had to guess, though facial recognition hasn't identified any of them. It's not often someone's able to get one past me. I don't know what you're into, but I want no part of it."

"I don't have time for this right now. Can you get me in the door or not?"

"Not this time. I'm fond of my bones remaining where they belong and undamaged. If you want to continue down that path, be my guest. I won't be going with you!"

"Can you at least give me a name? If someone came after you, you had to have touched a nerve."

"You really don't know when to quit, do you? Fine. Look into a guy named Alexander Volk. But good luck keeping your legs. I wash my hands of it." The call ended.

Ray took a deep breath, realizing he was back to square one. Closing his eyes, he waited a moment before tucking his phone away and returning to the depot.

Kel'Gos watched him enter, seeming undisturbed by the annoying runt on the other side of the counter, still rambling away as if Ray had never left. "Everything okay?"

Ray extended the card to Kel'Gos. "My guy backed out. Looks like I won't be needing this."

"Hang onto it. Everyone finds themself here at one point or another."

"—and another thing, the gyrochopper is off limits to everyone except gnome personnel. No questions. No negotiations. No barter. Are we understood?"

"Gnome?" Ray asked Kel'Gos.

The grizzled orc nodded.

Ray smiled and approached the counter a second time. "You know, I've heard about the joys of gnome punting but I never thought I'd understand it firsthand." Ray stated casually.

The gnome's face turned bright red, but it stopped his talking. His clenched fists shook. It took everything not to jump over the counter and throttle the human. He stomped his foot onto the wooden stool beneath him.

Ray waited a long moment for something— anything to happen. The creature would start to say something and then stop. After about the third failed attempt, it turned around and jumped off the stool, disappearing back inside the quartermaster's shack.

"I think you pissed him off. Gnomes are a little temperamental. Their feelings get hurt easily." Kel'Gos stated with no emotion whatsoever.

"Better his feelings than his face. How do you guys deal with them?"

"Patience and selective listening mostly. If neither of those work, there's always vast amounts of alcohol."

Ray laughed at Kel'Gos' joke, though he suspected there was more truth to it than he realized.

"So, what were you aiming for before your deal fell through? The WMD has many resources at its disposal. More than say a narcotics detective from Miami PD."

"That casino I mentioned, Club Vice. I don't know if there's anything there worth taking a look at, but I believe they're on the receiving end of that schedule that disappeared. I won't know for certain unless I can get inside and take a look. The trouble is you have to be on a member's list. The only person I know who could have pulled those strings was on the other end of that call."

After a short consideration, Kel'Gos offered his thoughts. "Seems to me most of this, including your lack of direction in our fair complex, can be attributed to an untrained way of thinking. You still think like a local cop. That doesn't work here. Local cops think local. You have to assume you already know everything. You have to convince yourself of it. If you're always right, even when you're wrong, you'll find your way."

"I'm afraid I don't understand."

"Call Roderick. Tell him what you need." Without another word on the subject, Kel'Gos disappeared through the metal door and got into the elevator.

The 95th District

Levi Samuel

Chapter 14
Sins of Man

A pink and orange glow rapidly descended the horizon and night was on the way.

Sitting in his car a block from the site, Ray watched with earnest. An armored truck had been sitting near the back lot for more than an hour now. It wasn't the first he'd seen and likely wouldn't be the last.

Quickly scribbling the final details into a notebook, he watched the driver return to the cab by means of an internal door, never once leaving the truck. The engine started and it pulled away, revealing no trace of what it was carrying or why it had been parked so long.

Scanning his notes, this was the third armored truck today. There had also been two black cargo vans with dark tinted windows, and a couple catering trucks. Of them all, the vans were most suspicious. Neither displayed license plates and one of the shotgun passengers let his concealed pistol slip when he climbed out.

Traffic was picking up on the opposite end of the building, a massive warehouse with rusted tin siding that hung loose in many places. It was time.

Ray glanced at the text message he'd received a few hours prior and silently recited the directions for what had to have been the thousandth time. They were long committed to memory but the final words of his predecessor kept ringing in his ear. At the time, Ray hadn't understood the context.

Carrying an old printer paper box full of his personal possessions, Detective Jim Watson, now retired, had taken a moment to stop beside Ray's desk. "No matter what it is, believe the lie. If you don't believe it, no one else will." The grizzled old detective muttered. He then turned and marched straight into the department's single elevator, never to be seen again.

Ray had never asked but he was fairly certain the grouchy old man recommended him as replacement. The fact that Anderson called him into his office moments later nearly solidified the theory.

Returning to the task at hand, Ray started his car and pulled onto the street. It was a short hop and around the bend to reach the entrance drive. Thus far there had been two ways he'd seen people do this. Most were chauffeured in, their driver leaving once they got inside the door. The other, as Ray was doing now.

He turned and pulled to the guard shack at the entrance of the six-story parking garage just across the street.

A young colored man stepped out, dressed in a fine looking suit and a glimmering diamond in his ear. "Name please."

Minor panic took hold. He hadn't been undercover in so long. He didn't even know if his cover was still good. "Ra—" Ray cleared his throat, forcing confidence into his voice. He knew how to do this. He'd done it numerous times. Why was now any different? "Ray Bradley!"

The guard scanned a large tablet. "I'm sorry, Mister Bradley, you're not on the list."

He silently cursed himself. He'd forgotten all about the directions. "I'm a guest of Senator Jones."

"Oh?" The guard scrolled his list once again. "You're good to go, sir. Enjoy your evening."

The boom raised and Ray pulled through.

Inside the garage was nearly as magnificent as the USMS impound hanger. The first three floors were packed with the most exotic and beautiful cars ever engineered. A part of him wanted to go back to the hanger to see what some of these were capable of.

Finding a series of open spots on the fourth loop, Ray pulled between a Lamborghini Veneno and a Tesla Roadster, leaving an open space on each side.

Rather than taking the elevator, Ray decided to walk. He wanted to survey the beauties around him. He wondered what it would have been like if he'd chosen something else. A car needed to be flashy enough to get attention but not so much as to create a problem. In his line of work not just any car would suffice. The relationship between car and driver was a special one. It had to be something felt. These cars, while gorgeous, offered little more than a fun time. His Aston Martin on the other hand spoke to him. It was his even before he knew it existed. Ray nodded, knowing he made the right decision. Without so much as a second glance at the surrounding cars, he made for the exit.

Traffic on the small street wasn't much of a concern. Ray hurried across, forcing himself to walk casually instead of march.

He'd been out of the army for several years now, yet the habit remained. It was something he had to keep an active mind about. Military life meant structured hierarchy. Most of the people he dealt with were opposed to anything of the sort. Never mind the fact many of their own guys served at one point or another and their own systems operated on the very principle to which they were opposed. The only difference being, they were at the top. That was the hypocrisy of it. They hated hierarchy when forced into it. Ruling it was another story.

The front of the old factory warehouse wasn't much to look at. Most of the exterior walls were dirty and rust covered. There were several pieces of loose tin siding that hung at awkward angles or rattled when the wind blew. A small sign hung over the entrance that was much easier to read in the daylight. Club Vice was scribed in black lettering on a dark background. Once yellow handrails that, like the door, needed a fresh coat of paint lined both sides of the concrete steps.

Ray climbed them and approached the faded green doors. Bubbled rust spots showed through where the paint was thin. Hesitantly, he reached out and pressed the doorbell, reciting his directions one final time. Ray took a deep breath and stepped back, awaiting entry.

A series of slides and latches echoed behind the metal barrier and the door swung open. A large bald man wearing a black suit with a lime green dress shirt and dark blue tie stared menacingly at him.

If for no other reason than his size, and the Veil unopen to him, Ray would have guessed this man to be an orc. As it were, that was not the case. He was simply a hulking behemoth of a man. The perfect type for security.

The guard's deep voice echoed. "Guest of Senator Jones?"

"I—Um—Yes?"

"You're unsure?" His eyebrow raised.

"I—No. I'm sure. I wasn't prepared for the question."

The doorman glanced Ray up and down. Nodding, he stepped aside, allowing him to pass.

Once clear, Ray took a deep breath. He'd been expecting to recite his directions at the door, not the guard shack. That meant they either radioed his arrival or the checklist was automated and instantly updated. Either way, this place was more secure than he'd hoped. Extreme caution would be needed if he was going to find anything without drawing attention to himself.

The hallway just past the entrance was dimly lit by overhead red lights. The air smelled sweet, like flowers in spring and the temperature was perfect. It had an ominous feel though. It was the lack of noise. From the number of people he'd watched enter, there should have at minimum been some chatter, though he could feel slight vibrations in the carpeted floor.

Reaching the end, Ray found a small room with two elevator openings. The left side was sealed. The right, open and waiting. Stepping into the box, Ray turned and pulled the top portion of the door. Counterweights allowed it to move slow and smooth, nearly seamless as the lower half raised. An indicator light flashed into existence and Ray pushed the selector lever to the *Up* position.

Slowly, the lift began to move, clanking and grinding its way up the shaft. He could hear its twin in the next shaft over. Unless someone was leaving at the exact same time, he guessed one or the other was always at each end of the spectrum.

The lift came to a stop and the wall behind him split open. Ray turned, seeing the large half-circle shaped room. He was dumbfounded by the sheer magnitude of the place. This was only the first room and it easily filled the warehouse in width, though length wasn't close.

Stepping out of the lift, he found he was standing at the center of the curved wall. There were a set of glass elevators directly across from him, disappearing somewhere below. It made sense now why the hall had taken him to a lift. The second floor was for the main festivities, while everything else happened at ground level.

Quickly scanning the room, Ray noticed the left half was mostly dining. There was also a long bar and plenty of seating. The center and right were filled with card tables, roulette wheels, slot machines, and the typical casino scene.

Ray hadn't spent much time in casinos, maybe twice in his life, and never more than a few hours. Despite all that, there was a weird dynamic happening around him.

It seemed all the money spenders were human, not all of them Caucasian, but a vast majority. Some were accompanied by pretty women. Many more, by women who were maybe once pretty but had since tried too hard to maintain it.

This was everything he'd expected to see. It was the perfect illusion. Lifestyles of the rich and powerful. But it wasn't these men or their women that caught his attention. It was the help.

Ray studied the numerous workers. The well-dressed barkeep pouring drinks, the waitresses scrambling to deliver food or beverage, every table dealer, the barhop across the room. Every single one of them was far from human.

The barkeep was a gray-skinned elf wearing a white buttoned shirt and a maroon waist coat with dark slacks. The waitresses appeared to be split evenly between elven and faerie, all female, all attractive, and all wearing just enough to be considered clothed.

One of the faerie waitresses flew past, her wings fluttering faster than the eye could see. She delivered a tray of drinks to one of the card tables. Despite the hands grabbing at her, she appeared unphased. She unloaded the drinks, grabbed the tray and flew off, out one of the many doors.

A gnome stood on an overturned crate, sliding the dice to a man across the craps table. The list went on. What was most intriguing though was the silver platters carried here and there. Each one held a pyramid of chalky tablets being passed out like candy.

Knowing he couldn't stand in the doorway and watch all night, Ray slowly made his way around the perimeter.

"Good evening, sir. I hope you're having a wonderful time at Vice City Casino and Lounge. Can I help you with anything?" The voice was high pitched, belonging to a faerie just over six-foot-tall and weighing maybe ninety pounds. Her pointed ears poked through her sparkly gray hair and her skin was a pale white.

Ray turned, realizing he'd stopped in front of a cashier booth. "Um—Yes, I was wondering, where do I buy chips?" Ray asked, reaching for his wallet.

"Any of the dealers can exchange cash for chips. All payouts are exchanged here."

"Okay. Would you happen to know the minimum buy in?"

"Two-hundred is the minimum."

"That's a little steep. I was thinking maybe fifty at most."

A mild smirk crossed the faerie's thin blue lips. "Thousand. That's two-hundred-thousand minimum buy in."

"You're joking, right? How the hell does anyone have two-hundred-thousand to throw away?"

The faerie shrugged. Her wings flickered a moment before falling docile behind her once again. "Don't know. I just know what I'm told." Her facial expression shifted from forced welcoming to sorrowful. He could tell she wanted to say something else, something unscripted, but decided against it.

"Well, thank you for the information."

"You're welcome. Feel free to approach any of our staff with questions or concerns and enjoy your time at Vice City."

Making a path around the roulette and craps tables, Ray decided it was best to watch the place for a bit. He had a gut feeling something wasn't right, something more serious than Pandora tablets.

His path led him to the slots. Following it around through rows and islands, he found a machine perfectly located. It was a variable-pay at the end of one of the central islands. From here he'd be able to survey most of the room with a simple glance.

The slot was fairly straight forward. It had a bill reader on the front face as well as an inset scanner. Glancing around, seeing some of the other patrons, Ray grabbed his wallet and loaded a twenty. Selecting one of the cheaper per spin options, the wheels began to rotate, their depictions flashing nearly faster than he could see. Giving it a few seconds he tapped the button and one by one they came to a stop. *Seven,*

Cherries, Bar. No luck. Pressing the spin button again, he repeated the process.

About twenty minutes passed and he'd managed to hang on to just under thirteen of the twenty. Cashing out, he grabbed the printed ticket and tucked it away. Ray marched straight across to the bar and took a seat on one of the high-top chairs.

"What can I get for you?" The gray-skinned elf asked, setting a freshly wiped cup into the shelf.

"How much is a Brown Pelican?"

The barkeep cocked his head at the question. "Like the bird?"

A soft chuckle escaped until Ray realize the gray-elf was serious. "It's a drink. Cider and ginger beer over ice."

"Oh, okay. To answer your question, all drinks are on the house."

"With a two-hundred-grand buy in, that's awful generous."

"I assume that's what you want?" The barkeep replied, glancing toward the end where a fat man was waving excessively.

"Yes please." Ray watched him rush off, tending the needs of the plump balding guy in a knockoff Gucci suit.

A moment later the elf returned, drink in hand. "Here you are, sir. Is there anything else I can get for you?"

"Yeah. I was curious what he ordered?" Ray subtly gestured to the guy.

The gray elf took a deep breath. His eyes narrowed and he leaned in close to speak just over a whisper. "With all due respect, sir. You asked about the drink prices. That alone says you don't have enough money to even think about what he ordered." There was a coldness to his tone, though it was clear it wasn't in insult to the amount of money Ray possessed. It was more akin to reaction of personal insult.

"My apologies. I didn't mean to offend you."

"You want to know what he ordered? Watch. They're prompt on deliveries for multimillion-dollar orders." The elf turned away, tending one of the middle-aged women who'd had a little too much artificial beauty performed.

A set of swing doors opened and one of the faerie waitresses appeared carrying a small glass saucer on a tray. She was careful to avoid entering within six feet of anybody. Approaching the man who'd ordered the delicacy, she sat the saucer on the bar and turned to leave as quickly as possible.

Ray stole a glance of the item on the plate. It wasn't much to look at, reminding him of a single tiny stuffed mushroom.

The portly man lifted the tiny à la carte and placed it in his mouth.

A sudden cold came over the room and Ray felt as if he were witnessing an atrocity of untold horror. He glanced around, realizing everything had stopped. Every worker in the house was glaring his direction, ignoring those around them.

Shaking the chill from his spine, Ray returned his focus, watching the man wipe the corner of his mouth with a cloth napkin.

The man tossed the cloth atop the small platter and extended his hand toward a wine glass that rested in front of him. It hesitated for an instant and then flew into his grip like a piece of metal drawn to a magnet. He closed his grip and brought it to his lips.

"What the hell?" Ray asked aloud.

"Abomination!" The gray elf spat under his breath, nose scrunched in distaste.

"Tha—That was—was magic?" Ray stuttered, having trouble accepting what he'd just witnessed.

"Stolen magic! Theft of the most sacred resource imaginable. And these pigs are bartering it like some cheap whore!" The elf's voice grew loud. He chucked the glass he'd been cleaning across the room. It shattered on the floor, not far from the source of his frustration.

One of the waitresses rushed over. "Jacob, contain yourself. You know better than to—"

"No, I'm done playing these stupid games!" The gray elf jumped onto the bar top. Throwing his arms overhead he addressed the growing mass of patrons. "Ladies and gentlemen, I wish death upon each of you! There will come a day when my kind rises up and slaughters you in your sleep!"

"Jacob!" The elven waitress pleaded, trying to pull him down.

Several metal prongs impacted his torso and he convulsed, landing hard on the countertop before falling again to the floor.

Ray turned to see two human security guards near an open door that wasn't there a moment ago.

Shutting off their tasers, they approached and easily drug the unconscious elf through one of the other doors.

A smug looking man with greasy hair stepped forward and gestured to the crowd. He could have been any one of them but he commanded a presence that few others mastered. "Esteemed guests, we apologize for that unfortunate business. Please know everything is under control and we'll be doubling all payouts for the remainder of the evening." Turning, he marched back into the secluded room.

Ray peeked around the corner before the door closed. There were several monitors and at least three other guards, though he couldn't see what else.

"Poor guy. That happens about once a week." One of the passing women said.

"Such a shame. How are they expected to make any money when they're constantly having to provide refunds and offer discounts? Good help is so hard to find these days." Her companion replied.

Knowing he needed to expand beyond the main room, Ray followed a group of people into the glass elevator at the center of the rear wall. It began to lower. No sooner than it was clear of the casino floor, Ray got a feel for just how big this place actually was.

The central wall was little more than a divider. The back half of the complex contained another half circle, this one at ground level. A balcony wrapped the top with curved bleachers stacked arena style along all but the far wall. The floor was covered in sand and at its center Ray noticed something larger than any orc. It was thrashing wildly at what appeared to be a group of elves carrying swords and shields.

The window to the arena passed out of view and the elevator stopped. Whistles from the men around him echoed inside their glass container and the musty scent of cologne began to fill the air.

The elevator emptied and suddenly Ray understood what was happening. He was in a large lounge, not quite as grand as the upstairs but about half the size. There were numerous couches, recliners, giant bean bag chairs, and an area with nothing but fur covering every available surface.

Ray had the unfortunate privilege of witnessing a half-dressed fully-grown man bent over a fuzzy pony while a faerie, seemingly of the female variety, whipped him with a riding crop. Shaking his head, he stepped out of the elevator and casually made his way around the room.

He wasn't one to shame anyone. Hell, he'd had his own out of the box experiences, but he wasn't about to open the lid in a place like this. A smile crept to his face, recalling what Lilian had done to him. He found it interesting how much he missed her, especially with so much—potential around him.

Surveying the *merchandise*, Ray counted at least thirty women and about half as many men searching for a playmate. Most were occupied with someone, light comforts at the moment. Occasionally a pair or more would disappear behind one of two purple curtains that hung at the rear corners of the room.

The air was filled with smoke. Between that and the strobing lights, it was hard to see much further than about halfway across. Even then it was a hazy blur. Full detail was limited to roughly ten feet.

Staying to the left, Ray spotted someone with authority. He wasn't sure what title worked best. Madam seemed appropriate for a female boss but this was a straight faced human male making the rounds. He wondered if pimp was a more suitable term. He had a '70s pornstache and yellow tinted Ray-Bans with an aloha shirt. It wouldn't have been a stretch to say this guy idolized Ron Jeremy.

Skirting the man's path, Ray ducked behind one of the thick curtains and found himself in a narrow corridor. Several other curtains hung along both sides, fixed to metal rods atop the entryways. Some were open, many were closed, and a few halfway in between. An array of noises radiated from within the small bedrooms, leaving no question about what was happening inside.

Ray passed one of the partially opened curtains, catching a glance. A faerie was vigorously riding some guy. Her wings were outstretched, fluttering and changing color in time with her soft moans. Hurriedly, he passed and bumped into a man wearing a black coat and priest's collar. He was buttoning his pants.

The man stopped, stunned at the sight of another. Without word, he brought his fingers to his forehead and promptly gestured away his sins. Stepping around Ray, he rushed out as quick as possible.

Watching the priest leave, Ray glanced around the open curtain seeing a gnome lying face down on the bed. His back side was exposed and bloody. Ray could hear the small creature sob into the pillow.

Hesitantly, he stepped into the room and closed the curtain behind him. His brain was screaming at him. He didn't have time for this. He needed to get in and out without drawing attention. This was anything but.

Unfortunately, he wasn't always known for thinking with his brain. He slowly approached, scanning for cameras along the ceiling and walls.

"Hey." Ray said softly, trying not to scare the poor thing.

The gnome stifled his tears and wiped his cheeks. Rolling over, he stared up at the newcomer. "I suppose you're next? I need a minute to clean up. The last guy was—" He trailed off, attempting to wipe away the stains.

"No. I'm not here for that. I— I heard you crying. I— I know nothing can make any of this okay. I just wanted to check on you."

The gnome surveyed him skeptically. "If you're not here for this—" He gestured to the bed. "—what are you here for?"

Ray glanced around a second time, desperately hoping he wasn't being watched. Even the lack of evident cameras didn't have him convinced. Porn was too big of an industry to miss out on that market. "Can you keep a secret?" He leaned in close, speaking in a lower tone.

The gnome nodded vigorously, seemingly more interested in the prospect of a secret than his torn backside.

"I work with the WMD. I'm going to bring this place to its knees. So if you hear any alarms go off tonight, I want you to flee. Get out of here as quick as you can and don't look back."

The gnome nodded. "If only it were possible. I'm probably going to die in here."

"Why do you say that?"

"In case you haven't noticed, it's not like we're doing this for fun. We're slaves. We do what we're told or we disappear."

"Disappear? Relocated or killed?"

"I don't know. Probably both. I just know those who get taken away don't come back."

"Well, I promise I'm going to do everything I can to help. I have to go now but I want you to remember what I said. I don't know if you'll get another chance." Ray picked himself up and made for the curtain. It wasn't much but the gnome seemed to have a glimmer of hope in his eyes, if only for a second.

Stepping back into the hall, Ray continued down the path, finding another curtain guarding an intersection. He could hear the lounge off to his right. There was no sense in going that way. He really wanted to go to the arena, or more aptly, the ground level outside it. If he was going to find anything substantial, it was likely to be there, under heavy security. If his bearings were accurate, left would take him toward the front of the building. That meant straight was the only feasible option. Decided, Ray continued straight.

Almost immediately the path veered right. He passed the entrance to another large room, this one was relatively dark, save for a few lights on the floor. Curious, he stepped in and found a movie theater in session. It was playing some Errol Flynn movie from the 1930s. The theater was empty save for a few seats toward the front.

Continuing on, passing several other doors, Ray eventually heard cheering and the sound of metal on metal. The corridor began to gradually incline and the lights got brighter. Making his way to the top, he realized where he was.

Ray emerged on the left side of the arena balcony. An entrance from the central floor stood beside him, leading into the dining section of the casino. Another door like it, and he suspected another ramp, were on the opposite side, not far from the opening near the slots.

Maneuvering his way into the crowd, Ray glanced at the battle going on below. The combatants had changed. It was now two female elves. One, redheaded, swung a sword at the other, brunette, who dodged. In turn, the dark-haired beauty jabbed a spear at the first. It grazed her left arm, spilling a thin stream of blood. Both were wearing little more than leather straps over their crotch and backside, leaving them completely unprotected against the sharpened instruments.

The crowd erupted in cheer. Bookkeepers rushed through the bleacher rows, collecting and recording bets.

A sudden sensation overcame him. He couldn't explain it but there was something here, something he could feel. Looking around, Ray found his query almost immediately.

Lilian stood a few rows away, staring intently at the fight. Her demeanor was calm, though Ray could feel the disgust within her. She was hurt, angry, and a little confused, though he didn't know how he knew all that from a single glance.

As if he'd called to her, her eyes shot up, focusing on him. She waved him over, offering a false smile.

People crowded the walkway and guardrail making it difficult to pass but he managed. Ray started up the steps and fell in beside her. "What are you doing here?" He had to shout to be heard.

"I could ask you the same."

"Long story. How are you able—" Ray glanced around, making sure no one was paying attention. Cautiously, he gestured to her ears. "—you know?"

"Hide?" Lilian responded more in his mind than aloud. "Ancestry. I'll explain when we have some privacy."

Ray nodded agreement. "I'm happy to see you. I wanted to call earlier but I didn't want to come across as clingy." His mouth was moving again.

Lilian's cheeks flushed. "And showing up in person is less clingy?" She broke into a laugh, which felt good considering what was happening around her. Throwing her arms around him, she pressed her lips to his. "Thank you."

"For what?"

"You didn't answer my question." She changed the subject, her eyes returning to the fight.

The brunette elf suffered a deep gash across her ribs. Holding the wound, having lost her spear, she fell to her knees, pleading for mercy.

"Fin—ish—her! Fin—ish—her! Fin—ish—her!" The crowd began to chant.

The redheaded elf twisted around, sword extended. The impact sent the brunette into a spin. She landed hard in the sand and her head rolled a short distance away.

Lilian buried her face in Ray's chest, as the crowd cheered.

"This place isn't good, Lilian. You shouldn't be here."

The victorious elf reached down and locked her fingers into the severed appendage. Several shallow wounds covered her legs and arms but she appeared otherwise unharmed. Raising both it and her sword overhead, she yelled and tossed the head at the crowd. It was short, bouncing harmlessly off the stone wall and fell back to the sand.

A voice echoed over the loudspeaker. "Let's hear it for the luscious Alexus!" He drew the last syllable out, renewing the crowd's excitement.

The topless elf circled the sandpit in victory before disappearing into one of two heavy portcullises along the sidewalls.

"And remember ladies and gentlemen, you can auction for a private 'anything goes' audience with any of our gladiators after their fight. Submit your silent bids at any time."

Sections of spectators turned into a mosh pit of people trying to place bids. Judging by their shouting and vulgar movements, Ray suspected what many of the men had in mind for the elf named Alexus.

"And now it's time for our main event. The reason you all came here tonight. Get ready for the undefeated champion. A creature so powerful, so vicious that we've had to build a special cell just to contain him."

Lilian stared into Ray's eyes, saying more in a glance than she could with words. Finally, after a long moment, she spoke. "Did you see the security room?"

"Yeah. There were four guys in there earlier. Oh, I almost forgot. I saw a guy use magic. Not sure how that happened. It seemed to upset the elf at the bar. What kind of elf was he anyway? He had dark-gray skin."

Lilian nodded, acknowledging she understood but either couldn't or didn't want to explain.

Catching unusual movement, Ray watched out the corner of his eye. "Two guards by the door. They're looking directly toward us. Please be careful, Lilian." He lifted onto his toes, hoping to shield her from sight. Whatever was happening here he didn't want them to drag her away.

The announcer continued talking, pumping up the crowd while a group of gnomes rushed onto the sand and began collecting discarded weapons, severed body parts, and dragging the dead body off. One of the others went to work raking the bloody sand over, providing a nice even layer for the next combatants to churn. They hurried back through the lattice gate as it began to close. "Before we bring him out, please feast your eyes on the only opponents capable of withstanding our champion's wrath. They've mastered every weapon known to man. Their hands are hard as stone. Ladies and gentlemen, give it up for the Devil Twins!"

One of the bookkeepers passed buy, collecting a folded paper from a guy on the next row up. "Three-fifty on the Champion."

Still watching the entrance, Ray noticed the guards were no longer there. "They're gone." He let his guard down, happy Lilian was safe.

"I hate this."

He placed his arm around her, hoping it would provide comfort. Even in human society this was unacceptable. Everyone had a right to live free of oppression.

"All that time we spent in the shadows dreaming of a day we could walk freely. This is but a taste and look at what they do with it." She shook her head, disappointed.

The ground beneath them shook and the gate closest to them began to open. Two stout dwarves came running out, eliciting cheers from those who'd placed bets on the twins.

They looked nearly identical with their jet-black hair and thick braided beards hanging to their waists. Their stocky physique left them broader than the average man, yet slightly shorter. A tattered loincloth was all that covered them, revealing much of their thick skin, heavily covered in tattoos and scars. They certainly looked like an intimidating duo.

"I'm sorry. I know how hard this must be." Ray watched intently seeing the far portcullis clank open. Four identically dressed men came marching into sight. They looked like prison guards in riot gear. Taking position on each side of the large opening, another two came into sight. They wielded thick batons with metal prongs on the end. Reaching the edge of the sand, they turned and waited.

A large creature was brought through. It was easily six-foot-five though the distance made it difficult to estimate. Much of its body was concealed in a heavy metal suit. Both arms were locked in an uncomfortable forward position and the metal straight jacket was bolted into place. It appeared as if any movement from the waist up was impossible.

The creature's legs were fixed to rods, limiting their range of motion and its head was sealed in a steel mask with a single slit near the eyes. Two more guards appeared, hands locked around heavy poles that were hooked to the metal suit.

"I wonder what's in that." Ray said aloud.

"He's angry." Lilian replied. "I can feel it."

One of the guards issued a command and the others snapped to defensive positions. The two forward guards, first to enter, cautiously approached and moved up beside the subdued creature. Working as best they could from the blind spots, they began removing the bolts that kept the constraints in place.

The brace on the creature's right leg fell free. Instantly, the man went flying from a kick to the ribs. He crashed into the chain link fence just beyond the guardrails. Sparks shot through his body and he crashed to the sand, smoke rising from his prone form.

"Let that be a reminder for you folks, stay clear of the guardrails. This is for your protection. But don't let that deter you from placing those last minute bids. If our champion can kick a man that far while still under constraint—well, let's just say the devil twins have their work cut out for them."

The shock guards pressed their batons against the suit and activated them. The creature roared in pain, dropping to its knees. Using the momentary distraction to their advantage, they removed the last bolts and backed through the gate as it began to lower.

The crowd was silent for the first time since Ray's arrival. They watched in anticipation as the brute picked himself up, pulling the armored suit free. It crashed to the sand in front of him and the angry green face of an orc appeared from behind the metal mask.

"Holy shit!" Ray announced.

"What?"

"That's Crum."

"Your partner, Crum?"

"Yeah."

The 95th District

Levi Samuel

Chapter 15
Prison Break

"Looks like he's given as good as he got." Lilian stated, inspecting the battered orc.

His dark hair had been chopped roughly and was extremely uneven. Several cuts and bruises covered his green flesh and he had a blood-soaked bandage wrapped around his left thigh, partially covered by a stained loincloth.

"I have to get him out of here!"

Lilian squeezed Ray's arm, offering warning. "Believe me, I'd love to see these people pay for what they've done. But how do you plan to do that? I've been watching this place. It's a fortress. It would take a full militarized strike. Even then it's unlikely they could breach the doors before they disposed—"

"I'll sneak in." Ray interjected. His mind went into overdrive, attempting to formulate a plan. "But I can't do it alone."

A mild drumroll echoed through the speakers and the announcer stepped into a small alcove along the central wall. Two scantily clad faeries appeared from the ceiling and flew over the open pit. Doing a full revolution, spiraling opposite each other, one landed near the opening where Ray had come up and the other landed in the same place on the other side.

The crowd went wild, pawing and shouting as the faeries passed.

Ray studied her as she went by. Each time someone grabbed her thin iridescent wings they changed color. Despite the seductive smile she presented there was no ignoring the pain and fear behind her eyes.

A subtle flash erupted and an image appeared on the wall for all to see. It looked just like the slot machines Ray had messed with earlier, though this one had cartoon figures above each row and the wheels themselves had depictions of weapons rather than cherries, sevens, or bars. The outside two looked like the dwarves from Snow White. Ray guessed Grumpy and Bashful, though he hadn't seen it in such a long time. The orc in the center looked more like Shrek than anything.

The twin faeries, as one of the patrons had labeled them, along with what he wanted to do with them, met near the projection and for the first time Ray noticed a chrome handle protruding from the wall. It was maybe a couple inches diameter and about three-foot-long. It had a bright red ball on the end. Considering it was aligned perfectly to the digital wheels he knew its intent.

One of the faeries got on her hands and knees, displaying her mesh covered backside to the crowd behind her. Those in front got view of her other assets. Regardless, the stench of testosterone was growing stronger by the moment.

The other faerie fluttered up onto the back of the first and heaved against the protruding handle. Applying all her strength it began to move and finally, with all her weight, she pulled it down. The wheels began to spin.

Bashful's wheel was the first to come to a stop. It landed on an axe. The other dwarf landed on a morning star and a shield. And lastly, Crum was cursed to fight with fists only.

The crowd roared, altering bets and placing new ones. The nearly nude faeries danced and spun around each other, their sparkling wings carrying them into the air with a glowing trail. It was quite the sight to behold. Continuing their routine, a large bird cage lowered from the ceiling and they flew inside, disappearing. A moment later they returned, dropping the assigned weapons into the pit before retreating back into the holes from which they came.

A loud bell rang and the fight began.

In unison, the dwarves rushed forward and snatched up their weapons. They moved with deadly precision and speed, defying what should have been possible for their physique. It had only just begun and already they had Crum flanked and cornered at the gate.

"I can't let him die in there. I need a distraction of some kind. If I can get the announcer alone I can force him to take me to the lower level." Ray pleaded, staring intently into Lilian's almond-shaped eyes. He knew she understood.

"Okay. Wait for my signal."

"Your signal?" Before he could say another word an open-hand clapped against his cheek and a loud pop echoed above the cheers and battle.

"You son of a bitch! Did you think I wouldn't find out?" Lilian growled, drawing back. She swung, giving Ray ample time to dodge. Letting her fist carry it impacted the back of some random guy's head.

He stumbled and tripped over the seat in front of him. The people were packed so tight it created a domino effect and nearly half of them ended up a few rows ahead of where they'd been.

Lilian only cared about the front row. They were the target. Had the guardrail not been there several would have gone over. As it were, only two accomplished that and they were hanging by a thread. Others rushed to pull them away from certain doom.

"You aren't getting out of it that easy!" Lilian demanded, pursuing Ray again. She slapped at his chest, feeding the illusion. With a subtle change in stance she sidestepped and hooked the back of his leg. A gentle shove sent the both of them toppling over the already disoriented patrons.

Their spectacle was drawing more attention than the battle now, people turning to witness the domestic dispute. Rolling free, Lilian bounced to her feet with an ease as natural as breathing. "Fine! If that's the way you want it, good luck getting your shit. I'm setting it on fire!" She spun and stormed toward the exit just as a couple of the suited guards came rushing in.

It was dark, though not so much that he didn't know where he was. Ray glanced around the support braces and brackets under the stadium bleachers. A single square of light beamed down atop him from the access hole where he'd fallen. He laid there a long moment, partially catching his breath, partially trying to figure out what had happened. Had Lilian intended for this? Was it part of her plan, whatever her plan was? He couldn't say. If it had been intentional, he realized just how outclassed he was. He never would have thought about the underside of the seats, even if he'd realized there was space to move unseen.

Crawling to his knees, Ray peeked through the opening, locating Lilian. She was walking straight toward two guards. His heart raced. He hoped she wouldn't have any trouble with them. That was the last thing he wanted. Though there was no denying she could handle herself. Realizing it was out of his hands, he grabbed the cover plate teetering at the edge of the hole and slid it into place.

It was now exceptionally dark. He couldn't see anything. Not the beams or bars. Not the excessive dust, nor the unknown sticky substance clinging to the floor and ruining his suit. Nothing. Ray grabbed his cellphone. The display was blinding. He thrashed, trying to block the excessive light. Finally, it faded, adjusting to his surroundings.

Realizing it wasn't so bad anymore, Ray hit the call button and selected Kel'Gos from the *Recents* log. The display flashed and a *No Signal* alert appeared. "Dammit!" He exhaled sharply, realizing he was in this alone. Turning on his flashlight app he started crawling.

An extremely loud and excited cheer erupted overhead and the ceiling shook from various stomping feet. Ray desperately hoped it didn't mean anything bad. Fortunately, the sounds of battle continued. That was a good sign. It meant Crum was still up and fighting.

Reaching the rear wall, Ray got to his feet and quickly navigated the path toward the end. He could see an outline of dim light that looked about the shape of a door. Provided it wasn't blocked, that was fantastic news. It would provide an exit as well as a place for cover. He was upon it faster than expected. Tracing it, Ray discovered the back side of two hinges and a simple bar latch. Better yet, the mechanism was on his side and unshielded. For once he felt like luck was on his side. Carefully, he pried it open and the door gently swung free.

Stealing a glance, Ray wasn't entirely sure where he was. He was on the end. He knew that much. What confused him was the fact that he wasn't in the arena room. He could hear the sounds of it, somewhere behind him. This was somewhere else. Somewhere with a narrow hallway.

Turning off his phone, Ray stepped out and walked toward the only source of light he saw. The noise got louder as he neared. A few steps from the threshold, the far side of the arena came into view. This was better than he could have hoped for. He was in the little alcove where the announcer had disappeared a few times already. A realization hit him. If he could see people, they could see him. Ray took a step back. There was no sense in ruining such an advantage by careless placement. More careful this time, he inched closer, trying to locate his target.

The announcer was no more than ten steps away, near the unprotected ledge overlooking the fight. All he had to do now was get close without being seen. Take him hostage, without being seen. And extort him, again, without being seen. Easy as pie!

The announcer jumped back, reactionary to something Ray couldn't see. He heard it though. The familiar rattling and zap of the electrified fence. His target inched forward once again, attentions firmly set on the fight below.

Ray prepared himself, butterflies swarming in his stomach. When the next cheer erupted and everyone was distracted, that was when he'd strike. He'd grab him and pull him into the shadows.

Hearing the excitement rise, Ray started for the opening. Lilian's voice echoed in his head. *Wait for my signal.* He froze, heeding her warning. He didn't know if she was actually talking or if it was memory from before she'd slapped him. Either way it was too clear, too crisp. He needed to wait.

Out of nowhere the alarms sounded, drowning out all other noise. Ray could see strobing flashes bounce off the walls and the announcer's voice echoed through the speakers.

"Ladies and gentlemen, please calmly make your way toward the exit."

Naturally, it was an uproar. Stomping feet echoed on the stands and floor. Voices shouted over one another. From the sound they were all trying to leave at the same time, while others argued and fought over money, owed or dissatisfied, it made no difference.

Seeing his opportunity Ray drew his Colt and stepped from his hiding spot. He locked his left arm over the announcer's shoulder and drug him into the cover of shadow, discarding his microphone along the way. Ray pressed the muzzle of his firearm into the fleshy spot under the man's right ear. Despite the chaos outside, he heard the trickle of liquid hit the floor and he realized the man had pissed himself.

"What do you want?"

"How do I get into the lower level?" Ray backed against the wall, covering his flank and granting a wide enough view to watch both entrances.

"There—There's a door right over there." The man gestured to his left. "Please don't kill me."

"Is it locked?"

"Magnetic keycode."

"Do you have the code?"

"Who are you?"

"That's not the answer." Ray jabbed the gun a little more forcefully.

The announcer straightened his posture slightly, requiring Ray to stand on his toes to contain him efficiently. He wasn't much taller but it was enough to make a difference. As if the man suddenly grew some balls the announcer quit quivering and relaxed. "I don't think you're going to shoot me. You would have done it by now. And from the sound of it you need me to get through the door."

Sighing, Ray had to think fast. He was right. He wouldn't shoot him. At least not without proper reasoning. Suddenly realizing the arena was eerily quiet, aside from the alarms, an idea came to mind. "You're right." Ray released him.

The announcer took a step forward and started to turn.

Before he could finish his revolution, Ray slammed his shoulder into the guy's gut and forced him into the open. He stopped just shy of the ledge, the only area without a guardrail. Ray reached out and snatched the man's tie. It instantly tightened under the weight.

The announcer teetered on the edge, his locked legs and improvised noose keeping him from certain death.

"The way I see it you're on limited time. If you don't answer my question my grip is going to loosen and you're going to fall. I doubt you'll survive the electric fence. If you take too long to answer your tie will continue to get tighter. Eventually you'll lose consciousness and your knees will buckle, resulting in the same. So, again, do you have the code?"

"This isn't cool. Pull me up!"

"What's the code?" Ray let the tie slip just enough to cause fear.

"Security is on their way. You're a dead man!"

"You know the worst thing about silk?" It slipped a bit further. "It's so damn slick."

"All right! Fine. I'll open the door. Just pull me up!"

"I didn't ask you to open the door. I asked for the code. For all I know you'll sound an alarm and this entire place will lock down."

"How do I know you won't drop me once I give it to you?" The man pleaded. His face was turning a deep shade of red and his knees were shaking.

"If I was going to kill you, I could have just as easily shot you. You'll just have to trust me."

"One-six-one-eight." The guy struggled to recite, red turning purple.

Ray caught him just as his legs buckled and pulled him in. Quickly loosening the tie, the man regained consciousness.

Coughing, he massaged his throat and took the tie off completely, tossing it over the ledge.

"Smart move. Now, get up and open the door." Ray gestured with his gun.

Picking himself up, the man led the way.

On the back side Ray was now able to see why the faerie had had such trouble with the lever. It had springs about as thick as his arm pulling against it and massive counterweights to make it raise slowly. Seeing it himself he was surprised she'd been able to pull it at all. Just across from the weight and spring system a solid metal door was set into the wall with a fixed keypad.

The hostage slowly pressed the numbers he'd given and stepped aside, opening the door. "Are you satisfied?"

"Not yet. You go first."

Reluctantly he did so, sighing his annoyance.

Ray was on his heels, closing the door behind them. They were standing on a landing at the top of a stairwell. It went down several steps to another landing before continuing to the floor below. Ray searched the shadows overhead and around the walls looking for cameras. "How much security is on site?"

"I don't know man. I just want to get out of here."

"And you can, after you've answered my questions."

The man sighed. "Somewhere around twenty I reckon."

"You reckon? That's not very helpful. I've seen at least sixteen. You're telling me I've already encountered eighty percent of the security force? I don't think so." Ray shook his head.

"Look man, I just work here. It's not like I plan to attend the Christmas party or anything. There's a hand full of guys that watch the top, and a bunch more that watch the bottom."

"So all this discrimination and slaughter happening, and you just work here? It doesn't bother you that they're kidnapping people off the streets and murdering or raping them for sport?" Ray was starting to get angry. No, that wasn't right. He was already angry. He was becoming furious.

"It's a paycheck, and a damn good one. I make in a night what I used to make in a month. Do I like what happens? Not really, but I can't do anything about it. They'd kill me if I tried."

Ray wanted so badly to beat this guy within an inch of his life, to make him see what it was like to have all control stripped away from him. Unfortunately, he was a cop. He was sworn to put his personal feelings aside and uphold the law. Taking a deep breath, tempering the rage building within him, he retrieved one of his two sets of handcuffs. "You have two options. I can't have you running off and telling the first guard you come across that I'm here. I can either beat you to a pulp until you physically can't go anywhere." He let the contained rage escape just enough to get his point across. "Or you can cuff yourself to the rail and wait it out. Which do you prefer?" Ray tossed the handcuffs to him.

"Seriously?"

All it took was a glance and he clamped himself to the railing. Ray reached down and tightened both cuffs, ensuring he didn't slip free. "When you get out of here I suggest you find another job. If I ever hear of you in this line of work again I promise you'll wish you'd never met me."

"I already wish that. Guess I can go back to radio. The money isn't as good but I never had anyone put a gun to my head."

"You do that." Turning away, Ray rushed down the stairs, two at a time. Cautiously, he approached the lower door and slowly turned the knob.

His view was limited. He was at the head of an intersection. The spacious area just outside seemed to be a staging area. It was a polished concrete floor and a cinderblock wall that seemed to run the entire width of the building. Judging from the ceiling mounted motors, there were three overhead doors, one at each end and one near the center. Slight protrusions suggested there were at least a few smaller doors like the one he was hiding in now.

Straight ahead was somewhat different. The corridor was roughly eight-yards-wide with a row of six-foot-deep prison cells along each side. The walkway down the center was just wide enough to avoid being touched by the numerous occupants in the event they were crowding the front bars.

There were several of them, docile and reserved. Dwarves, elves of light and dark skin, faeries, gnomes. He couldn't tell how many of each. Some had two or more per cell. Others were solitary, but they all looked defeated. Those he could see anyway.

Seeing one of the wall mounted boxes, Ray was surprised the strobes and alarms weren't going off. He could still hear those upstairs. Why were these ones dormant? More importantly, why weren't they evacuating anyone?

Running footsteps echoed somewhere to his right. Ray ducked behind the door and pulled it nearly closed just as a guard came into view. He watched the man, out of breath and dressed in tactical clothing, run right past where he was hiding.

He turned down the hall where the cells were and opened a glass door. "We need more men! The orc's not cooperating."

"God damn it! I wish they'd just shoot him and get it over with. We can't keep doing this every damn night!" Another replied inside the room. He sighed. "Fine. I'll call Volk and see what he wants to do. Grab the tranq guns. I've got fifty saying the dumb sum bitch drops after the third shot."

The other guard chuckled. "You're on." He turned, headed back the way he'd come only to stop just short of the corner. Veering, he disappeared into an opening Ray hadn't seen.

They had to be talking about Crum. If that was the case, this guard was likely headed straight to him. That was his best lead yet. But first he needed to disable the guard in the room. And hopefully before they brought the tranquilizers out. There was no way he'd be able to carry Crum's heavy ass to safety.

Ray stepped out, letting the door close behind him. Gun in hand, he stalked forward pausing at the opening where the guard had gone through. There wasn't much to see. It was another hall, though the back wall was curved. He could see straight through to another opening just like the one he was standing at. He guessed it wrapped the entire arena, providing a barrier between the wall and the rest of the complex. There were a few tables with an assortment of blood coated weapons piled atop. Likely those that had been used this evening.

"Hey!" A voice shouted.

Ray turned, seeing a guard at the end of the cells drawing his gun. He'd been sloppy, too focused on locating Crum that he'd let his guard down. There was no way he'd be able to get a shot off before the sentry fired.

A sudden bang rang in his ears, though it wasn't that of a gunshot. Ray watched the guard hit the ground, refusing to get back up. A set of slender yet muscular arms protruded through the cage, fiddling with the locking mechanism. Ray couldn't be sure due to distance but judging from the fiery red hair he assumed it was the elf victor preceding Crum's appearance. Alexus, if memory served.

Ray rushed forward, reaching the glass door just as it opened. The guard who'd been inside was carrying a shock stick. His eyes widened seeing Ray right on top of him.

With no time to think Ray kicked the metal framed door. The glass shattered on impact. His fist was right behind it, landing a solid punch on the guy's cheek bone. Unfortunately the surprise blow didn't drop him.

The guard threw his arm up, blocking the following punch. He twisted and jabbed the electrified baton at the intruder. It passed harmlessly through the ruined door.

It snapped and crackled near his face, making his hair stand on end. Ray brought the grip of his pistol down, hitting the guard on his collar bone. It would hurt but it wouldn't kill him. Another hit weakened his hold on the shock stick, still zapping and popping, trying to get at him. Seeing his opportunity, Ray stepped through the frame, locking it in place with his foot. Raising the other, he kneed his opponent in the stomach. It served its purpose.

The guard bent at the waist trying to absorb the blow. It had given Ray the leverage he needed. He forced the baton into the metal frame. The crackling prongs made contact and the guard fell limp in a pile of shattered glass.

Disarming him and tossing both his shock stick and sidearm aside, Ray stepped through the ruined door and took a look around. It was a control room of some kind. There were a few security monitors, though less than he'd expected. These just watched the cells and the arena openings. There were a lot more cells than he'd expected, and more than just the barred type outside this room. If the cameras were accurate, and he was sure they were, there were plastic, or maybe plexiglass cells, metal plated ones, and even one that looked like a public swimming pool with an iron domed lid. He had no clue what was inside but he didn't want to find out. Quickly scanning the switchboard, Ray found the cell release switches. He went down the rows and opened every single one of them.

Hearing the cell doors clank open, he returned his attention to the monitors. He needed to locate Crum sooner rather than later.

Movement started to swarm the screens. Hundreds of prisoners were loose and starting to explore. Some seemed to be looking for an exit while others went after the few patrolling guards. He couldn't say he blamed them, though unfortunately it wouldn't help the cause. Most here would likely develop a deep hatred for humans, strengthening the very reason Pandora was put on the streets in the first place. The last thing they needed was all out war between the races.

Ray saw a guard go flying past a camera. It looked like the ones he'd seen at the portcullis door when Crum was brought out. That had to be him. There wasn't time for the released slaves to make it that far.

Ray turned, seeing the elven warrior standing at the broken door. She watched him in silence, studying him. "I mean you no harm." He said, hoping she understood English. He had no desire to fight but the rage in her eyes told him it might not be a possibility. She had every right to hate humans. She'd been enslaved, forced to fight, forced to do things he couldn't and didn't want to imagine. "I'm sorry for what's happened to you but I have to go. My friend needs help. I can't abandon him."

"Who's your friend?" She asked through a cold expressionless glare.

"His name's Crum'Bul. He's the orc they brought out after you. Please, I need to find him." Ray's hand was getting sweaty around his pistol. That wasn't good. A sweaty palm meant more chance for mistake.

"Follow me." Alexus said, reaching down and grabbing the guard's shock stick. She turned and rushed down the hall.

Ray followed, keeping a safe distance. He didn't know what to think about her. She was attractive but in a scary way. She was just as likely to turn on him as she was to help, and even though her body was exposed for the world to see he had no trouble keeping his eyes in a safe direction.

Turning into the sub-hall Ray had spotted earlier, Alexus paused at one of the tables and grabbed a sword. Paired with the shock stick she was a force to be reckoned with. "This way." She turned and followed the narrow corridor behind where the control room was located.

Ray saw numerous doors here and there along the curved wall. Occasional bloody footprints stained the otherwise clean floor leading away from them. He'd assumed the curved portion was the only thing separating the arena walls. This proved his theory wrong. "What's in there?" He asked, pointing to one of the doors with the footprints.

She slowed and turned to look. "I've never been inside."

Curious, Ray inched forward and reached for the knob. Just as he was about to push the door open, Alexus grabbed his arm and shook her head no. "Why not?"

"You don't want to know." She said coldly. He couldn't tell through the grime clinging to her but it looked almost like tears.

"I'm a United States Marshal. I work with the WMD. I have to know."

She took a deep breath, steeling herself and nodded.

Slowly Ray pushed the door open and looked inside. The floor was dark and slick, glistening in the low light. It gradually sloped toward a drain at the center. Beside the entrance a bloody yellow apron and matching pair of rubber gloves hung from a coat hook mounted to the wall. Lights and cameras were dormant but fixed to numerous booms and extended in various ways. Ray flipped the switch at the edge of the apron, careful to keep from touching anything. The lights came to life and he nearly vomited.

A surgeon's table stood upright over the drain. What was left of a gray-skinned elf was strapped in place. His arms and legs had been chopped and flayed and were dangling from suspended hooks. Chunks of bloody gray hair and pieces of flesh were plastered about the floor. Resting on a metal roll around cart loaded with bloody tools was the head of the barkeeper, Jacob.

Ray was at a loss for words. How could anyone do this? It wasn't right. He felt a surprisingly gentle hand grab his arm and pull him away from the grisly scene.

"Come on. You can't do anything for him."

She was right. It was over. There was no fixing it. But he could still save Crum. Summoning his fortitude, Ray turned off the light and closed the door, wiping his own tears away.

A sudden roar echoed down the hall. "That's him." Alexus stated plainly, walking toward the unseen commotion.

The alarms came to life and what sounded like freefalling chains echoed through the corridor. Whatever was happening didn't sound good.

"Come on!" Alexus broke into a run.

Ray was right behind her. They followed the curve around, hearing the fighting become more intense, though it wasn't just straight ahead. It was all around. To the left, behind them, everywhere. It sounded like a complete and total uprising.

Weightlessness claimed him and Ray crashed into the stone wall, hitting the ground before he knew what happened. He stared up, dazed, seeing a huge behemoth of an orc step into his sight. The creature was several inches taller than Crum and its thick tusks were much larger and capped in metal bands. It had a short scraggly beard with beads braided into it and its ashen skin was covered in a collection of carved scars that looked more akin to welted tattoos.

The beast roared and charged him.

There was nothing he could do. If it landed he was dead. No questions, no doubts. Ray weakly raised his gun, surprised he hadn't dropped it when he got hit. It was so heavy. Straining, he took aim, feeling the ground beneath him shake.

A flash of green flew past and the gray orc was no longer charging. Ray shifted his weight, trying to see what was happening. It hurt to move. He realized now that he was about half embedded into the cinderblock wall, chunks of rubble and dust around and atop him.

Alexus knelt and began digging him out.

With limited freedom Ray moved just enough to see what was happening.

Crum slammed the gray orc's face into the wall. Grabbing its tusks, he spun him around and body slammed him to the floor. Placing his bare foot on the creature's throat, he glared into its eyes. "This is my human!"

The gray orc strained under the weight. Realizing he was defeated, it made some strange grunting sound and quit struggling.

Crum roared so loud the walls shook. He removed his foot and took a step back, sinking into a defensive posture in front of Ray.

The gray orc picked itself up, bowed respectfully, and backed away.

Watching the larger orc leave, Crum turned and approached the pile where Ray was still half buried. Kneeling down, he extended a meaty hand. "Are you okay?"

"I'll live." Ray groaned, wishing he was dead.

Ensuring the damaging and jagged rubble was clear, Crum pulled him free. "I thought that was you during my fight. Thanks for finding me. It took you long enough."

"I had to stop and ask for directions." Ray joked, though it hurt to laugh. His suit was most certainly ruined now. "What the hell happened?"

Crum shook his head. "I don't know."

"How can you not know?"

The orc shrugged. "I was following someone. I don't remember who or why. Next thing I know I woke up here."

"Any ideas about this place?"

"They justify fear with hate. Someone will always find a way to profit from the fear of others."

"Excuse me, boys. We need to get out of here." Alexus prompted, gesturing down the hall with the baton.

"I agree." Ray tried to walk but it didn't work so well.

Crum put his arm around him, giving him support.

"And here I thought I was going to have to carry you out."

"In your dreams, puny boy." Crum joked.

The three of them made their way to the staging area with little issue. Most of the prisoners were heading that way as well. Reaching the overhead door a chain curtain had fallen over it, though someone had had the foresight to turn one of the tables on end and bar it from sealing. Elves, gnomes, faeries, everyone who wanted out had either already gone or was in the process.

Ray looked around at the mass of freed slaves filing out. "Do you think we need to do anything for them?"

Crum watched them for a long moment. "No. If they need something they know where to go. Most are going to find their way home and try to forget any of this happened. Some will lash out and hold the human race responsible. Unfortunately they'll become exactly like those who wronged them. In turn they'll be treated the same and the cycle will begin again."

Reaching the loading docks, one of the doors had been completely dismounted from its track and was lying crinkled on the floor. Realizing he was outside Crum jumped down and drew in a deep breath of city air. He stood tall. It was good to be free.

Talking to Alexus who was patiently waiting for him, Ray slowly descended the steps one at a time. "What will you do?" She was still scary but he trusted her now. And hopefully she trusted him. Crum was right. Many would strike at humanity for the actions of a few. The elf could have been one of them. With any luck he'd saved her from that path.

She took a deep breath and looked around. "I don't know. I think I want a cheeseburger." Alexus dropped her weapons and skipped the last couple steps, bypassing the human. Without another word she started walking.

Ray watched her leave, never looking back. "I think she needs to find some clothes first."

"She'll be okay." Crum added.

Exiting the steps Ray hobbled toward the street. "I'm parked in the garage out front. Do you want to wait here or go with me? I don't know if the top side security is still active or not."

"If you can make it, I'll wait here. I need some time to clear my head."

"I get it. Once you've cleared your head try to find some tarps or something. I don't want your bare ass or my filthy suit touching my seats." Limping up the street, Ray hoped Lilian made it out all right.

Chapter 16
Dinner and a Show

"Your toxicology report came back clean. We're still analyzing a few tests but overall, aside from some minor bruising you'll be fine." The doctor set the otoscope she'd been using on the counter and removed her gloves.

Ray watched the large orc sitting at the end of the paper covered examination bed. The light blue gown that covered his otherwise naked form was huge, even for him. His legs dangled over the stepstool, mindlessly kicking like an oversized green child. They'd been sitting in the medical room for several hours and neither of them had slept a wink, despite Crum's insistence that he should go home. Lack of sleep was just something he was going to have to get used to.

This was Ray's first time on the fifth sublevel and it filled him with a dread all hospitals did. Granted, this wasn't a full fledge hospital, even though it had literally everything all hospitals did, as well as some stuff most did not. As far as *nonhospitals* went, this one was more than typical nurses rushing about and strange machines reading people's vitals. It was the medical floor of Department 10, which, according to the sign posted just outside the elevator, was the Science and Technology department.

That didn't mean much to him, but he was still a little loopy from the pain meds. On a positive note, the soreness was all but gone. It only hurt when he made sudden movements now. Regardless of his understanding about the various departments, Ray was beginning to realized just how big the WMD was as an organization.

The single door creaked open and Kel'Gos stepped in. "How's our little soldier doing today, doc?"

"I was just about to update his file. Aside from malnourishment and a few healing wounds, he's in good shape. I'd say a few days bed rest, a high protein diet with plenty of water, and he'll be back fit for duty by the end of the week."

"Excellent. How do you feel about that, Crum?"

Ray was somewhat taken back by the old orc's question. He'd gotten to know Kel'Gos a bit over the past few days. Such a question didn't seem out of character, at least with the knowledge he'd obtained thus far. He just thought it rare for a boss to consider the input of their employees. Thinking back, Ray recalled numerous jobs he'd had where the company didn't care if he lived or died, just so long as his job was completed on time. Anderson had been an exception to that. The Captain always appeared to have a genuine concern for the wellbeing of his people.

"Honestly, boss, I just want to get back to work and find whoever's responsible for all of this." Crum answered, rubbing his sore muscles. "Have any of the others shown up yet?"

Kel'Gos hesitated. "We've had a few turn up, but nowhere near the quantity I anticipated. Medical, lodging, and food have been provided to those who requested."

"And the club? Or any news on this Volk guy?" Ray asked, wondering if anything had turned up. He was thinking of Lilian again. She hadn't returned any of his calls or texts and he was starting to overthink.

"Alexander Volk is a career criminal. He's supposed to be in lockup at ADX but was reported absent six months ago. We're running a thorough background. The only personnel on site when we arrived were a few casualties and the guy you cuffed to the banister. Unfortunately, nothing more than a few mundane infractions turned up. The stiffs have all been identified. We had a couple opulent individuals. It seems most of the guards were blue collar workers up until a few months ago. Those who had family have been contacted. Next of kin had no knowledge of their career change. The wives and girlfriends have reported the same story.

'Mandatory shift change at work'. They claim their lives were relatively unchanged. They still came home and spent time with their families until it was time to go to work again. As far as I can tell they were your everyday average Americans."

"Except for secretly exploiting, raping, and murdering an untold number of nonhumans." Ray added. "Do any of the refugees remember anything?"

After a few moment's silence the doctor was the one to speak. "Those I've examined have reported the same story as Agent Crum'Bul. I can add, temporary memory loss is not uncommon under such circumstances. The stress involved with abductions oftentimes leaves the victim confused or disoriented. They're sometimes unable to recall the events of what happened even years later. Though usually these repressed memories return within a few days. What I find odd is the fact none of them seem to recall a single detail about their abduction. If I had to guess, I'd say they were drugged immediately following. That's the only logical explanation for such mass memory loss. Unfortunately, nothing has shown up in any toxicology reports to validate that theory. Of course, a psychologist would be better equipped to determine if it's mental repression or chemical alteration." She quickly added something into Crum's file. "Which reminds me. I've recommended scheduling a session with Doctor Hurst."

"Thank you, Doctor." Kel'Gos said, pulling the door open for her to exit.

She left without question.

Inching off the table, Crum stepped down and grabbed the change of clothes he'd requested some hours earlier. All modesty gone, he dropped the gown and began dressing. Having his undershorts and tee shirt in place, he stepped into his jeans and pulled them up. "I wish I knew who they were. I remember I was following someone. I don't remember who. I could hear waves on the shore. And I remember a gunshot and the clanking of boots on metal." Buttoning his pants, Crum closed his eyes trying to locate something at the edge of his cognitive thought. "I have nothing after that. Next thing I remember is waking up naked in a barred cell. I ripped them out of the ground and was running for the first door I saw when they hit me with a tranquilizer. The next time I woke up they had me in a metal suit and were leading me to the arena."

"It's all right, son. We'll find whoever's responsible. When we do we'll deal with them accordingly. I won't have slavers targeting my people. Not again."

Upbeat music erupted from Ray's pocket, ruining the dark mood settling over the room. Grabbing his phone, Ray glanced at the screen seeing Lilian's picture. A smile formed on his lips. Seeing her name and picture relieved all the worry that had been building in his gut. "Excuse me. I need to take this."

Rushing out the door, he couldn't swipe the answer bubble quick enough. "Hello? Lilian? Are you all right?"

"Hi. Yeah. I'm fine. Sorry I couldn't answer when you called. I was in a tight spot. Were you able to get your friend out?"

"I did. And we freed most of the prisoners in the process. Thank you for the help, though I wouldn't object to a little warning next time."

"Oh, come on you big baby. It wasn't that bad. I even held back." She laughed. It was always nice to hear her laugh.

Chuckling, Ray looked around, making sure no one was paying him attention. "So, when can I see you again? Preferably not when we're following a lead."

"Well, I was going to invite you to lunch but your stipulation creates a conflict."

"Why? What's going on?"

"I'm following a lead. I've been tracking the pit boss since last night. I thought you might like to get in on it. Plus, it's an excuse for me to see you. Two birds."

A laugh escaped him. "I suppose I can forego my requirements this one time. Where would you like to meet?"

"The Lido? Forty-five minutes?"

"I'll see you then. Oh, and Lilian."

"Yes?"

"I expect a kiss when I get there. I didn't get to fish for one last night."

Lilian laughed. "I'll see if I can bring myself to bear. See you soon." She made a smooch sound before ending the call.

Floating on air, Ray returned to the room. Realizing the two orcs were staring at him he found something to ground him. Clearing his throat, he spoke. "Lilian is tracking the pit boss from last night. I'm off to meet her. Do you guys need anything while I'm out?"

"I'm okay, thank you. I'm just going to head home and get some sleep." Crum said, limping toward the door.

Kel'Gos stared at the human for a long quiet moment, studying his demeanor. "Ray, I would urge caution. Don't forget she's an ICPC agent. Just because we're working toward the same goal doesn't mean we're on the same team. There's always an ulterior motive at play."

"Understood, s— Kel'Gos." Ray pulled the door open, waiting for the pair to pass. Crum was much slower than usual, though he couldn't blame him. Getting tossed around like a ragdoll had had a similar effect on him. He could only imagine what the orc was feeling.

Reaching the elevator, the three of them stepped inside. Kel'Gos pressed the display for floors eight, B3, and B9. The door closed and a moment later they parted ways.

Entering Belle Isle, Ray turned off Venetian Way and veered onto Island Avenue. It was an almost immediate left into The Standard Spa Hotel. Finding a parking spot, he locked the doors and stepped out.

The overhead palms provided much shade in the midday sun. Ray quickly crossed the lot and entered the hotel lobby. It would have been nice if they'd included a direct path to the beach side bar but apparently that was too much to ask for.

Following the signs, Ray exited a side door and found himself on a tiled path that cut through a garden. Ivy grew up the walls on either side and arched overhead. The whole experience felt like something out of a cheesy romance.

Reaching the end, Ray approached the wood topped counter under the covered bar. A waitress was occupied typing something into the touch screen before her.

Glancing up, she gave a welcoming smile. "Welcome to the Lido. Will you be dining in?"

"I'm actually meeting someone here." Glancing around, Ray spotted Lilian toward the backside near the wire rail that separated the stilted patio from the water and rocks below. "She's right over there."

The waitress smiled, nodding her understanding.

Without delay, Ray made his way around the support columns and wooden barriers that separated the walkway from the booths. A wide smile formed, seeing Lilian's eyes meet his.

Getting to her feet, she threw her arms around him and planted a big kiss on his lips. "Does that make up for what you were so callously denied last night?" She smiled.

Ray nodded excessively. "Yes. Though I think I need another just to be sure."

A cute chuckle escaped her and she kissed him again. "Now, sit down before we make a scene."

Finding his seat, Ray stared in silence, unable to take his gaze away from her. "I think you get more stunning every time I see you."

Lilian rolled her eyes, forcing herself not to blush. "You've already gotten in my pants. There's no need for added flattery."

"Of course there is. I may want in them again." Uncontrollable giggling overcame him. Each time he tried to stop it began again.

"It's not that funny." Lilian announced, though she was having trouble not laughing at his response. Exhaling, regaining her composure, she lifted the menu and began scanning the items. "Have you ever been here?"

It was still difficult to contain himself but the obnoxious laughter shifted to little more than minor chuckling. He knew the joke wasn't that funny, yet he couldn't stop laughing about it. Finally, he was able to stop long enough to reply. "No. I can't say I have." A few more chuckles resonated. "I did take the liberty of reading some Google reviews. There appears to be a high opinion of the Lobster Roll Sliders."

"Perhaps we'll have to see if we agree with that review." Lilian returned the menu to the table and fixed her longing gaze upon him.

"God, you're gorgeous." Ray shook his head as if still in disbelief. "As much as I would love to sit here and stare at you all day, you said you were following a lead?"

Taking a sip of water, Lilian nodded out to sea. "Do you see the yacht anchored just offshore? Three shirtless men lounging under a blue and white umbrella."

Indirectly glancing that direction, Ray located the yacht to which she was referring. "Yeah." The glimmering necklaces displayed amidst a forest of thick chest hair, shining rings, and wait staff dressed in full tuxedoes despite the temperature told him they were his kind of target. He squinted, trying not to be obvious about it. It was hard to tell from the distance but the man on the right looked an awful lot like the guy who'd had Jacob, the gray elf, taken away. "Any idea what they're saying?"

"They're talking about the lost product last night. As of right now they don't know who was behind it or how it happened. The current theory is a faulty electromagnetic lock which allowed the prisoners to escape and overpower the guards. Though I'm willing to bet they'll piece something together as soon as they recover their security data."

"Two questions. First, how do you know that in such great detail. And secondly, shouldn't they have already done that?"

"You're so cute when you're trying to keep up." A smile formed on her lips, though it was hard to tell if she was playing or being serious. "I know because I have ears on the boat. And normally, yes. They would have viewed the security. But I couldn't rightly have you walking into an ambush. After I pulled the fire alarm I decided to take a minor detour." Lilian reached into her inner jacket pocket and placed a small plastic case on the table. Sliding it toward him, she placed her hand on his for a short moment.

He wished she would have kept her hand there, though they were discussing business. Hand holding could wait. Unsnapping the black plastic tab, Ray opened the case and stole a glance inside. A hard drive was secured firmly within a bed of foam insulation. "How can someone so beautiful be so equally smart? I wouldn't have thought of that until after the fact." It was true. It'd been a problem for him on more than one occasion. "Do you mind if I take this for review?"

"Be my guest. I've already made a copy."

"Anything worth note?"

"Only a meeting scheduled for today, at this time and that location." She nodded toward the boat a second time.

Placing the case into his pocket, Ray returned his hand to Lilian's. Staring into her eyes he located the spark that so easily allured him, the same spark that called to him what felt like a lifetime ago. For the first time in as long as he could remember, he didn't have anything to say. Words were meaningless. He just wanted to admire those beautiful brown orbs.

"What?" She blushed, feeling his desire.

"Nothing. I'm just admiring you."

A waitress approached and Lilian pulled her hand away. "What can I get for you two today?"

"We'll take an order of the Lobster Roll Sliders and two beers."

"What type? We have—"

"I'm not partial. Just so long as it's in a bottle."

The waitress turned to Ray.

"She pretty much covered it, though I'll take water as well if you don't mind."

The waitress rushed off.

Resuming his obsession, Ray watched how her ears poked through her hair. It reminded him of what she'd said last night. "You said ancestry was how you were able to hide. How's that work? That place was crawling with Pandora. I thought it allowed—" Ray peeked around, continuing in a hushed tone. "—humans to see through the Veil?"

"It does, but it's more complicated than that. Were you aware that the drug you call Pandora has different effects depending on who takes it?"

"I think I remember Crum mentioning something about that. He said it makes him stronger than usual but extremely angry, which is why orcs aren't supposed to take it."

"An overly simplified explanation, but yes. It puts them in a rage that death itself cannot stop. For elves it does something entirely different. Our strengths are more empathic by nature. That's why humans are so susceptible to elven influence."

"I remember that conversation. When Crum and I were searching for his old partner, Wright. He had a whole team of humans under his control. Hell, he even tried to get me to kill myself."

"Kilian Wright? Yes, I recall reading that report. I was the one who collected him from the WMD and transported him to The Hague for trial."

"The Hague? Why there?"

"The ICC is the home of the Eldar Council. All nonhuman races are subject to its law."

"I wasn't aware of that. It seems problematic."

"It can be, though the US is the only country with its own justice system. Everywhere else is enforced by the ICPC." She paused. "We're getting off topic. Do you remember our conversation about magic?"

"Yeah."

"Do you remember me telling you how elves, like faeries, are an innately magical race?"

"I do."

"Okay, and with your knowledge of the Veil, are you aware how Pandora is weakening it?"

"That part I don't think we covered." Ray released her hand, sitting back to absorb as much information as she was willing to give.

"You know that magic is basically a natural resource. The pools have been depleted and are in a state of constant drain. That's what keeps the Veil working. With Pandora the Veil isn't able to do its job. It's starting to fade. If, or more accurately when it fails, magic will return."

"I saw a guy using magic last night?" Ray interjected, forgetting he'd already told her about it.

"You saw the remnants of magic. Faerie magic to be exact. An abomination against nature and a crime too extreme to put into words." Lilian snapped.

"I'm confused?"

Pausing, Lilian took a deep breath. She steeled herself and stared intently into his eyes revealing barely contained tears. "They were serving faerie flesh. Like I told you in Brussels, they're the only magical race which has retained their innate abilities. What you witnessed was a human consuming part of a faerie and stealing their innate magic for little more than a cheap trick. It's one of the four forbidden crimes and one I never expected to witness firsthand." She faded off, staring her hatred at the men on the boat.

"I'm sorry." Gently interlocking his fingers with hers a warmth radiated between them. He felt that strange sensation again, like he was part of her thoughts.

Lilian shook her head, forcing memory of the event to subside. "No, I'm sorry. It's not your fault. I know the tax of this job. I shouldn't allow it to affect me so deeply."

"You have every right to be angry. Just know we're going to get these bastards."

A false smile came to her lips. Solemnly, she continued. "Many of the elves are happy about Pandora. They don't understand the danger it represents."

"I'm afraid I'm not following."

"Well, we're similar to faeries in the use of innate magic, though not all elves are capable of harnessing it. That's why they seek Pandora. For us, it gives an artificial boost. It amplifies, allowing one who has never grasped the spark the ability to do so."

"You're saying elves can use magic if they take Pandora?"

"Yes and no. It depends on how close to pureblood they are. A pureblood can harness their innate magic just like a faerie, though there are differences between the two. I don't know what Pandora would do for a pureblood. Like I told you before, they're all missing. What I didn't tell you was how the generations work."

"Oh, I know this part." Ray threw in. "First generation half-elf, then second generation can either be nearly pureblood or closer to quarter-blood, depending on a human or pureblood mate."

"Pretty much. There's more there, if for instance two half-bloods were to reproduce, but you get the idea.

Depending on the generation and blood strength most elves third generation or higher have at least some connection to their magics, albeit extremely limited. Under the effects of Pandora those limits are greatly reduced. A third or fourth gen could potentially become as powerful, if not more so than a pureblood. To my knowledge, it can't do much for anyone lower than seventh gen but that opens many doors for a lot of elves. That's why so many of my kind have jumped on the bandwagon."

"Wow." It wasn't much but it summed up everything. There was so much more to this than he ever realized. Not knowing what to say a question popped out of his mouth before he could stop it. "What generation are you? I mean, I know you're a half-elf, but if I'm understanding correctly, with all the purebloods missing wouldn't the bloodline just continue to get weaker?"

She smiled at his ignorance. "It would, and it has since they disappeared. Elven blood is stronger than human blood. It has a tendency to override the weaker of the two. That's why half-elves are physically indistinguishable from purebloods. But just because the physical attributes are identical doesn't mean the others are. Besides, time works differently for elves."

"How so?"

"How old do you think I am?"

"That's a trick question and I refuse to answer!" Ray spouted on instinct.

Lilian laughed, which was a nice change from the somber mood she'd slipped into moments ago. "I'm six-hundred- and fifty-one of your human years old."

"Damn!" As usual his mouth didn't know when to quit talking. "I banged an old lady."

"Shut up! I'm not that old." Smiling, Lilian lightly punched his shoulder. "I'm only 93 elven years. Compared to the human lifespan that's like the range between teenager and young adult stage."

"Does this mean you're going to start clubbing and hooking up with strange men? I really don't think I can handle that again."

Lilian laughed. "No. Even with my relatively *young* age, I'm not much for the club scene. And as far as hooking up, you're my first in a long time." She leaned over the table to kiss him.

"Tell me more about this elven age. How's that work? And not the age of elves. I've had that threat already."

"There isn't much to say about it. We simply age slower. I think it's like one elven year for every seven human years right now. It used to be less. Like how in the Christian bible people were living to be nearly a thousand years old. Climate shift and pollution has made a major impact on all our lifespans."

"Are you saying I age in doggy years to you?"

Laughter escaped her with the revelation. "Oh my god, you *are* like a dog to me." Playfully, she reached over and petted him.

"I just want to go on record and say I don't find this amusing." Ray said with a flat expression, allowing her to ruffle his hair.

"That's a good doggy." Lilian jabbed one last time, lowering her hand.

"Keep it up." Ray threatened with a smile.

Abandoning her good mood, Lilian's attention shifted to the yacht in the distance. Snapping her fingers, she gestured.

Turning his attention, Ray watched one of the men, now wearing a flower print blue Aloha shirt, climb down the ladder and into a dinghy that had been tethered at its base. He was carrying a manilla envelope in his right hand.

Starting the motor, he crossed the short distance to the dock where he tied off and climbed out.

The yacht came to life and began to pull away.

Staring intently, Ray located the name and hull number, writing both on the paper napkin in front of him. He wasn't certain but it looked almost like the snake logo was painted beside the name. "I'm pretty sure that's the same logo on the Pandora tablets."

"It is." She stated flatly.

"Since we're both on the case would you like to join forces and share resources? I mean, we're obviously after the same target."

Lilian turned away, looking at anything except him. Fixated on the table she spoke more timidly than he'd ever heard her. "Ray, I would love nothing more. Unfortunately I'm under specific instruction to work this independent from the WMD and Marshals Service. The ICPC believes there's a leak in the system and many believe that leak is you. For the record, I'm not one of them." She twisted her wrist, taking the dominant role in their handholding. Slowly bringing her gaze to his, she continued. "I wish I could, and I'm happy to share whatever I find. But I cannot release anything without reporting first."

"What happens if you reach the end of this before I do?" Ray asked, assuming the answer was going to be ill-favored. "I hate to point out the obvious but your agency is a guest of this country, much the same way I was a guest when I met you. If I were to apprehend a wanted criminal in your jurisdiction I'm fairly certain your people would demand he be arrested and detained by one of their agents. Do you expect any different from us?"

Lilian remained silent for a long moment. "No. You're right. And I know the WMD and U.S. government have been extremely lenient with my investigation thus far. I promise you when I come across something useful, or if I manage to apprehend this guy before you I will share. I hope you'd be willing to do the same for me."

Ray could sense the conflict inside her. On one hand there was nothing she could do within the confines of her position. On the other she was used to being top dog and everyone staying out of her way. It was a horrible position to be in but a necessary one. "I'll do what I can. I would like to make a request though."

"What's that?"

"If we continue this thing we have going on, I think we need to try to keep work and play separate. At least as much as possible. I don't think competing for a case is going to help us in the long run."

Lilian smiled. "The long run, huh? I was hoping I could just sleep with you a few more times and then send you packing." Kissing him, she scratched under his chin. "I'm just kidding. I could never abandon my little puppers."

"Very funny." Glancing to the yacht, now little more than a blip on the horizon, Ray considered the agreement they'd just made. "There's something you should know."

"What's that?"

"Crum overheard something while he was in captivity. There's another shipment arriving tonight. We're planning to stake it out. You're welcome to join us if you'd like. I'd appreciate your company."

Watching the envelope toting pit boss, Lilian turned her attention back to Ray. "I would love to come. Unfortunately I have a meet and greet this evening. With any luck by this time tomorrow I'll have a time and location to nail Ezekiel." Her lips curled into a smile. "Besides, you and your partner need time to talk. I sense you haven't seen him for quite some time."

"Not since Pandora got out and we caught Wright."

Lilian nodded, content in her decision. "You need to spend the time catching up. I'm only a phone call away if you need me." Kissing his cheek, she stood. "Good luck tonight, love. I need to tail our friend there before he gets too far away. I promise I'll let you know if I get anything of value."

Before Ray could say a word, Lilian was gone. He wanted to go with her. If not for the company, the evidence she was surely tracking. Unfortunately he'd been too distracted by her presence to make such a logical decision. Moreover, the waitress was headed his way with food.

Chapter 17
Catch and Release

Moonlight cascaded along the gentle rolling waves. The anchored dock bobbed melodically. Connected cables and a long gangway clanked and groaned in time with the lapping water breaking against the pontoons.

A faint whirling buzz carried atop the water as Ray cast into the distance. Hearing it hit more than seeing, he waited for the sinker to descend a fair distance before giving a partial turn on the crank, locking the string into place.

"You know you don't have to cast every five minutes. We're not using bait, or hook for that matter. The purpose of reeling is to attract predators on the drag." Crum offered from the chair beside him.

"I know. It gives me something to do." Ray sighed heavily. "I hate stakeouts. They're always so boring." Raising the night-vision scope he scanned the shipping yard not far from their position. A suspicious red car was parked outside the fenced yard, between a stack of containers and the shore. He twisted the dial and zoomed in, getting a closer look. An amused chuckle escaped him and he offered the monocular to Crum.

"I don't need them."

"I forget you can see in the dark. Either way, check out the car over there."

Crum lifted a regular pair of binoculars and located the source of Ray's interest. No sooner than he spotted it he lowered them and turned to Ray. "There's something wrong with you."

"What?"

"What two consenting people do in privacy is none of my business."

"Okay, mom." Ray joked casting his weight into the ocean again.

Crum tapped the screen on his new phone, revealing the time. It was nearing oh-four-hundred. Rubbing his eyes, he leaned over and grabbed the thermos. "You want some coffee?"

"No thanks. I need sugar in mine." Hearing his phone vibrate Ray wedged his fishing rod into the cupholder mounted at the side of his chair and unlocked the device, careful to keep the illuminated screen hidden. Swiping, he saw the waiting email notification. It wasn't what he'd hoped for but at least it was something. Opening it he read the tiny text. "Looks like they've finished restoring the hard drive. Facial recognition has picked up a few people worth talking to but it still has a long way to go." Tapping a link, Ray followed to a secure server and input his login information. A dossier came up on the owner of the yacht. Quickly scanning the information, he sighed. "I just don't get it."

"What's that?"

"Everything appears legit. The registration matches. There's even a picture here. I guarantee this is the same yacht. I just don't get how someone who has no criminal record to speak of could be tied to this whole slave ring."

"There's plenty of criminals who have no record. And don't forget what Kel'Gos said about the guards. Those we identified were everyday Joes. Hell, you're probably closer to more criminals now than you've ever been in the past. Politicians are some of the biggest crooks I've ever seen, yet their records are spotless because they have the influence and money to keep them that way."

"I suppose you're right." Ray tucked his phone away. Grabbing his rod he began to reel in once again. After a long moment of silence, he turned to face Crum. The orc looked menacing in the low light. "What do you know of elves?"

"Can you be more specific? That's a pretty large topic to cover in a single setting?"

"Well, I'm sure it's probably against regulations somewhere but I've been sleeping with Lilian."

A guttural chuckle echoed from Crum. For its relatively low volume it made the dock shake. "I'll never understand you humans and your desire for elves. Besides, you act like I didn't already know that."

"First off, she's half-elf." Ray corrected. "And secondly, how could you know? I haven't told anyone."

"I know because you've been checking your phone every fifteen minutes. When she calls your face turns red. And you talk about her nonstop unless Kel'Gos or Arthur Roderick are around. And how does being half-elf make a difference?"

"I guess it doesn't, especially since they're all basically half-elf or less. But I'm not that bad. I guess I talk about her more than I should. I can't help it. I really like her. We get along great. In fact, she's the first woman I've been with in a long time that I wanted more than a one night thing with."

"It sounds serious."

"I don't know if I'd go that far. She's just enjoyable to be around. Like a friend who— does extra stuff." Ray paused. "I probably shouldn't even be talking about it."

"I agree with you. You shouldn't be talking about it. But for what it's worth your secret is safe with me. I once had an affair."

"Oh?" Ray asked surprised. This was the first time the orc had really opened up about any of his personal life. It took heavy restraint to resist giving him shit about it.

"Yeah. We met by chance in May of 1905. I was working a job on a train running from Los Angeles to Salt Lake City. We stopped in this little settlement called Las Vegas. They made some big deal about it being founded, but it looked like it had been there a while to me. The population is apparently much larger now but I haven't been back to see it."

Ray silently waited an uncomfortable length of time for the orc to finish. Finally, he couldn't take it anymore. "Is that seriously the end of the story?"

"Yeah?"

"Dude, you really need to learn some basic etiquette. You can't just lead up to something like that and leave me hanging. I need some detail. Some excitement. Like this girl, I'm assuming she's a girl. No judgement if she's not."

"She's a girl."

"Does she have a name?"

"Yes."

"And?"

Crum stared blankly for a moment. "Why do you want to know about my sex life?"

"Okay, first off, if the last time you got laid was 1905 you don't have a sex life. You have a tragedy. Secondly, you had sex so that's something to the story. How did you meet her?"

Crum took a deep breath, clearly unenthused about the direction of the conversation. "There was a celebration. I was trying to go around but I got too close. She grabbed me and pulled me into a mob of dancing people. She was the most beautiful participant at the party and she chose me. I'll never forget the yellow of her tusks or the way her brown lips parted when she smiled."

"So, she was an orc?"

"Was that not clear?"

"And, did you—?"

"Did I what?"

"Have dinner? Hold hands? Maybe some heavy petting?"

"That's none of your business." Crum stated flatly.

"Oh, you did, you dog. I knew there was more than you let on. So, what happened? Did you leave town and never see her again? Did she give up life in Vegas and come with you?"

"She died."

"What? How? You really need to learn how to tell a story. That's fucking sad, man."

"She was working in a mine and it collapsed on her. I had planned to see her again when I was passing through. We talked about going to Los Angeles together when I returned."

"Damn. I'm sorry to hear that. And there's been no one since?"

"Orcs are nearly extinct. There's only a few hundred of us left. Reproduction doesn't happen like it used to. We're lucky to get ten orclings in a generation."

"Now you made me feel bad."

"Sorry."

Bellowing laughter escaped Ray, though he was trying to stifle it. "I'm sorry Crum. I don't mean to laugh. It's not about your kind, it's the way you react to things." Straightening himself, forcing the laughter to subside, he shook his head. "And don't be sorry. You haven't done anything wrong."

"Sorry." Crum repeated.

"That's what I'm talking about. Don't apologize for something—anything you didn't do. You can show sympathy without claiming the accountability that comes with an apology." Had Lilian really had that much of an impact on him? He was now repeating something she'd said to him.

"Okay." Crum stared at Ray for a moment before returning his attention to the water. "You had a question about elves." He prompted, hoping it would change the topic.

"Oh yeah. So, the first time Lilian and I had sex this weird thing happened. I don't even know how to describe it. I guess—Did you ever see the movie Demolition Man?"

Thinking for a moment, Crum ran through most of the movies he'd ever taken the time to watch. "I don't recall the name. What's it about?"

"Well, it's a great movie. If you've never seen it you should. And if you have, you'll know my opinion to be fact. I have it on DVD. I'll let you borrow it. Anyway, there's this scene where Sandra Bullock's character invites Sylvester Stallone's character to have sex. Okay, so before that part, you need to know that it's a futuristic setting where touching is frowned upon, as is pretty much anything fun. In fact, it's kind of how these people are reacting to Pandora outbreaks.

"Anyway, Sylvester Stallone's character, John Spartan, is from the past and was frozen in a cryogenic prison. Skip forward a few decades and a criminal from his time, played by Westley Snipes, escapes and starts laying waste. The police are now a bunch of pacifists and have no idea how to fight such a primitive criminal. They decide to thaw John Spartan out and send him after the bad guy since he's the one who captured him last time. About halfway through the movie Sandra Bullock's character invites him to have sex. Naturally, he's thinking sex in the manner we know it. But in a time where physical contact is frowned upon, her idea of sex is connecting them to this machine which allows them to experience pleasure without the physical contact part.

"That's kind of what sex with Lilian was like, only I could feel the physical side too. It was like a mind entanglement while doing the deed. Honestly, it's the best sex I've ever had. But it was weird, like I could feel it from her perspective as well as my own. You know anything about that?"

"I've never had sex with an elf. Even if I found them attractive I'd be afraid to. They're much smaller than I."

"That's not what I meant but thank you. I'll never be able to get that image out of my head."

"It sounds like their little mind meld trick, only I've never heard of it happening like that. Most of the time they just use it to make their enemies see or do things they normally wouldn't. That's the danger of Pandora. Humans were protected before they could see through the Veil. Now that the curtain is cracked there's no telling what could happen."

"Do you think it's something I should ask her about?"

"I think it's something you should be careful about. A mind meld isn't just one way. If you can see into her, she can see into you. It will be hard to keep secrets from her if she's bonded with you."

"Bonded? What's that?"

"I don't really know how to describe it. I guess it would be like—" Thinking for a long moment, searching for an accurate analogy, Crum settled on one. "I guess it would be like connecting two computers together. Both are capable of working independent but by being connected they're able to share information and communicate back and forth faster."

"Are you saying she's hooked into my brain? Like she can see and hear everything that happens up there?"

"I'm not saying that but the possibility does exist. I wouldn't be overly concerned. There isn't much that happens up there." A wide grin cracked on the orc's face and he began laughing, shaking the entire dock once again.

"Ha-ha, very funny. I'm glad you finally developed a sense of humor. It only took a couple hundred years and becoming a gladiator but it finally happened."

A horn echoed in the distance and a moment later lights came into view. The pair watched a small feeder glide ever closer.

"Do you think that's our mark?" Ray asked, watching the container ship carefully. For being one of the smallest of its type, it was still able to haul over a hundred intermodals.

"Possible. I guess we'll know when something happens." Crum reeled his fishing pole and set it aside.

Locating the registration number, Ray quickly scribbled it into his notepad. This had to be what they were waiting for. Nothing else had moved all night and he was tired of sitting. Watching intently, several men, both ashore and on the ship began preparing for dock. One of the gantry cranes pivoted over the water and began lowering a harness.

No sooner than it was stopped, both teams jumped into action, exchanging the cargo. An intermodal would touch the ground just long enough to be disconnected and an oversized forklift would snatch it up and disappear along one of the many rows. Over and again they repeated the process until just a few containers remained.

"Eleven-thirty." Crum stated flatly, peering through his binoculars.

Searching where the orc was referring, Ray zoomed, adjusting the night optics for lens flare of the overhead lights. It took a moment for his sight to clear but not long after he located the focus of Crum's attention. One of the ship's men had gone ashore and was talking to three of the dock workers. That wouldn't have been such an odd thing except they kept glancing around as if searching for eavesdroppers. Ray watched the shipman gesture toward the incoming container. It was a pale yellow with several faded graffiti tags along the sides.

Instead of the metal box being dropped and scooped up as the others had, this one was immediately secured by the shore crane and loaded onto the back of a long truck. It was little more than a cab and frame, making it perfect for hauling the steel boxes. It touched down and two of the men locked the four corners into the frame while the third climbed into the cab.

"What do you want to bet that's our mark?" Ray asked, watching for any identifying features.

"I see no reason to gamble. It likely is our query though I don't think it's a smart idea to rush off until we're certain there's nothing else to see."

"Maybe not, but did you notice the perimeter security prior to a few minutes ago?" Ray asked, watching the heavily armed guards standing at the edge of the light.

Doing a quick sweep, Crum let out a hiss.

"You okay?"

"Yeah. Memory flash. I think this is what it was like when I was snatched. And yeah. They weren't there a few minutes ago."

"I take that as a confirmation of shipment. When's the last time you saw a fully militarized security unit for a load of anything short of weapons. Even then they wouldn't be coming by private cargo. Whatever's in that container they don't want to lose."

One of the men shook hands with the shipman and handed him a folded envelope. He climbed abord just as the final container touched down. Waving the truck off it began to leave.

Ray watched it turn longways, displaying a decal along the driver door. The familiar snake logo was tucked neatly between the curved blue lettering in the form of *Anaconda Excavating*. "We need to follow that truck."

Early morning traffic wasn't bad. Most were either still in bed or had no intention of leaving their homes. Though there was still enough happening to blend in.

Ray lowered his visor to block the sun's blinding rays. It made the truck in the distance a little hard to see but it was better than being too close. Fortunately, it was also slow enough he didn't have to worry too much about it getting away.

Seeing traffic slow for a red light, Ray changed to the center lane about ten cars directly behind. It only took a moment for the others to close in around them.

"Um, Ray." Crum stated with a slight fluctuation in his usual bass.

"Yeah?" Glancing at his companion Ray realized pretty quickly what had caused the orc's concern. Sitting next to them was a blacked-out Chevy Yukon and at least three armed men dressed in full tactical gear. To make matters worse, their eyes were all set on them.

"We need to get out of here." Crum advised.

Seeing the machine guns come into view, Ray glanced around. There was nowhere to go. Two identical SUVs had them surrounded, one on each side and the last directly behind. "How the hell did they make us?"

Fortune smiled upon them. The light changed and traffic began to move. It presented a small window of opportunity. Ray slammed on the gas pedal and cranked the wheel to the right. The rear wheels of the Vantage Roadster came to life and he drifted sideways, sliding directly in front of their would-be assassins. Hearing the repetitive echoing pop of gunfire, Ray glanced behind him. "Please tell me they didn't shoot my car!" Cutting the wheel back to the left he sped around the outside of the car now directly ahead of the SUV. It was a tight fit but he managed to squeeze through without touching either the car or the curb. Ray mashed the gas, hoping to gain some distance.

"I think they missed." Crum replied, looking back.

A gray Nissan Altima slammed on its brakes, opening a path. Ray wasted no time slipping into it. It wasn't much but it provided a little space cushion. The Yukons weren't nearly as maneuverable and unless they decided to go off-road they'd be delayed at least for a few seconds.

Whipping between cars, hoping to add as many obstacles between them as possible, Ray got right behind the intermodal truck. It had picked up speed and was now barreling its way through traffic. He glanced into the rearview mirror seeing the first SUV break through.

Ray pressed the call button on his steering wheel. "Call D.A.G.!"

The speakers cut out their music and began to ring.

"Do you have any idea what time it is? This better be good!" Roderick's voice boomed.

"Sir, this is Ray."

"No shit! What do you want? I'm not supposed to be awake for another hour."

"Well, you know how you told me not to blow up half the city?"

"God damn it, what have you done this time?"

"Nothing yet, sir. Crum and I are in pursuit of a container truck heading west on 36th. They have a heavy security team and we've been made. They've already opened fire."

A heavy sigh echoed through the speakers. "Where are you now?"

"Still on 36th. We just passed the McDonalds on 22nd. I don't know how to ditch the team while staying on the truck. Any advice, sir?"

Vigorous audible clicking echoed on Roderick's end and a moment of silence passed before he came back on. "Hang tight. I'll make a phone call. Do everything you can to keep the truck on 36th. Try to direct it toward the airport. Minimize damage. I'm contacting local PD and DHS to get you some backup. This is now a containment op. Avoid collateral damage at all cost. If they get away, so be it."

"But, sir, we need—"

"Don't make me repeat myself. Containment *is* your first priority!" Roderick interrupted.

Sighing, Ray whipped around a car that just got side swiped and spun in front of him. "Understood, sir." A click told him the call was over. Glancing at Crum, Ray knew the orc could tell what he was thinking. "We aren't letting them get away!"

"Just don't do anything too reckless."

"What, like jump a car off a bridge?" Ray dodged another wreck.

"Yeah. I'd consider that reckless."

Ray shook his head. "I'm beginning to not like this job. How am I supposed to get anything done with my hands tied?"

The overly calm orc shrugged, glancing in the mirror at what was behind them. "Don't know. You may want to do something though. They're catching up."

Ray mashed the gas and sped around the truck, blocking the intersection. The sad reality was he couldn't do much to stop it if they decided to turn. He'd be smooshed like a fly on a windshield. The only thing he had going for him was the truck was moving too fast and was too big to make sudden turns. So long as he could maintain that he'd be able to subtly direct it. That was until the SUVs caught up. Things wouldn't be so easy then.

Pulling ahead, Ray glanced back seeing the two men inside. The one on the passenger's side had what appeared to be a pump action in-hand, though he was doing little more than watching at the moment. Locating the SUVs, one fell in on either side and the last brought up the rear.

Seeing another intersection, Ray waited until they were near. Slamming on his brakes, he forced the driver's instincts to dodge, missing the turn. It was a useful ploy once. There was no delusion it would work a second time. More than that, he'd shown his hand. Now that they knew he was directing them, it was going to be hard to keep them in line. Though he could see the airport ahead. One intersection to go and he'd have them in the best position he was going to get. "I need you to lay some cover fire on my mark. Preferably along the driver's side."

"On it." Crum drew his Desert Eagle and twisted around in the seat. It was a tight fit. The car was too small for someone of his size but he managed to place his knees in the seat and face rearward. Rolling down the window, chilly morning wind rushed through.

"Ready—Now!" Ray ordered, swerving into position.

Crum squeezed the trigger twice. The first bullet spiderwebbed the windshield in the top left corner and the second appeared to hit the driver's mirror. In response, the driver jerked the wheel right, missing the turn.

That's what he'd been aiming for. It was time to end this. Scanning the buildings along both sides, Ray searched for any place he could ground the truck without causing too much damage. On the left, there was a large opening between the air strip and the buildings. Unfortunately there was no way of reaching it. He needed to get the truck into the grass.

As if the desire had manifested itself he saw an opportunity. Just past one of the approaching structures there was a grassy field and a gravel lot beyond that. That was likely the best he was going to get. "I have a plan but it's a little reckless."

"How reckless?"

"Just a little. How good of a shot are you?"

"I can hold my own. What are you thinking?"

"We're closing in on a small field. We need to disable the truck there. I don't think a tire shot would do much more than slowly deflate but if you can put a hole in the driver front rim it should drop quick enough to force a hard left into the grass."

"That's going to be a near impossible shot from where I am. I could barely hit the windshield from here."

"That's where the reckless part comes in. Do you think you can manage the shot if I get you in position?"

"Maybe. Don't you think it'd be easier to shoot the driver though?"

"That's your call. Doesn't matter to me how it happens. We just need a hard left on my mark."

"I'll do what I can." Crum replaced his magazine with a full one, preparing himself.

"All right. Here we go." Ray gained some distance ahead of the truck. Checking clearance, he exhaled, mentally preparing himself. Veering right, he suddenly cut the wheel left and tapped the brakes. The car spun around in a one-eighty, repeating the trick exactly how the young wheelman had shown him. Just before the car straightened and the tires grabbed, Ray pressed the reverse selector and mashed the gas once again. He was driving backward, facing the approaching truck. "Wait for it!"

Crum held fast, awaiting command.

Seeing the grass come into his peripheral vision, Ray cut the wheel again, sliding sideways. Crum was closer to the front left corner of the truck than he was comfortable being.

"Now!"

Seeing his opportunity, and realizing he was too close to get a good shot on the driver, Crum took aim. He fired three shots into the driver's front wheel. Air hissed immediately and the front corner dropped.

The truck cut suddenly left and hit the ditch. Its heavy weight carried around and it flipped on its side, sliding across the lot, uprooting grass and churning dirt.

Pulling out of his slide in a reverse-J, Ray hit the gas and returned to drive. He narrowly missed the tail end of the truck as it plowed by. Reclaiming full control of his car, Ray hooked into the gravel drive along the bottom side of the truck and stopped. Drawing his Colt, he waited for the shootout that was likely to follow.

Sirens echoed in the distance and flashing lights topped the hill from both directions. The SUVs slowed, surveying the lost load. Realizing there was no chance at recovery, they turned onto a side street and disappeared.

Staring at his orc friend, Ray took a deep breath pleased there wouldn't be any gunfights at the moment. He'd already reached his getting-shot-at quota for the week. A wide smile settled on his lips. "That was crazy. I wasn't sure it would work."

"Nor was I. We aren't finished yet though." Crum opened the door and climbed out. Weapon at the ready, he tactically approached the overturned truck.

A shotgun blast echoed from the cab.

Bringing up the rear, Ray filed in behind Crum just as Customs and Miami Police were arriving on scene. They slowly approached the cab, moving in a blind spot.

Crum peeked through the broken glass. Turning to Ray he shook his head.

Looking for himself, Ray realized the driver was dead from the crash. His head had somehow gotten smashed between the truck and the ground. The passenger immobilized himself by a shotgun blast to his chin. "Another lead evaporates."

"Perhaps. Perhaps not. They were trying to keep us from seeing what's inside." Crum gestured to the scraped yet still fully intact box. Making his way to the rear, he grabbed the lock rod and released it. The rod flexed under his strength and the heavy door cracked open. Getting his fingers into the gap, he strained to lift the solid metal door, gravity working against him.

Activating his flashlight app, Ray slipped under the partially open door and stole a glance inside. Several fearful eyes stared back at him. Crates of drugs and money were scattered and broken. Many of the occupants were in disarray, some wounded but they all appeared alive. "Hang tight. We'll get you guys out of there."

The 95th District

Levi Samuel

Chapter 18
Heating Up

"Seventeen captives and no one remembers a damn thing! It's almost like we've heard this one before." Ray fumed, throwing his file off the table. The loose pages fluttered and flipped, scattering to the floor in varying intervals.

"Calm yourself. Rome wasn't built in a day." Roderick watched him jump up and pace the room.

"Why? It doesn't seem to matter what we do. These assholes continue to slip through the cracks. How are we supposed to catch them when we can't even get a solid lead?"

"You've made progress. You found Crum'Bul. Now we just have to cross the finish line."

"What turned up on Anaconda Excavating?" Kel'Gos asked, scanning his copy of the report.

"Another dead end. There's no business license on file. The plates were reported stolen from a garbage truck in Panama City a few months ago." Ray sighed, squeezing the bridge of his nose. His frustrations were growing and he was losing sight on the big picture. "Honestly guys, I don't know where to go from here. I've followed every lead I've come across and nothing aside from the word of a dwarf and a scribbled note ties anything to Ezekiel."

"There may be a little more than that." Crum added, pulling a picture from his file. Laying it on the table he pointed to a man in one of the casino security photos. "I remember seeing this guy when I was caged. He walked through at least once a day, surveying the stock. I found it strange because he's an elf but the guards didn't seem to question it. I remember one of them calling him Mister Ezekiel."

Ray studied the picture. The sad truth was he didn't even know what Ezekiel looked like. The only photos he'd seen were at odd angles or exceptionally blurry. This one wasn't much better. It was a wide angle and half his face was obscured by lens flare. All he could really tell was he was Caucasian with blonde hair. No other details were visible. "Why don't pictures match what they really look like? I've seen tons of them. Even Crum looks human in a picture."

Kel'Gos inspected the image. Turning his attention to Ray he replied simply. "The Veil."

"How so?"

Roderick sighed. "It wouldn't do much good if all it took was an untimely picture to out an entire world of inhabitants, now would it? The Veil hides all perception, even for those of us who can see through it. Belief allows you to see with the naked eye. Nothing more."

"Most of us don't know what we look like." Kel'Gos added. "When I look in a mirror, I see a human staring back at me."

"That's interesting. Though it makes our jobs much harder. It'd be nice if we could always see things as they truly are. Those of us who can see through it anyway."

"It is the way it is." Roderick retorted. Directing his attention to Crum, he continued. "You're sure about the picture? I don't mean to be skeptical or discredit your report, which didn't contain that piece of information. I fear with your medical ruling any judge will be hesitant to give us a warrant based on so many uncertainties."

"We may have a way around that." All eyes turned to Kel'Gos. "Linguistics has been studying the letter brought back from Brussels. This morning we got a ninety-eight percent match on a signature from his bust in '98. That confirms its authenticity. If nothing else we can bring him in on murder in the first degree."

Gathering his scattered file, Ray glanced up. "That's good news but there's still more to this than we know. Murder is great—well, not great like that. What I'm saying is, we need to get him anyway we can, but it'd be nice to nail him for everything at once. Distribution, smuggling, money laundering, kidnapping, human trafficking, just to name a few. Murder's little more than a slap on the wrist compared to the accompanying charges."

"Don't forget, Capone was brought down by tax evasion. With the slippery ones sometimes you have to take what you can get. And if this guy's an elf he won't have the luxuries and loopholes provided by the human justice system. The Eldar Council is old world. There's less red tape for him to slip through." Roderick offered with a smile.

"Are you talking about the court in the Netherlands?"

"The International Criminal Court oversees all trials for nonhuman races." Crum explained. "That's where Wright was tried."

"I heard. So, what happens after the trial? Like, if someone is found guilty?"

"It depends on the crime. The council has seven members who overhear the case reports, listen to testimonies, and consider all evidence provided. Once all sides have been heard they adjourn and make a decision. A guilty charge requires a unanimous vote, penalty decided at time of judgment. If the vote is split or agreed of innocence, all charges are dropped and the defendant is provided compensation for any lost wages and travel arrangements to their place of domicile. Everything happens relatively quick, making the entire process less cumbersome on all involved." Kel'Gos explained.

"Okay, but like, what about those who are found guilty? What happens to them? Like death row inmates or something like that?" Ray asked. He hadn't heard much about their justice but it sounded like it had its benefits.

"It depends on the punishment given by the council. We only imprison our criminals until their trial. Once they're judged their infractions are placed into one of three categories depending on severity. All debts will be paid be they monetary, time, or life. Unlike the human justice system, life in prison does not exist. If life is required it happens swiftly, the day of the ruling."

"Damn!" Ray was stunned. It sounded slightly archaic but at the same time refreshing. It made no sense eating up tax dollars letting someone spend life in prison. If they were going to require life they should just get it over with and move on. "What happens if someone turns out to be innocent afterward?"

"The Eldar Council has never been known to vote incorrectly. If it's happened conflicting evidence has never been presented as proof."

"I guess it helps you don't have social justice warriors crying about cruel and unusual punishment either."

"All punishment must be cruel and unusual. If it's not cruel, it's not effective. And if it's not unusual, it's not working." Kel'Gos added.

"Thanks for the education, boys. While you were talking I was able to get a judge to sign off on a delayed notification search warrant. Go into Ezekiel's. Find anything you can, including proof of identity. If you get that he'll sign an arrest warrant in the morning." Roderick interjected, returning his phone to his pocket.

Ray paced from his bedroom to the living room and back again. "Yeah, the stakeout was a bust. I mean, shit happened but we didn't get anything. A shipment of slaves, a few crates of Pandora tablets, and right at fifty-thousand cash. But no leads, no idea where it was headed, and no evidence as to who's unhappy about it."

"It sounds like I need to come over and make you feel better." Lilian teased from the other end.

"That would be amazing. Crum and I have a sneak and peek into Ezekiel's mansion this evening, but I'm good until sundown. Sleep is for the weak." Ray laughed. "I just hope we find something to nail this bastard."

"You'll get him, but you need to sleep too. I take it you haven't gotten any in a while?"

"A few naps here and there. I think I'm still just adjusting to the job. Everything seems to happen all the time. Makes it hard to shut off."

"I get it, though I don't fully understand. Elves don't sleep like humans do."

"What do you mean? I thought they did that torpor thing."

"We do but it's not an everyday thing like you need. We run for months, sometimes years at a time before going into torpor. Unlike your daily sleep we do a meditation. It allows us to align our energy and keep us focused. An elf who ignores meditation must take torpor more frequently. But enough about me and mine. Let me finish what I'm doing here and I'll be over in about an hour. I'll make sure you forget all about your bad day. When I'm done you'll want to go to sleep."

Ray smiled, unable to say anything in response.

"I can sense your grin."

"Can you? I've actually been meaning to ask you about that."

"About what?"

"Ever since we— you know." He paused. "It's almost like I can feel what you feel. Like I know what you're thinking. Sometimes I hear your voice in my head." His words echoed like feedback only they weren't distorted. Unsure if it was another symptom of the very topic he was discussing or something technical Ray stopped pacing and fell backward onto his bed.

"Oh my god, you felt that too?"

"Too? You mean it's not just me?"

"I'm so embarrassed."

"What? Why?" Attempting to get up, Ray rolled to his side. A small black dot under the lampshade caught his attention. Half rolling, half crawling, he reached the lamp and plucked the tiny device free. It wasn't much larger than an ear bud with little pin holes in the center. A protruding wire hung from the side, running beneath the light bulb. He'd changed the bulb from incandescent to LED when he moved in. The device wasn't present then, but then again, he wouldn't have seen it without being on the other side of the bed. Regardless, if it had been there a year or more recently, it still raised questions. He'd done a lot of things in this bedroom other people had no business listening to.

"It's— it's something that happens sometimes when I really like someone." Lilian finally managed to get out. It was almost like she was searching for the proper words.

Leaving the mic dangling from its wire, Ray got up and began searching for others. "So, you like me, huh? That's good."

"Of course I like you, silly. Do you think I'd do that thing you liked with my tongue if I didn't?"

"I sense that's a loaded question." Climbing onto a chair, Ray untwisted the smoke alarm just past the sliding door that closed off his bedroom. A similar device rested beneath it, wired to the power supply. Shaking his head, he climbed down, setting the now removed alarm on the coffee table.

"This conversation is better had in person. I have too many people around me right now. I'll see you when I get there, okay?"

"Okay. I'll meet you in the lobby. Take care, beautiful." A kissing sound echoed on the other end and Ray ended the call. Tossing his phone onto the couch he frantically searched every place his vast knowledge of spy movies provided. To his relief most were exactly how he'd hoped to find them, filled with dust but otherwise empty. Unfortunately, he'd located two others, one in the air vent near the kitchen, and the last behind his stereo system.

Prior to now, Ray had never seen an actual surveillance bug before, not out of the movies anyway. It was possible he could have mistaken the first for simple paranoia, but the second, and the one after that—There was no mistake. He'd both installed and replaced batteries in many smoke alarms. Just because this one was wired in didn't mean it was any different. Ray grabbed his effects and headed for the door. He had questions but there was no way to call or even research if his place was bugged.

Riding the elevator to the lobby Ray hurried to his car, keeping an eye on his surroundings. No one out of the ordinary seemed to be paying him any attention. Climbing in, he pressed the brake pedal and the start button. His car came to life, idling in his usual parking spot. A thought came to him. If his loft was bugged, likely his phone was as well, and the GPS in his car. There was literally no place he could go to escape surveillance. Things were getting rapidly complicated. Taking a deep breath, he put the car in drive and pulled out. There was only one place he could think to go.

Reaching the downtown police department, Ray parked along the side of the building and quickly fell into his usual path. The mad house was as chaotic as always but it held a comfort he was desperately missing. He passed Katelynn's desk.

She was on a call but waved at him.

He returned it and continued past toward his destination. Reaching it, he knocked on Anderson's door.

The old captain waved him in through the glass pane. Ray opened it and stepped inside, taking his usual seat. "I'm sorry to barge in, sir. I didn't know where else to go or who to talk to."

Anderson closed the file he'd been reviewing and directed his full attention to Ray. "What can I do for you today?"

"I found a bug in my loft. Multiple bugs actually."

Seemingly amused Anderson leaned back, taking a less formal approach. "Ray, when your transfer to the Marshals Service was processed possession of all in-use assets transferred with you. If you have a bug problem, you'd be better served to take it up with them."

"You misunderstand, sir. I'm not talking about roaches or anything like that. I'm talking like spy shit— surveillance bugs."

"Oh!" A puzzled look settled on Anderson's face. "I'm afraid I don't have much to offer in that regard. Police captains are typically low enough on the totem pole that such has never happened to me. Though as a cop and the direct superior to a team of detectives, if you intend to investigate the matter, I would advise handle it like you would any other case. Keep your personal emotions out of it and build a list of possible suspects. Motive and reach are going to be your biggest clues here."

"What should I do about the bugs?"

"That's a tough one. My first instinct would be to get rid of them. The problem with that is whoever installed them will know they've been found out. They'll respond by either upping the stakes or disappearing altogether. Neither are good for building a case. With that in mind you'd be better off leaving them for the time being. Limit what you say and do. If your home is under surveillance it stands to reason everywhere else you go is too."

Ray took a deep breath, letting the realization settle in. "I miss being just a regular cop. Things were so much simpler back then."

A hearty chuckle escaped Anderson. "True, but think of it this way. You're living your life in a manner most only dream about. Normal is often boring. You can't have excitement without having struggle."

Ray nodded subtly. Getting to his feet he extended his hand. "Thank you for the advice, sir."

"Anytime. Just remember, no matter how difficult things get you always have a friend here."

Grabbing the doorknob, Ray's phone began to ring. Glancing at the display Lilian's name and picture showed. "Shit!" Stepping out, he answered the call. "I'm so sorry. Something came up and I completely forgot you were coming over."

"Oh? Does this mean I don't get to spend the rest of the day with you?" There was a disappointment in her voice that made him feel both powerful and sad.

"Not at all. I'm on my way right now, though I'd ask we go to your place if that's okay?"

"I suppose. Do you want to meet there or do you need to come here first?"

"What's the address. It would probably be quicker if I just meet you there."

"Okay. I'm staying at the Rodeway on 4th Street. I'll be watching for you."

Ray stared at the plain white ceiling of the small motel room. The quilted blanket that covered the still made bed was wrinkled beneath him, standing out in stark contrast to his light blue boxer shorts. Glancing around the room he couldn't help but find peace in its relatively simple décor.

The single full-sized bed took up one half of the room. A couch, recliner, and coffee table occupied the other. The desk, dresser and flatscreen took up the wall beside the wooden door, sharing commonality with almost every cheap hotel across the United States.

His arm was wrapped around Lilian, holding her against him. Her dark hair cascaded about his chest and her shallow breath felt good against his skin. Lifting his head slightly, he stared down at the beauty beside and partially atop him. She wore only a pair of black lace underwear, looking magnificent as ever.

Lilian gently ran her finger along Ray's sternum, listening to his heartbeat, cherishing its rhythmic thumping. Kissing his chest, she suddenly shot up and looked into his eyes. "You still haven't told me why we couldn't have done this at your place."

"I just wanted a change of scenery." Ray lied. He hated himself for it but it was necessary. He had to keep quiet until he discovered who was watching and listening to him. Bringing his lips to her forehead, he kissed her. "Besides, this way I get to share a bed other than my own with you."

His phone rang, echoing from his discarded pants lying somewhere between the bed and air conditioner. He groaned and stretched to reach them, wishing he could have done so without requiring Lilian to move. She was so peaceful he wanted her to stay there forever. Securing his phone, he saw Crum's name and swiped the green icon. "Hello?"

"Ray, this is Crum. Everything's good to go. Kel'Gos has given the green light and surveillance just reported that Ezekiel left the property. If we're going to do this there isn't a better time than now. I have all the gear with me. Where are you? I'll pick you up on my way."

"I'm at the Rodeway Inn on 4th Street. Room 102. Give me five minutes to get dressed."

"Okay." Crum hung up the phone.

"I'm sorry but I have to go. We just got authorization for our sneak and peek. You're welcome to come with us if you'd like." Ray slipped his legs into his pants and hopped, pulling them up.

Stepping out of bed, Lilian circled the foot and wrapped her arms around him. Pressing her lips to his she smiled softly. "It's okay. You go. Have fun. I have a meeting with some of his people tomorrow. I don't want to risk blowing it by being identified tonight."

Running his hands along her bare back, Ray cupped her perfect ass and lifted her, falling backward onto the bed. Her smile was more than he could have hoped for. Her hair draped down around him, sealing them in a perfect world. Staring into her eyes, he softly kissed her nose, wishing he could stay. "I must be insane, leaving you here while I go to work."

"I know. I wish you didn't have to go either but it's the job. I'd do the same." Lilian returned the nose kiss playfully. Anticipating his attempt, she giggled and turned her head shielding herself with her long dark hair.

Ray tried to kiss her, getting tangled in the defending locks. After a few failed attempts, he tickled her and planted a passionate kiss on her lips when her defenses were broken.

"No!" She demanded playfully. "Get dressed. You can't rightly storm the castle in your skivvies." Straddling, she grinded hard against him, ensuring he knew what he would be missing.

"I see how it is. You're gonna pay for that."

"Oh really? How?"

Ray grabbed her and rolled, placing her beneath him. Bringing his lips to her neck, he kissed, and bit, and sucked all the places that would make her squirm.

"Ray!" She squealed. "We don't have time. You have to get dressed."

A knock at the door confirmed her statement.

"Grrr!" Ray grumbled climbing off of her. Pulling his shirt on, he waited for Lilian to disappear into the bathroom. Drawing his gun, he stole a glance through the peep hole. Crum waited patiently on the other side. He opened it and returned his Colt to its holster while slipping on his shoes.

Crum stepped in and glanced around. "You ready?"

"Almost."

Lilian stepped out of the bathroom wearing a tee shirt and a pair of black yoga pants. Approaching the large orc she extended her hand. "Hi. You must be Crum. Ray's told me quite a bit about you."

Accepting it, Crum returned the gesture noticing her exceptionally strong grip. "Pleasure. I've heard a little about you myself."

"Not all bad I hope." She winked at Ray.

"No. Not bad." Glancing from Lilian to Ray, Crum arched an eyebrow. "If you're coming with us I need to make a detour. I only brought gear for two."

"No. She has a meet tomorrow. Doesn't want to risk discovery." Ray answered.

"I understand that." Crum glanced at his watch. "We should get going. We're on limited time."

"I'll meet you in the car." Ray waited for the orc to leave. Turning to Lilian he placed his hands on her hips and kissed her again. "Do you want me to come back when we're done?"

"No. Go home and get some sleep. You need your rest. I'll let you know how my meeting goes tomorrow. Maybe once all this is over you and I can take a vacation. My family has a villa in Cancún that I'd love to visit with you."

"A villa, huh? You didn't tell me your family was rich." A smile formed on his lips. He only hoped she knew he was joking. Money was nice but there were so many more important things. Though there was no denying that lack of money could make problems bigger.

"You never asked. I saw no reason to tell. Now go." Lilian kissed him once more, pushing him toward the door. "Good luck. I hope you find what you need."

Chapter 19
Stormin' the Castle

Ray tossed his jacket around his shoulders and skipped down the last few steps. He reached the bottom and rounded the corner to find what may as well have been a monster truck. Okay, so it wasn't quite that bad but it wasn't far from it.

The meaty tires made the aluminum outlaw rims look small by comparison. The square shaped body and patchy black paint made it stick out like a sore thumb. It had a flat iron brush guard, also painted black, that covered the grill and was packed full of lights and an electric wench. There were a few other trinkets mounted here and there but Ray had no idea what they were. One looked like a siren or speaker of some kind. Another was some kind of shallow box with a splined hole in the center. He'd used some pretty archaic tools when he was in the Army but this thing was a fossil long before his era of service.

The diesel engine running and waiting, Crum sat in the driver's seat watching the human approach.

Against his better judgment Ray climbed in and sank into the bouncy bucket seat. Pulling the door closed the hinge groaned under the strain and it sealed with a crash. "Have you heard the term discreet? It's this thing where you don't draw unneeded attention to yourself."

"I know what discreet means. It's along the lines of sleeping with someone whom would be in your best interest to keep at a professional distance. Opposite of having your partner pick you up at a motel room where yourself and the agent in question have been clearly in the throes of passion." Crum put the K5 Blazer in gear and pulled onto the road.

"I suppose you have a point there. All I'm saying is this death trap is too conspicuous. If they don't see us coming, they'll damn sure hear us."

The orc shrugged. "I like it. I don't have enough room to move in your little cars. I can breathe in here. Plus, there's plenty of room for any gear I need to haul. And since you like convertibles so much the back half can come off."

"That doesn't make it a convertible. It makes it a half cab. And I don't know how you can breathe with all this diesel smoke." Ray grabbed hold of the bouncing seat, trying to stabilize himself. Quickly, he buckled the seatbelt though it didn't relieve his worries.

Crum glanced at the nervous human. His lips tightened around his tusks in a big grin. Finally, he was going to get a taste of his own medicine. "Relax. This thing tops out at about the slowest speed you've ever driven. And in the highly unlikely case we have a rollover, it has a roll cage."

"That doesn't change the fact that we're driving through Miami in a fucking tank."

"It's not a tank. Only the undercarriage is armor plated and it doesn't have any heavy firepower. I think you underestimate how many of these are on the road."

"Maybe in middle America or even in the glades. I doubt the market for spray painted rust buckets is overly large on Millionaire's Row."

"First of all, there isn't a speck of rust on this thing. I rebuilt it myself to make sure of it. Even the leaf springs are powder-coated. Secondly, Millionaire's Row doesn't exist anymore. It's all condos now. Thomas Ezekiel's place is off a sub street beside what used to be known as Millionaire's Row. And for the record, just because you don't pay attention to anything that isn't red, shiny, and shaped like a penis doesn't mean there aren't a bunch of four-wheel-drives out there. Every time I'm out I see at least two other K5s."

"Red, shiny, and shaped like a penis? No more TV for you!" Ray laughed, glancing out the window at their surroundings. They were nearing the Venetian Causeway. The site brought back memories. The fact that he'd been driving a shiny red car at the time had no bearing on the conversation. "Speaking of TV, what would you say if I told you someone bugged my loft?"

Crum was silent for a moment, following the road. "I wouldn't know what to say. I suppose it would be worth knowing who did it. More importantly, knowing what information had been gained from such a thing."

"I don't know. I don't know how long it's been that way. I can't imagine much of anything confidential being overheard. Maybe a location and time if I was arranging a meet over the phone. Prior to recent I haven't been home for a few months."

"We can probably arrange for a sweep team to come through. At least then you'd know it's clean."

"Maybe. I'm more curious as to who installed them. They got in once I'm sure they can do it again. Only a second time they're bound to be more careful about location."

"I can see that. I'd still recommend a sweep team. Even if you don't have them removed it would be good to know what's there. Speaking of bugs, it would probably be a good idea to plant a few of our own tonight."

"Does our warrant allow for that?" Ray asked. He was still new at this entry without permission bit. Most of his searches were initiated by invitation. There was nothing worse than having a solid case thrown out due to improper collection of evidence. "Having ears inside would be useful but think of it like my loft. I accidently found the first bug. That sent me searching for more. We can't have this guy any more paranoid than he already is. If we spook him there's no telling where he'll turn up next. Hell, he fled Europe simply because someone tipped him off that we were coming."

"Our warrant covers it. We also have a surveillance van on site, but nothing inside. I see your point though. We'll take a few with us whether we use them or not. Better to have and not need than need and not have." Crum turned onto the side street off Collins Avenue. Several cars were parked along both sides and it held a strange calm otherwise absent on the strip previously known as Millionaire's Row.

A yellow van with a cleaning company logo was parked in the shadow of a large oak. That was one thing about this little strip. It had plenty of upscale homes but was far less crowded unlike other places in the area. Most of these estates were wrapped in a perimeter wall with a fair number of trees sprouting all around. If not for frequent cultivating it wouldn't take long for nature to reclaim the area.

Crum parked directly behind the van and turned off the ignition. The engine rattled and fell silent. A moment later the yellow rear door opened and a man peeked out, shotgun in-hand. He glanced around and waved the pair toward him.

"I assume that's our surveillance?'

"You assume correctly." Crum opened the door and stepped out. Going to the rear of his vehicle he unrolled the back glass and reached inside, securing two black duffle bags.

Ray waited near the front bumper. Seeing Crum, he approached the open van. "I'm a little surprised you're human." Ray said without thinking. This new world he'd been thrust into was blending together so frequently he was starting to forget not everyone knew.

"Of course I'm human. Michaels here is human too. What'd you think, everyone who works for the WMD is a pointy-eared arrogant prick?"

Crum chuckled. "Ray, this is Derrick Lowe. He works Department 8. That's Roger Michaels inside. He's Department 11."

Inside the faintly illuminated van a series of switchboards, controls, and monitors occupied the entire left wall. The man in front of them turned and waved at the pair.

It had a domed roof but it was the floor that made it unique. Instead of being flat a central channel dropped nearly a foot further, allowing the occupants to move without squatting or ducking. It was sure to be a tight fit but even Crum would be able to stand comfortably inside.

"I haven't learned what all the departments mean yet." Ray stated, slightly embarrassed.

"Eight is Intelligence and eleven is Information Technology."

"Come on in guys. We need to keep the door closed as much as possible." Derrick unlatched the secondary door and pushed it aside. A small set of steps unfolded and bridged the gap to the road.

Ray climbed in realizing how spacious the surveillance van actually was. With the mainframe and systems on the left and the equipment loaded shelf on the right, all four of them could sit without feeling crowded for quite some time. Though sitting wasn't likely to be on the agenda for long.

As soon as the stairs had folded and the rear doors were sealed, Derrick retrieved a pair of stools for the newcomers before returning to his own. "All right, guys. We've watched the place most of the day. The security system is tight but not perfect. I don't want to bore you with the details but let's just say I could talk for hours about every problem you're likely to face while getting into this place unseen. Even then, you'd still fail."

"That bad, huh?" Ray asked, glancing at the numerous screens. Multiple video feeds displayed nearly every inch of the massive complex. The sheer volume told him there had to be at least sixty cameras in use.

"You don't know the half of it. I've read both of your reports. From what I've seen there's no physical way for the two of you to get into this place by yourselves undetected."

"What now? The job is scrapped?" Ray asked, unsure what was happening. If they couldn't get in how were they going to get the evidence they needed?

"That's where I come in." A thin smile stretched across Derrick's lips. "I'll be with you the whole time. It's the only way to get you in and out, but I have to insist you do exactly what I say when I say it. If you hesitate for even a second, you'd be better off staying here. Can you both agree to that?"

Crum nodded.

"What about you?" Derrick's attention was firmly on Ray.

"I think so, though it'd be good to know the plan beforehand. Hesitance comes from uncertainty."

"We don't have time to discuss every detail. The target left the property at twenty-one-sixteen. It took you forty-seven minutes to arrive. Each second we delay is a second less from our search time. I will say we're going to enter from the southeast corner. A design flaw in their security makes that the optimal breech point. We'll temporarily disable the camera, scale the wall, and enter the complex through the left side bay windows of the sitting room." Derrick gestured to one of the monitors displaying an overview of the property. Numerous rotating cones faded from red to yellow and eventually to transparent.

Ray assumed that was the camera range being displayed.

"Having thoroughly studied the structure it stands to reason any evidence you can hope to find will be located in the study. That's where the target retreats each time he receives a business communication. Now, to repeat my question, are you capable of doing what I say when I say it?"

"Yes?"

"Good. Let's get suited up. And make sure you leave your weapons here. You won't have any way to properly equip them and we won't be needing them."

Crum handed one of the duffels to Ray and unzipped his own. Pulling out the black tactical clothing he went to work replacing his street clothes.

Ray glanced in the bag seeing a smaller set of the same. Their host was dressing in his own suit, though he'd already been partially there upon their arrival. Ray removed his suit jacket and hung it on a hook near the shelf. If he'd anticipated a full change of clothes he would have happily worn something less delicate. As it were, he hadn't planned for this. He hadn't planned for a lot of things. Especially leaving his gun behind.

"I don't foresee the need for these but I'd rather have extra if something unexpected happens." Derrick handed a bundle to the orc and another to Ray.

Unrolling the bundle, Ray inspected each item. There was a small box about the size of a deck of cards. It had four indicator lights on the side, a switch, and a button. There was also a holstered gun of some kind though it didn't match any model he'd seen before. The barrel was exceptionally long and instead of a magazine it had a solid pistol grip. In many ways it reminded him of a paintball gun without all the extra accessories. Lastly, there was a black plastic case. Opening it, he peered inside seeing a communications earbud and microphone. "I get the earpiece but what's the rest of this?"

Velcroing the kydex holster into place, Crum did a test draw ensuring it was properly positioned. "Knockout gas gun. They released the prototype a couple months ago."

"Knockout gas gun? So you just shoot someone and it knocks them out?" Ray studied the device, curious as to what was going on under the hood. Knockout gas was nothing new. Hell, a similar effect was achieved with a mixture of bleach and toothpaste, not that it was advised. The curious thing was why he was just now learning about it. If a capable gas had been around so long, surely it would have been weaponized not long thereafter. "How does it work?"

Derrick, growing annoyed with the constant questions, drew the gun at his side. In the blink of an eye it was field stripped and resting disassembled at the table's edge. Quickly reassembling, he gave a walkthrough of the basics. "It uses a carbon dioxide propulsion with a spring assisted backup. The gun itself does little more than deliver the pellet unbroken. The pellets themselves are where the magic happens. All you need to know is when you shoot, don't do it closer than ten yards. And if you're in a sealed room get out as fast as possible. A gentle breeze will dissolve the lingering gas within five minutes." Holstering the tool, he lifted the box. "This is a jammer. It has a range of twenty feet and will interrupt the electrical signal of any device, hard wired or wireless within range. If show and tell is over can we go now?"

"I'm ready." Crum offered, getting to his feet in full tactical gear.

Ray hurried to get the last few elements into place. These people seemed to forget that he wasn't a heavy assault kind of guy. He was the one who talked his way into their circle and got arrested with them. Gun fights, while more frequent of late, were usually small arms. Not signal jammers, gas guns, and high-tech equipment. He was an undercover, not a spy. At least until recent anyway. His new duties were apparently going to broaden his horizons. "I think I'm ready." He finally added, getting things to stay in place.

Crum grabbed the body armor of his human friend and jerked the tabs into place. "Now you're ready."

Ray was surprised by the sudden comfort. The thick covering was no longer pressing into his sides as it had been. "Excellent. Lead the way." He gestured toward the rear doors, watching Derrick sweep past him with ease. "I guess you'll be keeping watch from here?" He asked the other man, Michaels.

The quiet communications tech pulled a cigarette from an unseen pack and nodded his answer. Lighting up, he blew a wispy cloud of white smoke into the air.

The scent reached Ray just as the doors were closing. It had been a few months since his last smoke. It wasn't something he missed. At least not anymore, but he'd be lying if he said the smell didn't make him desire one. He knew it would taste horrible. The last time he'd given in had been a testament to that. Forcing temptation aside, Ray raced to catch up with Crum and Derrick who were already across the street and somewhere in the shadows of the partially neglected vegetation.

Patches of oak, palmettos, cactus and several others Ray didn't know the names to had overtaken the landscape just outside the walled property. In many ways it looked as if someone had tried to tame it some years past but had simply given up. Nearing his companions who'd come to a stop behind one of the thicker trees, Ray ducked down and awaited command.

Derrick glanced back at him. "Do you have your earpiece in?"

"Not yet. You didn't tell me to."

A sigh escaped him. "Go ahead and put it in. We won't have time to stop and explain things. The comms are open. If you need something, say it as quiet as possible. If something requires immediate action, do what you have to do. We'll deal with the consequences afterward."

Ray nodded and slipped the earpiece into place.

Derrick reached over and pressed a small button, bringing the device online. "Can you hear me?"

Ray nodded, surprised at just how well he could. He'd seen Derrick's lips move but the only audible noise came directly from the speaker.

"There's a corner post about thirty yards behind this tree. Michaels is going to give us the signal. When that happens run as fast as you can directly to that post. Do not veer or delay in any direction. Do you understand?"

Again, Ray nodded. Inspecting the gear their guide had equipped made him feel somewhat naked. He had the basic stuff they'd provided and nothing else. Even Crum wore more than the bare minimum, leaving him the odd one out. This was the most naked he'd ever felt and he was fully clothed.

"Rotation in three—two—one—Move!" A previously unheard voice echoed through the comms.

The 95th District

Levi Samuel

Chapter 20
Unexpected Heroics

In unison the three broke into a sprint, reaching the corner in a matter of seconds. Crum hit the wall first, his longer legs granting him a natural advantage. Wasting no time he grabbed hold of Ray as soon as he was in range and threw him up and over.

Ray hit the ground, landing on his hands and knees. He hadn't expected the sudden flight. He was just glad he hadn't landed some other way. The walls were right at eight feet tall. That could have seriously hurt.

"On your feet. Move to the left side of the pool." Derrick demanded, landing beside him. He was much more graceful about it, letting his legs absorb the blow.

Crum was the last to hit, having to climb over. Though his height removed much of that concern. He could reach the top standing flat footed. Someone of Ray's height would have had to jump.

White curtains fluttered in the breeze outside the open bay windows. The air was cool and the lights from the pool put a glowing blue haze in the air. Aiming for the open space between the thin drapes, Ray dove inside the house. He didn't need direction to tell him they were running out of time. It had been Derricks increasing pace that had done that. Ray landed awkwardly on a suede ottoman which slid under the sudden force.

Crum hit the ground beside him, landing roughly on a white fur that lined the center floor. It bunched under his momentum and drug the couch and ottoman, and by extension Ray, several inches toward the far wall.

"You hear that?" An unfamiliar voice asked somewhere in the distance.

"Probably just Elian walking around upstairs. Quit stalling and deal the cards."

Rolling from the footstool, careful to avoid the mass of Crum beneath him, Ray got to his feet and glanced around the room. The three bay windows where they'd entered were overlooking the pool. The wall to his right was decorated by a single canvas painting of flowers which took up a large area. A sectional sat center room, misaligned and offset now due to Crum and the rug.

Derrick stood behind the angled couch seeming as if he'd never left his feet even with the mandatory dive. He brought his finger to his lips and gestured above Ray's head.

Glancing behind and up Ray spotted the camera he was being warned about. They were just out of view, the stationary device focused solely on the door that sat mid-wall. Backing toward the only remaining path, Ray arced wide to ensure he didn't come into view.

The room adjoined to what he could only assume was the master bedroom. He was noticing a theme with the interior. Everything upholstered or painted was white. Everything else was a light shade of wood, glass, or chromed metal. It had been extremely prominent in the sitting room but now in the bedroom he was seeing more of the same. The vaulted ceiling was trimmed in wood, exposed rafters giving it an elegant feel. A king-sized bed sat along the center west wall with folded corners and a mountain of pillows at the head. The chest of drawers across from the foot had an oval mirror mounted to the white wall. Every available surface had a vase or a decorative bowl of some type or another filled with flowers or perfectly preserved plastic fruit. The whole place looked like something out of a Home-Living magazine rather than a criminal mastermind's place of residence.

Derrick marched through the room, giving it a quick once over. Passing into the narrow hall on the far side he stole a quick look into the twin walk in closets. "If we don't find anything in the study we'll have to come back here."

"Why?" Ray couldn't help himself. Such a statement wouldn't have been made had it not been fueled by additional knowledge.

"The back side of this closet has a false wall that leads into either a safe or panic room. I'd rather not disturb it unless we have no other choice. There's a camera watching that wall."

"Understood."

Continuing on, as if he knew exactly where he was going, Derrick turned at a vestibule and slowly opened the large double doors that separated the master wing from the rest of the house. There were at least three distinct voices, possibly more, echoing around the corner. Throwing his hand up, Derrick called for a halt.

Ray could hear water running in the room to their left. He couldn't tell if it was a recently flushed toilet refilling or a sink in use. Either way someone was in that room. If they stepped out, they'd be caught red-handed. "Fall back." Ray whispered, bumping into Crum.

The orc filed back behind the double doors giving enough room for the others.

Getting clear, Ray watched Derrick. The man hadn't heard him or refused to listen. Either way, it presented a problem. As if moving in slow motion the side door opened and one of the guards appeared. He was dressed in a simple suit with a radio clipped to his side pocket. A pistol was holstered to his other hip.

"Hey, what are you—"

Ray squeezed the trigger of the gas gun. It clicked making no more sound than a snapped twig and a small oblong shell that looked more like a bird's egg erupted from the muzzle. It impacted the man in the back and exploded in a thick cloud of blueish-white fog. It was impossible to see anything through the growing haze. Hearing something, or more aptly someone hit the ground, Ray signaled Crum to back away even further. If this stuff continued to grow it would engulf where they were standing.

"That's not good." Crum stated, unsure what to do now.

"Derrick, can you hear me?" Ray asked, hoping their guide had been able to move out of range before the shot. Silence suggested that had not been the case.

"Roger, we have a bit of a problem." Crum stated, revealing no worry in his voice.

"What's going on?"

"Derrick is possibly down from a knockout round. He—"

Uncontrolled laughter echoed through the comms. After several long moments it finally subsided though labored breathing could still be heard. 'You're shitting me? That know-it-all got taken down by a knockout? That's hilarious!"

"Maybe so. It doesn't change the fact that our only route has been closed by the gas and we have a man down in an unprotected hall with multiple hostiles not far away."

"All right. I'll see if there's anything I can—Shit!"

"What?" Crum and Ray asked in unison.

"Um—Things just got quite a bit more complicated. So— the target."

"What about him?" Crum didn't need to ask to know what was about to be said.

"He's pulling in now."

"I thought you guys had a tail on him? I thought you were going to give us a heads up before he got back?"

"We did, and we were. I don't know what's happened or why he's back. I'm calling our guy now."

"Screw that. Whatever he has to say is irrelevant right now. How do we fix this before we're discovered?"

Ray was somewhat surprised to hear the emotion growing in Crum's voice. He'd heard it a few times but it always seemed to be a last resort. The orc was one of the most controlled and collected people he knew. "We can't leave him. If Ezekiel finds him he'll run before we ever get a chance to get this close again. Not to mention he'll probably kill what's his name. We also can't leave the hall full of sleepy-time fog."

"Okay. So, the stuff is water soluble. If you can dose it with a misting spray it will literally fall out of the air and dissipate."

"How are we supposed to spray water all over it with guards in the next room?" Ray asked, seeing no good way around any of this. Like every other aspect of this case it was turning into an unmitigated disaster.

A sigh echoed in their earbuds. "Give me a minute."

"Roger, Roger."

"Say that again and you're on your own!"

"Sorry." Ray couldn't help but chuckle. He stood a short distance from the door watching the fog seep through the cracks. Thus far not much had gotten in but he wasn't keen on the idea of getting much closer. A voice echoed through the radio on the other side of the door. It was distorted, keeping him from hearing what was said but the other guards, seeming oblivious to their predicament cleared up the confusion.

"Shit! Boss is back. We need to get back to the control room."

Crum tapped Ray on the shoulder and pointed up.

Curious as to what the orc was telling him about Ray glanced at the ceiling seeing a small drone hovering overhead. It had a centralized body with four spinning blades that kept it up. Strange looking instruments were mounted to the underside and four wheels dangled reminding him of the remote-controlled cars he'd played with as a kid. Though the oddest thing about the contraption, he couldn't hear it. His experience with drones was still fairly limited. He'd seen a handful in action but it was still one of those things that, while he knew they were out there, he didn't think of them as common just yet.

"Would you mind opening the door for my little friend?" Roger asked, the drone waiting patiently.

"Um—sure." Ray covered his mouth and nose and inched forward, pulling the door toward him just enough for the device to slip through. He took the opportunity to steal a glance. Much of the fog had settled though the hall was still too dense to enter. The drone flew straight through unaffected, one of the bottom mounted instruments unfolding. A mist began to spray in a radius, visibly settling the lingering fog. In no time it was little more than a minor haze a few inches off the floor and still fading.

"The guards are headed your way. Don't move."

The drone fell the remaining couple feet it had been hovering and bounced harmlessly on its now extended wheels. A light erupted from a bulb on the top and a projection shot out, blending in seamlessly with the walls.

Ray studied it as best he could, refusing to move. It appeared as if the drone was taking samples from its surroundings and creating a fake hallway to coverup the two bodies lying on the floor. Hearing the guards moments before he saw them, they rushed around the corner and turned right, disappearing with a left turn at the end.

"They just entered the elevator. I recommend doing whatever it is you need to do and getting out. Ezekiel is pulling through the front gate right now."

"What about Derrick?" Ray asked, studying the unconscious man before him. The sleeping guard was another problem but he only had room to process one at a time right now.

As if Crum had been thinking the same, he pushed past Ray and grabbed the guard. Heaving him with ease he slung him over his shoulder and carried him to the master bedroom. Throwing back the blankets he laid the man down and tucked him in. It was unlikely to be good for the man's career but it was better he be caught sleeping than to be found unconscious in the hall.

Watching his friend, Ray suddenly understood, though there was still a question weighing on him. "Won't he still be able to tell them about Derrick? He clearly saw him."

"The knockout gas is potent. It's highly unlikely he'll remember anything for at least an hour before he was knocked out. Hell, I got hit with one once. It took me forty-eight hours before I remembered what I had for breakfast that day." Roger replied.

"I've got Derrick. You head to the study. We only have a few minutes. Let's make them count." Snatching up their unconscious guide, Crum pointed down the hall where the guards had disappeared moments earlier. "It's the double doors at the end."

Ray stepped into the lead position seeing the now grounded drone take off ahead of him. Quickly crossing the open area at the center of the massive complex, he was glad they waited. The left side contained a stairwell, the foyer, and a large dining room, all accented in glass and the ever present white and wood theme. A balcony overlooked the top of the stairs, overseeing much of the grand room that adjoined all of it as well as the living room and a breakfast nook beside the kitchen. Beyond that appeared to be several more exits to the pool area, along with more rooms. For as simple of a layout as this place had it was overly complex. Ray reached the twin doors and pulled them open.

The drone raced inside. "The room is clean. Enter at will."

Ray was already on his way in when the report had been delivered. It was nice to have a heads up but they were running out of time. Glancing around, it was simple yet elegant.

A desk sat center room with a single white leather chair at its head. The left wall was filled by a large hutch that stretched from floor to ceiling. The cabinet doors on the bottom were closed and the scaling shelves were filled loosely with books, trophies, and a wide variety of bladed weapons that didn't appear to have collected a single speck of dust. The right side was much the same with the exception of another desk between the twin towers and another set of cabinets bridging the top. Four flat screen monitors were assembled in the space between, looping a vibrant meteor shower over an ocean sunset from one screen to the next.

Crum closed the door behind him and gently placed Derrick in the office chair. "Found anything yet?"

"Not yet. Nothing looks out of place. It's going to be hard to find anything without letting him know someone was here." Ray searched for anything out of the ordinary. The wall opposite the doors held four windows that ran side by side from floor to ceiling. Thick drapes partially covered them though the tinted glass was probably more helpful in blocking light than the curtains were. While it was unlikely he'd find anything of importance near the windows he felt the need to inspect them. They were undoubtedly going to have to make a hasty retreat and the glass panes looked as good a place as any, provided the jammers were strong enough to kill any cameras in the area.

Content in his exit strategy, Ray returned to the central desk and silently pulled the top right drawer open. Picking through the various items, odd trinkets and office tools, he closed the drawer. It clearly didn't contain the sort of stuff he was looking for.

"Ezekiel's Mercedes is pulling into the garage." Roger announced.

"Dammit! Is there any way to wake Derrick?" Ray pulled the bottom drawer open. It was packed full of organized files though he didn't have time to go through them one by one.

"Most wake on their own after about twenty minutes. A glass of cold water to the face or smelling salts might work though."

"Sternal rub?"

"That might do it but I'd recommend caution. He's likely to be disoriented when he awakes. It might trigger an attack."

"I see. Crum, do you want to do the honors?"

The orc chuckled. "So it's okay if he hits me?"

"Look at you. Of the two of us you can take a lot more abuse."

"That doesn't mean I want to get hit. It still hurts, regardless of size or strength." Crum pulled open the unconscious guide's shirt, exposing his chest. Balling his fist he vigorously rubbed his knuckles against the man's sternum, applying steady pressure.

Groggily, Derrick turned his head and batted at the irritant. He opened his eyes and glared at the orc towering over him. Suddenly, he kicked away and slammed the back of the chair into the furniture behind him. A loud crash echoed and one of the displayed placards fell forward. It landed on the wood floor and shattered.

"Easy." Crum cautiously approached. His hands were open signaling no threat. "Do you remember where you are?"

"I—" Derrick closed his eyes, trying to remember. "I'm on a job. I don't remember where."

Ray stared helplessly at the broken placard. They may as well have left a business card telling him to give them a call.

"You're in Thomas Ezekiel's estate in South Beach, Miami. We're on a covert search looking for evidence. The guards are upstairs and Ezekiel himself will be in the house in a matter of seconds. I need you to pull yourself together so we can get out of here." Crum backed away. He'd learned some time ago that his sight wasn't easily accepted by humans. It was best to give them some processing time before coming on too strong. Of course, he'd never read Derrick's file. It was confidential, even to him. Just because he worked for the WMD didn't mean he was on the enlightened side of things, but their previous dialogue suggested he was aware.

"Not to add to the problem but Ezekiel just entered the house. I have him near the ground floor elevator. He's right around the corner from you."

"Shit! We need to hide." Ray glanced around for any place to do so. They still didn't have anything. Leaving was

not an option, not yet. "Quick, behind the curtains."
Without a second thought, Ray climbed into the windowsill
and pulled one of the thick drapes over him.

"I highly doubt I'll fit in the window." Crum replied.

"I may be able to help. Find the nearest corner and press
your back into it. Do not move. If you move it will not
work." The drone's propellers began to spin and it took to
the sky, the lights it had projected in the hallway coming to
life.

Watching Derrick climb into one of the other windows,
Crum selected the southeast corner. Judging from the layout
of the room that was the one place least likely to be viewed
from the central chair. Pressing his shoulders between the
hutch tier and the corner wall, he wedged himself into place,
seeing the drone's light scan him.

The door cracked open and the overhead LEDs came on.
An elven male wearing a pair of kakis, flipflops, and a baby
blue button up shirt stepped inside. His blonde hair was well
manicured and combed neatly. Seeing the broken glass on
the floor he approached and picked up the largest chunks,
inspecting them. "Worthless sonsabitches!" Placing what was
left of the placard on the desk he turned toward the single
hutch on the north wall and knelt in front of it. Pulling the
cabinet doors open he reached inside.

Crum took several short breaths through his nose,
employing every trick he knew to keep from moving. He
couldn't verify if this was Ezekiel. It didn't look like the elf
he'd seen in the lower level of Club Vice, not that his
memory of the encounter was that great to begin with.
Whether this was the supposed kingpin or not, he clearly
knew the combination to the safe he'd just opened. There
was no telling what was inside but a hidden safe was a good
indicator their query was near.

"Boss!" A voice called from outside the door.

"What!" The elf snapped, flipping through a handful of
papers.

"Um—you're going to want to see this."

"What now?" He tossed the papers back inside and closed the safe, resetting the lock. Getting to his feet he followed the guard down the hall.

Crum stepped from his nook and closed the study door. "We need to get out of here now."

"What about the evidence? If we leave empty handed all of this was for nothing?" Ray replied, peeking around the curtain.

"He locked the safe. Unless you can break in, we're done here."

"I may be able to help with that." Roger replied, his drone taking position above the double doors. "I record everything. Got a clear shot of the combination."

Derrick pulled a pair of latex gloves from a pocket in his tactical vest and quickly put them on. Kneeling in front of the insulated box, he studied the lock. "It's got a thumbprint scanner, but I think I can handle that. What's the combo?"

"Twenty-five—fifty-one—thirty-five—fourteen!"

Typing the code, Derrick gently placed a thin plastic strip over the glass sensor and pressed his gloved thumb over it. Twisting the lever, it clicked and he pulled the door open. "Anything in particular you boys looking for? We've got money, guns, what looks like some drugs, and a lot of paper."

"Do you mind if I take a look?" Ray waited for Derrick to move and crouched down. Snatching the small bag of familiar coiled snake tablets, he inspected them. These were mixed between blue and pink, though both were a much darker shade than the others he'd seen, and less chalky. Pulling his cell phone, he snapped a few pictures and handed the bag to Crum. Turning his attention to the papers he quickly scanned their contents. Most were nonincriminating but a few held some questionable details. He took pictures of each for good measure. One in particular caught his attention. "Crum, I think we've got him. This looks to be the original shipping schedule I found a few days ago. It's circumstantial but I'm willing to bet the amounts paid match what's in this money log." Handing the schedule to Crum, Ray flipped through the leather-bound book. The records inside were much larger than he'd expected. That in itself was suspicious. Locating the date of Crum's disappearance there were two payouts, both to numbered recipients. The first was just shy of twenty-million-dollars. The second wasn't in traditional currency, paid in a share of some kind. It had a US dollar amount in parenthesis beside it, reading four-hundred-million.

"I hate to cut it short but you have people headed your way."

Ray snapped a couple shots of the log. Doing the same for the schedule and collecting the bag, he slipped a couple of the tablets into his pocket and returned it all to the safe. Closing the door, he got to his feet. "I think we can escape out the windows but the cameras along the east wall are going to cause a problem. Any advice?"

"I need a pay raise. Stand by. You'll know when to move."

Almost instantly, a loud boom shook the house and all the lights went out.

"That's our cue." Derrick lifted the dual paned glass and stepped through. "Let's go."

Chapter 21
Rounding the Posse

The grating beeps of Ray's alarm sounded in the dark. He sat up and glanced at the time. It was fifteen-till-six and he felt like he hadn't slept a wink. With a sigh, he got to his feet and carefully made his way across the storage unit apartment. Finding the pull cord, the small space illuminated and he located his shoes. Today was the big day. With the evidence they'd found they had everything they needed to bring Ezekiel down once and for all.

Taking a moment, Ray stared at the question marked silhouette atop his wall diagram. This was it. He was finally going to put an end to this several month obsession. Maybe then he could direct his attention to whoever had bugged his loft.

Making his way to the door, Ray holstered his Colt and stepped into the morning light. He sent a quick text to Lilian as he approached his car. He desperately wanted to hear her voice but didn't want to risk compromising anything she had going on by an untimely phone call. It was better for her to respond at her convenience. He reread the message, making sure he hadn't said anything too stupid.

Good morning, beautiful. Just wanted to let you know we got what we were looking for last night. Things are moving forward. I hope you have a wonderful day. I miss you.

Happy with the message Ray hit send and climbed into the driver's seat. Within minutes he was parked in the sublevel parking garage of the WMD and headed toward the elevator. It still baffled him how so much was underground, especially here. But then again there were still many factors of the WMD that alluded him. One of which being the view outside the eighth floor windows. The elevator dinged and Ray made the increasingly familiar trek toward the old orc's office. Before he reached the door his phone rang.

"Hello?" He answered without looking, hoping it was Lilian. His hopes were dashed.

"Kel'Gos tells me you had some success last night."

"Yes, sir. Everything's been submitted for review. I think we've got him, though I wasn't able to confirm identity."

"I guess something is better than nothing. Head down to the first floor, Auditorium B, as soon as you can."

"Yes, sir. I'll be down in a few minutes." Ray hung up the phone and glanced through the tinted glass of the old orc's office. As far as he could tell, Kel'Gos wasn't there. Turning around, he returned to the elevator and was off to the first floor. He wasn't sure how but navigating the mysterious complex was beginning to get easier.

Locating the auditorium Roderick had told him about Ray squeezed through the throng of people gathered in the hall and stepped inside. It was a huge amphitheater with an elevated stage at the center of the bowl-shaped room. He wasn't sure how many seats were available but it could have easily hosted the largest concert he'd ever attended.

Ray made his way along the descending pathway toward the center. Crum and Kel'Gos were seated a few rows from the front in section seven. Ray rounded the inner ring and took a seat beside them. "Good morning, gentlemen. What's going on here?"

"Interdepartmental briefing. We have one of these before each raid." Crum answered.

"I guess that makes sense. We do the same thing in PD though it's usually held in a training room, and only includes those who will be participating. Who are all these people?" Ray glanced around seeing far more in attendance than he'd expected. Of the thirteen sections which ran from center to top, including balcony seating, numerous members of every race were present and discussing among themselves. The chatter of voices growing outside told him many more were on their way.

"The WMD has a mandatory open door policy for all interdepartmental operations. Most of the time it's just the department heads and a few representatives from each. This is a big one though. They need the additional seating and the acoustics are far better. From the stage your voice can be heard in every corner without shouting. Plus, sometimes the big wigs want to sit in. This allows them to check things out without being crowded." Kel'Gos replied.

Ray glanced around the circular room finding his choice of words amusing. "So it's basically a free for all? How do you maintain discretion? It seems to me this is the same error the ICPC made when we were preparing to move on Ezekiel. Had they kept it isolated it would have been easier to discover who tipped him off."

"I don't disagree. Unfortunately this operation is much larger than Department 7 can handle independently. The fact that you're here is in part the reason for this."

"How so?"

"Roderick insists this is a Marshals case. I concede it is as much yours as it is ours. Though from what Crum'Bul here tells me, Ezekiel is confirmed of elven descent. That places his arrest and conviction solely on our department. ICPC also has their hand out. We're likely to have some of their representatives here as well." Kel'Gos added. "Plus, this is the easiest way to manage cooperation between agencies and departments."

He didn't like it. There were too many loose ends. Too many chances for leaks, especially if ICPC was going to be in the audience. Realizing there wasn't anything he could do about it, Ray took a deep breath and exhaled. "So what can we expect from all of this?" He gestured around them.

Kel'Gos shrugged. "It's pretty much going to be a boring couple of hours. Collected evidence from all involved parties will be presented, reviewed, and discussed. We're going to study every inch of the floor plans, camera locations, security count, and pretty much every aspect of the site we can think of. Once that's been firmly established, we'll formulate a plan of entry and assign teams. I imagine sometime around noon we'll adjourn for a two-hour break. Those who will be in active participation will then return for a complete recap, at which time we'll divide into our teams, gather our gear, and prepare to roll."

"Oh, so basically we spend the day planning and then we strike afterward while it's still fresh in everyone's mind?"

"Pretty much." Crum concluded.

"So I don't really need to be here since we went through most of the layout stuff last night?"

Kel'Gos chuckled. "I've a feeling Roderick would— How would he put it? —shit a brick if you skipped out on this."

Various people began to filter into the room taking seats near people they knew. It seemed fairly divided, much of the like races sitting with their own kind, though it was still intermingled by department. Seeing them all together in one place made the world feel equally large and small at the same time. Ray realized how tiny his little piece of it was, but it was also interesting to witness it firsthand. Departments 2, 3, and 4 looked to be mostly lawyers and accountant types. It was evident they had the cushy desk jobs.

The representatives from Department 1 were an odd sort. They carried poorly concealed guns though Ray suspected it was his training that gave it away. Their eyes constantly wandered, surveying each and every person in the massive room. "Who are those guys?"

"Internal Control. They're the ones who ensure the WMD remain honest. They police us." Crum answered honestly.

"Okay so the internal affairs department. Got it."

Entering the conversation, Kel'Gos elaborated. "All case reports go through them before being sent to archives. Aside from a question here or there we don't usually have to worry much about them. Though that ordeal with Wright stirred up some trouble. That made us all look stupid, especially them since it's their job to identify that sort of activity before it comes to a head. Speaking from experience, they don't like to look stupid."

"I imagine not." Continuing his tour around the various departments Ray saw both Roger and Derrick from the night before sitting with their groups. It seemed the vast majority of the people in the room were either in tactical or intelligence though the former outnumbered two to one.

Seeing Ray's curiosity, Kel'Gos provided some insight. "Classified information isn't something we throw on each and every document to come through here. It's counterproductive to having a fair and equal organization. Sensitive data, sure. There's always 'need to know' information that's held until a case is resolved, but as soon as it's been filed all information becomes public access, within the WMD anyway. Transparency is required for an honest work environment. We have enough secrets from the world, we don't need to keep them from each other."

"I guess that makes sense. I don't know. I guess I don't understand how—" Ray paused, thinking through the questions piling in his brain. "Okay, so, we know this guy's slippery. We also know he has someone in ICPC who alerted him last time. How are we going to ensure there isn't a repeat if this briefing is open to everyone?"

"That's why Internal Control is here. They're the only department who has unlimited access to the ICPC database. They inspect and verify every person who walks through those doors. If someone arrives who isn't authorized, they'll handle it."

Ray sighed. "I suppose that's better than nothing. I still don't like it. I'd prefer as few people as possible on this."

"I understand. This is simply how we do things here. It's worked pretty well thus far. If there comes a time when we can't trust our own we may as well close our doors and let the ICPC take over. They certainly want to."

"I trust you. And I trust Crum. Most recently, I suppose I trust Roger over there. I can't say the same for anyone else here." Ray's phone rang. Glancing at the screen he saw Lilian's picture. "Excuse me."

"Hurry back. We'll be starting in a few minutes." Kel'Gos called after him.

Ray answered before he reached the door. "Hey! How are you?"

"I'm fine. Thank you for the text earlier. I'm sorry I couldn't answer right then. I was working."

"No need to apologize. I assumed as much. That's why I texted instead of calling. Though I have to admit I'm happy to hear your voice."

"You're sweet. So, tell me about the search. You found something?"

"Yeah. Some drugs and money, as well as a bunch of paperwork that ties him down. We're gearing up for the raid right now. Kel'Gos says it's going to take a few hours but we're probably going to hit this evening."

"That's wonderful. I got to meet with some of his people this morning. It opened the door to some of his middlemen. If you cut off the head, I may have just gained the key to killing the body. I'll find out in a couple hours but I'm pretty sure they're going to play ball."

"That's awesome! It looks like all of this is finally coming together for both of us."

"It looks that way."

"Kel'Gos said your people have been invited to join the briefing. I was kind of hoping I'd see you here."

"I got the message but unfortunately I can't make it. Two of my surveillance team will be there though."

"I forgot you weren't alone. I guess that makes sense though."

"Hey, listen, I'm sorry I have to cut this short. One of Ezekiel's people is calling. I love you and I miss you and I'll call you again as soon as I can."

Ray heard the call end though he was still stuck on her words. "She loves me?" He said aloud to no one in particular. A smile formed on his lips and his legs floated across the floor carrying him back into the auditorium. "She loves me!" He repeated, unable to contain his smile. This could have been the worst day he'd ever experienced and she just flipped it on him. Even the gloomy shadows of the amphitheater seemed suddenly bright. Nothing could bring him down.

Returning to his seat Ray watched the oldest elf he'd ever seen climb onto the stage. He looked like an elf anyway. His ears weren't nearly as long but he had every other feature so commonly found in them. He found himself wondering just how old an elf had to be to show signs of aging. Lilian was over six-hundred and she looked like she was maybe twenty.

"Ladies and gentlemen of the audience, we ask you silence your phones and hold no congress outside this chamber while we're in session. Please remember these briefings are held for the safety of all involved. If you have questions or concerns there will be an appointed time for such at the end of each section. You'll find quill and parchment in the right side pocket of your seats. Now, if you'll please invite Director Kel'Gos of Tactical Response to the front, we'll get this shindy started."

Kel'Gos picked himself up and made for the center. "Greetings, friends and visitors. We're here today to discuss and arrange the apprehension of a criminal who has long evaded justice. This entity operates under the identity of Thomas Ezekiel. By all accounts we believe Mister Ezekiel to be of elven descent. Unfortunately this has been neither confirmed nor denied. I would invite each of you to direct your attention to the overhead screens in review of evidence and allegations."

"I have to tell you, that was the most grueling, boring, mind numbing experience of my life. I'll literally never get that time back." Ray exasperated, taking a drink from his water bottle.

"It wasn't that bad. It had a few moments. You want to talk about a boring briefing, I sat through one in 1962. Three guys broke out of a prison on this small island in the San Francisco Bay. Nobody knew how." Crum rebutted.

"Are you talking about Alcatraz?"

"Yes. I guess it's not surprising you've heard of it."

"Heard of it? It's one of the most well-known prison breaks in history. Hell, there's been movies and books written about it, not to mention every few years someone digs into it trying to prove or disprove what happened."

"The case is still open if you feel like having a look. I'm pretty sure it's a Marshals case right now, though I don't think your jurisdiction will allow you to work it."

"I've got better things to do than worry about a couple geriatrics who clearly haven't been causing problems since their escape. How did they end up on your radar anyway?"

"Back then things were less black and white than they are now. Anytime something unexplained happened we were called in to investigate. Sometimes it became our case. Most of the time, not. Technological advances have eliminated much of the guess work. We pretty much know what we're walking into now."

"I guess that makes sense."

Kel'Gos approached the pair. "You boys ready to do this?"

"Yes." Crum answered.

"Where's Roderick? He called me this morning. I would have expected him to be here."

"No clue. He doesn't work field anymore. Now that you're here it wouldn't surprise me if he stops coming in altogether. I think it's mostly a transitional adjustment. He wants to make sure you're well established before leaving you to the wolves."

"That's mighty nice of him. I assumed he was— I don't know. —always around, watching things from on high."

"Just between you and me—" Kel'Gos glanced around, making sure no one else was listening. "—I think he has a little separation anxiety. He was doing your job for nearly thirty years. That isn't much for one of my kind but that's like a third of the average human's lifespan."

"When you put it like that it does seem like a long time."

Kel'Gos nodded and began to walk away. "Anyway, get geared up. Boats are rolling in fifteen."

"Yes, sir—" Ray cut himself off, seeing the orc pause. Turning to Crum, he shook his head. "I'm never going to get used to that. It was so different in the Army. Officers were addressed either by rank or Sir. Enlisted were rank only. I don't know why but the absence of insignia makes it so much harder to drop the habit."

The green orc shrugged. "I don't know. I don't know how I address him. I've never thought about it."

"Probably one of those raising things. My parents always made me say sir or ma'am, depending on the situation. Anyway, I'm going to make a phone call real quick. I'll be down in a few minutes. It's basement level seven, right?"

"Correct. I'll start pulling gear for you."

"Thanks." Ray drew his phone and hit the recent calls, dialing Lilian. The phone rang several times. Finally, a voice came across the line.

"The person you are calling has a voice mailbox that has not been set up. Please try your call again later."

Ending the call, Ray quickly typed a text.

Hey beautiful, just wanted to let you know we're rolling in the next few minutes. I don't know what your plans are but be careful. I'd hate for you to be in the crosshairs. I miss you.

Making his way through the crowd, Ray climbed into the elevator. It seemed everyone was going to the same floor though that was a bit of an exaggeration. It did make him realize a flaw in security though. The private system required ID to operate, all except department heads. If anyone could just climb in they practically had access to any floor so long as it was already headed there. Then again, how did they know if a department head was present? Glancing around, no cameras were outwardly visible but that didn't mean anything. There was plenty of discrete technology around this place. A camera could be hidden anywhere.

The elevator stopped many times unloading passengers until only a few remained. It finally reached subfloor seven. Two elves and three humans, including Ray filed out into the concrete parking garage. Ray had driven through this level a few times headed to the lower floor's parking. It seemed like an entirely different place now.

It still retained the chain link fencing and stone walls of the other levels but the ceiling was much higher and the vehicles were much larger. It now looked more like a military base. Groups marched in all directions, albeit not in cadence. They were dressed for action. Many of the vehicles, most of them armored assault trucks or large tactical vans, were being filled with soldiers, for lack of a better term.

Spotting Crum near one of the vans where a few men and elves were loading up, Ray started toward them, avoiding the units getting ready for the assault.

Crum looked up as he neared. "Get suited up. I didn't know what weapon you like to carry, but considering you never shut up about being in the army, I got you an M4."

"We used M16s when I was in."

"We have some of those. Though I recommend trying it. The M4 does everything the M16 can, only better."

"I see you're not biased. What are you using?"

"An HK MP5."

Shaking his head, Ray grabbed the gear set aside for him and climbed into the van.

"You boys got room for one more?" Kel'Gos approached, dressed in full tactical gear with a shotgun slung across his back.

"There's plenty of room, Director." The supposed driver offered a quick salute, standing down when the brown orc waved it away.

"Good." Kel'Gos pulled himself inside and took a seat next to Ray.

The team piled in and the rear doors sealed as the engine roared to life.

Feeling the first sign of movement the old orc surveyed those around him. They were all quiet, awaiting whatever hell was going to unleash within the next thirty minutes. Quietly, he retrieved an audio recorder from one of his pockets. "Ray, I'm going to need you to state your name and ID number for the record. Are you okay with that?"

"Yes s—. I am." Ray fixed the buckles as Crum had shown him the night before. He was nearly ready, he just needed to add the last few elements to his ensemble. Unlike the others, his flak jacket read *US Marshals* across the chest and back rather than *WMD* as the others had. He knew there were a few deputy marshals here and there, though as far as he could tell they weren't stationed within the WMD and likely had no knowledge beyond the Veil. He needed to ask Roderick about it when time permitted.

Pressing the record button, the older orc held the device in front of him and began speaking clearly and concisely. "This is Director Kel'Gos of Tactical Divisions within the WMD. The day is Sunday, September 30th, 2019, at approximately eighteen-thirty. We're en route to the estate of one Mister Thomas Ezekiel for the purpose of serving a search and seizure warrant along with apprehension of

Mister Ezekiel himself. With me and serving as liaison to the United States Government is US Marshal Rayford Scott Bradley." Kel'Gos signaled Ray to speak.

"Marshal Bradley. ID eight-six-seven-seven-six-seven."

"This recording will continue until the estate has been secured."

Chapter 22
Collateral Damage

Aside from the engine's hum and the roar of knobby tires on pavement the ride was deathly quiet. Nobody said anything. They'd heard it all before, many times in fact. The briefing left no detail unattended.

Ray mentally recited the floorplan, now converted to memory though by no choice of his own. He wondered how many of the others were doing the same. The combination to the office safe rang out in his mind. Today it would all be over. He couldn't help but think about what came next. Would the WMD and all those living on the other side of the Veil disappear back into the shadows? Would the Veil itself start to heal once the threat of Pandora was contained? Would it force him back to the other side? Or was he truly a believer now, stuck between both worlds? This was the day all those questions would be answered. But first they had to deal with Ezekiel.

"Arriving in thirty seconds." One of the men up front announced.

Seeing the others chamber their weapons Ray grabbed the M4 carbine Crum had picked for him. It took him back to his days in the sandbox. The anticipation, the growing anxiety, the fear of the unknown. He hoped it would be an easy bust. Quick in and quick out. Unfortunately he feared otherwise. Security was too heavy, too tight. Ezekiel wasn't going to go down without a fight.

Ray felt more than heard them come to a stop and the rear doors flew open. An army of trained soldiers wearing WMD across their gear rushed passed, out of view.

"Let's do this, boys." Kel'Gos picked himself up and jumped out the back doors, joining the flood.

Ray was quick to follow, shortly behind Crum. He couldn't help but feel like Crum was guarding him. The orc could have easily left him in the dust. Instead he walked just fast enough for Ray to keep pace.

"We've got a warrant. What do you mean we can't go in?" Kel'Gos asked, his deep voice carrying over the pounding of boots on concrete.

They weren't close enough to the compound for it to be the guards. Who had the authority to tell them no?

"I don't give a damn who authorized it. You're not permitted to operate without sanction. All operations go through us!"

Ray stepped through the path Crum had made, coming up behind Kel'Gos. "What's going on?"

Kel'Gos glanced at the human and grabbed his phone. It looked like an old gray brick with about a mile of antenna protruding from the top. "He says they have a UC inside."

Ray studied the man for a moment. He couldn't help but feel he'd seen him somewhere before. Suddenly it dawned on him. This was the guy driving the day he'd discovered Lilian under the bridge. He was frozen. If Lilian was the one inside how were they going to move without her getting caught in the middle of it? He wanted to ask but the answer was scarier than the uncertainty.

"Yes sir! I understand sir. But—" Kel'Gos glanced at the van the man had come from. "Yes sir!" Turning to the man in front of him he put his phone away. "You have five minutes. Whether they're out or not, we're going in."

"Understood." The man climbed back into the van, leaving the door open. Taking a seat, he placed a pair of thick headphones over his ears and began typing.

Studying the interior, Ray couldn't help but notice it was eerily similar to the surveillance van he'd been in the night before. There was less room in this one, set up for two, maybe three people tops, but it had just as many screens and boards doing all kinds of things he could only speculate about. Subconsciously Ray pulled his phone. There were no notifications telling him Lilian hadn't responded yet.

Kel'Gos counted down the time on his watch. "Five—four—three—." Raising his hand, he gave the signal when it hit zero.

One of the forward trucks equipped with heavy armor and a huge bull bar started down the drive into the complex. Several soldiers fell in behind, marching discretely toward the gate.

Doing likewise, Ray took position with Kel'Gos and Crum as they neared.

The truck picked up speed and rammed directly into the gate, battering it open. Gunshots echoed.

Strategically the footmen swarmed around the truck, targeting the guards. Distant gunfire echoed from the south side of the property and a voice came through the comms. "Mission leader, the rear gate is breeched."

Kel'Gos grabbed his radio. "Breech at the front. Move in!"

Guards fired from windows and doors and behind trees. Any place they could get a shot they took it.

Seeing one of the armed men between two stocks of an Adonidia palm, Ray took aim and released a three round burst. The man hit the ground. Amidst all the excitement a strange sensation overcame him. He was hearing the echoing pops all around, though not through his own ears. He was someplace nearby, out of sight, though far from safe. He could see a phone in front of him. It wasn't his own. Feminine thumbs quickly typed out a message. Ray tried to focus through the haze. It was difficult to see, like he was staring through a blurry fog. Squinting, he could just barely make out the words. *Run! The place is going to—*.

Returned to his own surroundings, a vibration in his pocket called to him. A quick look around told him he had enough cover to check it. Ray snatched his phone seeing a text from Lilian. Opening it, the message he'd witnessed being typed displayed warning. It was the final word that demanded attention.

—blow!

Panic erupted inside him. Locating Crum, Ray found him near the far side of the roundabout drive. Kel'gos, along with several others were approaching the steps that led up the front patio. "Crum!"

The green orc fired a few more shots at one of the upper windows.

"Crum'Bul!" Ray screamed again, feeling the strain in his voice.

Turning back, the orc located the source of his name.

Ray waved vigorously demanding he fall back. "The place is going to blow!"

"What?"

"The place is going to—"

The shockwave sent Ray flying backward. He slammed into the grass and rolled end over end more times than he could count. A loud ringing echoed in his ears and his vision went black. He could feel people touching him though he wasn't sure who. Slowly peeking beneath his eyelids, blinding light overpowered his senses. Towering shadows hovered over him. He could hear them talking though their words were muffled, distant.

"Oun ohh eor hu. oue any fungers mam ey oledn up. Uro ou all right, sir?"

Slowly, the shadows came into focus and Ray was able to make out the faces staring at him. Straining, he tried to pick himself up.

"Slow down. You got blown back pretty hard."

It hurt all over, though he wasn't exactly sure where all over was. It was safer to say everything hurt. Breathing heavy, Ray finally managed a thought. "Where's—" He had to pause to take a breath. "—Where's Crum?"

"Don't worry about that right now, sir. Are you okay?"

Despite the pain, Ray twisted around and started to push himself up. His eyes fell on the aftermath of the explosion. A flaming pile of scattered rubble was all that remained where the mansion used to be. Debris littered the ground as far as the eye could see. Paramedics and flashing lights filled every open area. There were more gurneys than people, though not by many. More than he cared to witness were loaded with black bags zipped to the top. "Where's Crum?" He repeated.

"Agent Crum'Bul is— I don't know how to tell you this sir."

Ray winced, getting his knees beneath him. Somebody, he didn't know who, helped him to his feet. "Spit it out!"

"Crum'Bul is on his way to the hospital. He's under critical condition. We don't know if he's going to make it."

"What about Kel'Gos?" Ray limped toward the destruction. After about his third exhausting step, he felt something crunch beneath his foot. Glancing down, he found his cellphone. The screen was shattered but it was still backlit. Carefully trying to keep his balance, he picked it up.

"Kel'Gos is gone. He was too close to the blast."

Ray shot around glaring at the man who'd delivered the news. He looked young, though his pointed ears told him he was likely older than every human he knew. "You're sure? He isn't just missing?"

"Unfortunately."

Ray's phone rang, though the tones were distorted. He stared blankly at the dancing device, surprised it still worked. Unable to swipe the screen he pressed the button on the side hoping the other features were still useable. "Hello?"

"Are you the one who's been snooping around my place?" The voice was smooth and powerful. Ray couldn't place the accent but he knew he'd heard it before.

"If I am?"

"You've cost me quite a bit of money over the past few days. I want it back."

It was all he could do to contain his anger. Kel'Gos was gone. Crum was in critical condition. Lilian was inside when it happened. There was no telling how many were dead. This guy had literally taken everything away from him and all he cared about was his money. The only thing that kept him in check was the fact this phone call was likely the last piece of evidence he'd get. He'd need it to track him down and put a bullet between his eyes. "You blew up your place. Not me."

"Semantics. I'm willing to work out a trade."

"A trade for what?"

"Your girlfriend, of course. You want the girl. I want my money. Five-hundred-million cash delivered to the South Florida Container Terminal, D7."

"How do I know she's still alive?"

"Ray?" Lilian's voice echoed through the phone.

"Lilian! Where are you? Are you okay?"

"Ray, don't—"

"You have twenty-four hours!" The call ended.

Taking a deep breath, Ray stared intently at the broken screen. There was no way he'd be able to get that much money in his life, never mind by sundown tomorrow.

"Sir, we really should get you to the hospital and have you checked out."

"There's no time." Ray turned, limping toward the broken front gate. It took longer to get there than he preferred but there was someone he needed to talk to. Locating the ICPC surveillance van he approached the man who'd been inside. "Lilian's alive."

"What? How?"

"Do you have any way to tap into my phone and find the location of the last call?"

"Jesus!" He took the shattered device, inspecting it. "Maybe. We won't know unless we try. Though if it came from Lilian's number it won't work. Her phone is custom made with no GPS tracking capabilities. It'd be like tracing a landline. Without the call being active there's no way to guarantee a location." Plugging it into his system and tapping away on keys the display appeared on screen.

Ray wasn't sure what he was doing. It was happening faster than he could comprehend but it was clear that Lilian's phone had been the last to call. He sighed, faced with the most recent on the long list of dead ends.

"Here he is, sir." A voice called from the rear of the van.

"Bradley! I got here as fast as I could. What the hell happened?" Roderick spoke louder than required, stepping around the door. Glancing into the back of the van he noticed the technician. "Who's this?"

"He's ICPC. I just got a call from Ezekiel. Lilian's still alive. He want's five-hundred-mil in exchange for her."

Roderick stared him up and down, surveying the battered detective turned marshal. "I don't have the juice to pull that kind of cash, son."

Ray stared into his eyes, allowing his rage to flash to the surface. It wasn't rage toward the old marshal turned politician. No, this was a rage of passion. It was personal now. "They killed Kel'Gos. Crum is lying in a hospital bed, likely to die any minute. I need this, sir. I need to kill this motherfucker!"

"I understand, son. Kel'Gos has been a friend of mine longer than you've been alive. I want him just as bad as you. Unfortunately our hands are tied. Do you recall that code Kel'Gos mentioned a few days ago? Code thirty-five-twenty-one."

"Vaguely. It was something unknown if memory serves."

The old politician nodded. "Not anymore. It's an archaic *Do Not Apprehend* status. Some extremely influential people reached out to me. I have direct orders to stand down on this investigation."

"What? Fuck that! This guy's going to pay!" Ray was livid. How could they simply turn their backs on what was happening? This guy was responsible for so much pain, so much death. There was no way he could let it go.

"Listen, son. I understand your position, I really do. But I need you to understand that going in halfcocked is a surefire way to get yourself killed. I cannot sanction it. But I also cannot stop you. Therefore, I urge you to do what you've got to do. Just do it with your head. Not your heart."

"I don't even know where to begin. We know he was home. We know Lilian was inside. How did he get out? The floorplans don't show a basement. Hell, I don't even know if he can build one. I've suspected something underground for a while but everything I've seen says it would take a lot of time and money. Even then it's not guaranteed.

"He's an elf. He has time. And he clearly has money. The way I understand it you breeched this question with Kel'Gos a few days ago. You're a detective. If you have a hunch he's underground there's a reason for it, wouldn't you say?"

"I suppose so. But how? Even if we clear away all that rubble—" Ray gestured to the smoldering cloud billowing from the piles of wood, stone, and bodies. "—even if we find an entrance, how am I going to locate him before he kills Lilian?"

"Son, I was doing this job long before you came along. Over the years I started to notice a pattern. In nearly every case I worked the initial evidence always told a story. You don't always notice it upon first glance. Like everything perspectives change. If I were in your shoes, and I was not long ago, I'd review the initial reports again. See if there's anything you missed."

Ray nodded. There wasn't anything else to say.

"Come on. I'll give you a lift back to the office. But I want you to promise me you'll swing by the medic. Let them give you a good once over. I can't have my replacement dying from internal bleeding a week after I sign him."

The thumping tick of a clock echoed in the quiet exam room. Ray flipped the page and continued scanning the contents. He recalled reading it before, a few times in fact, but it felt fresh. He was undecided if it was due to Roderick's advice or that so much had happened since then. Either way it was almost like he was seeing it for the first time. In a way he was. When he'd agreed to take the case it had been for the purpose of finding Crum. That purpose had shifted.

Hearing the door open, Ray closed the file and looked up at the doctor who had tended him.

"Good news, Mister Bradley. There's no lingering damage we can see. It'll take a few days for your hearing to return to normal, and I can't promise you won't be sore for a while but barring any infections you'll make a full recovery. I've taken the liberty of filling a prescription for you." She tossed an orange bottle with a white cap to him.

Instinctively, Ray caught it, wincing at the sudden pain. "Thanks." He read the label and glanced up at her. "Eight-hundred milligram Ibuprofen? Couldn't have sprung for something a little stronger?"

"I could have. I won't. The way I understand it you're still working. It's hazardous enough out there. So unless you want to be placed in off duty status, I refuse to accept responsibility for giving you anything that might further jeopardize your reaction time."

"Understood, Doc. Am I free to go?"

She nodded and opened the door. "Be safe out there. There's been enough casualties already.

"Yes, ma'am." Ray grabbed the file and stepped into the hallway. A nurse pushing a cart loaded with insulated containers forced him to jump aside, which hurt. Ray couldn't help but notice the handwritten name on one of the labels. He hadn't thought much about Crum being here. He'd forced himself not to. Worrying about Crum would distract him from what he had to do. Unfortunately seeing his name forced it upon him. Taking a deep breath, Ray followed, seeing her turn into one of the surgical rooms.

Ray approached the tempered glass and peered through. He was surprised they didn't have curtains or blinds preventing witness but the WMD was big about transparency. Ray watched a team of doctors and nurses hard at work. There was no mistaking the large orc laying on the table, though his usual intimidating demeanor was absent. He was utterly helpless, lying there with pieces of his body being explored and worked on.

Hearing the door open Ray glanced to his left seeing the nurse he'd followed step out, minus her cart.

She paused, looking at him before approaching. "Friend of yours?"

"Yes ma'am."

She was silent for a long moment, selecting the right words. "He has a collapsed lung, severe trauma to his right eye, multiple deep lacerations, and a ruptured spleen. I wish I could deliver better news but it's too soon. We're doing everything we can."

Ray nodded, unable to take his eyes off his friend. "I—I should have been right beside him. I—" He trailed off, lost in emotion. Turning away, Ray stared at the nurse for a long moment. "When he wakes up will you tell him I went to kill Ezekiel?"

"Um—okay?"

Without another word Ray marched past her, headed for the elevators.

Chapter 23
It's the Little Things

The radio was off. Ray couldn't remember the last time that had happened. Music was a part of the job. It was how he got into the zone. Even if it wasn't blaring the subtle beats calmed his mind. That wasn't the case this evening. He didn't want the distraction. He had one job to do and he was going to do it, clear headed, emotionless, and without hesitation.

Creeping past the decrepit buildings and refuse littering the street, Ray searched for the address. This was one of the few times in his relatively short career that a contact's name and location was openly included in the report. It simply didn't happen on the mundane side of things. Once another officer discovered who your informants were, they'd ride them into the ground. That was the key to good informants. You had to keep them to yourself. This was apparently not the case in the WMD. But then again there were far fewer agents in the discrete operation than in most precincts. That made for less competition and therefore easier working conditions.

Locating the faded numbers he'd been searching for, Ray pulled to the side of the road and parked his car. Normally in a place like this he wouldn't have considered leaving such a beautiful machine unattended but something told him it'd be okay. There was a calm over the area he hadn't felt elsewhere. It was almost as if a gentle music floated in the breeze, tugging at the anger burning inside him. It made him want to leave. He needed that anger if he was to succeed.

Unscrewing the lid to his medicine, he swallowed two of the large pills and climbed out. Glowing eyes peered from every shadow, nook, and cranny in sight. He wasn't alone though none stepped into view. He was an outsider here, a visitor who didn't belong, but that wasn't going to stop him. He needed information and he was going to get it one way or another, haunting music be damned.

The building looked like it had once been a restaurant or convenience store of some kind. It was clearly unfit for the job now but the red and white striped awning and painted cinderblock walls, albeit stained from dirt and despair over the years, retained that quaint charm such ma-and-pa shops often held. The windows were still present though each was cracked thoroughly, the broken pieces held in place by generous portions of clear tape.

Pulling the door aside Ray stepped in hearing the overhead bell ding. The inside was filled with long banquet tables, the type he'd always seen at church functions when he was a kid. Several mismatched chairs, the majority being folding metal or sun-bleached plastic, were stacked neatly atop the numerous surfaces. This left the black and white checkered floor open and glistening from a thin layer of liquid that had mostly evaporated.

"The kitchens closed for the evening but something tells me you're not here for food."

Ray turned toward the low countertop seeing a man nearly two-foot taller than himself. His skin was sparkled and dark blue, nearly purple, and his pointed ears and iridescent wings were laid back at a strange angle reminiscent of an agitated cat's ears. Ray couldn't help but feel like it was a defensive pose though he had no evidence to support that theory. "You would be correct in that assumption. I apologize for the intrusion but I have a few questions to ask you."

The faerie studied the man before him. It was a quick glance, nothing too telling, but he stood to his full height having clearly measured him fully. "You're not from the WMD yet you carry fae magic. And judging by your line of sight I know you can see me for what I truly am."

"My name is Marshal Ray Bradley. You gave information to a friend of mine a little over a month ago. I wanted to ask you a few additional questions." Hearing something outside, Ray's attention snapped to the window. It was odd how the shadows seemed to move. He could see the glowing eyes just outside the edge of moonlight, yet when he focused they were gone.

"I remember the orc. If you're here for a follow up I'm afraid I have nothing to add."

"Then what you told him. Please, I need to hear it."

The faerie looked him over once again, studying more carefully this time. "You're in duress. How can a few words aid your situation?"

"Please, sir. The orc you spoke to, he's— he's in surgery right now. I need to find the man responsible and I think something you told my partner—my friend may be of help."

"Crum's in surgery?"

"He is. Please sir, I'm begging you. Any information you have might help."

Glancing out the window the faerie signaled and turned, disappearing into the kitchen.

Ray followed watching his beautiful wings shimmer. They moved so fast it was almost as if they weren't moving at all. His host nearly glided with each step, majestically celestial. Passing the threshold, the kitchen was messy but not dirty. Huge stock pots and stacked bowls covered every surface. Steam rose from a large tank, two blue flames burning beneath it. "What do you do here? I mean, I see it's a kitchen. I guess my question is who do you feed?"

Taking a seat near one of the walls the faerie looked around. "Everyone who comes. I serve breakfast between six and ten and dinner between four and eight."

"And you do this alone?"

"I have a few volunteers who help me occasionally but most of the time it's just me."

"And how many come per meal?"

"It varies day to day but it's usually about two-hundred per meal on average. Those numbers spiked nearly twenty-five percent over the last week though."

"Damn. You know, I'm sure the WMD would help if you asked. From what I've gathered they're willing to provide medical assistance and lodging for those who need it."

"They already help. They purchase much of the food I serve. That's why I invited you to speak. I consider Agent Crum'Bul a friend as well. He helped arrange the funding to make this place happen. For that, I'll answer your questions but please understand I'm doing so for him. Not for you. Though I fear I won't be as much help as you think. I've already given him everything I know."

"I understand. Can you please recap what you told him?"

"I was one of the first to report the abductions. I hadn't witnessed them myself but I knew something wasn't right. Faces whom I'd seen every day for months simply vanished. One or two is no big deal. Situations change or people move on. But those numbers kept growing. Eventually rumors began to spread that someone was kidnapping the homeless. There was no evidence of this of course. Then we started having unexpected visitors driving through. Mostly men but sometimes elves. They'd watch and study, never taking the time to stop. After a few weeks it became routine. Four or five would disappear within the next couple days after they came through. We started calling them the hunters."

"What about the drugs?"

The faerie shook his head, his nose wrinkling. "They've tried to deal here a few times but there's no money to be made. Like anywhere I suppose there's always a few who get hooked and want more, but the people here have nothing. They're defeated, unwilling to get up and build. Most who have that ambition left a long time ago."

"You said you had a spike within the last week. Do you know anything about that?"

"Several who'd disappeared came back. Most refuse to speak about it. The few who have are typically silenced by the others. They fear whoever took them is going to come again. I've had more than one warn me to watch my back. Apparently, my kind are highly sought after."

"And of those who returned. Do any of them remember being abducted?"

There was an awkward pause. Finally, the faerie continued. "I can only think of one but I doubt he'll tell you anything. He's refused to talk to anyone since he got back. I don't know how much you know about my kind but we're rather good at reading emotion. I could tell he was hiding something—something none of the others possess."

"Do you know where I might find this survivor?"

"His name is Girden Shodknot. He lives under a pile of garbage just east of here. But like I said, I don't think you'll get much out of him. He's likely to take one look at you and run. The way I understand it many of the slavers were dressed as you are now."

"I wish I had an option. I'm on limited time. Thank you for the information."

The faerie nodded. "If Crum survives please give him my regards."

"I will, thank you." Ray got up and made for the front door. Stepping outside, he saw the shadows retreat. Stealing a glance at his car nobody appeared to have touched it. Glancing east he noticed a rather large pile of refuse against an old privacy fence. That had to be it. Ray approached a piece of plywood that was wedged into the frame of some unrecognizable piece of furniture. That was the closest to a door he saw. Kneeling down, he gently rapped on the board and took a step back.

Hearing grumbling on the other side the wood began to rotate and a small burrow was revealed. What was even more surprising was the creature staring up at him.

"It's you!" The squeaky voice announced, throwing his stubby arms around Ray's legs in an affectionate hug.

"Um, hello?" Suddenly Ray remembered the gnome he'd consoled in the brothel a few days prior. "Are you Girden?" It was odd, trying to talk while the small being clung to his legs.

"You know my name?" Girden released and took a step back. "You wanna come inside. I don't have much but some tea, but you're welcome to it." Halfway through his makeshift door, the gnome stopped and turned to face the human once again. "Sadly, I don't think you'll fit. It's okay though. I can bring some tea out." His smile widened with the new thought.

"No, Girden, it's okay. I actually have a question for you. About the night you were abducted. Do you remember what happened?"

The friendly smile faded and the gnome seemed lost in his own mind. "You wanna talk about that?"

"I'm sorry to ask you to recall such painful memories but I'm afraid I have to insist. Some friends of mine are in danger. I can't help them without knowing what you know."

Girden glanced around. "Come with me."

Ray had to take half steps to avoid running over the child-sized creature. Every time they neared a shadow it seemed to flee to another darker area. "Girden, can you tell me why the shadows keep moving?"

"Don't worry about them. They're just trying to see what's going on."

"What are they?"

Girden stopped, turning to look at his friend. "Dark elves, of course. But don't try to play hide and seek with them after dark. They win every time." Seemingly content in his answer he turned and continued along the narrow alley between shacks and rubble. Finally, after several minutes, he came to a stop at the entrance of what looked to have been an old abandoned mall.

Ray was taken back by the sight. It may as well have been a city. An undercity anyway. Elves, both dark and otherwise were watching from all directions. The numerous shops, that at one time had been full of life, were cluttered with discarded and broken furniture and serving as homes. This was a community if ever he saw one. The population seemed to be mostly elves but there were several gnomes and faeries as well. In some cases entire families huddled together. There was only one orc as far as he could see. Ray prayed it wasn't the gray one who'd nearly killed him. If it was, the brutish creature didn't bother getting out of its La-Z-Boy recliner. It simply watched him walk by, glaring the entire time. "Where are we going?"

"Just this way." The gnome hurried up a stationary escalader and across the overlook. Much of the safety glass was busted out leaving metal poles where it had been braced. They continued around the upper level and down another inoperable escalator into what might have been a food court. It was hard to tell without the numerous signs, but the walls were discolored above each of the many alcoves and the floor was littered with broken machinery and items typically found in a kitchen. Finally, the gnome turned and rushed under a security grille that was stuck near the midway point.

"What are we doing here?" Ray asked glancing around. Nobody appeared to have followed but they were still being watched.

"I brought you here so we could talk without nosey people listening in."

"Is it safe here?" Ray glanced at the skylight overhead. The moon wasn't quite full but its glow illuminated much of the central area within the mall. There were still plenty of shadows but not near the extent he'd seen outside. Even the moving ones were keeping their distance now.

"Safer than outside. The hunters haven't been back since you freed us but everyone's been on edge. We have guards in here. They'd rather die than let the hunters grab any more of us." Girden took a deep breath, thinking about his own predicament.

"Is that how you were captured? Were you grabbed by the hunters?"

"No." The gnome slowly shook his head. "I was taken in a much scarier way."

"How so?" Ray couldn't imagine what was scarier than being kidnapped. At least not being abducted. There were much scarier things that followed. The gnome was living proof of that.

"I was minding my own business. Out having fun and exploring. I found this really cool place where a bunch of water went into this really big building. The guy who found me kept smiling but it wasn't a nice smile. He told me I was in a lot of trouble and that I would wish he killed me. He was right."

"Can you tell me what happened? Do you know where you were exploring?"

"I already told you. I was exploring this really big cave. It went down a long way and I could hear the rumble all around me. Cars were driving by. It was really cool."

"And then what happened?"

"There was this path off to the side. I got on it since the cars were honking at me. There was some stairs and the floor was springy. Not like a trampoline but like on a bridge when the wind blows really hard. I was taller than most of the cars so I sat down to watch them for a bit. I don't know why but when I leaned against the wall it opened and I was laying inside a small room with buttons on the wall.

"Like an elevator?"

"I guess. I don't think I've ever been in one of those, so it could be. Anyway, I wanted to know what the buttons did so I pushed them. And then the wall in front of me opened and I was in an even bigger cave. The one with the big building and the water. There were these tall pipes coming out the top with thick clouds of white smoke and in the middle of the river there was this big spinning wheel. The water would hit it and spiral down into the center. Then it would come out of other pipes and shoot back into the river. I wanted to jump in and see if it would shoot me out too but it was spinning really fast and I got scared."

"Go on." Ray urged, feeling the gnome was getting somewhere. At the very least his story sounded like a water treatment plant. That sounded about right for siphoning Pandora from the water supply.

"I was getting cold standing next to the water so I went into the building. It was really boring in there. Most of the doors were locked and the ones that weren't had a bunch of boring stuff, like tables and medicine and machines without any buttons. I did find one cool room though. It had a big window staring down at the water and a bunch of buttons and switches. I started playing with them and these red lights started to flash and the water stopped shooting out of the pipes. People came running in and yelling at me. I tried to hide under the big table with all the switches but they found me." Girden was nearly in tears, as if he were reliving the experience. "They put a bag over my head and when they took it off I was in a small room and chained to the floor. The mean smiling guy came in and told me what I told you. And then he stuck a needle in my neck and I woke up on a bed with some guy I didn't know on top of me."

Ray was silent for a long while, watching the gnome wipe his tears away. "Thank you for telling me. I'm sorry you had to experience that."

Girden sniffed, though he didn't say anything.

"I need to find this building. Can you tell me how to get to the first cave? The one you were walking in with the cars driving by?"

"There are two of them, right next to each other. I think it was called Port Dodge or something like that. There were a bunch of signs but they're all boring and green. I don't like boring signs."

"The Port Miami Tunnel?"

"I think one might have said that."

"Thank you, Girden. I hate to cut our visit short but I really need to check this out. My friends need my help."

"Just keep what happened to me from happening to anyone else."

"I'll do my best. Thank you again." Ray got up and made for the door. Stopping just outside, he turned back. "Hey Girden, did you happen to see any signs in the big cave where the building was?"

"Yeah. That one wasn't boring. It had a big snake on it."

"Thank you. I know you probably like living here, but if you go to the WMD I'm sure they can help you. They're friends of mine."

"Oh? I guess I can talk to them. My cousin works there but I never thought about it."

Ray nodded. "Take care of yourself, Girden." Turning, he rushed toward the mall's exit as fast as his sore muscles would carry him. He wasn't sure how the locals would respond without a guide but with any luck he'd get out without any issues. It was getting late and he needed to handle a few last-minute details before heading into the underbelly to face the beast.

The Port Miami Tunnel was much different on foot than it had been by car. It had a strict thirty-five mile-per-hour limit but that didn't make it feel any less intimidating.

It was approaching midnight and he was starting to hurt again. Retrieving the orange bottle from his pocket, Ray unscrewed the cap and tipped it back, swallowing another large white pill. It was times like these he wished he'd had a cigarette.

Forcibly pushing the thought from his mind, Ray continued along the railed walkway. Already he was questioning the gnome's recount. He was nearing the midway point and hadn't seen one set of stairs, though there had been a few doors. Initial inspection showed they were no more complex than some kind of emergency exit leading to an insulated chamber with several stainless-steel doors inside and lots of exit signs. Though without walking it there was no way to be certain where it came out.

Sighing, Ray leaned against the wall and wiped the sweat from his forehead. It was remarkably hotter in the tunnel than he'd realized, even with the overhead fans every so often. He was rapidly feeling tired and the painkillers weren't doing much of anything as far as he could tell. A car flew past and the floor bounced slightly. That reminded him of what Girden had said. Something about a springy floor.

With renewed vigor, though far from maximum, he began searching the wall behind him. It was comprised of several concrete slabs that ran from floor to ceiling. Feeling his way along, the ground became more springy, noticeable only when a car passed. He had to be getting close. Suddenly, the texture changed. It was no longer the coarse grit he'd expected. This was smoother, more like a hard rubber or even plastic. It still looked the same as far as he could tell but it certainly didn't feel the same. Carefully, Ray pushed against the odd slab feeling it sink slightly.

An audible click echoed inside and it slid out of the way granting access to a wide corridor that ended at a set of elevator doors. Ray glanced around, searching for any form of surveillance. The tunnel was too large to know for sure but the gnome had made it undetected. With any luck he'd be able to do the same.

Ray stepped inside, feeling the floor plate sink under him and the door sealed itself behind him. Red lights flashed into view, illuminating the short passage. The walls were simple, using the same concrete slabs outside. An interesting thought came to him. If the same materials had been used, who was to say this hidden passage and whatever secrets lay at the bottom weren't part of the tunnel planning from the start? There had been quite a bit of cloak and dagger stuff surrounding the tunnel project, including a lot of money funded by private contracts.

Shaking his head, clearing the concept away, Ray pressed the button outside the elevator. Even if his gut was right, and it usually was, now was not the time for unraveling greater mysteries. He had one job to do. Find Lilian and put a bullet in Ezekiel's head. The doors opened and Ray stepped inside.

It was a long and dreary ride and Ray wasn't quite sure where he was going, but it was clear he was moving. It felt like a downward motion though the sudden forward jolt caught him off guard. He suspected the elevator might be traveling more at an angle instead of straight down. Finally, it came to a stop and the doors opened.

A cool breeze washed over him. Staring out into a massive cavern, Ray was at a loss for words. It was much larger than anything he'd imagined. Another discrepancy with the gnome's tale. How could someone so small leave out such a major detail. Moreover, the building and river were nowhere in sight.

The thought triggered something he'd completely overlooked. Sight. He could see. Ray glanced to the ceiling far overhead. Light tracks ran both directions, hanging from embedded mounts. He stepped out of the elevator taking it all in.

The walls, floor, and as far as he could tell, ceiling weren't jagged or porous. Quite the opposite. They were smooth and solid almost as if they'd been melted or eroded somehow. A wavy texture wrapped rhythmically around almost like rings on an earthworm. Of course, this wasn't an earthworm hole. At least he hoped not. It would have been one huge worm. Maybe a graboid or sandworm. He'd seen some strange things over the past year. Neither could be completely ruled out.

Kneeling, Ray placed his hand on the floor. It was hard to see with the naked eye but there were wear marks where wheels had repeatedly traveled. That meant there had to be an access tunnel somewhere. If he could find it just maybe there was a way to call in some backup before the shit hit the fan. Suddenly he knew what the abbreviation Roderick had added to his phone meant, though it didn't do him much good now. His phone was broken and there wasn't much hope of getting a new one until this was over.

Ray got to his feet and closed his eyes. They wouldn't serve him. He needed his other senses. He could feel the breeze, though it was difficult to tell from which direction it was coming. Possibly both? There was too much space to make that determination. He needed some place with closer walls. Of course, if he had a cigarette it would be much easier. Just light it and watch which direction the smoke traveled. He silently cursed himself on two fronts. One for quitting. The other for reminding himself about it.

With that option out, sound was the only way to go. He could hear water echoing off the walls. Not just a little trickle so commonly found in caves. This was a raging flow, like that associated with a large stream or even a small river. His senses told him right though the echo made it hard to be certain. Still, he'd always trusted his gut and it had served him pretty well up until this point. His gut said it was right. Decided, Ray turned and made his way along the smooth tunnel listening for any change.

He walked for what had to have been a mile, maybe two. Girden hadn't said anything about all this walking, though the rushing water was getting louder. Ray rounded the bend, finally finding what he'd hoped to see from the start. It, like the cavern itself, was larger than he could have imagined. This section of the cave was much wider and more open than the tunnel he'd come from. The towering structure was embedded into the ceiling in places and stretched on for nearly as far as the eye could see.

Water poured from a large hole in the wall, shooting out with such force that it ran nearly horizontal before arcing down into the flowing pool. Ray couldn't see much of the river but what he could cut a deep ridged channel into the rocks before disappearing behind the massive structure.

The wall to his left had several metal doors embedded into the stone. It reminded him of the underground docks in Brussels, though these went all the way to the ground. If he had to guess it served as either a garage or a storage facility, possibly both.

One of the doors began to open and light spilled from beneath. Ray heard the sound of an engine start. Looking around, there wasn't anywhere to hide. There was too much open space to reach the structure and he couldn't rightly stay where he was. Even if whoever was in the vehicle turned the other way they were bound to see him.

With no other option, Ray rushed toward the opening door. Just before he reached it, he spun and slammed his back into the shallow corner of its neighbor. It wasn't much but it was the best he could do given the circumstances.

A flatbed truck pulled from the opening. It was loaded with plastic wrapped pallets and had the Anaconda Excavating logo on the door. To Ray's relief, it turned left and followed the road along the building. That answered his earlier question. Wherever it was going, that was the way to the surface.

The door began to close beside him. Ray waited for the truck to gain some distance. He'd gotten lucky the driver wasn't paying much attention. He didn't want to risk it by moving prematurely.

Seeing it reach a safe distance and with no time to delay, Ray wrapped the corner and ducked under the closing door with inches to spare. Instantly he realized that was a mistake. Ray stared helplessly at a warehouse full of workers and armed guards, many of which staring intently back at him.

Chapter 24
Belly of the Beast

Three scenarios flashed through Ray's mind, each one in elaborate detail and none better than the rest. First, he could fight. This was a poor option as he was outmanned, outgunned, and outclassed in nearly every way. A quick head count told him there were at minimum eight guards and twice as many workers in this area alone. There was no telling how many more were nearby. Any one of them could sound an alarm and call hell down upon him, likely resulting in the immediate execution of Lilian, as well as his own death.

Second, he could flee. This wasn't much better than the first idea and would likely result in the immediate sounding of the aforementioned alarms. To make matters worse it would also evoke any lockdown procedures, severely limit his options, and cause doors that might otherwise be open to barricade until his capture or death. There was also a fair chance they would execute Lilian.

And lastly, he could surrender. This was by far the simplest solution and the only one he could think of that would prevent alarms, locks, and Lilian's immediate death. On the other hand, there was no guarantee he'd be able to escape and exact his revenge. Nobody but a tormented gnome knew the location. That left exactly zero chance for any kind of rescue. They'd likely torture him which would definitely ruin his suit. Blood stains were a nightmare to get out and he'd lost enough of them in the past week alone. After all that unpleasantness they'd ultimately kill both him and Lilian and the bad guys would still get away. This wasn't even an option.

Decided, Ray broke into a sprint and ran straight toward the largest group of people he could see. He would have made the gunslingers of ole proud. The details were a bit hazy. Everything happened so fast. He wasn't sure if he'd fired the first shot or if they had, but his Colt was in hand and bullets were flying. If he was going down it was best to do so in a blaze of glory.

Powder exploded and rained down over the area. Ray duck behind one of many wrapped pallets awaiting shipment. Blue and pink tablets poured from the numerous holes riddling his cover. All things considered it wasn't the greatest protection. Bullets passed straight through without resistance but it obscured his location. That was better than nothing.

This particular load appeared to have just finished wrapping and hadn't been unloaded from the machine yet. Digging his loafers into the bottom run, Ray held tight to the wrapped plastic. Stretching as far as he could, though not so much as to expose himself, he pressed the muzzle of his pistol into the square green button on the control panel. The wrapping machine started to spin. It rotated slowly at first, picking up speed. Ray squeezed off two shots, dropping two guards. The roll of cling wrap was nearing. He dismounted just before it reached him. Hitting the ground, Ray sprinted as fast as his sore body would allow.

Flatbed trucks, empty intermodal haulers, cargo vans, and even a few motorcycles were parked here and there. Bullets whizzed past him. With nowhere to go, Ray aimed for the nearest truck. He dropped to his knees and half slid, half rolled, ducking beneath the frame.

It was a brand new white F350 with the Anaconda Excavating logo on the door and a glossy black flatbed. Popping up on the other side he rushed to shelter behind the driver's front tire. That was always the safest place when using a vehicle for shelter. It was a fair distance from the fuel tank and the solid engine was most likely to stop a bullet.

Hearing a pause in the symphony of gunshots, Ray stole a glance beneath the truck. Four sets of legs were slowly approaching. The way they moved suggested they were tactically trained. Two broke toward the rear, one down the center, and the last moved toward the front. They were going to flank him.

Taking aim at the central legs, though it was an awkward angle to be shooting from, Ray squeezed off a round. The pop was answered by imminent screams and the guard dropped to the smooth floor clutching his left shin. Ray would have shot a few more in the same manner except his slide was locked in the open position telling him he was out of ammo. The empty magazine hit the floor and Ray grabbed a fresh one from his waistline and slammed it into place. The flip of his thumb sent the slide rocketing forward and a new round was chambered.

Automatic fire peppered the truck and at least one of the tires began to hiss, rapidly deflating. Judging by the angle, Ray suspected the front right though he couldn't risk stealing a glance. He'd inadvertently cornered himself. The wounded guard, once he quit screaming about his leg, would be able to report his movement to the others. And considering he was effectively flanked, there was no place to go. He'd be shot the moment he tried to make a run for it. Whatever he did next would have to be extremely clever or it would all be over before he even reached Ezekiel.

Glancing around, Ray took a quick inventory of his surroundings. The warehouse was set up as a packing and distribution center. Aside from the various vehicles and numerous pallets awaiting shipment, several hoppers hung from metal bracing in the ceiling. Each one was centered over what he guessed to be a bagging machine. It had a shoot at the top and several discs with conveyor belts and trays. Beneath that was a cylinder with empty bags and another conveyor assembly under that. For the most part he wasn't seeing much he could use, though a thought came to mind.

Locating the hopper nearest the truck's rear, Ray took aim at the control arm. It was a simple rod that had a spring on one side and ran to an actuating roller at the top of the bagging machine. Steadying himself, he squeezed the trigger. His bullet hit just left of its mark.

He could hear staggered footsteps behind him. The guard at the front was near the hood. Just a few more seconds and he'd be out of time and options. There was just enough for one more shot. If he missed this time it would be game over.

Lining up, remembering his coaching, Ray took aim and forced his breath to calm. His heart pounded in his chest making it the hardest aspect to control. Seeing where he needed to hit, he exhaled and fluidly squeezed the trigger. He was out of time. If he waited to see the result he was dead.

Ray twisted on his backside and kicked hard against the chrome covered wheel, sending himself backsliding away from the truck. To his surprise, the guard was right there. He'd climbed over the hood and was staring down where Ray had been just a moment before. Weapon in hand, Ray placed two well aimed shots under the towering guard's chin.

A loud commotion echoed near the flatbed and the front guard collapsed, tumbling off the hood, over the extended bumper, and to the floor.

Rolling from his slide, Ray flipped to his stomach and took aim on the massive pile of chalky blue tablets mounted over the machine and the previously empty flatbed. The rear guards, if they'd been there, were unseen, trapped somewhere beneath the growing heap. Ray wasn't sure if it was enough to kill them but it would certainly take some time to dig out. With any luck he'd be long gone before that happened.

A bullet pinged off the hubcap. It destroyed the mirrored finish and ricocheted narrowly missing him by an inch. He searched for its source acutely aware he was in the open. The angle suggested it was somewhere to his right and elevated. Another round of automatic fire rang out and bits of stone and dust exploded around him. He knew where that one came from.

Rolling to his side, Ray fired beneath the truck silencing the already wounded guard. He didn't overly enjoy having to put the man down, but he couldn't risk letting him fire again. This was a game of life and death. There were only winners and losers. Cheating or cheap shots didn't exist.

A burning pain erupted long before he heard the shot. Ray instantly knew he was hit. He didn't know exactly where or how many times but there was no denying it. Someone had gotten the drop on him. The trouble was he still didn't know where they were. There couldn't be more than one or two of the local guard remaining. Though with all the gunfire, he'd be surprised if more weren't on the way, if not already here.

Seeing no alternative, he forced the pain aside and dug his knees and elbows into the hard floor. Crawling as fast as his injured body would allow, Ray twisted and aligned himself to the flatbed, rolling beneath a second time. Bullets struck all around him, blowing stinging chunks of concrete into his skin. How he hadn't been hit more than he already had, he couldn't answer. Under cover, Ray checked his perimeter in search of any ground level hostiles.

Most of the workers had already cleared out and to his surprised no audible alarms had sounded. That didn't mean anything though. Just because there weren't flashing lights and sirens didn't mean his presence was unknown. He'd never encountered a security team that didn't have radios. For all he knew reinforcements were already here and he was down more than half his ammo minus one. The final bullet was reserved for Ezekiel. He only hoped they hadn't killed Lilian yet.

The stone floor chipped away to his left. Ray was able to see the bullets bounce toward the front. That confirmed his theory. The shooter was toward the rear of the truck and somewhere up high. A ground level shot would have had more of a glancing ricochet than a solid hit and bounce. He was dealing with a sniper type, though clearly a poor one. When he was in the army, if a sniper set his sights you were dead before you knew he was there. On the other hand, this left him in a difficult situation. Both sides of the truck would be in clear view and the rear was blocked by the spilled drugs. That left only one option and the least favorable among them.

Gritting his teeth, Ray rolled to his back. He now realized most of the new pain was coming from his legs. Three bullets, maybe four. One was just below his left butt cheek and two, maybe three, in his right leg though he still didn't know exactly where. There were also a couple grazing wounds along his right arm and at least one burning spot on the right half of his ribcage.

Forcing the pain aside, Ray arched his back and kicked with his heels. It hurt tremendously but he had to do it. Back crawling, he twisted and pushed again making his way toward the nose of the truck. The underside of the engine compartment and front axle passed overhead, dragging against him with almost no room to move. He was happy the driver's side tire remained inflated. If it hadn't been, there wouldn't have been room to pass. Most grating of all, there was no such thing as a clean undercarriage. If his suit hadn't been ruined from blood and bullet holes the grease guaranteed it was now.

Breaking through, he grabbed hold of the front bumper and pulled himself the rest of the way out. It hurt less than twisting. Ensuring he was still hidden from the overhead shooter. Ray realized he was in a new predicament. The moment his head popped into the open he would have a fraction of a second to locate and eliminate the threat before it eliminated him. He had to find *and* eliminate at the same time. One without the other was folly, especially considering a good sniper would move the moment location was established.

Ray locked eyes on the dead guard beside him. He desperately needed resources. Unfortunately he couldn't just drag the body into cover with him. To do so would give away his position. There was another option though.

Ray fell onto his back and stretched toward the dead guard, instantly regretting the decision. Blinding pain erupted in the left side of his face. His hands locked over the wound and he curled at the waist, hissing in agony. It took several long moments to calm himself and get his body under control. Those were several moments he didn't have.

Opening his eyes he was startled to realize he only had vision out the right side. Moreover, he'd dropped his gun near the dead guard's feet but at least he himself wasn't dead. Not yet anyway. Ray located the fresh gouge in the truck's hood. All things considered he'd been extremely lucky. Such a shot should have finished him. From where he lay, it looked like the bullet had dropped just low enough to hit the truck instead of him. That didn't prevent the shredded metal from flying at him though.

More careful this time, knowing his position was made, Ray grabbed the guard's feet and drug both the body and his Colt toward him. Securing both his own and the guard's weapon, a CZ Scorpion 9mm pistol converted to full auto, Ray released the sling holding it to the guard's arm. Quickly, he went to work searching the numerous pockets for anything he could use.

Most of his findings were useless, at least under his current circumstances. There were two pair of rubber gloves, a book of matches, some nylon cord, and various trinkets he'd carried himself at one point in time. The bottom left pocket of the flak jacket proved to be more useful. Inside were two metal canisters, one olive drab with a white band and the other a light gray with red lettering. Both had pull rings and fixed levers.

It had been some time since he'd last played with either but there was no forgetting, especially the gray and red one.

It brought back many memories, most of them unpleasant. Ray tucked the M7A3 CS grenade back into the pocket and turned his attention to the other. Pulling the pin on the M18 he depressed the lever and rolled the smoke grenade under the truck, watching the billowing cloud engulf the area. He had no delusions it was going to limit any shot he could potentially take but it was more important to gain a strategic advantage.

Stripping his suit jacket, Ray wasted no time removing the guard's armor. He threw it around himself and buckled it into place as a rain of bullets cut through the fog around him, many hitting the truck in the process. He had only a few moments before the smoke would start to thin. That didn't leave much time to get into position.

Dropping the Scorpion's mag, Ray did a quick ammo check. The current magazine was a thirty shot and about half full. He found one additional mag in the vest, fully loaded with 9mm rounds tipped by a tapered shank. That sent a shiver down his spine. He hoped not everyone was sporting the same. If so, the armored vest was useless as was pretty much anything except an engine block.

Ray slipped the nylon sling around his arm and tightened it into place, testing his movement. He'd used similar weapons before but never one of these. Hopefully it was sighted halfway accurate.

Forcing a few quick breaths for preparation's sake, Ray rushed around the side of the truck and pulled the driver's door open. Bullets continued to blindly spray around him though their increasingly familiar sting was not felt. Weakly pulling himself inside, he closed the door and moved into position behind the flatbed's bulkhead. The rear glass had already been busted out. That was fortunate. It saved him from having to do it. Ray pressed his chest against the rear of the bench seat and extended the muzzle through the metal slots. Silently, carefully, he waited for the smoke to clear.

There was no wind in the warehouse. No ventilation ports aside from whatever fed the overhead hoppers. No large fans moving air. The temperature within the sub terrain system was comfortable. These factors made the smoke linger long after the grenade had quit burning, though it was now beginning to spread wide and thin.

Ray knew this was a game. The last game. Winner take all. Either himself or the shooter would come out the victor, and both were on borrowed time. His eyes scanned the upper level, searching through the cloud. He needed to find his target. A subtle movement, light reflected off a glistening bead of sweat, an untimely cough, anything that would betray location. He was restricted to the same. The very act of breathing was dangerous at this point.

He suddenly found himself wishing the guard had been carrying a bouncing betty. He'd seen the damage they could do firsthand, though it wasn't likely to do him much good in this scenario. Landmines were entirely different beasts than grenades. The German S-mine would have served him well when all this began. It was similar to a claymore mine in regard to an explosion that fired numerous ball bearings, but unlike the claymore's *FRONT TOWARD ENEMY*, the bouncing betty shot up about three feet and exploded out in all directions.

Ray stopped searching just long enough to consider the thoughts going through his head. These were thoughts of war. He wasn't a soldier any longer. He was a police officer, or federal agent more accurately. Why was he regressing? Was it because they'd struck first? Was it because they'd killed Kel'Gos, possibly killed Crum? Wounded him? Endangered Lilian? If this wasn't war, what was? There were still rules of engagement. There always were. That was what separated the good guys from the bad guys. The only exception was Thomas Ezekiel. By the end of this day he would die, be it in battle or execution. There was no negotiation on the matter.

With renewed focus, Ray's keen eyes searched the settling smoke. He was finally at a greater advantage than his target. Something dark caught his attention, something buried in the shadows.

A metal catwalk ran along the stone wall at the rear of the warehouse. He'd noticed the stairs leading to it before all of this started. Many of the workers had fled up them and disappeared, though a few ran for the overhead doors behind him. Where they'd gone from there, he couldn't say. None of that concerned him now. His target had been located.

The would-be sniper was hidden among the steel framework that braced the catwalk to one of the hopper systems. There was nowhere for him to move without climbing down. That was the only logical reason he hadn't done so. It didn't matter though. Not anymore. Ray had him in his sights.

Lining up, Ray pulled the trigger. The not-so-hidden guard released a final volley of shots and fell limp, dangling from his hiding place. It didn't last long. Gravity claimed him and he landed face first with a sickening thud on the stone floor.

Allowing himself to breathe, Ray relaxed against the glass covered seat. His left eye was swollen shut and he wanted nothing more than to take a nap. Unfortunately there wasn't time. Groaning, he pulled himself up and climbed out of the cab, realizing how much damage had been caused in the last few minutes.

Bullet holes and their debris were everywhere. All but the driver's front tire of the truck had been blown out. Even the metal bed which had shielded him so well was riddled with holes. It was a miracle he didn't have more holes in himself than he did. Stealing a quick glance in the driver's mirror, surprised it hadn't been shot out, he was pleased to see his eye wasn't as bad as he'd thought. It was swollen and bruised and there was a deep cut on his eyebrow, but it appeared the eye itself was relatively undamaged.

Slowly circling the truck, Ray noticed many of the workers huddled near the front corner, near one of the closed doors. Why they hadn't fled he couldn't say. Any one of them could have taken a shot at him and he wouldn't have been the wiser. So why were they cowering there?

They didn't look like much. Elves, one faerie, a handful of gnomes, all huddled together with fear on their faces. Suddenly he realized the slaves weren't limited to the casino. They were here as well.

Nodding his understanding, Ray turned away from them and limped toward the stairs. It took far longer to climb them than he desired but there was nothing he could do about that. Both legs were severely damaged. He was lucky he could even walk. Each step took tremendous effort but after a lot of swearing and a fair amount of grunting and hissing, he ascended the catwalk.

It was much larger than he'd realized. He'd assumed it was more of a supervisory position but now that he was here it served a more practical function as well. The warehouse had twelve bagging machines, each with its own hopper and conveyor system. The catwalk bridged them all. Moreover, two man-sized doors were set into the stone wall on the other side, above the bay doors. Ray wasn't thrilled with the new set of stairs that led to them, but he'd have to bear it. The fleeing workers who had run this direction had to have gone somewhere. That was the only logical direction. Ray sighed and started toward them.

These steps weren't any easier, but there were about half as many and the handrails were more comfortable to pull against. That relieved some of the strain. He was growing increasingly weak and the trail of blood that followed his every move told him he was running out of time.

The top ended at a narrow shelf with twin metal doors roughly twenty foot apart. It was an even guess as to which way to go. He was hugging the right side rail, that placed him a couple steps closer to that door. That's the way he went.

Reaching it after several long grueling minutes, Ray was pleased to discover it wasn't locked. He would have rather thrown himself over the railing than to traverse the steps again. Pulling it aside, he was taken back by the sights before him. He tripped, catching himself just enough to land on his back and knock the wind out of him.

Gasping for breath, he lay there, staring up at his surroundings. As far as hallways went it was relatively mundane. There were three wooden doors along both walls, each with a diamond shaped window toward the top. A final door at the far end was identical to the one he'd just fallen through. As for the floor where he lay, it was either a polished hardwood or a thick laminate that mimicked such. It didn't matter either way. He was bleeding all over it. What really caught his attention was directly above.

Ray stared intently at the ceiling. He was on the seabed of Biscayne Bay, peering up through thick domed glass. It was a spectacular sight. A school of blue and yellow fish casually swam overhead, disappearing in a hurry as a fair-sized bull shark came into view. There were a few boats leaving trails of white bubbles in their wake. A strange clicking grew distant as they passed. Several more boats floated gently where they were docked or anchored, though none overly close to where he was now. He was a little surprised nobody had reported the undersea complex from the surface. The water in the bay wasn't that deep, maybe twelve foot in most places. Something like that would have brought in some big money. Though the more he thought about it, it was probably hard to see. The reflection through the water would have caused quite a bit of distortion unless you were right on top of it. What really caught him by surprise though was the sunlight.

It was late when he'd started this little journey into the unknown and it hadn't felt that long ago since he'd entered the Port Miami Tunnel. That left only two answers. Either he was already dead and this was the afterlife, or it'd taken far longer to walk the cavern than he'd realized. Judging from the throbbing pain, as well as his need for air he suspected he wasn't quite dead yet.

Groaning, Ray forced himself to breathe and rolled to his stomach. Getting his arms beneath him he slowly pushed himself up and clawed at the wooden door to his right. It came open and he found himself in an office room with stiff blue carpet. It had the same glass ceiling as the hall but was overall just like any other office. It had a wooden desk, a few chairs, a shelf, and various odds and ends valuable only to their owner. The only thing he was pleased to see was a white metal box with a red plus fixed to the wall.

It took some effort but Ray managed to get to his feet. Opening the box he emptied the contents onto the floor and picked out what he needed. Judging by the entry and exit wounds, it didn't appear any of the bullets were still inside. That was good but it meant twice as much damage. There wasn't quite enough gauze to wrap everything, though at least he'd be able to slow the bleeding.

Ray used every drop of saline and packet of sterile wipes he could find. There was some peroxide but that was a last resort. It was good for cleaning but also had a tendency to inhibit healing. In truth, there wasn't much to clean. A little dried blood here and there but most of it was still fresh, flowing quicker than he could wipe it away.

Out of options, Ray folded one of the empty boxes and placed it between his teeth. He had no delusions this was going to hurt and the improvised bit gave him some comfort. Chomping down, he applied a moderate layer of antibiotic ointment to a wad of gauze and pressed it into the exit wound on his left thigh. He screamed, barely able to remain conscious. Labored breaths and rapidly beating heart blurred his senses but he had to keep going.

It felt like an eternity spent in hell by the time he got the last plug into place. Ray awoke on the floor, uncertain how long he'd been out. He was weak but the cold that had surrounded him was starting to feel distant. He glanced at the packaged wounds, pleased the puffy flesh around them had turned a deep purple rather than the pale white they had been. He was confused though. He didn't remember cleaning after the plugs or applying pads and tape.

"Ah, you're awake. I was starting to think that wasn't going to happen." The voice was calm, full of assurance.

Ray shot up, instantly wishing he hadn't. Instinctively he reached for his Colt. It wasn't there. None of it was there. He was in nothing but his blood-stained boxer shorts and bandages. Searching the room he found his gear, both original and borrowed, folded and resting neatly on a chair that had been overturned but now sat upright.

"I assure you, I intend no harm." The elf stated from behind the desk. His blue eyes were calm, calculating, studying the injured man before him. "Quite the contrary as it were." He stretched his arms behind his blonde head and leaned back in the chair. "You passed out before you were able to stop the bleeding. I took the liberty of finishing it for you. I also stitched your wounds and gave you a blood transfusion. It'll take some time to heal but you're further along that road than you were."

"What blood did you give me? I'm O-Positive." Ray's senses were beginning to focus. His disorientation fading. Soon he'd try to pick himself up.

A knowing smirk appeared on the elf's rapidly clearing face. "Elven blood is universal. If I'm being honest it's the only reason you're still alive. You'd lost too much by the time I found you."

"Do I know you? Your voice sounds familiar." Ray started to get up.

"We've never met before. My name is—"

"Frank Elliott!" Ray interjected, getting to his feet. He staggered toward his effects and grabbed his bloody pants.

"I—well—yes, but—"

"You're that wordy religious nut who's always on the radio. I can't check social media without your name appearing at least once."

The elf shrugged. "I suppose some of my messages receive more attention than others."

"What are you doing here?" Ray pulled his shirt into place and was working on the tac vest. "Why did you help me?"

The elf lowered his arms to the desk and interlocked his fingers. With a heavy sigh, he answered. "That's a more complicated answer. One might say I've been betrayed."

Ray froze, staring at the cunning elf before him. It was obvious there was much he wasn't saying. It seemed more an issue of how to say it. That was an oddity for one who made a living spewing bullshit.

"I assume you weren't alive in 1928."

"No."

"I was. I knew even then that I had a gift for communication. I could verbalize the most ridiculous concept and people would gather near and far to listen to me. It was only natural I decided to use my gifts to better my status in life. Up until that point I was little more than a street kid. That's how they perceived me anyway." The elf leaned against the rear of the chair a second time, getting comfortable in the recount of his tale. "I won't bore you with the details. I ended up at the head of a small gang during the height of Prohibition. And I managed to do so without spilling a single drop of blood. Needless to say, my status didn't last."

"That's a great story but confessions aside, I don't understand why you're telling me." Ray was growing increasingly suspicious. His gun was within reach, he had but to take it.

"I'm getting there. I need you to understand how things came-to-be before you can understand how they got where they are." He waited for Ray's consent before continuing. "The night everything changed, I was in negotiations to absorb a rival gang. Things went south. They killed my men and beat me to a pulp. As I lay dying in the sewer, this old orc approached. I remember staring up at him through swollen cheeks and gasping breaths. His face was grim and covered in scars. He had this— fire that burned in his cold gray eyes. It was a fire that had always eluded me. I'll never forget what he said to me. 'You can't keep what you have unless you're willing to fight for it. If you can't fight, you must instill such a fear that your friends and enemies alike would never consider trying.'—" The elf paused, thinking over the words he'd just uttered. "It took a few years but in time, with the help of my orc friend, I built one of the largest criminal empires this country has ever seen. I had my hands in everything. Hell, even Capone came to pay his respects and ask my advice once.

"We, my orc friend and I, carved out a piece of history for ourselves. I was the head. He was the body. Anytime someone thought they could cross us, he moved against them while I tailored the next piece on the board. We were ghosts. We ruled from the shadow, never lingering in one place longer than a few years. We'd claim power, put our people into place, and move to another. When one location would settle, we'd return and take it again. Tho'Mas—" He gestured elsewhere. "—and Ezekiel" He gestured to himself.

Hearing the name, Ray ripped his pistol from its holster. He spun, aimed, and pulled the trigger. The hammer fell and a resounding click trailed to silence. Ray stared helplessly at his gun. It had been unloaded and he'd just wasted his only chance.

Refusing to show the slightest hint of fear the elf reached into the central drawer and retrieved a handful of bullets. He placed them on the desk top for the human to see. "I need you to hear my story. If, by the end, you don't like what I have to say then by all means shoot me. But I believe we both have something to offer one another."

Eyes narrowed, Ray leaned against the desk glaring his hatred at the elf. Reaching out, he plucked the first bullet from the desk and loaded it into his magazine. "Get to the point quickly. You have until I've reloaded."

Ezekiel nodded. "Tho'Mas and I are at odds. We agree Pandora is useful. It weakens the Veil. When it falls magic will return. Our disagreements lay in what comes after. I want peace. I want to retire and live a life of solitude. To be left alone and to leave others alone. Tho'Mas desires one thing— War. He's from one of those old orc tribes. The ones that believed only the strongest have the right to rule. He has no appreciation for a strong mind, only a strong arm."

"Ten seconds." Ray prompted, still loading bullets.

"I'll face any judgment for my actions, but you'll need my help to get close to Tho'Mas. I cannot kill him. You can."

Ray racked his slide and took aim at the elf's face. "I have one very important question for you, Ezekiel. Consider it carefully. Your response will determine whether you live or die." He paused, letting the severity of the situation set in. "Is Lilian alive?"

The 95th District

Levi Samuel

Chapter 25
Head of the Snake

"You'd better not be lying to me!" Ray demanded, pulling the door open. Despite his anger and lingering pain there was no denying he was feeling significantly better. One could even speculate that he felt well.

"I'm aware of the seriousness of the situation, Mister Bradley. I have no reason to lie." Ezekiel marched through the door and turned right. Reaching the metal door at the end of the undersea hallway, he paused. "Be on your guard. I arranged the shootout in the warehouse to look like an unruly slave got the upper hand before meeting his demise, though I doubt Tho'mas will remain convinced. For all I know he still has guards searching the premises."

Ray nodded. He could hear a loud humming through the metal barrier which grew in intensity the moment the door was opened. Following his guide onto the elevated walkway, Ray paused, realizing they were suspended nearly fifty foot over a huge spinning turbine.

The walkway was little more than perforated mesh with steel reinforcement beams and a round tube railing that guarded the ledge.

"Remarkable isn't it?" Ezekiel smiled, overlooking the massive machine beneath them. "Three identical machines, each drawing clean water from the aquifer and aerating it to blend seamlessly with Pandora Type One."

From a series of pipes Ray watched the gushing water spill onto the back-spinning serrated blades. It swirled around creating a vicious looking whirlpool at the center. One set of blades rose and another retreated, sloshing the liquid back and forth as it went around. He could almost see particulates dropping into the glimmering trap beneath.

Hearing a buzz, a pink mist exploded from a series of sprayers and drifted down a top the agitated liquid. It disappeared no sooner than it touched the surface. There was no mistaking the smell. Ray had encountered it a few times before. Strawberries and sunshine, playing under a field tree in his childhood. It was the same memory he'd had when he tasted Pandora for the first time.

The sprayers quit and a beeping replaced the buzzing. Ray watched the dark and glistening tray under the drum start to collect water, spilling over the top. A set of arms rose up and separated into two long spikes that looked like the outer prongs of a fork. They closed in and latched onto the filter, plucking it from its frame. The filter spun out of its gap, slinging water back into the trough. From the other side a clean filter settled into place and the water began to pass once again.

"This is my favorite part." Ezekiel prompted, gesturing below.

Ray watched the automated arms carry it to a glowing orange box on the far side of the room. He could feel the heat even from where he stood. Bright blue flames erupted from the numerous port holes and sparks danced into the air around it. It took but a few seconds and the now glowing sheet dropped out the bottom, splashing into a basin beneath. It sizzled and cooled instantly, all the cooked resin separating and floating gently atop the surface. The now clean filter sank and settled onto a conveyor belt and was carried up and out, disappearing under another section of the machine.

Ray heard rattling and clanking echo through a square shaped duct running overhead and into the wall. He didn't have to ask to know a finished batch of Pandora tablets were traveling to the bagging hoppers in the other room.

"All that stuff floating on the surface is pure Pandora resin. From there it's transported to the ovens and baked into Pandora Type Two." Ezekiel said with pride in his voice.

"And what about all the people who've been hurt because of that shit? Did you ever once stop to think about them?" Ray turned away in disgust. "Quit bragging and lead the way. I still haven't decided if you've earned a bullet or not."

Ezekiel followed the path to the right, walking with confidence.

Ray stole a look behind them. The only people he saw were far below, tending the machines. If they knew of his presence they didn't show it. None bothered to glance his direction, even if they could see that far. A fair amount of steam rose from the hotbox, clouding the upper level. It was difficult to see a short distance ahead, let alone halfway across the factory.

The wall curved around and Ezekiel stopped at the second door on the right. Hesitating, he turned to Ray. "Beyond this point is mostly office space. We don't keep a large staff but we're bound to encounter at least a few innocents between here and our destination. I hope you're everything I've heard you are. Enough people have died already."

It was an odd request from the self-admitted criminal, one Ray had already considered. That was a major part of gun safety. Confirm your target before pulling the trigger. In a small way it almost humanized the monster before him. He'd said he wanted peace but up until this point it was only words. This request, at least on the surface, felt more than that. It was concern. A concern Ray struggled with every day he got up and put on the badge. He and his fellow officers went out and faced the scum of the earth on a daily basis. And most people hated them because of it. A simple nod was all he could manage. Anything more was liable to betray him.

Ezekiel opened the door. To everyone's surprise an elven guard was standing on the other side, hand extended toward the knob.

Recovering nearly as quick, Ray reached out and grabbed the guard's rapidly rising gun. Ripping it away he twisted and landed an elbow to his exposed head. The sudden movement hurt but not nearly as much as he'd anticipated. Whatever Ezekiel had done to him was working fast and effective.

The guard staggered back, his weapon no longer in hand.

Using the opportunity to his advantage, Ray shouldered Ezekiel out of the way and slammed the door in the guard's face. Bringing the stolen Scorpion to bear, he released a volley of bullets through the metal barrier. The armor piercing rounds penetrated with ease. Dropping the spent mag, he loaded the final one and slapped the bolt. It sprang forward, reloaded.

There was no telling how he knew. It could have been the sound of movement, or maybe a minute vibration in the mesh beneath his feet. It could have been anything. The only thing Ray knew for certain was the guard was not dead. He jumped sideways as three bullets tore through about knee level. Throwing his back against the wall between the door and Ezekiel, Ray raised the modified machine pistol and waited for him to emerge.

Like clockwork the door slowly opened. Primed and in position, Ray squeezed the trigger.

Seeing the gun, the guard shoved it from the bottom and a single round expelled, nicking the door.

To Ray's horror the bolt was locked to the rear and the mag slipped free, disappearing between the metal runs at his feet. Whether it was due to a loading error or the guard pulled the release, he couldn't say. Either were equally plausible. He'd lost a lot of blood and he wasn't feeling entirely himself.

A boot impacted his chest and Ray stumbled backward into Ezekiel. It took everything to maintain his composure, though he still had his wits about him. Discarding the useless weapon, Ray locked both hands around the guard's foot and rebounded. Shoving as hard as he could he ushered the unbalanced guard toward the railing.

The guard hopped, managing to keep his free foot beneath him. It wasn't enough. The rail impacted his grounded leg and it buckled.

Using the disbalance to his advantage, Ray released the foot and rapidly drew his Colt. He fired three rounds point blank into the elven guard's chest. The slide locked to the rear and the guard tumbled over the rail.

A sudden and unexpected jerk yanked Ray toward the railing. He struggled against the weight, dropping the nickel-plated 1911 in the process. It bounced near his feet, luckily too wide to slip through the gaps. Catching himself against the yellow painted tubing, Ray strained to hold himself up, staring down at the spinning turbine and the dangling guard beneath him.

The guard had a firm grip on the empty machine pistol tethered to Ray's arm. He silently cursed himself. Had he not attached the sling this would have already been over, but then again there was no denying the benefits the simple accessory provided. Seeing no alternative, Ray braced himself. "If you promise you won't shoot me, I'll pull you up."

A quick and unexpected knife slice answered his statement. Ray jumped back, avoiding the wild blade. He slipped between the rails and felt the pop as he slammed to the metal floor. The nylon strap was frayed, useless and ruined. Ray glanced down, seeing both the guard and the machine pistol disappear into the turbine.

For the brief second the elf was visible, Ray watched the dancing blades tear into his skin. His mutilated body was torn apart and gone before he had time to scream out. The gun on the other hand, while damaged beyond repair, danced around a top the spinning gears and sawing blades. Each time a piece caught it locked up and began to squeal.

Ezekiel approached the rail and stared down. "Do you realize what you've done?"

"I'm guessing your machine doesn't agree with metal. Tough shit. Keep moving." Ray snatched his pistol up and got to his feet, replacing the final mag. He had seven shots remaining. Gesturing toward the door, Ezekiel pulled it open and stepped through, clearly unhappy about whatever was happening below.

A harsh and loud thud echoed and the floor shook. Ray took one final glance at the seized turbine before stepping through the door. Whistles could be heard down below and numerous technicians—workers—slaves—whatever they were, rushed around trying to open valves and hit switches, each one searching for the source of the problem. Shrugging it off, Ray followed his guide into the complex interior.

The hall went on a short distance before they passed the first room. Ezekiel didn't appear to show any concern or worry. Ray on the other hand had his head on a swivel, searching every corner and doorway they came across. The last thing he wanted was another unexpected encounter.

Ray glanced into the room on their left. It had large windows on each side, those closest peering into the hall. The others faced the outside cavern wall. As far as he could tell there were two desks in the room. An older man, elven possibly, though his long brown hair covered his ears, and a female gnome with curly white hair looked up as they passed. Ray could see the fear in their eyes. They had every right to be afraid. Gunshots had just passed through this hall moments before.

The next opening was to the right. It was little more than a small kitchen area with a larger break room on the back side. It was clear there were other doors around the corner.

Ezekiel continued straight.

There were more people than Ray had expected, though no humans aside from himself. They passed numerous offices, most of them filled with boxes and file cabinets, though many had workers in them as well. What they were doing, he couldn't say. It looked like the typical everyday desk job. Only why an evil lair required office workers was beyond him.

Finally, after a mostly straight hall and a few zig zags, they were nearing the main control room. Flashing red lights and an annoying siren echoed just as they passed the threshold.

"God damn it!" Ezekiel sighed.

"What?" Ray looked around the large empty room. It was oval shaped and a wall of windows sat just over the control board which ran nearly the length of the room. He couldn't see the river from where he stood but the initial inlet was plainly visible.

"Those alarms only happen when one of the machines is malfunctioning. Your little stunt back there probably sheered one of the gears. That'll take months to fix."

"I don't give a damn about your machine! I'd destroy all three of them if I could. Now show me to Tho'Mas or I'll deal with you now." Ray jabbed his pistol into the elf's ribs for good measure.

"He's in there." Ezekiel said, pointing to a sliding glass door set in an equally glass rear wall. There wasn't much that could be seen due to the thick drapes covering all but a small section near the center.

Cautiously, Ray approached the door, unsure what was to happen next. Movement caught his attention and he jumped back seeing an armed guard step into view. "Drop your weapon!"

The guard stepped through as if he was fast enough to get the first shot off. Ray proved him wrong. Two rounds connected and the glass door shattered. The guard fell through, ripping several of the curtain hooks loose in the process.

"What the hell's going on out here!" The voice was deep but incredibly smooth. Ray recognized it from the phone call he'd received.

The oldest orc Ray had ever seen came into view, casually stepping over the dead guard. His skin, while brown, was pale compared to the other brown orcs he'd seen. Not much of it was visible from the bulging gray suit that wrapped his wide frame. What could be seen was covered in discolored pockmarks and ancient scars. Some looked ritualistic in nature, others naturally received. Thick yellow tusks protruded from his lower jaw, jutting out and protecting his angry face along both sides. Ray couldn't help but notice they were larger than both Kel'Gos and Crum's tusks combined. The old orc couldn't have been taller than six-foot but he had to weigh at least four-hundred-pounds of solid muscle.

"Tho'Mas, you're under arrest for the murder of Kel'Gos, kidnapping an ICPC agent, production and distribution of narcotics, and a bunch of other stuff I don't have the patience to list. Get on the ground and tell me where Lilian is or I will open fire!"

A hearty laugh echoed from the intimidating orc. "You really think you can bring me down so easily? I've taken shits bigger than you."

"I will not say it again. Get on the ground and answer my question!"

The orc leaned forward, taunting him. "The elf girl is dead. I watched the life leave her eyes as my fingers tightened around her throat. I felt the snap of her neck."

Ray felt his hands shaking. He wanted nothing more than to blow a hole through the orc's massive chest. His hands were sweating, finger on the trigger. Just a little further and he'd have revenge.

Amidst his rage, a piece of broken glass crunched on the floor behind him. Before he could turn, a sudden impact landed at the base of his skull. Ray collapsed to the floor and lost consciousness.

A splash of cold water roused his senses. Ray's eyes shot open and he struggled to move. He was bound to a chair at the center of the control room. Footsteps could be heard somewhere behind him, though they stopped before entering his peripherals. Struggling with his bonds, Ray realized both wrists and ankles were tied to the wooden frame. "Ezekiel, you piece of shit. I knew I couldn't trust you!"

The elf rounded and stopped just in front of him. "It's nothing personal. You had your shot and you didn't take it." He leaned in close, speaking just over a whisper. "I wish you had. I wouldn't have to do this."

"Ezekiel, get on with it!" The orc snapped from inside the curtained room. "The quicker I see you're capable of snuffing his light, the quicker we can move on to the next stage of the plan."

"You're a coward!" Ray challenged. "You can't even kill a man standing on his own two feet. You have to tie him up like a dog." Ray shook his head in disgust.

"Get on with it!" Tho'Mas roared, clearly growing impatient. Thundering footsteps drowned out the persistent bells and whistles echoing around the room and the orc appeared at the broken door. "A hundred-years of this shit and you still can't pull the trigger?"

Ezekiel snapped around, glaring at the orc. "I'm working on it!"

"Just kill him and be done with it. We wouldn't even be in this situation if you'd just killed the green skin to begin with. Instead you had to ship em off to whatsisname."

"Volk. Alexander Volk! We've only discussed it a thousand times!" Ezekiel pleaded, showing his frustration. Returning his attention to Ray he lifted the wood handled Colt and pointed it at the restrained detective's head.

"Shoot 'em already! I ain't gettin' any younger."

"Any last requests?" Ezekiel asked, seeming more for the orc's sake than Ray's.

"Yeah. Take a peek down the barrel and pull the trigger." Ray pulled against the ropes, hoping for any give whatsoever. Unfortunately they held tight.

Taking a deep breath Ezekiel stared into Ray's eyes. His words weren't on his lips. They were in his head. "I'm sorry."

Hearing a series of pops, Ray jumped, surprised he wasn't dead. He glanced up finding Ezekiel turned, the gun aimed at the old orc. Tho'Mas collapsed to the floor, two to the chest, one to the head.

Ezekiel dropped the gun where he stood and staggered toward the dead orc.

"What are you doing, Ezekiel?" Ray asked, tugging on his binds. He was starting to notice some slack in his right wrist, though it was far from loose.

"I told you I wasn't a tyrant." The elf replied, dropping to his knees beside his once friend's body. It wasn't clear if he was speaking to Ray or the orc. "All I wanted was peace. To be left alone and enjoy my life. I never asked for any of this."

Ray's spine was tingling. He didn't know if the elf was on the verge of a mental breakdown or really what was to follow. The only thing that mattered was getting out of his bonds and finishing this once and for all.

A final tug freed his wrist and Ray reached into the lower pouch of the tactical vest. Wrapping his fingers around the gray canister, he yanked the ring free and prepared himself.

Burning gas filled the air around him, emanating from the pocket. Ray breathed deep, letting it fill his lungs. It hit almost immediately, stinging on the inside. His nose began to run and his eyes watered. For the briefest moment he felt like he couldn't breathe. It was an illusion though. He'd been through this before. Many times in fact. Forcing himself to remain calm, Ray tore at the ropes binding his other arm and legs.

"What are you doi—" Ezekiel started to ask. His words gave way to violent coughing as the tear gas reached him. Crawling, he tripped over his former partner's bulky body in a desperate attempt to evade the growing cloud.

Ray got the final knot loose and climbed to his feet. The burning gas didn't bother him. Not anymore. He blocked it out. He couldn't feel anything at the moment. Ezekiel may not have been the one to physically kill Lilian but he was as much responsible for her death as Tho'Mas. The two were one in the same. Thomas Ezekiel. Snatching his pistol off the floor, Ray did a quick count. If he was correct he had two rounds left and he knew where he was going to use them. Death itself couldn't stop him.

Ray walked through the hazy fog, approaching the doubled over elf. His eyes were teary and he had a long trail of snot dangling from his nose. For as posh as the elf seemed to be, in the moment he wasn't much to look at. Ray's knuckles popped in protest, wrapped tightly around the wood grips of his Colt. He wanted nothing more than to expend his last rounds and end this. Placing the muzzle against the elf's head, he stared coldly into those pleading tear-streaked blue eyes. All he had to do was pull the trigger.

All you have to do is pull the trigger, he repeated to himself. Why was he not responding? He wanted to do it. A part of him needed to. It was certainly within his right. So why couldn't he?

Lilian's voice popped into his head. "The old code, which all knights were sworn to uphold—If they broke the code the runes quit working for them."

It wasn't much but it was enough to stop him. Ray was a cop. He swore an oath to the badge. Executing Ezekiel here and now would be a betrayal of that oath. Sighing, Ray lowered his gun. "Thomas Ezekiel, Frank Elliott, whatever your name is, you're under arrest for the—" An unexpected punch came out of nowhere, silencing him.

Ray flew across the room, landing near the chair he'd been bound to moments before. "What the hell?" Half dazed, he rolled and got to his hands and knees just as Ezekiel was stalking toward him.

"It didn't have to be this way. If only you'd killed him when you had the chance!" A pristine shoe stomped down beside were Ray had been a fraction of a second earlier.

He'd avoided the stomp but wasn't quick enough to evade the next. Ezekiel kneed him hard in the chest. For a moment Ray was weightless, flying through the air. He crashed down on something hard.

Ray groaned, twisting just enough to realize he was on the control board. Ezekiel lumbered toward him, vengeance in his suddenly cold eyes. Bracing himself, a fast and hard jab busted his face. He absorbed it as best he could. He didn't have anywhere to go and no time to change the odds. The only thing he could do was bide his time. He needed to remember everything Ezekiel was responsible for. He could use it to hold on.

Another blow landed in his gut and he felt the wind escape him. *Ezekiel killed Kel'Gos!* He gasped for breath and his head rocked sideways from a powerful strike to the jaw. *He hospitalized Crum!* Another blow to his face. *He kidnapped Lilian!* A quick jab to the right side of his head. *Blew me up!* An upper cut launched him into the air and he slammed down onto the control panel a second time.

Ray stared at the ceiling, watching the smug elf step into his line of sight.

"Pathetic! And to think I actually believed you'd be a worthy adversary. Had I known you were just going to rollover I wouldn't have bothered with you in the first place." Ezekiel shook his head, raising a slender knife with a wavy edge.

"This is Thomas Ezekiel and he's going to pay!" Ray shouted, catching the elf's wrist and twisting it backward. Pulling himself up, he delivered a solid punch to Ezekiel's unprotected face. It didn't take much to force him backward, his arm locked. A side hand chop at his bulging arm muscles sent the blade skittering across the floor. Ray wasted no time bringing his knee up, landing a solid blow to the elf's ribs. He forced him backward, near where his gun rested unattended.

Suddenly, in a manner beyond Ray's comprehension, Ezekiel flipped sideways. He untwisted his arm and jerked it free of the human's grasp. He brought his leg up, returning the rib shot Ray had previously delivered.

It was painful but he didn't have time to feel pain right now. Ezekiel was here, right in front of him. He had a job to do.

Ezekiel looked less sure of himself now, though he had speed and agility on his side. Ray didn't have much of anything. He was of average strength, average agility, maybe a hair over average intelligence, but not much else. He was simply average. What he did have though was determination. That in itself would see him through.

Ezekiel paced a semicircle, watching the human. It took little more than a sidestep to scoop his knife from the floor. He flipped it between his fingers, awaiting Ray to make his move. When he did he'd slide the blade between his ribs.

Stealing a quick glance behind him, Ray was still too far from his gun. He could probably reach it if he rolled but Ezekiel would be upon him in the blink of an eye. He needed more time. "Tell me honestly. Was anything you said true? Or were those just the words of a little prick coward trying to manipulate the situation?"

Ezekiel's lip curled and anger flashed in his eyes.

That's what Ray wanted. He needed to make the elf angry. It had its uses, but not in a precision fight. It was something he had to keep in check himself. He'd used it to escape a complete disadvantage, but now he was only slightly disadvantaged.

"I wish your girlfriend was still alive. I'd love to slide this little prick inside her." Ezekiel waved the small blade between his fingers, making it dance from one to the next. "I could probably slip it in three or four times. I bet she'd cry out like a whore. And just as consciousness slipped away from her, I'd slit her throat."

That was the wrong thing to say. Ray wasn't entirely sure how, but he had Ezekiel by the throat. He'd fallen into his own trap, losing himself to anger. Fortunately, he didn't care about himself. The knife didn't hurt so bad. It only landed once before he tore it out of his grip.

He wasn't certain if Ezekiel recognized his mistake or not. It was all about the eyes. It didn't matter how good an actor was, if their eyes didn't tell the story, they weren't convincing. Ezekiel knew that. It was Ray's eyes that announced his error. Neither pain nor exhaustion could hold him back. Blood trickled down his face, though he didn't know if it was his own or the elf's. He had Ezekiel's wrist locked in a death grip in one hand and the other around his throat, dragging him toward his doom. Again, Ray slammed his head forward, landing solid.

Ezekiel stumbled under the force of the blow. He had to get free. There was no way he could take another hit like that.

The enraged detective didn't give him the option. His forehead landed a third time, dropping the elf to his knees. Seeing defeat, Ray dropped him and turned, snatching his gun off the floor. He could have shot him then and there. There was one problem. It wasn't personal enough. And since he'd made the mistake of bringing Lilian into it, his morals were no longer stopping him. Ray pressed the muzzle against the dazed elf's forehead and pulled the trigger.

An explosion shook the entire structure. Fire and debris could be seen out the rattling windows overlooking the river far below. One of them shattered, though not from the blast.

Ray picked himself up. He had no idea how he'd missed so close, explosion or not. Still, he had. Swinging around to take his last shot, the gun was knocked from his grip.

Ezekiel, having regained his senses, thrust his palm into Ray's chest and knocked him back a few steps. Springing to his feet, he flipped and brought the heel of his loafer down on Ray's shoulder. It wasn't enough to stop him but it did knock him to the floor. Rolling, he was back on his feet in no time. Ezekiel grabbed hold of the prone human and pulled him to his feet. Keeping him off balance he escorted him to the broken window and slammed his unprotected face onto the metal frame.

Ray struggled against the elf's leverage, getting his feet beneath him. He was stronger but not by much, and not even a candle compared to Crum's strength. Ray could feel the broken glass cutting into his face, though it was nothing compared to the jagged shard less than an inch away and closing. If the elf won out that would be the end of it. He would have failed. Kel'Gos and Lilian would have died for nothing. Crum's injuries would have been unavenged. All of it would have been wasted. That could not happen!

Stomping Ezekiel's foot, Ray ripped himself free and stood to his full height. He pulled back to deliver the final blow as a gunshot echoed in his ears. He stood stunned, unsure what had just happened.

Ezekiel froze, equally surprised. He placed his fingers to a bleeding hole in his chest. Removing them he stared at the blood for a long moment before turning to see who'd pulled the trigger.

Lilian stood in the middle of the room, Ray's Colt in hand and still aimed. A wisp of smoke drifted from the barrel and the slide was locked open.

Gasping his surprise, Ezekiel staggered backward. Tripping over the ledge, he tumbled out the window.

Ray watched him disappear into the rushing river. He searched for several long moments but the elf didn't resurface. Turning away, his attention solely on Lilian, he limped toward her and threw his arms around, hugging tight.

Lilian dropped the gun, returning his embrace.

"I thought I'd lost you." He was torn between hugs and kisses, doing both repeatedly in no specific order. "They told me you were dead!" Tears welled in his eyes.

A gentle smile crept to her lips and she placed her hands against the sides of his face, staring intently into his swollen eyes. "You won't get rid of me that easily, Ray Bradley." She planted a tender kiss on his lips and took a step back, surveying the room around them. "It's all here."

"What? What is?"

"The entire empire. The drugs, the money, all their plans, names of associates, contact information, who they'll work with, who they refuse to work with. All of it!"

Ray shook his head, surprised how fast she was back into work mode. "Lilian, to be perfectly honest, I don't give a damn about any of that. I just wanted you to be all right."

She blushed. "I'm all right. Better than you anyway. What happened? I saw you just last night, or the night before anyway. You're bleeding all over the place."

"I got blown up, technically twice now. I got stabbed. And I don't even know how many times I've been shot." He sighed. "It's been a rough couple of days."

"You shouldn't be walking around, silly. You need a hospital."

"I'll be all right. What I really need is that vacation with you."

"I don't know if you can handle a vacation with me right now." She smiled and kissed one of the less bloody spots on his cheek, leading him toward one of the many doors. "I did get something for you though."

"Really? What?"

Lilian reached into her back pocket and retrieved a crumpled brown envelope. Handing it to him, she continued. "I wanted to surprise you but then all this happened."

Ray opened it seeing two plane tickets to Cancún. "It's perfect." He leaned over, doing his best to contain his weight and gently kissed her.

"I didn't know when your schedule would permit so I got them open ended. We can go whenever you want."

Ray tucked the tickets away and pulled her close, slowly making his way toward the door. "How's tomorrow sound?"

"Tomorrow is fine, but I don't think you'll be able to enjoy it until you're properly healed."

"I guess we'll have to stay for a while then."

"If you're sure."

"I am."

"Then I'll meet you at the airport tomorrow morning, zero-six-hundred."

"But—It's so early." Ray trailed off in a whimper.

"You big baby." Playfully, Lilian pushed him, forgetting just how hurt he was. "Sorry!" Giggling, she wrapped her arms around him. "So, what are we going to do about all this evidence lying around?"

"Once we get to the surface we're going to call for backup and let someone else clean up this mess. There're a few trucks in the warehouse. I'm sure no one will object to us borrowing one for a few hours. Oh, by the way, my phone's broken. It got shattered when I got blown up the first time. I don't know if yours will work down here."

"It won't. I tried when I got free."

"How'd you manage that anyway?"

"It's an elf thing. You wouldn't understand."

The 95th District

Levi Samuel

Chapter 26
More than Words

A knock at the door called Ray from his slumber. He hadn't opened his eyes yet and he was already wishing he was still asleep. Pain was no stranger but he'd never experienced anything quite like what he was feeling at the moment. It was tenfold worse than what he'd felt lying in an office floor bleeding out. "Who is it?" He managed, though it wasn't nearly as loud as he'd intended.

The door cracked open and a familiar face poked through. "Good morning, Marshal Bradley. Sorry to wake you. I'm told you requested a driver?"

Ray groaned, memories filling the dark spots. "What time is it?"

"Five-fifteen."

"Okay." Pulling the blanket from himself Ray noticed the numerous wires and tubes connected to him. The room was bright white and the beeping machines were growing rapidly annoying. "Can you do me a favor and have one of those people out there come and get this needle out of my arm?"

The young wheelman ducked out and approached a counter where a few nurses were talking amongst themselves. Ray watched him point to the room and exchange a few brief words. Coming back, he poked his head in once again. "They'll be here in a moment."

"Thank you." Ray pulled the sticky sensors from his skin and searched the room for his clothes. He was incredibly stiff, every movement slow and aching.

One of the nurses pressed past the awaiting driver and stepped inside. "How's our patient this morning?"

"Leaving. Can you get this thing out of me?" He extended his arm.

"Um—I wouldn't recommend checking out just yet. Your bullet wounds were tended quite well, but whoever ga—"

"Look, Doc—"

"I'm an LPN."

"Whatever. Look, I appreciate the fix up, I really do. But I have other plans. Plans that don't include me laying in a hospital bed for the foreseeable future. So unless something inside me is broken or requires surgery I'm out of here."

"No, *sir*, nothing currently requires surgery. You do have a fractured fibula from one of your bullet wounds but it's already started to mend. Damage to the lower extremities is always a serious issue, one that can become potentially life threatening if not monitored closely. And the elven blood flowing through you has nearly replaced the original. We don't know what's going to happen with that. To our knowledge it's never been done before. I would urge you to remain here."

"Noted. Is there anything else?"

The nurse shook her head. "Apparently nothing you're going to listen to."

Ray could hear the growing irritation in her voice. He liked her. "Excellent. Now, if you'd please?" He extended his left arm a little further.

Sighing, the nurse grabbed a pair of latex gloves from the countertop and quickly applied them. As if on instinct she kinked the rubber hose leading to his arm and clamped it. "Do you want tape or a wrap?"

"Tape is fine."

She nodded and placed a small roll on the table beside his bed, laying a couple packs of gauze beside it. Carefully she removed the thin strips holding the IV in place and pressed a cotton ball over the entry point.

It was all over before Ray knew what happened. Probably for the best. Needles didn't make him feel so good, though as he understood it the needle was retracted as soon as the tubing was set. In moments he had a new makeshift bandage matching his numerous others, and the nurse was leaving the room without so much as a word. "Thank you." He weakly called after her.

With the help of the driver, Ray got dressed and found himself in a wheelchair. It wasn't that he couldn't walk. He could. It just took so much effort for so little progress. The chair was the fastest means of travel until some of his soreness wore off.

In minutes they were out the door, and minutes after that they were on the road.

Ray sat in the back seat watching the early morning scenery fly by. If all went according to plan he'd soon be on a plane with no idea when he was returning. He was nearly in a dream, watching the world drift by. Before he knew it they were pulling into the terminal. He was pleased the driver took it much easier this time. He wasn't currently up for donuts or sliding around corners as they'd done on their previous venture.

Reaching the drop-off line, the driver popped the trunk and unfolded the wheelchair. He brought it around to the rear passenger door.

Ray navigated himself into it. He wasn't too keen on this needing help stuff but with any luck it wouldn't last much longer. Getting settled, he dug around in the satchel he'd thrown together the night before. It contained the basics. Soap, toothbrush, his shaving kit, a few other items he'd decided to bring. Clothes were the last thing on his mind. He was going on vacation. Clothes would make him want to work. He felt it was better to purchase whatever he needed once he was there. Finding his query, he retracted the brown envelope Lilian had given him. Both tickets remained inside, awaiting use.

"Name?"

Ray glanced up realizing they were at the check-in desk. "Ray Bradley. I'm awaiting Lilian Lambrino."

"Nobody by that name has checked in yet."

Ray nodded and backed out of the line. Glancing to his driver, he smiled. "I guess she's running a little late." He looked at the green dots mounted on the wall, reading the time. She was only a few minutes late. Nothing to be concerned about. "I appreciate you bringing me. You can go ahead and take off if you want."

"Thank you, but I think I'll stick around. At least until your companion arrives."

Minutes ticked by. People came and went. Planes arrived while others departed. Ray glanced at the clock for what had to have been the thousandth time. He'd been waiting for just over two hours. Taking a deep breath, he rotated the chair to where his driver was sitting valiantly by his side. "If she was coming she would have been here by now. Would you mind taking me back to the office?"

"No worries." The driver stood and grabbed the handles of Ray's chair. Gently, he rolled him back to where they'd parked.

Ray spent the return trip staring at the unused tickets. He didn't want to talk. There wasn't anything to say. Scenarios flashed through his mind. Had she run into trouble? Did one of Ezekiel's men find her? Had she changed her mind last minute? There were thousands of possibilities and he didn't have a phone to get answers.

"We're here, sir." Again, the driver prepared the chair and helped him get seated.

Moving clear of the door, Ray turned. "Thank you— I'm sorry, I don't think I ever caught your name."

"It's Dusty, sir."

"Thank you, Dusty." Ray handed him the brown envelope.

"What's this?"

"Take someone you care about on a vacation."

Dusty opened the flap and stared at the tickets within. "I appreciate the offer but I can't—"

"Yes you can." Ray offered a false smile. "Consider it compensation for the stunt driving lessons. I've used them at least twice this past week." Refusing to take no for an answer, Ray rolled himself into the elevator. He scanned his ID and pressed the display for the fourth floor. The doors opened and an instant later two security guards, one human, the other orc, were blocking the exit.

"Ray Bradley?"

"Yes?"

"We need you to come with us."

Ray knew it wasn't a question. The way they'd stepped in and taken possession of his chair and by extension, him, said that much. Something terribly wrong had happened. The only question was, what?

Ray found himself handcuffed to a table in what he could only describe as an interrogation room. He'd been in enough of them to know what was about to happen.

After what had to have been an hour, maybe more, the only door opened and a smug elf stepped in. Ray recognized it for what it was. They were trying to make him sweat. He'd done the same thing on more than one occasion.

The elf pulled up a chair and casually plopped down. The file he'd been holding clapped to the table and a heavy sigh escaped the elf, shaking his head. "Marshal Bradley, you're in a lot of trouble."

Ray nearly smiled. Had it not been for the ridiculousness of it all, he would have. "Look, I know what you're playing at. I've used these little games myself. So instead of fishing for whatever information you want to know, quit wasting both our time and just come out and say it."

The elf cocked his head, silently studying the human. The movement was subtle. Most would have missed it. Ray might have as well except he was looking for it. "The problem is—" He drug out the last word for effect. "—I have a lot of people dead, a lot of evidence missing, and quite frankly a lot of questions. So why don't you start by telling me what happened yesterday."

"Which part? Yesterday started about a week ago."

"Let's begin with how you found your way into the tunnels under Biscayne Bay."

Ray recounted his trip into the Port Miami Tunnel, giving as much detail as he could remember. A lot of it had happened so fast he wasn't sure he'd told it all in the correct order, but his story eventually led to Ezekiel being shot and falling out the window. "I filed my report last night. If you've bothered to read it I'm sure you'll notice I left no detail unattended." Except for the part about the kissing, he thought to himself.

"I've read your report. I also went through the evidence list you signed off on."

"And?"

The elf looked puzzled for a moment. "It's gone."

"What's gone?"

"The evidence."

Now Ray was the one who was puzzled. "What do you mean it's gone?"

The elf opened the file between them and retrieved an envelope. Ensuring it was what he'd intended, he slid it within range of Ray's restrained hands.

Struggling against his handcuffs, Ray opened the flap and sorted through the stack of pictures within. They were arranged as before and after shots of file cabinets, computers, pallets of drugs, and every other point of interest he'd encountered the previous morning. "I'm confused. I was there when these were taken. Both before collection and after. They loaded all the evidence into a white van. I signed as witness. Clearly, I did my job. If someone else failed in theirs why do you have me handcuffed to a table?"

"It's about more than the missing evidence, Marshal Bradley. Would you do me a favor and have a look at these?" The elf slid another envelope to him.

This one had numerous pictures of both him and Lilian, some in private and others from their various public meetings. The one that caught his attention and, judging from the wear this picture had above the rest, apparently the attention of most others was Lilian sliding a small black box across the table to him.

Ray recalled that incident. "I remember this. She was giving me a hard drive taken from Club Vice. It was submitted as evidence a few days ago."

"I'm well aware of the hard drive. While forensics was recovering the contents they inadvertently activated some unexpected malware. There's no telling how much information was accessed before we got it shut down. We also know you've been sleeping with Agent Lilian Lambrino of the Interspecies Criminal Police Commission. These recordings go into great detail of your various endeavors." He lifted a catalogue of micro SD cards with numerous dates and times written on them.

Ray glared at the elf. Suddenly he knew who was responsible for bugging his loft. "So, what is this? Blackmail? Are you trying to get something out of me?"

"You misunderstand, Marshal Bradley. I have no care who you're screwing any more than a moth cares for a bug zapper. What concerns me is two agents from various institutions forming a romantic relationship and trading confidential information."

"Have you listened to those tapes?"

"Many times, in great detail."

"Then you should know that confidential information isn't what we discuss. We even agreed to leave work at the door. At times our cases intersected which required minor information exchange, but never anything confidential."

"Marshal Bradley, would you mind explaining to me why you attempted to leave the country this morning?"

"I—" Ray froze. He'd been on the other end of this conversation. This was the point where they believed they had a slam dunk and any excuse he gave was subject to speculation. "I evoke my right to refuse answering any further questions until my lawyer is present."

"Very well, Mister Bradley." The fact he'd said mister instead of Marshal wasn't missed. "Seeing as you have no lawyer on retainer, and even if you did it's unlikely they have clearance to view the details of this case, might I provide you with a list of qualified individuals who may assist you?"

Ray nodded, refusing to speak another word.

"I shall return momentarily. In the meantime feel free to look through the information I've collected against you. It's never right to hang a man without him knowing what he's being hanged for." The elf slid the rest of the packet across the table.

Ray sat still until the elf left the room. He knew he was being watched. Glass walls were installed in most interrogation rooms for a reason. Additionally, he's spotted the button camera in the corner above the door the moment he was brought in.

Grabbing the file, Ray slid it off the table and into his hands. It was a little more complicated to scan the contents with his hands bound but he made do. If they seriously had a case against him, it was time to see exactly what they had, and it seemed they had a lot.

Ray scanned the transcripts of conversations, both verbal and texts. There were hundreds of pictures as far back as the day he returned from Brussels. That told him they'd opened the case the moment ICPC accused him of conspiring with Ezekiel. There were samples of his blood, lab results, even a used condom that had somehow found its way into their possession. But none of it bothered him so much as a file faxed over about the time he awoke that morning.

It was from ICPC and held a brief message before several pages of encrypted data. Ray read it aloud, hoping the words would somehow make sense. "Analytics came back from a terminal used exclusively by Senior Agent Lilian Lambrino. Agent Lambrino has failed to check in for multiple days. Consider her armed and extremely dangerous. Apprehend with extreme caution." Ray didn't have to be a code reader to know the following encryption was the transfer of her full and complete file. Part of him wanted to see it. Lilian betrayed him, quite possibly bringing him down in the process, but a part of him knew it had to be a mistake. He knew Lilian. She knew him. Hell, he'd been in her head. Never once had he sensed the slightest deception, though there was no denying she was good about changing the subject.

Hearing the door open, Ray closed the file and tossed it back onto the table.

The elf smiled. "Good reading?"

"It's missing key elements." Ray replied. "I have a question."

"What's that?" The elf laid a freshly printed sheet of paper on the table in front of Ray.

"If Lilian went rogue, what about her team?"

"What team?"

"The team she was here with. One of them was on location when we went in to raid Ezekiel's place. Lots of people saw him. Hell even Roderick talked to him."

"ICPC reports that she was here alone. We'll look into your claim though." The elf gestured to the paper he'd placed in front of Ray. "This is a list of every criminal attorney with clearance to review your case."

Ray glanced at it. It wasn't much to work with, taking up less than half a page and more than half of those worked for the WMD. Ray was reviewing the names when the door opened and Roderick stepped in.

"What the hell's going on here?"

"I'm questioning a suspect." The elf replied indignantly.

"No you're not! He's one of mine and you don't question the tail end of a horse if it belongs to me, do I make myself understood?" Roderick reached into his pocket and removed a set of keys. Selecting a strange one Ray had never seen before, he slipped it into the metal cuffs and both sides fell free in unison.

"Sir, you can't just—"

Roderick stood to his full height and turned on the elf. "Don't 'Sir' me! I can do whatever I damn well please. Now take a hike."

"Sir?"

"You heard me. Git!"

The elf gathered his paperwork and rushed out of the room.

Watching the door close, Roderick's facial expression became less commanding and a light smile broke when he met Ray's gaze. "What kind of trouble have you gotten yourself into?"

"Honestly, sir, I don't know. I was leaving the elevator when security grabbed me and brought me here."

Roderick shook his head as if his question had pertained to something else entirely. "I'm pretty sure I warned you about sleeping with that girl."

For the first time Ray felt ashamed. It was a simple statement but the tone made it sting more than a whip could have.

A heavy sigh escaped the old politician. "I suppose we were all young once, thinking with the wrong head. We'll just chalk it up to experience and call it a day."

"Sir?"

"These boys from Department 1 will crucify you without so much as a thought and justify it with half-assed evidence. For all the ways nonhuman culture has surpassed what we've come up with, in many ways they could learn a thing or two. For starters, how to do real police work."

"I'm afraid I don't understand, sir."

"Don't worry about it. For now, go home and get some rest. Let those legs of yours heal up while I get all this bullshit straightened out."

"Yes sir." Free of the table, Ray rolled his chair toward the door.

"That doesn't mean you're getting a break. I still expect daily check-ins and staying on top of your case work. Just because you can't chase em down on foot for a little while doesn't mean you're getting out of the brain work."

Ray couldn't help but smile. "Understood, sir." He left the interrogation room, making his way toward the elevator. The place was a bit of a maze but he'd made sure to memorize it on his way in. In many ways it felt like a police station. There were file rooms and cubicles, and numerous phones ringing. And most notably, a revolving line to the coffee pot. Finally, he got through all the people and rolled into the elevator, swiping his card.

The office remained much the way he'd left it. His dirty suits were hanging separate from the only remaining clean one he had available. The ever growing stack of case files rested in the wire basket at the far right corner. Other than that, things were the same.

Ray pushed his office chair aside, making room for the wheelchair. He wouldn't be able to use the computer but that didn't bother him. He was only here for a few things anyway.

Staring over the quiet room, Ray pulled his top right drawer open and set eyes on the felt covered blue box within. With a heavy sigh he tucked it into his pocket and grabbed the stack of case files. A white envelope fell from between them and landed on the desk in front of him. He separated the new files from the old and set them aside.

Snatching up the envelope, he inspected it. There was no name, no postage, no writing of any kind. That meant it was hand delivered. He grabbed his letter opener, a dull knife that stayed in his pocket except for when he needed a screwdriver, bottle opener, nail file, or any other assortment of tools a pocketknife should never be used for, and slipped it under the fold. The paper tore easily.

Ray reached inside, removing the folded parchment with elegant yet hastily written handwriting that filled the page.

Ray, I'm so sorry. I never meant for you to get involved in this. I'm sure you have many questions and I wish I was able to provide answers. As I'm sure you're aware by now, I'm the one who tipped Ezekiel off about the raid in Brussels. As bad as that sounds, I want you to know that I do not work for that pig. He was an instrument. A tool. I needed to come to America and he was the vessel which delivered me. I want you to know that I really do love you and I wish we could have met under different circumstances.
With all my love, Lilian.

Ray inspected the letter several times over, reading a different interpretation each time. None of them made him feel any better. A lipstick kiss rested at the bottom under her name, seemingly her trademark from the previous message he'd received.

He sat there, quiet, letter in hand. Questions raced through his mind, none of them answered. At the very least the letter would be an excellent cherry atop the elf's stack of evidence. It confirmed he had no knowledge of Lilian's scheme, though some would certainly claim it was planted to redirect blame. The only thing he got from it was that Lilian had in fact been using him.

Unable to read the words again, he let if fall to the glass surface. Grabbing his stack of case files, he rolled toward the door. Reaching the elevator, Ray hesitated on the selection panel. On one hand he wanted to inform Roderick of the new evidence. On the other he just wanted to leave.

Making his selection, the doors opened and Ray found himself in the lowest floor garage. He pocketed his phone, confident in the voicemail he'd left Roderick. Too much had gone wrong too fast. The old man needed to know about the letter but he didn't have the energy to deliver it personally. Reaching his car, Ray pulled the door open and carefully climbed inside. Now came the hard part of folding and storing his wheelchair without scratching the paint.

Several curse words and severe exhaustion later, Ray was on the road. A song played on the radio, one he'd never heard before. It was a sad tune but it spoke directly to him. It was funny how that worked, though he didn't find humor in it.

Reaching the only place he wanted to be, Ray turned on to Bayshore Drive and pulled into his favorite lot. The sun was just a few feet over the horizon when he pressed the off button and climbed out of the Vantage Roadster. Hobbling to a nearby park bench, he plopped down as the sun made contact. He hadn't actively watched it set in so long it was almost a new experience.

Taking a deep breath, Ray reached into his pocket and removed the blue box. The hinge groaned and it clapped open, revealing a glimmering ring within. It wasn't much but it once belonged to his grandmother. He'd intended to give it to Lilian when they returned from their vacation. It seemed none of that was possible now.

The sun was fading fast. It had only been a few seconds and already over half of it was out of sight. An old man approached the bench and took a seat at the end opposite Ray. He was wearing a tattered green coat that hung down to his knees and his hair was slightly unkempt.

Ray got the sense he was homeless but it was difficult to tell. He wasn't dirty by any means but he was also far from pristine. His clothing was hidden beneath the coat and the five o'clock shadow was more akin to a few weeks of neglect and laziness. Ray nodded to the man, turning back to finish the sunset.

"It's a wonderful sight, isn't it?" His voice was raspy but strong.

"What is?"

The man gestured to the sunset.

"Oh. Yeah, I suppose it is."

They sat in silence, watching the last slither disappear in a hue of pink and orange. Finally, the old man spoke. "So, what's your plan now, Ray?"

"I'm sorry, do I know you?" He hadn't expected the man to say his name.

"Not yet, but you will."

"What's that supposed to mean?"

"Let's just say I've come to offer you some advice."

Ray picked himself up, letting his tight muscles stretch, wishing he hadn't. "Listen guy, I've had a rough few days and I'm really not in the mood for a bunch of cryptic bullshit right now. So either tell me what you want or leave me alone?"

The old man shrugged and retrieved a pack of cigarettes from his inner pocket. Placing one in his mouth, he extended the pack to Ray.

"No thanks." It seemed his desire had finally faded.

The man returned the pack to his pocket and waved his free hand over the tip of the cigarette. It flared to life and the orange glow grew bright with the steady initial puff. He exhaled a thick cloud of smoke. "You know, people are so impatient these days. They—"

"Whoa! What the hell was that? How did you do that?" Ray searched the man's hand seeing no lighter, match, or any other fire creating device. He knew he hadn't been seeing things. That left only one explanation. Reaching for his gun, he suddenly remembered stashing it in his car before going to the hospital.

"Relax, Ray. I'm not here to harm you."

"Oh yeah? So why are you here?"

"What if I were to tell you there's so much about this world that you don't know?"

"What, like eating faeries? Sorry but I've kicked the habit. How about you get the hell out of here and leave me alone!"

The old man chuckled. "An archaic practice. The price is too high and the reach too limiting. Not to mention it's unacceptable in most cultures."

"Munching down on faeries is the only way I've seen anything like that happen." He gestured to the burning cigarette. "You'd better start talking real quick."

"Like I said, I'm here to offer you some advice."

"And what advice is that?" His question went unanswered. Ray glanced around, confused as to where the mysterious man had gone. He was nowhere in sight, a feat made impossible by the lack of cover. Instead, a business card stood on edge where the man had been sitting moments before. Ray snatched the card, still searching his surroundings. Bringing his gaze to the beautiful black calligraphy scrawled across the white stock, a single message greeted him. *Don't Despair!*

Slightly on edge, and a little more than uncertain, Ray took a final look around before limping to his car. Climbing in, he started the engine. It had been a long week and he needed some rest.

The 95th District

Levi Samuel

Author's Notes

I always say this, and somehow it's always true. This was the hardest book I've ever written, though I'm not entirely sure why.

I'm constantly learning the craft and trying to apply everything in the first draft. I'm sure that has a lot to do with it. It could be because I'm seeing the world around me and using my stories to express myself. Or, it could also be that this particular story kept evolving throughout the entire writing process, ending with multiple rewrites, restructures, and entire new chapters that weren't part of the original plan. In truth, I believe it's a mixture of them all, including many more I don't yet understand.

Writing used to feel so easy. My first book was a long process but thinking back it was remarkably easy to write. Of course, it was complete and utter shit. Not the story itself, but the execution. I didn't know how to be a writer at the time. I discovered something I enjoyed and simply let myself enjoy it. The rules were unknown to me. I didn't think about the millions of things that flood my thought process now, each one with the single goal of crafting a marketable product. None of it mattered because I was ignorant, creating for the sake of creating.

I made an effort to go back to basics with this book. I threw out the rules and I crafted an enjoyable story for the sake of telling a good story. It wasn't until I'd finished the first draft that I then went through and tailored the rules to fit.

Our world has slipped into a bit of a shit show this past year. Between isolation, riots, race wars, murder hornets, and the other stuff that's likely on the way, it's been interesting to say the least. This book is what I have to show for it.

In truth, the isolation side of things didn't impact me toward the beginning. It made my weekly trip to the grocery store more difficult as the shelves were barren. Other than that, there was no change to my daily life. My daughter couldn't go to school, so it felt more like a weekend. I didn't really start to feel it until my backup became unavailable to watch my grandpa and give me a break. He's an 84-year-old man with dementia and currently requires 24/7 supervision. I'm sure many of you don't understand how difficult it can be to tend to someone like that but if it gives you an idea, I've been here for just over a year and a half and I've been able to use the restroom without interruption maybe three times total. If I'm not sitting in my chair constantly keeping a watchful eye, he's up and into everything.

By the time I finally got some relief, I was ready to get out of here and never look back. I spent the first week doing a bunch of nothing. Everywhere was still closed. I couldn't visit most of my friends. I couldn't enjoy dining out. For the most part, I didn't do much of anything except work on this book and spend some time with family.

The second week was another story. I hadn't taken a vacation since I was a kid. So rather than spending another week doing nothing, I took the opportunity to drive down to Florida and spend time with my sister. I was still greatly restricted by closed businesses, but it was a fun time nonetheless, and even though it wasn't Miami, I was able to do a fair amount of hands on research for this book. I studied palm trees and the various vegetation. I got to see a fair amount of sea life and other legged creatures. I wasn't aware just how many lizards hung out around the beach. And I got to enjoy the culture and foods of the area. Over all, I had a great time and I came back feeling renewed. I also managed to listen to two writing courses during my drive, and overcame an exceptionally difficult chapter in this book—Seriously, I spent nearly two weeks rewriting the sneak and peak chapter and none of them worked. It finally clicked one night when I was about half drunk and staring out into the ocean.

You've probably noticed I took the liberty of including some of our modern-day issues into this story. It's weird to explain it, and while the extent was done purposely, the issues themselves were part of the original plan, long before any of this crap was happening around us. The end of The Pandora Gambit left the world at a transitional phase. It would have been strange if I'd ignored those details and started anew. It just so happened the events coincide with what we're facing in the real world so I used it to strengthen the story.

I had some trouble deciding on a title. I turned it over in my head for a few months, seemingly never making progress. Finally, one night after writing, I was doing the dishes and thinking about it. I asked myself what I was hoping to achieve with the title. My answer was simple. I wanted it to be mysterious enough to denote it wasn't just a normal everyday story. But I also wanted the formality of organization. Once I'd answered that question, The 95th District instantly jumped into my head. There are 94 districts in the United States which are overseen by the US Marshals Service. Since I'd made beyond the Veil the 95th, it worked perfectly. I ran the title past a few people who I talk to about these sorts of things and after good feedback, I considered it set in stone.

I've read this book many times over. I believe it has the potential to go far, but I need readers to make that happen. There are always a few places I wish I had to ability to write smoother, but at some point you have to stop fixing things and let it go. That's the curse of being a writer. We always feel we can do better — So begins the repetitive cycle; Write—fix—rewrite—fix… Whatever I decide to write next will employ the skills I've strengthened with this one, and by default be better. The next book is always better than the last.

Whatever the next project it, be it the conclusion to Rise of the Nightkings, another part of the Eldarlands Saga, or something I haven't considered yet, I hope you'll do me the favor of leaving a review for this book. Reviews don't seem like they're that big of a deal but as an author they can make the difference between success and failure. Additionally, if you liked this book and want the latest news on others, as well as a free download for a book unavailable through any other media outlets, please subscribe to my monthly newsletter. http://eepurl.com/dxRUvL

I give a little insight to what's going on in my life, talk about new books, news with old books, provide exclusive content, and overall give my subscribers things that aren't provided elsewhere. Happy reading and I look forward to hearing from you.

Levi Samuel
June 2020